Cats in the Belfry

Mary Lu Warstler

Mary Lu Warstler
8-23-08

PublishAmerica
Baltimore

ISBN: 1-4241-4667-4
PUBLISHED BY PUBLISHAMERICA, LLLP
www.publishamerica.com
Baltimore

Printed in the United States of America

To:
My family and my friends from
Kenmore United Methodist Church,
who encouraged me with love and
prayers.

Preface

I want to take this opportunity to thank all the wonderful folks in the Kenmore United Methodist Church (now closed), Bucyrus United Methodist Church and the Winterset/Antrim Charge for all their help and support. The church is a marvelous place to meet people because we are all sinners saved by grace. We all have our faults and yet we are accepted.

Also, I want to thank my husband who gave me the idea for this book—sort of. He suggested I write a mystery. I remembered from conferences that I should write what I know—the church, cats, and mysteries. My children have been an encouragement to me. My son, Tim, put in hours editing then advising me with the first drafts. My daughter, Liz, read it and said, "Wow! It actually came together at the end!" My other daughter, Martha, gave me some insight into the characters, how to make them more real. And my youngest son, James has always been my encourager.

Even though I was born in southern West Virginia, am an ordained United Methodist minister (retired), and have three cats (not two), that is where the resemblance to Laura Kenzel ends. This is not a story about me. It is pure fiction from beginning to end. I did use some scenes from my ministry—and that of pastor friends—but they are universal to most churches. Only one character intentionally resembles a former parishioner. She encouraged me, prodded me to learn more, and reminded me that

I should write. Often she would call me out of the blue—early morning or late at night—and say, "The Lord told me you needed prayer." She would pray for me and hang up. I always new I had a prayer warrior on my side.

Any other resemblance to persons, living or dead, is purely coincidental.

1

"Laura, I won't be home for dinner. I'll just grab a sandwich somewhere. Butch called. He's drunk again—needs me to pick him up and take him home. See you after the trustee meeting."

Harold Kenzel spoke quickly into the answering machine. He thought he heard the click as someone picked up the phone at the other end on the last word. He cut the connection before Laura could say anything, then left the receiver off the hook before she could call back. He didn't have time or patience to explain. In his haste to leave, he replaced the receiver and forgot he had a call in for the bishop.

Twenty-five minutes later, he was at the four-way stop at the intersection of County Roads 13 and 26. Thinking only of his tight schedule, he started across the intersection. Suddenly bright beams blinded him, causing him to swerve. As if the gas pedal were stuck, the car sped forward. Harold swerved again to get out of its way. The car swerved again. Harold tried to miss the car and at the same time avoid the ditch at the side of the road, but the car rammed into his door forcing his car into the ditch. Everything went black.

The driver of the speeding car climbed out, removed his protective head and chest gear, and pushed his long, oily hair out of his face. He reached into the car and pulled his unconscious passenger under the steering wheel, yanked his head back, and slammed it forward.

Then he went to Reverend Kenzel's car. A passerby—had there been one—would have thought he was going to help. Instead, he smashed the window then cupped his gloved hands around the pastor's neck. He laughed—a harsh, maniacal sound—as the neck snapped. Headlights approached. The man ducked. The oncoming vehicle stopped, blinked his lights twice and waited. The oily-haired man picked up his protective gear and ran to the passenger's side of the waiting vehicle. He hardly had the door closed, before the impatient driver spoke. "Well?"

"Don't worry, Uncle. He's dead. If the kid ain't dead, he won't know what hit him when he wakes in a jail cell for drunk driving and vehicular homicide."

"Good job, Randy. Now, let's find a place to make our call before that kid wakes."

"He ain't gonna wake for days, if he ever wakes." Randy laughed again his harsh cackling sound. As if the young man had told a very funny joke, the man behind the wheel laughed with him and pressed on the gas. He drove to a turnoff lane to an old abandoned apple orchard. Turning the ignition off, he pulled out his cell phone and called 911.

"Give me your name and the nature of your emergency, please." The faraway voice of the police dispatcher crackled over the phone.

"There's been an accident at the intersection of county roads thirteen and twenty-six. You don't need my name." He disconnected and replaced the phone in his pocket. The two men waited, wordlessly—about ten minutes—until flashing lights sped past them toward the scene of the accident.

Finally, all was clear. The driver backed onto the highway. "You need to get back before anyone misses you," he said to the younger man. "There's an envelope in the glove box."

Randy hungrily opened the little door and picked up the fat envelope. His mouth turned up into a crooked grin as he placed the bundle in his shirt pocket. "Thanks, Uncle," he said.

"I trust you won't share this night with anyone—not even your old man."

"Sure, my old man wouldn't understand. He's not cool like you."

The man laughed and sped down the highway and was soon far away from the scene of death. He dropped Randy off in a secluded, dark country road. The boy jumped in his own car and sped out of sight.

Randy's a good boy. He'll be useful to me, but I'll have to watch his erratic behavior. Too much desire for using drugs, not enough for selling them. Could be trouble down the road. With this self-warning, the driver returned to his home.

* * *

Laura Kenzel stared at the phone, an angry scowl on her face. She had hurried to catch it before the answering machine. Intuitively she knew it would be Harold, but why had he deliberately refused to talk to her? She heard the click as he broke the connection, but when she tried to call him back, all she got was a busy tone. When she did get a ring, there was no answer. She could have dropped him off at the church and gone after Butch, but with only one car, Harold would have to wait until she returned for him. He didn't like to wait for anyone. Maybe Butch was drunker than usual. When would that kid ever grow up? His parents had given up on him long ago.

Laura sighed and combed her fingers through her short auburn hair. I really need to talk to him. Oh, well, later, I suppose.

Laura took the meatloaf from the oven then drained the potatoes and put them in a bowl. She covered the salad bowls with plastic wrap. The refrigerator received that meal—as it had many others. Even the aroma filling the kitchen did nothing to encourage her appetite, which was suddenly gone. Maybe she would have a sandwich later. This wasn't the first time Harold called at the last minute; probably wouldn't be the last. She should be used to it by now.

Some *friends* from the church had hinted that maybe Harold was seeing another woman. Laura ignored them and refused to speak to him about it. While they didn't have the best marriage in the world, Laura knew her husband wasn't interested in other women.

Sirens wailed in a distance and Laura automatically breathed a prayer for the one in the ambulance. She picked up her cup of coffee and started to her reading and studying space in the corner of the family room. When Harold got home, she would tell him of her desire to go to seminary. They would argue. He didn't want her out of his sight—especially around young, ambitious men.

She paused at the full-length mirror on the hallway closet door. At forty-five, she was still a pretty woman—slim, five foot six, auburn hair, brown eyes, and fair skin. She had an eye for colors and clothes and often received compliments which made Harold beam as if he were somehow responsible for her choices. Truth was, he didn't care what she wore as long as it was fashionable, made him look good and didn't embarrass him.

Finishing high school at sixteen, Laura had worked her way through college and had a degree in teaching before her marriage. Harold never wanted her to work outside the home; said he needed her at his side. That was all he wanted her for, since he insisted on doing everything else alone—paying the bills, doing the shopping. He did leave the raising of their daughter, Susan, to her and the supervision of the housekeeper. Laura would rather have done her own cleaning, but he wanted her to be a decorative piece of his picture. She kept her driver's license up to date, even if she didn't have much use for it.

Laura shook her head to chase away the growing depression. She had everything a woman could want—well almost. Why wasn't she happy? Sighing deeply, she moved on into her reading room and picked up the book she had been reading. Before she had read more than a paragraph, the phone rang. Believing it was Harold, she was tempted to let the machine answer it. At the last minute, she rushed to answer. It might be Susan, or an emergency of some kind.

"Kenzel residence."

"Mrs. Kenzel, this is Trudy at the hospital. We need you in the emergency room."

Trudy? Oh yes, she's a member of our congregation that we rarely see. As a single mom, she works a lot of the time. "Harold isn't here, Trudy. He had a call to make before the meeting at the church. He has the car. Does someone from our church need him?"

"Reverend Kenzel is already here, but we need you to come right away."

Must be something serious. The siren I heard a few minutes ago? "All right," she said, "I'll call Barbara from across the street. I'll be there in about five minutes."

The anger at Harold that she had pushed aside earlier returned. He knew she didn't have a car. How did he expect her to…? While she grumbled to herself, Laura dialed her friend's number. "Barbara, do you have time to run me over to the hospital? Apparently, there's an emergency. Harold is already there. Trudy just called—said they needed me."

"I heard the siren. Meet you out front."

Five minutes later, Laura jumped from Barbara's car. "I'll ride back with Harold." She closed the car door and hurried to the emergency entrance. She had hardly entered the building when the strong odor of antiseptic and fear caused her to stop. Antiseptic she understood. Fear was a new sensation. Can you smell fear? Maybe, maybe not, but she was sure she could smell fear in the air as clearly as an animal would if it were cornered. Something on Trudy's face made Laura suddenly wary. Where was Harold? Why wasn't he there to meet her? Who did they need her to see?

Not explaining why she called, Trudy and the state highway patrolman led Laura to a room down a long narrow corridor. In the center of the otherwise empty room was a gurney which obviously held the covered form of a dead person.

Why was she here? She should be in the emergency room to help Harold counsel the accident victims. They wouldn't have called her unless there was an accident with several victims. The patrolman pulled back the cover exposing the cold, gray face of her husband, Harold.

11

"Is this man your husband, ma'am?"

Feeling the blood drain from her face, Laura stared, first at Harold then at the patrolman. She struggled to understand. Her knees began to feel like putty. She took a deep breath and turned to face Trudy. She would not pass out. She had learned long ago to hide her emotions. She would not lose control now—not here in front of strangers.

"Why didn't you warn me?" Anger flashed in her eyes, her fists clenched at her side.

"You could have…never mind." She had to get out of that room. Those spotless, glaring white walls were pressing around her, squeezing the oxygen from the air.

"I'm sorry Mrs. Kenzel" the patrolman was saying. She struggled to focus on him—on his words that would hopefully explain this bizarre situation. "There was an accident. It looks as though the other car ran into the side of Kenzel's and forced him off the road."

"And the other driver?" Laura gathered all her willpower to make her voice sound calm.

"Butch Martin—a young kid. He's still unconscious. We won't know much until he wakes—if he ever does."

Laura blinked and shook her head. Something didn't make sense. Trudy saw her blink and offered her a box of tissues.

"I don't need those." Laura's words were sharper than she'd intended.

Trudy ignored Laura's curtness. "I've called Reverend Collins, the district superintendent, for you," she said.

"Why?" Laura reacted as if Trudy had slapped her.

Confused, Trudy said,"As a minister's wife, you don't have a pastor, so I thought…"

"Well, you thought wrong. I don't want to see that man."

"Laura?"

Laura whirled around. It was too late. District Superintendent Bill Collins stood in the open door. He stepped closer and reached to put an arm around her shoulders. "Laura, dear, I'm so sorry about this. Come, let me take you home and…"

Laura backed up and glared at him. Her brown eyes snapped with rage, but she forced her voice to be civil.

"I'm not going home at the minute. I'll call my friend, Barbara when I'm ready."

"Laura, you aren't thinking clearly. You need someone to…"

"I don't need *any*one to do *any*thing for me. Please just leave me alone." She turned to the patrolman. "If you need more information, you have my address and phone number."

"Yes ma'am."

"Laura, we need to talk, whether you want to or not. You know I'll have to send another pastor to the church. He'll need the parsonage. By the way, was Harold working on anything I need to know about?"

"Harold never talked to me about his church business unless I could help him with something. When do you want me out of the parsonage? Tonight? In the morning? Do you suppose I can I wait until after the funeral?"

"Laura, don't be sarcastic. Of course you'll have some time. You can work it out with the personnel committee."

Without another word, Laura turned, walked away to call her friend. While she waited for Barbara, the night's events seemed to float about in her mind like puzzle pieces in a violent windstorm. How could Butch have killed Harold? Why was Harold out there in the first place?

She turned back to the patrolman. "Excuse me, but something isn't right about this accident."

"I understand ma'am. Accidents are always…"

"No, the accident I understand. What I don't understand is why Butch Martin was driving a car. He called my husband maybe an hour ago and asked him to come to a bar and take him home. He was too drunk to drive and felt sick."

"We'll certainly check that out, ma'am."

She saw Barbara pull up at the door. She nodded to the patrolman and left.

"Why don't I stay with you tonight? You've had quite a shock."

"Thanks," said Laura, "but, I really need to be alone—to think and try to make sense of it all. I'll call Susan. She and Norman should be here by morning."

"If you're sure…"

"I'm sure."

"Well, all right, but call me if you need me during the night."

"I will. Thanks again."

The phone was ringing as Laura opened the door. She hurried expecting it to be Harold. Suddenly she remembered that he would never call her again. She hesitated, and then cautiously picked up the receiver.

"Laura, this is Bishop Jarvis. Is Harold there? He called me this afternoon and I'm returning his call." There was such a long silence that he asked, "Laura? Is something wrong?"

"Harold is dead, Bishop," she said. "He was killed in a car accident about an hour ago."

"Oh, Laura, I'm so sorry. Did you call Bill?"

"Bishop, I don't want to be rude, but I don't care if Bill Collins never comes near me again. I don't like the man. I have never liked him and…" For the first time since the strange ordeal began, her voice faltered.

"Laura, I'm sorry. What can I do to help you?"

"Would you do the service?"

"Certainly. Let me know about the details."

2

Randy paced in front of the upstairs window. The heat was excessive—humid. His uncle hadn't given him much work since the Kenzel job. That was over a year ago. The money was long gone. His old man was a tightwad. His other uncle was still in prison.

"Hey, stop all that stomping around up there," Randy's father called from the foot of the stairs. "You're making the lights flicker."

"Yeah, yeah." Randy slammed his hand into the palm of his other hand and screwed up his face like a three-year-old. He even stuck out his tongue then muttered to himself. "I got to get out of this hole. Got to get away from that old man and those stupid cats. Maybe I could sneak one out and sell it. But who would buy a stupid animal?"

The phone shattered his grumbling. He heard his father answer and waited to see if it was anything important before returning to his lead-footed pacing—just to annoy the old man.

"Hey kid. Your uncle wants to talk to you."

Randy suddenly perked up. Maybe he had another good-paying job for him. He ran down the stairs, jumping over the third one from the bottom, which was cracked and ready to break with too much weight. He grabbed the phone and turned his back on his father hoping he would go away. He heard the footsteps moving toward the kitchen.

"Yeah?"

"Is that any way to answer a phone?"

Randy laughed—his normal cackle. "Sorry, Uncle. I'm getting cabin fever cooped up here with my old man and those darn cats."

"Well, maybe I can help. Got another job for you."

"Yeah? Who do you want me to whack this time?"

"Randy, do learn to be a little more civilized. You sound like a street bum. No killing this time—unless, of course, it's necessary. Your dad still there?"

"He went to the kitchen to start something for supper."

"I need both of you. Bring him to our meeting place. Make sure no one follows you. I'll explain then."

"When? Can't you just tell me?"

"No, I want to talk to both of you together to make sure you understand the problem and what I want done about it. Three o'clock in the morning. Don't be late."

"But..." Randy was holding a buzzing phone when his father stuck his head around the door.

"What'd he want?"

"Wants us to meet him at the cabin three o'clock in the morning."

"Then we better eat a bite and get moving. That's a five hour drive."

Randy groaned. Five hours cooped up in a car with his old man and..."Are you taking those cats?"

"No. We'll lock them in the basement."

* * *

"You sure he said three o'clock?"

"What do you think, Pop? I'm stupid or something? Yeah, he said three o'clock in the morning." He glanced at the clock on the dash. "It's only two-thirty. He's probably already there."

"Yeah, he only has three hours to drive, not five. There's county road 15. Don't miss your turn."

"I see it, Pop. I ain't blind."

16

"Don't talk to me in that tone of voice. I am your father."

"Cool it, Pop. You ain't got no hold on me no more. I'm a big guy now."

The car lurched over the unpaved and uncared-for road. Randy slammed on the brake as two deer ran across the road in front of him. Had he been home he would have just hit them. But he was afraid his uncle would be angry if they were late because he was careless. He cursed under his breath and continued until the turnoff appeared. Ten minutes and they were at the cabin. No lights were visible, but a darker bulge beside the house must be his uncle's car.

They got out and approached the cabin door with caution. Randy gave their signal knock—three short taps, a pause then two more short taps. The door opened a crack, sending a sharp arrow of light across the porch. Randy and his father squeezed through the narrow opening and the door closed behind them. A lock clicked in place.

Randy looked around surprised at the light when he had seen none. A double layer of heavy black cloth of some kind covered every window.

"What took you so long? I don't have all night. I've got a nine a.m. meeting."

"Sorry, Uncle. Deer slowed us down."

"Well, let's get down to business. I need you two in a little town south of here. Perfect hiding place for our stash of heroine between runs. I need you to keep people away from it."

"No problem, Bro. Tell us where and how."

Twenty minutes the uncle left. Randy and his father waited ten more minutes, giving his uncle time to get out of sight before they left. They drove back home to prepare for their new assignment. Randy was excited. Finally, his uncle had given him a job he could really get in to. His father pretended to sleep, not wanting to talk. He wasn't so sure about the new job. He had a bad feeling about it. He didn't like messing with religion.

* * *

Jeb—as he was known in this little town—was even more sure his brother's idea was not a good one. He had been here nearly two years, living at a poverty level, always cold in winter and hot in summer. Randy lived in that big mansion on the hill—never cold, never hungry, never lacking for anything. Something had to change. Maybe he could call his brother, except he had no idea where he was or what name he used. He would have to wait for him to call.

"Hey there old man, let's see those cats dance." Randy threw a dollar in the old man's hat. Jeb cranked up his wind-up music box and the cats danced for them. A few other passersby threw some coins and bills in the hat.

"Thank you sonny," he said and laughed. Randy scowled. He hated for his old man, or anyone for that matter, to call him that. Jeb knew he couldn't complain, because he called all young men, son.

Later he unrolled the bill to read the note enclosed. "Uncle says one more is coming—a woman. When we get rid of her—dead or alive—we're home free."

Another? A woman yet? With all the trouble here, why would they send a woman? They must want to get rid of her for some reason. Maybe she's a troublemaker. Well, I'll sure be glad when it's over and I can live like a normal man again.

3

Laura had sold most of her furniture and moved into a small efficiency apartment until she could sort out her life. Susan had been upset because she didn't go live with them. As much as she loved her grandson, Laura would not tie herself down as a permanent live-in babysitter. She intended to go to seminary in the fall. Susan had been upset about that, also.

Laura remembered the conversation as if it had been yesterday. "You know Daddy never would have allowed that," Susan had said.

"I'm sure we would have worked it out." Laura wasn't sure they could have worked it out without a major argument, but it was a moot point since she didn't need his approval now—even if Susan thought she did.

"Mother, how could you...?"

"Susan, I certainly didn't want your father to die. I don't especially enjoy being a widow. But, it's what I am and I will not sit back and pine away. I have to move on with my life. I believe God is directing. I must follow."

"But..."

"Never mind, Susan, I'm your mother, not your child. I think I'm capable of making decisions concerning my life."

Laura smiled. That had been three years ago. Now she was

packing and getting ready for graduation. The cabinet was still meeting preparing for the Ohio Annual Conference. Surely, they would come up with something for her. She was ready to move on. She had learned to live alone and do all the things Harold had insisted on doing before his death. She just wished she could call that chapter of her life closed, but until they found the person who killed him, she would forever wonder.

She'd learned that Harold's death was no accident. Butch remembered calling Harold from the bar. While he waited, some man bought him another drink. He remembered nothing after that until he awoke in the hospital. The bartender confirmed his story. His attorney proved that in his drunken state, to say nothing of his concussion, he could not possibly have gotten out of the car, killed Harold then got back in his car. The doctor confirmed the impossibility of the act.

Still, if he hadn't been such a problem drinker and hadn't called Harold that night, Harold would still be alive. Or would he? Someone deliberately broke his neck. Why? Did it have something to do with what he wanted to talk to the bishop about? After all this time, Laura found herself still fighting the anger. Could she ever forgive Butch or the person who murdered her husband?

Laura had finally been able to let go of her anger at God for allowing the tragedy. She sought His help in deciding her future. She heard, or thought she heard, or felt, what she could only think of as a spiritual mirth within her soul. She knew God was with her.

Now, with graduation near, Laura waited again for God's direction. "Where do I go from here?"

Deep in her soul, she felt the answer as if a friend stood before her speaking. "I have work for you Laura Kenzel. There's a special little church nestled down in the hills that needs you and you need them to complete your healing. Will you go?"

Laura thought she was losing her mind, but found herself saying, "I will go where You lead me." Had she but known the trials she would endure on the way to healing!

* * *

"The cabinet members are all waiting for you, Bishop." Sally held out a stack of folders for Bishop Matthew Giles as he straightened his tie and smoothed back his hair. Still in his first year at that conference, he was learning his way around.

"Sorry I'm late," he said without offering an excuse. He took the folders and proceeded to the cabinet room where twelve district superintendents sat around the table looking expectantly for his excuse. He gave none, but opened the first folder and went right to the point.

"What is the problem with this Cottonville church? I just received a call from Tom Howell, whom we sent down there last week. He says the Staff Relation Committee refused to even meet with him. How many does that make in the last year? Or is it two years?"

Groans sounded around the room. "That makes close to a hundred pastors we've sent there in the last—what—two and a half years? Isn't that your district, Bill?"

Bill Collins grunted an answer. "Don't know what their problem is. They tell me that ever since John Lakeland hung himself in the belfry over two years ago, they've had all kinds of troubles. They're hill people—believe the place is haunted."

"Why would they believe that?" Bishop Giles locked eyes with him expecting an answer.

Bill pulled at his collar which suddenly felt tight. "I'm not sure. They hear noises in the belfry like a man moaning and chains rattling. They see lights flickering. The chief of police had checked numerous times, but can never find anything. People are afraid to go into the church. The secretary won't go in there by herself. The church and parsonage are falling down around them."

"Maybe we ought to just close it," suggested Karen.

"We can't do that," said Bishop Giles, "not without going through the proper channels. Any other suggestions?"

"I say give them one more try. Don't give them any choice, just appoint someone and send him there. Make them understand that if that person doesn't stay, we'll start proceedings to close the church." George had been on the cabinet longer than the other superintendents and knew many of the pastors who had been sent there and refused to stay.

"That's a little drastic," said the bishop, "but maybe we're at the point of being drastic. A name *has* been suggested—a seminary student ready for graduation."

Bill Collins frowned. The rest of the cabinet looked surprised and waited for Bishop Giles to give them the name. He was still new, so they would have to let him know if it would work or not. Surely if seasoned pastors couldn't stay, a seminary graduate had no chance.

"Her name is Kenzel," said the bishop. "What do we know about her?"

"A woman? Are you sure she...?"

Bill Collins' brow creased into a greater frown. "Her husband was one of our pastors. He died in an automobile accident about three or four years ago. She went to seminary the following fall. I guess she would be happy for any appointment."

"We've tried everything else," said Karen. "Maybe a woman could make it work."

"She's not a risk taker," said Bill. "She won't last any longer than the rest. They won't accept a woman down there."

"What about all the rumors? You say her husband died. Is she alone, or does she have children?"

"She has a married daughter, but she lives alone. All those rumors might be stories to keep people away from the church," said Bill.

"Who would want to do that, and why?" The bishop frowned.

"Who knows? Someone's disgruntled with the church and doesn't want it to survive. Maybe even one of the other churches in town."

"Very well," said Bishop Giles, "call her and make certain she understands this is the church's last chance. We'll make an exception in this special case. She will be under appointment beginning the first of the month. She will not meet with the committee until she arrives. There is no choice in this appointment."

"I suppose she'll go. She does need a home. She's desperate." Karen looked uncertain.

"You will keep tabs on her, Bill, and if there is any hint of trouble you will pull her out of there immediately. I'll talk with her later. Now, on to other business."

4

"We're getting closer, Shebop." The mountainous roads of southern Ohio didn't allow for much speed. They were much like the ones she learned to drive on in the hills of West Virginia. She experienced a small jab of homesickness. It had been years since she even thought about the old home place. Since her marriage to Harold and the death of her uncle, she'd had no reason to return.

Since early morning, Laura had been traveling from her seminary home in Illinois to her first appointment—a church that it seemed no one wanted. She wasn't exactly sure why. Bill Collins had told her very little about the church, nothing actually. But it didn't matter. As surely as God told Abraham and Moses to go to his respective assignment, she knew God was sending her to this church that no one wanted. She was excited, except...now Bill Collins was her district superintendent. He only had one more year unless he somehow finagled a second term, or an extension. She would simply ignore him.

She rounded one of the many curves and a dual-pump gas station sat at the side of the road like an island in a raging sea. Its sign over the door of the gas station/restaurant beckoned like a welcoming hand. SAMMY'S PLACE. Suddenly, Laura realized how tired and hungry she was. Her mind on many things, she hadn't noticed how close to empty the gas gauge pointed. Shebop, her ancient blue Chevette, rolled to a stop, sputtered, coughed, sputtered again then died beside the first of two pumps.

"I feel the same way," said Laura, patting the car's dash. She sat for a minute letting her body adjust to the non-movement of the car. She stood beside the car, stretched her arms skyward and wondered if her muscles would ever feel normal again.

She opened the gas cap, but before she could begin to fill the tank, a pleasant-looking young man ran from the building. He took the nozzle from her. "I'll do that, ma'am," he said. "If you want to get anything from inside, I'll just park her over by the window."

Laura, glad to turn the job over to him, smiled. "Thanks," she said and walked into the building. She paused to check out her surroundings—automotive needs to the left, cash register straight ahead, restaurant with tables and booths to the right, restrooms to the back of the restaurant area. She started in the direction of the restrooms. A very pregnant waitress not much more than eighteen or nineteen years old met her and took her order for coffee.

Coffee and a menu were on a table by the window when she returned. She glanced down the list of entrees and rubbed her aching temples. The smells of gasoline, frying foods—onions, fish, burgers—and an assortment of perfumed objects in the gift corner, made the thought of food almost intolerable. Cottonville was still several hours away. She had to have something, so settled for soup and coffee.

"We don't get many folks passing through here. Ya'll visitin' around here?" The pretty girl spoke with a drawl from much farther south. Laura smiled.

"Not visiting. I'm coming to stay. I'm the new pastor at the Cottonville United Methodist Church." Just saying the words gave Laura a tingle of excitement.

"Cottonville Methodist Church? Excuse me for saying so, ma'am, but ya'll don't want to go there. It's haunted, or demon-possessed, or something. Why they ain't had no preacher for nigh on to two years—not since one of the preachers hung himself. The last one came through here about six weeks back, stopped for supper and was back in about eight hours. Said the place was overrun with ghosts and eerie noises—chains rattling and screeching and the like from the belfry that made his hair stand on end. His wife, poor thing, was still trembling."

Laura smiled at the waitress, who rubbed her bulging midsection without a hint of embarrassment. Like many non United Methodists, she called the church by its former name. The young man who had pumped the gas approached her table.

The young waitress shook her head. "I know it's hard to believe, ma'am, but it's the gospel truth. Ain't it so, Sammy?" She patted her stomach and looked up at the young man who was obviously her husband—or significant other.

Sammy was more interested in Shebop than what the girl was saying, reluctantly handed Laura her keys. "I filled the gas tank and checked the oil, then parked her right outside the door," he said. "She sure is a beauty. You ever want to sell her, be glad to take her off your hands."

The keys jangled as Laura dropped them in her purse. She'd watched from the window as the young man caressed her Chevette as if it were a Mercedes. "Thank you Sammy, but it's not for sale."

The young waitress pulled at Sammy's sleeve to get his attention. "Sammy, this here's the new preacher in Cottonville. I was telling her about all the trouble they've been having over there."

"No kidding?" Sammy glanced at Laura. "Pardon me for saying so, ma'am, but you don't look like most preachers I know."

Laura laughed. Her jeans and pastel-plaid, short-sleeve shirt certainly wasn't the normal attire for a minister, but then, neither was being female the norm for pastors in this part of the state. She wasn't sure to which Sammy referred.

Sammy grinned. "Nancy gets a little carried away with her gossip sometimes, but she's right about this one. That church in Cottonville's had a rough time of it for a couple of years. No one stayed more than a few hours. If I were you, I'd just turn that pretty little car around and head her back the way you came. You don't want to get tangled up with that mess in Cottonville."

Laura, about to take a drink of coffee, held the cup mid-way to her mouth, steam rising, aroma wafting on the air. "Surely you're kidding," she said. "Ghosts?" She searched his face for a hint of teasing. He was serious.

"That's what they say, ma'am. I ain't never been there, but you sure wouldn't catch me going into that church, day or night." Sammy shook his head. "No sir, not me." He turned to greet another couple entering the store. Nancy took them a menu, leaving Laura alone with her unsettling thoughts which did nothing to help ease the mild headache or queasy feeling in the pit of her stomach. She finished her soup, not even sure what she had eaten and drained her coffee. She slid from the booth then waited while Sammy rang up another sale and went over a map with a customer.

"Thank you for looking after my car," she said when it was her turn. "With fuel in my car and food in me, I think I can make it the rest of the way." She smiled at the young man as he took her money. "By the way, how much farther is Cottonville? I have directions to the church after I get there, but my other directions are rather sketchy."

"You're on the right road, ma'am," Sammy answered shaking his head. "Just follow it through Glenville—that's about two and a half, maybe three hours away. Make a left at the west edge of town onto Gopher Mountain Road, just past the IGA. You can't miss it. Cottonville's about another forty-five minutes across the mountain. Just watch the sharp curves on Gopher Mountain. They don't say fifteen miles per hour for nothing and they don't have no guardrails on most of the road. I really would turn back if I were you."

Laura managed a smile and let her change slip into a pocket. "Thank you for your concern and thoughtfulness, but I've come too far to turn back now. Besides, I'm not afraid of ghosts."

The words sounded brave and confident, but the churning in her stomach and the shiver that crept down her spine didn't match the bravado. She wasn't afraid of ghosts, but there seemed to be something humanly evil about the rumors. That was a different story.

With one last glance at the still rolling clouds, Laura slid behind the steering wheel. She grumbled good-naturedly about the quarter-sized drops that dotted her car once again. "Beautiful day You gave me. You send me off to some god-forsaken place on the other side of Gopher Mountain, and now they tell me the place is haunted. At least You could give me decent traveling weather."

As if in answer to her complaint, a bright light flashed across the sky and thunder like a blast of dynamite boomed then rolled and bumped across the mountaintops. The convoy of clouds arrived, expelled its load, and moved on.

"All right. All right. Maybe You haven't forsaken it, but are You sure You're sending the right person to this little church?" In spite of her uneasiness, Laura felt a special thrill, which she could only describe as a chuckle deep within her soul—one which she identified as God's presence. The swishing of the windshield wipers lulled her into a pensive mood.

Three years ago last January the accident thrust her into singleness after twenty-five years of marriage. She had planned that night to tell Harold she intended to go to seminary in the fall. He never had the chance to try to dissuade her, which he would have done. But she had been determined then and would not have let him stop her. She was just sorry they never had the chance to talk about it.

Laura had done everything possible to forget that night—the feelings of guilt, anger, and remorse as well as the physical effects of the hospital visit. Even though she knew, as a pastor, she would have to visit hospitals, she avoided them. Once when she tried to visit a friend, she had a panic attack and returned home without stepping foot inside the building. She should have gotten counseling, but was too ashamed of her weakness, so she simply ignored the problem. She would deal with it later. Maybe it would be different when the patient was one of her own flock.

Laura shuddered. The memory of that night pushed into her consciousness without her permission—the hospital with all those white of uniforms, white walls, and white sheets. Even the windowsills and floor were white. The odor—she could still smell the antiseptic that mingled with blood and sweat. And sounds echoed in her memory as if they were in her car with her—bells, pagers, and IV's beeping from various rooms, carts needing oil on wheels, heels clacking down hard corridors.

Laura shook her head and blinked her eyes rapidly several times. Leaves and branches blew across the road in little circles like miniature tornadoes, but, even the stormy weather could not remove the memories. She had to pry her thoughts away from the past. This was the present.

Two hours later Laura saw the sign—Glenville 5 Miles. A few minutes later, the little car passed a park with swings and slides then rolled down Main Street. A hardware store, general store, and Alice's Restaurant were on one side of the street. A bank and a place called The Flower Pot were on the other side of the street. Not much activity at nine o'clock in the evening, except in the two-story, brick building beside the IGA. The words carved in the cement over the door said, Glenville Police Department. Lights and movement inside let the community know its protectors were on duty.

"Soon we'll be home, Shebop," Laura spoke to her faithful car as she turned left onto Gopher Mountain Road. "Doesn't that have a nice sound to it?" Of course, she got no response.

The road curved up and around the mountain. The sign at the bottom had said: Lookout Point 15 Miles; Cottonville 30 Miles. The road sometimes dipped with a steep slant, sometimes climbed upward. Laura's arms ached from all the turning. One final hairpin curve and she was at Lookout Point.

She couldn't resist stopping—even in the dark. She eased Shebop into one of the dozen parking spots. She got out and, glancing at the still rolling clouds, hastened to the rock wall topped with iron fencing. A pay-for-view telescope stood like a robot on its stand waiting for someone to feed it flat little bites of silver. In return, it would offer a magnified view of the valley. Laura ignored the telescope and leaned against the wall, gazing at the twinkling lights in the valley below. The scent of pine and other mountain greenery—freshly laundered by the rain—drifted across the mountain.

"God, it's so beautiful. Thank you for sending me here." Somewhere in the depth of her soul, she felt that spiritual mirth and she knew she was in God's hands.

In a brief flash or two of lightning Laura saw enough of the road behind her and before her to know she wouldn't want to go off the road anywhere along the way. She saw trees, bare mountain shrubbery and one huge boulder, about the size of a Volkswagen, which seemed out of place. Raindrops once again sent her back to her car.

"Well, Shebop, the sign over there says fifteen miles to Cottonville. If we're lucky, you can rest in a nice dry garage and I can sit in my favorite chair with a cup of something hot—tea, coffee, chocolate, or whatever I can find."

Laura chuckled to herself, knowing that wasn't likely to be the way it would work. The van would have left her furniture by now. Boxes would be stacked in every available spot. Various sizes and shapes of things waiting for her to put them away would make her chair inaccessible. She grinned anyway. She could always dream.

Close to twenty-five minutes later, the fifteen miles behind her, her faithful Chevette rolled past the sign that said, Welcome to Cottonville. Laura smiled in spite of her weariness. A tingle of excitement gripped her fingertips and ran down to her toes. She glanced at her sketchy map, which indicated she should turn right on Cotton Square North, go straight ahead on Second Street for two blocks and make a left on Cotton Avenue. Sure enough, there it was—The Cottonville United Methodist Church. The white frame building with its steeple and bell tower in the middle of the roof stood watch over its corner of Cotton Avenue like a tired sentinel.

Cotton Avenue. Church, parsonage, and another house about a football field's distance down the street. No sidewalks. One lone streetlight near the front of the church. She was home!

With a deep sigh of relief and joy, Laura turned into the driveway between the church and the parsonage. She stopped in a gravel-packed clearing. The garage was to the left and the parsonage to the right. Through the blur of raindrops on her window, she surveyed her new home. The garage looked more like a small barn that had seen much better days. Lighted by the beam of her headlights, one of the sliding, barn-type doors danced in the battering wind, shuddering and creaking on its only attached hinge. The other door rusted and frozen in place refused to dance with its partner.

"Sorry Shebop. Looks like you won't be there tonight. We'll see what we can do tomorrow.

"Bill said Frank and Martha Jennings lived nearby. That two-story house down the street must be theirs. They don't expect me until tomorrow, so maybe I can get a good night's sleep before meeting folks."

The parsonage, a two-story, white frame building stood waiting for its new occupants. The limited luminance of the headlights highlighted peeling and chipped paint, and a short length of spouting flapping in the wind. A narrow cement path connected the driveway to the house which seemed surrounded by a hay field.

Laura stared. "Well, God, it's not much to look at in the dark and the rain. I'm sure it will be better in the morning. Won't it?"

The soft feeling of spiritual mirth within her soul sent a grin across her lips. It didn't matter what it looked like, it was her first church and she was home. She turned off the engine, slipped her keys into her pocket, picked up her purse and reached for a flashlight from the glove compartment. She ran for the house, but was soaked by the time she reached the porch where she slowed to a fast walk. The beam of the flashlight fell across the doorknob which wasn't where it should have been. A three-inch open space yawned between the door and the doorframe.

The wind continued to blow and a noise from the church belfry sounded more like an odd combination of growling and moaning. Rattling of small chains accompanied the weird song from the belfry. Between the door, which should not be open, and the weird sounds, a chill slid down her spine. Had that waitress been right? Did ghosts occupy the house and the church? Laura shook herself—mentally and physically—then derided her fear. "Now cut that out, Laura Kenzel. You know better. No ghosts. Period!"

She pushed the door the rest of the way open and stepped inside the house. The strong odor of ammonia and other cleaning agents brought a short sneezing fit. At least someone had tried to clean up the inside. She located the light switch and flipped it. Nothing happened. Either the storm caused a power outage or the main switch was off.

"I'll have to find the main breaker box." Laura spoke softly to herself, hoping to chase away any of the ghosts she didn't believe in, or the subconscious foreboding that crept over her. She was more likely to stumble over boxes that cluttered the rooms than she was to run into a ghost. She aimed the flashlight beam at the floor.

In most homes, the main switch was usually in the basement. She would try there first. She stepped over a box into the dining room and picked her way toward what she assumed to be the kitchen. Something fell behind her. She turned to see who or what, was there and lost her balance A shadow loomed against the wall. Something hard, like a stick, or pipe, hit her arm. Pain shot up to her shoulder. Her purse fell among a stack of boxes that tumbled. The flashlight hit the floor and rolled away, its light extinguished as the bulb jarred loose.

"You miss your mister?" A weird sardonic, maniacal sound came close to her ear as an arm went around her waist. The combination of body odor and marijuana filled her nose and made it difficult to breathe. The intruder's other hand tightly clamped over her mouth and nose cutting off what little air she was able to suck in. "I killed him," a weird voice said. "I will send you to be with him." Laura struggled. The man dragged her toward the back door.

5

According to the weather report, the rain would last all day. "Heavy at times," the bubbly girl on News One had reported. Glenville Police Homicide Detective, Steve Morgan paced in front of the window of the office he shared with his long-time friend and colleague, Joe Baldwin. With each step, he sipped coffee that had long ago gone cold.

"What's up, Steve?"

Steve glanced at Joe. They had been partners and co-workers for almost a quarter of a century. Joe, a handsome black man, was tall, slim and kept in shape. He was a family man—wife, three kids. He knew his friend's moods well enough to know something was troubling Steve.

"Not sure, Joe." Steve ran his fingers through his thick, dark hair with specks of white around the edges. Could use a haircut, he thought. He turned his focus back to his edginess. "Ever have a feeling that something isn't quite right—like a picture hanging slightly off center?"

Joe laughed. "We've been in this business long enough to know the world is full of crazies. Nothing is ever quite right where crime is concerned."

"Yeah, but…there is no crime, at least none I'm aware of. It's almost like I can feel something more than just the rain coming down—almost like a premonition; and I don't believe in premonitions." He laughed at the expression on Joe's face. "Sorry, pal, don't mean to get psychic or philosophical. Maybe it's just the weather."

"Maybe you need a vacation. When's the last time you had one?" It was Joe's turn to laugh at his friend's expression. They both knew Steve never took a vacation. Maybe a day or two now and then, but never a real vacation. He had no family and wanted no part of women in his life, so where would he go?

Steve laughed. "Maybe you're right. I need a change. Maybe I'll go over to Cottonville and spend some time with Todd. He's been asking me to help him with some continuing education courses he's taking from Wheeling."

"I don't call that a vacation, but it would be a change of scenery and pace."

"Are you sure you can manage without me?" Steve laughed and Joe understood why women were so attracted to him. His blue eyes twinkled when he laughed and in his early fifties, he was a handsome man—tall, built like a quarterback. And yet as long as he had known Steve, there'd never been a woman in his life. After the divorce, he wasn't interested in women. Pity. Steve had so much to offer—honesty, integrity, compassion and understanding. Oh, well, it was Steve's choice. Joe brought his attention back to Steve's question.

"You wouldn't be that far away if we had a rash of murders."

Both men laughed. Although Steve was a homicide detective, they hardly ever had a real case in Glenville, or any of the surrounding area. He worked more with the FBI and the county sheriff's department than with local police on that front. The Feds had asked him many times to join them, but he thought he would be more help to them by working solo.

Steve called Cottonville Police Chief Todd Williams and arrived at Todd's office shortly after noon. Todd, a much younger man in his mid-thirties, met him at the door.

Steve smiled at Todd's boyish grin and grasped his extended hand. "Are you ready to work hard?"

"You bet," answered Todd. "I've been studying these books for the class in Wheeling. Got three weeks to finish the course for credit."

"What are we studying?"

"Violent crimes—murder, kidnapping, armed robberies— things we never see around here. But you never know and I want to be prepared."

Steve smiled at the younger man's enthusiasm, but remembered his own earlier restlessness. Once again he wondered if he was being paranoid. Maybe Joe was right. He needed a real vacation. He brought his attention back to Todd, who opened his book and started throwing questions at him so fast he had to laugh. "Whoa there, Todd. One at a time."

Todd laughed, too. "Sorry. I guess I can't believe you're really going to spend several days helping me. I want to get as much in as possible while you're here."

Time marched along and both men stood to stretch. Todd's brown hair looked like he had been caught in a wind storm from running his fingers through it while he struggled with concepts of police work. He glanced at the clock on the wall. "Six o'clock," he said. "No wonder I'm hungry. Want to try Charlie's? My treat."

"Sure, why not. That's the little diner at the edge of town near the park, isn't it?"

"Yeah, the only restaurant in town, so it has a steady business."

Steve and Todd found an empty booth in the far corner and continued their dialogue on crime while they ate. "What's the most violent crime you've investigated?" Steve leaned back in the corner of the booth and sipped his coffee.

"Probably when old man Morris got drunk and beat his wife a few years back. She divorced him and moved to Indiana with her parents. He spent a few years in prison for petty stuff. Never heard from either of them again."

"How about teen crimes—drugs, alcohol, car-related incidents?"

"Yeah, we have those. Nothing serious—yet. But I'm watching a couple of kids who are going to be in big trouble if their parents don't take them in hand."

"Shall we go back to your office and work a couple more hours, or have you had enough for one day?" Steve placed a tip on the table as they stood to leave.

"I'm game if you are, but are you driving back to Glenville tonight?"

"You got a better idea? Last I heard you don't have any motels in Cottonville."

"I've got a spare room if you want to stay. I'm not much of a host as far as cooking, but Charlie's is open at six a.m."

"Sounds good to me." Steve laughed. "This is my vacation."

Todd laughed with him. "I hear you, buddy. That's the kind I take, too."

Back at the office once again the two men attacked the books until Todd finally stood, stretched, combed his fingers through his hair, and said, "I don't know about you, pal, but that old clock is telling me it's time to quit. Ten o'clock. I don't think my brain can absorb another word."

Steve laughed, leaned back on his chair and nodded. "Tomorrow is another day. You're doing very well. You should have no trouble passing the exams."

"Thanks, Steve. I sure appreciate…" The phone rang, cutting off his words. He looked surprised. "Didn't think it was working. Haven't heard it all day."

"Cottonville Police Department, Chief Williams speaking…Frank, what's up?…I'll check it out."

"Trouble?"

"Probably not. Frank Jennings, over on Cotton Avenue. Says he saw a light in the Methodist parsonage. The new pastor's furniture is there and he's not due until sometime tomorrow. With all the trouble the church has had, Frank didn't want more before the pastor even gets here."

"Better go check it out," said Steve.

"Want to come along? My first B and E. Might need your expertise." Todd laughed.

"Sure, I'll tag along to see if you've learned anything from me. I'll stay in the background unless you need backup."

36

Todd stopped beside the car parked in the driveway. Steve waited to see what Todd would do about it and was pleased when Todd walked around the car, flashed his light on the contents. Then he made a note of the license number before they started for the house.

"We get transients parking here all the time—looking for a handout, or a place to sleep for the night. Car's packed for traveling, out of state license. Might be who Frank saw in the house."

"I hope you're right," said Steve fighting a stronger feeling of premonition. He followed Todd across the porch. The front door was open. No lights, but they heard scuffling in the back of the house."

Todd called out. "This is the police! Whoever you are come out with your hands up, or we'll come in shooting." He and Steve ran toward the kitchen, jumping over boxes and around scattered furniture.

* * *

The man jerked Laura toward the door and kicked it open. "Who called the cops?" he muttered. Laura had stopped struggling. She fell forward and began to lose consciousness. The man tightened his grip around her waist, but his hand over her mouth slipped enough for air to reach her lungs sending oxygen to her numbed brain.

Flashlight beams bounced across the floor and walls from the front room as the police officers ran. The man holding Laura muttered curses. "Can't let the cops see me. I'll take care of you another time."

Todd and Steve ran into the kitchen. The man shoved Laura away and ran out the door. Laura fell to her knees and Steve would have stumbled over her had he not seen something, or someone, fall. He stopped. Todd moved around her and ran after the man who disappeared into the darkness.

Steve stooped to help Laura, who still gasped for air, which left her light-headed. She fell against Steve, whose arms went around her to keep her from falling to the floor again. A faint aroma of Old Spice replaced the distinct smell of marijuana and extreme body odor.

"Sorry," she said, trying to stand without help.

"There's a chair. Lean against the wall while I clear it." He set his flashlight on the table and moved a box to the floor from the straight-backed kitchen chair.

Todd returned. "He got away. Must have gone through the woods. I heard a car on the other side peel out. Looks like we got one of them. We'll take him down to the station for questioning."

"I think you mean her," said Steve, "but I hardly think she's a burglar."

"Whoever she is she has no business in this house. We'll take her to the office and…"

"Maybe we should hear what she has to say first," said Steve.

"Won't make any difference. This is the church parsonage. It is full of the new pastor's belongings. Looks like someone wants to scare off another one. Maybe we'll get a lead on who they are and why they're terrorizing the pastors now that we have one of them. Let's go. We'll find out who this one is, then hunt down the other one."

Laura, still wheezing, tried to clear her head. The intent of Todd's words suddenly became clear. He's going to arrest her for trespassing—or worse!

"Wait a minute," she said. Her voice was raspy from the lack of oxygen. "Why don't you turn on the lights and we can talk here. I'm tired and I live here. Please, hear me out."

As hard as she tried, Laura couldn't prevent the sound of panic. She was disturbed by what her abductor had said and now she was threatened with spending the night in jail.

"Todd, maybe…"

"We can't do much here with no electricity," said Todd.

"Try the fuse box," said Laura, "and could you lower the flashlight beams a little." She shaded her eyes from the glare with her hand. Both Todd and Steve had been holding the lights on her like spotlights.

"Sorry," they said and set them on the table which sent the beam to the ceiling, lighting that corner of the kitchen.

"How do you know where the fuse box is, or even if that is the problem?" Steve asked.

"I don't. I was on my way to find it when that man grabbed me. I assume it's in the basement. Since there are lights outside and down the street, the power must be turned off here."

Steve laughed. Todd sputtered. "I think she has a point, Todd. Want me to check it out?"

"No, I'll go." He found the door and went to the basement, found the switch box, and pushed the master switch up. "Try the light switch," he called up to Steve.

Steve found the switch beside the outside door, flipped it and the kitchen was bathed in light. Laura couldn't help smiling. Somehow, the light made everything tolerable.

"All right," said Todd when he came back to the kitchen, "let's hear it. Who are you and why are you here?"

"I could ask you the same question," she answered, "considering I was nearly abducted and my life was threatened. I'm glad you showed up when you did, but for all I know you are with him and..."

Steve started laughing, sending the twinkle to his eyes, which caused Laura to catch her breath. She coughed to cover the unexpected feeling that overwhelmed her.

"Do you want to make the introductions, Todd, or shall I?"

Todd started to scowl then laughed with Steve. "Sorry, ma'am. Guess I got a little carried away on my first burglary. Cottonville Police Chief Todd Williams here. This is Glenville's homicide detective, Steve Morgan."

"Homicide? You've had a murder here?"

"No ma'am," said Steve. "I'm on vacation—just helping Todd with some studies."

"Oh," she said, a frown still furrowing her brow.

"Trouble with that?" Steve lifted his eyebrows and waited.

"No, I...I'm sorry. I'm still not thinking clearly. I couldn't breathe and that man said he killed my husband and would kill me too...But that doesn't make sense." Laura shivered and Steve slipped out of his cardigan. He handed it to her and she wrapped it around her shoulders. "Thanks."

"Maybe we better start at the beginning," said Todd. "Do you have a name?"

"Laurance Ellen Kenzel." She spelled it for him. "Laura, for short."

"Age?"

"Forty-nine."

"Married?"

"Widowed."

"Eyes?"

Laura smiled and began to relax. They were teasing her and she couldn't resist a sarcastic reply. "Of course! Two. Brown."

Steve leaned against the sink and laughed. Todd smiled and continued as if he were taking vital information.

"Hair, red," he said.

"It's *auburn*," she said, "not red. Would you like my fingerprints? They should be on file with the state police and the FBI."

"Why are you in this house tonight?"

At the same time, Steve asked, "Why would your fingerprints be registered with the state police and FBI? Sorry, Todd. I didn't mean to take over."

Laura laughed. "I can probably answer both questions at the same time. I'm the new pastor for the United Methodist Church and having fingerprints checked and on file is a new requirement for all pastors before being ordained."

Todd stared with mouth open. Laura's preconceived notion of a small town police chief was challenged. This man was slim, muscular, mid to late thirties, brown hair which was full and wavy—not thinning as she would have thought.

She turned to Steve who smiled at her. She noticed him—really noticed him—for the first time as well. He did not fit her preconceived notion of a homicide detective, either. No uniform—dressed in gray slacks, pale blue, button up shirt, no tie. She had on his navy blue cardigan. But beyond all that, for the first time since Harold's death, Laura felt attracted to another man. That unnerved her, sending a slight blush to her cheeks. She shook her head and hoped he didn't notice.

In the few seconds it took for her to size him up, Steve did his own evaluating, surprised by the pretty, auburn-haired woman. He could easily get lost in those deep brown eyes. She was slim, probably five-six or so, and couldn't weigh much more than a hundred and ten. He hoped *he* wasn't blushing. For almost thirty years, he had ignored women. Why was this one affecting him so?

"Pastor?" Todd's eyebrows shot up. "You can't be the new pastor they're looking for at the Methodist Church. Martha told me *he* would be here tomorrow sometime."

"Well, I don't know who they were expecting, but I'm it."

"Do you have any identification?" Todd pushed his hat back on his head and took a deep breath.

"In my purse that I dropped somewhere among the boxes in there." She nodded to the front room. "My seminary certificate is packed with my books—somewhere."

Steve went to the front room and found her purse and flashlight that had rolled under the dining room table. She showed them her driver's license and her Cokesbury card from the seminary.

"Reverend Kenzel," said Todd. "I don't know quite what to say. I'm sorry we mistook you for a burglar, but..."

Laura laughed a soft bubbly sound. She took Todd's extended hand in a firm handshake. "Chief," she said, "you were only doing your job and you did save me from the real burglar. You probably don't have a lot of crime to deal with in a small town."

"You have every reason to be upset, Reverend Kenzel," said Steve, extending his hand as well. He looked deep into her brown eyes and found it difficult to release her hand.

Laura grinned as he reluctantly released her hand. "Please, the name is Laura. It's nice to know I have a couple of friends to call on in an emergency—like chasing ghosts."

"You've heard about our ghosts and came anyway?"

"I heard stories from my seminary friends, but I didn't believe them. The waitress where I stopped about four hours ago told more. It was a little late to turn back then."

"Somehow, I think the folks here are going to be a bit surprised. I hope they don't give you a hard time."

"Oh, I think I can handle the congregation, but I'm sure glad you guys came along tonight. I don't think I could handle much of that kind of trouble. The folks are lucky to have such dedicated police officers—even if one is on vacation."

Steve and Todd both looked surprised and then laughed. "Steve and Todd here," said Todd. "You didn't have a very pleasant introduction to our community, but we'll do what we can to reverse our blunder."

Laura pulled Steve's sweater tighter around her, breathing in that faint aroma of Old Spice. Once again, a stab of memory shot through her—memory of her grandfather and uncle who had raised her.

"Are you all right?" Steve asked, but before she could answer, they heard footsteps on the front porch. A knock at the front door followed. Who would be visiting this time of night? Just what she needed—visitors!

6

"Yoo Hoo, anyone here?"

Todd moved to the living room and flipped on the light. "Martha, I was going to call you. We're just getting the story straightened out."

"Well you didn't call, so we thought we better come see if you needed some help." The woman was tall. Silver-blond hair adorned her head, not a single hair out of place. Blue eyes shone behind thick lenses framed by clear plastic which flattered the face. She glanced at Steve and Laura. "Didn't know you had Detective Morgan with you."

"Appreciate your concern Martha," said Todd, "but we've got things under control." He tried to edge her back out the door.

"We saw the car in the drive with Illinois plates. Is our new pastor here early?" She glanced around the room looking for Reverend Kenzel.

Laura took a deep breath and said, "I was just going to send the men out to my car for a couple of things—including a coffee pot. Would you folks like some coffee? I think I would."

Todd glanced at Laura. She still looked pale and even with Steve's sweater she was shivering. "Maybe we better..."

"I think that's a marvelous idea," said Martha. "Why don't you boys get the things from the car? I'll help Mrs. Kenzel in the kitchen. Where's your husband, honey? Upstairs getting beds set up? We're your neighbors down the street." She nodded toward the direction of the house Laura had seen from her car earlier. "I'm Martha Jennings—my husband Frank."

Laura wondered if the woman ever stopped for a breath.

Frank was tall with thinning hair. They were both mid to late sixties. Martha didn't wait for an answer, but took off her raincoat and laid it on the floor with her umbrella. "Frank, why don't you help them unpack the car?"

"Just the box, the cooler, and the suitcase from the hatchback," said Laura as she handed her keys to Steve.

"Are you sure you are up to this?"

"No, but I've got to face it sooner or later."

Frank went with Todd and Steve. He hadn't said a word, but the scowl on his face said volumes. They were back in minutes

"Frank thought we should wait 'til morning, but I thought we should come right over and make you feel welcome." Martha paused and looked around the room as if she had missed the entrance of another person.

The men carried in the requested items and Laura took the suitcase and set it at the foot of the stairs. "Where *is* Reverend Kenzel," asked Frank. "He's not outside and I don't hear anyone upstairs. Surely he wouldn't send you ahead to be alone in this house, not if Collins told him anything at all about what's been going on here."

Laura didn't dare look at Todd or Steve, who ducked into the kitchen with the cooler and the box marked COFFEE POT. She took a deep breath and silently prayed for help in saying the right things. Extending her hand first to Martha then Frank, she said, "I'm glad to meet you, Frank and Martha. There is no *Mister* Kenzel. *I* am you new pastor, Reverend Laura Kenzel."

Frank stared, mouth open. Finally, finding his voice, he stuttered, "But...we thought...that is...we were expecting Reverend *Mister* Lawrence Kenzel."

Laura smiled and glanced at Todd and Steve, who didn't even try to hide their amusement. "Surely District Superintendent William Collins wrote, or called you," she said to Frank.

"He called the other day and said Reverend Lawrence Kenzel would probably arrive sometime Wednesday," said Frank. "That's tomorrow. And pardon me for saying so, ma'am," he gulped hard as if something bitter had stuck in his throat, "but, you don't look like a Lawrence Kenzel to me."

"Mr. Jennings," Laura said, "trust me, I am your new pastor. I will be glad to explain in a few minutes, but if you don't mind, I'm cold and would like to get into something warm and dry. If someone would be so kind as to open that box Steve took into the kitchen and make some coffee and set out whatever is in the cooler, we can chat over a snack. Right now, I'm going upstairs and change clothes."

Laura didn't wait for an answer, but turned and hurried up the stairs, suitcase in hand. Frank and Martha Jennings stared after her as if time had suddenly stopped and caught them in the warp.

At to the top of the steps, Laura stopped to examine a worn spot on the carpet. Something didn't look right, so she called down to the men, "Todd? Steve? You got a minute?"

"I'll make the coffee," said Martha as Todd, Steve and Frank ran up the stairs.

"You afraid to go up there until we check it out?" Steve said.

"No, but I thought you might want to check out this step. It looks threadbare, but it looks like someone has cut it with something sharp—recently."

"You're right," said Todd as he examined the step. "Why would anyone do that?"

"It wasn't like that the other day when we cleaned up in here," said Frank as if they were accusing him of neglecting the parsonage.

Steve said nothing. He waited for Todd to discover the meaning and was surprised when Laura answered.

"Obviously it was meant to cause someone to trip and fall down the stairs. You're the detectives. You figure out who and why."

Laura moved on down the hall to the bathroom. Todd frowned and scratched his head. Steve laughed and slapped him on the back. "She's right, Todd. Possibly the burglar who got away."

"Maybe we better check the rest of the rooms," said Todd.

"Good idea."

"Looks like the movers put furniture up here, but didn't set up any of the beds," said Frank as he followed them in the search.

"Let's get one set up so she'll at least have a place to sleep," Steve said as they found the master bedroom

A hot shower would sure feel good, but Laura was afraid she would only get cold water. Getting out of her damp clothes and into her new sweat suit Susan had sent her for Mother's Day took away the chill. She liked the light teal color and softness of the material. Using her fingers as a comb, she ran them through her short hair then turned to go.

A sudden a movement behind the tub's sliding glass door caught her eye. Probably mold that looked like it moved because of the texture of the glass. Laura had to satisfy her curiosity, however, and slid the door to one side. At the end of the tub, two beady black eyes stared back at her and a forked tongue flicked from the grinning black mouth. A three-foot long blacksnake against the white tub was impossible to miss.

Laura blinked. Were her tired eyes playing tricks on her? The snake didn't go away. She shook her head, took a deep breath, and picked it up behind the jaws with one hand and the tail with the other. Someone had sure gone to a lot of trouble to scare her. They had to have looked hard to even find a snake this early in the year. She carried it from the bathroom and stopped at the bedroom door where the men worked on putting her bed together.

"Does this belong to anyone you know?"

All three men looked at her with open mouths. "Laura!" sputtered Todd. "Where did you get that?"

"In the bathtub," she said trying to look serious, but couldn't keep from laughing at their bewildered looks. "Do you think it might be trying to get in out of the rain? Then again, maybe he's hungry and looking for that mouse in the corner over there." She nodded toward the corner by the closet, where a mouse sat motionless. Again she laughed when they all turned to see the little gray creature in the corner by the closet.

"Where did he come from?" Frank looked at the two police officers expecting an answer from them.

"Don't know, Frank," said Todd laughing with Laura. "We didn't bring either of them in. Do you have any mouse traps? We can set it and..."

"Never mind the mouse," said Laura. "He'll get out eventually. I don't mind a live mouse in the house, but I don't want to find a dead one in my closet—or worse." She paused and sniffed the air. "I smell coffee. Care to join me?"

"We're almost done here." Steve shook his head and smiled at this most unusual preacher.

Laura took the snake downstairs. Someone had covered the frayed step with duct tape. At least she wouldn't trip and fall down the steps. Martha screamed as if a bat had attacked her when Laura walked through the kitchen to the back door. Laura laughed.

"It's only a harmless blacksnake, Martha. If you will open the door for me, I'll put him out in the backyard."

"How can you stand to touch that thing?" Martha finally got voice back.

Laura laughed again. "I grew up in an area where they were common. We often had to move them out of the way so we could play in the field. We didn't mind that kind," she said nodding toward the backyard where she had released the reptile. "It was the copperheads and rattlers that we had to watch out for."

"Well you wouldn't catch me touching them." Martha, having made her point, turned to filling coffee cups. "Coffee and food I understand. Snakes I don't." She shivered and reached for the coffee pot.

The men followed Laura downstairs and into the kitchen, where they found Martha good naturedly scolding Laura. "Didn't know we were getting a snake handler for a pastor."

Laura laughed that soft bubbly laugh Todd and Steve had heard earlier. She patted Martha on the shoulder and said, "Martha, I don't make a habit of it, and besides this fellow isn't the kind of snake used in some religions. He was probably more scared of us than we were of him—especially when you screamed at him."

She laughed again as Martha sputtered, "I doubt that. Pastor, you are certainly different."

"Yeah," said Frank. His face screwed up as if he had chomped down on a lemon when he was expecting a sweet orange.

Laura handed each of the men a mug of hot black liquid. "I'm sorry I can't offer you cream or sugar without searching for them," she said. "I don't use them, so they were packed in another box."

"Why ruin a good cup of coffee with cream and sugar?" Steve smiled as he took the cup.

Frank took a cup and grudgingly commented, "That's right, Detective. Good coffee is hot and black." Laura smiled at him trying to read the expression on his face. She could see a slight sign of admiration, but also skepticism and apprehension.

"Laura, are you always this kind and generous?"

Laura turned her attention from Frank to Steve. She didn't answer, only shrugged.

"If you are, your folks are going to love you before they realize they have a woman instead of a man." He grinned at Martha, who seemed to have recovered from the shock of seeing her pastor carrying a snake.

"It'll take more than a kind and generous spirit to convince some folks," said Frank. "But, I guess we'll have to wait and see. No one else has stayed longer than a few hours. If she's still here by morning, I'll be surprised."

Laura started to give him a sarcastic reply, but changed her mind. She clamped her jaws shut, took a deep breath, and turned to pick up her cup of coffee. She wouldn't get into a confrontation tonight.

Steve watched with interest. He figured she was gathering her self-control and admired her even more. He turned his attention back to the Jennings. "I don't know, Frank, a little kindness goes a long way in making friends and influencing people."

Martha returned his smile. "I hope you're right, Detective Morgan, but I'm not sure what folks will think about having a single woman living in the parsonage. Especially with all the weirdness we've had. Like Frank said, no man ever stayed. Maybe we'll just have to find her a husband. We have a couple of the most eligible bachelors in the area right here. Maybe…"

Laura turned so suddenly she almost dropped her cup.

Steve and Todd looked at each other. As if they had communicated by mental telepathy, they set their cups on the counter top. Before Steve could express his desire to leave, Laura faced her new neighbor.

"Martha, please don't misunderstand me. I will always appreciate anything you want to do for me in the line of church work, but please don't interfere with my personal life. I'm just getting used to being single, and I have no intention of changing that anytime soon. When, and if, God is ready for me to do something differently, He'll let me know. Until then, I am Reverend Laura Kenzel, single, and pastor of Cottonville United Methodist Church."

She gave Martha a charming smile. "I really appreciate your concern, though. It makes me feel wanted and loved."

Martha smiled at her. "Well, Reverend," she said. "If God ever needs any help, let me know. I know lots of good-looking men who would die for a pretty woman like you."

Laura laughed and changed the subject. "Do you suppose you could get the personnel committee and the trustees together for a meeting—say tomorrow night? We need to work out some of the kinks of getting a new pastor. I really wanted to meet with you before I came, but Reverend Collins said it would be best if the bishop just appointed me since I had so far to drive to get here."

"Well, Reverend, I thought it was a little strange that we didn't meet you before the appointment, but considering how we've had trouble getting a pastor for so long, we were just glad to get someone. We hope you can stay, but we won't blame you if you want to leave." Martha shook her head. A tear trickled down the side of one cheek.

Laura brushed it away with her finger. "Martha, Reverend Bill Collins and Bishop Matthew Giles think they sent me here, but they were only tools in the hands of God. I have no idea why God sent me here, but He did and here I will stay until He tells me to go, come what may. I don't scare off easily and I won't be intimidated."

"We'll see," said Frank. "We'll see."

Martha ignored him. Her eyes widened as her eyebrows went up. A smile slid across her face. "Reverend, I *like* you. If you ever feel frightened or anything, you just come next door. I know it's late, but I'm going home right now and call those committees. We'll have our meeting. I'll see you tomorrow and let you know how many will be there."

Martha patted Laura's cheek and left still smiling. "Come on Frank let's go get ready for those meetings." Frank followed her out. He didn't look quite as excited as his wife. He had a skeptical, wait-and-see look on his face.

Had she made friends or enemies? Or one of each?

7

When Frank and Martha left, Laura felt edgy—not scared, just in need of conversation. "I know it's late," she said, holding up the coffee pot, "but, would you care for some more coffee?"

"You're right," said Steve. "It is late. Aren't you tired? Or are you uneasy about tonight's earlier happenings?"

"Yes," she said and grinned. "To both."

"Laura, we fixed the step temporarily, but maybe you need to get yourself a cat to get rid of the mouse." Steve laughed. "You took care of the snake quiet nicely."

"I'm not afraid of mice or snakes and like I told Martha, that one was only a harmless blacksnake. I grew up with them in my backyard." Laura laughed again at their incredulous looks. A frown crossed her brow and she said, "The question is, why?"

"What do you mean, why?" asked Todd.

Steve looked at her with a mixture of curiosity and admiration. She didn't miss much. "She means someone put the mouse and the snake here and cut the carpet to help an accident occur. Who and why?"

Steve watched Laura, wondering if she really understood the full significance. She did. She stared into her cup as if the answer would be there in that black liquid.

"The real question," she said, "is who knew I was coming?"

"Laura the whole church knew you were coming. They just didn't expect you until tomorrow." Todd's face screwed into a frown.

"No, Todd," she looked into his perplexed eyes. "They expected a man. How did they know a woman would be coming? Very few men would be frightened by a mouse in the bedroom or a snake in the bathtub. And that step was rigged to catch the heel of a woman's shoe. So how did they—whoever *they* are—know a *woman* was coming? At the moment I know of only two people who had that information—my bishop and my district superintendent."

"Laura, are you sure you want to be a preacher? You're right on all counts, but surely there must be someone else who knew— maybe a seminary friend?" Steve sipped his coffee.

"I might have mentioned it to a friend, but didn't tell them the name of the town. I sincerely hope someone else found out. It really was no secret and I would hate to think my own bishop or district superintendent would even think of such a thing, much less do it. But *someone* knew and planted those little surprises."

Steve noticed a sudden surge of fear that reflected on her face. "You're right, Laura," he said. "Someone knew, but let's hope it wasn't your boss. Maybe the news was leaked, but maybe whoever is behind this assumed they could get rid of the pastor by scaring *his* wife."

"That's a possibility," said Laura, "but…"

Steve arched his eyebrows and waited. She shook her head and hunched her shoulders.

"If you ever want to change careers," he said, "I'm sure Todd could use your insight. And if he can't I could use you in Glenville."

Laura grinned. "I'm just beginning a career, thank you," she answered. "I think I have my hands full here. God and I will have a talk about my reception here tonight, though."

"Why *did* you decide to go into ministry, Laura? Surely you had other options," said Steve. "I'm not questioning your call—just curious."

"I grew up in the church. I married a pastor, so the church was all I ever knew. I worked other jobs to put myself through high school and college. I have a teaching degree, but the church is what I love. My husband was killed four years ago. At first it was assumed a drunk kid named Butch had run him off the road." Again that look of fear flickered in her eyes. "He was one of the youth in our church."

"Are you afraid of that kid?"

"No, not Butch. He was a good kid. He had—has—a problem with alcohol and drugs. It's just that…something seemed wrong that night and then tonight…" Laura took a deep breath. Todd and Steve waited.

She told them of Butch calling for Harold to take him home then seemed to have driven himself.

"The coroner said Harold's neck was broken—not unusual, but highly impossible in that accident. He said there were prints on Harold's neck consistent with someone very strong, wearing gloves and snapping his neck while he was unconscious. Butch's attorney gave a good case for Butch—said it was impossible for him to have gotten out of his car, kill Harold, then return to his car and pass out. He had too much alcohol and drugs in his system— and a concussion from hitting his head on the steering wheel. Even that seemed strange. How could he hit his head that hard on the steering wheel after the air bag had deflated? Anyway, the murder is still unsolved. When that man tonight said he killed my husband and…"

"Are you sure that's what he said?"

"Positive. Is it possible that man killed Harold and somehow made it look like Butch did it and is afraid I might know more than I do? Is he from around here? If he did kill my husband, what kind of coincidence—or God-incidence—would bring us together in a little town called Cottonville?"

"Do you always ask so many questions?" Todd rubbed his temples to ward off an encroaching headache.

Steve laughed. "I said before you would make a good detective, but you are right. Anything is possible. We'll check it out."

"Sorry, didn't mean to get sidetracked. Harold pretty much took care of me; he wanted it that way. After his death I had to learn to take care of myself again."

Laura smiled, took a sip of coffee and continued. "When I got through being angry with God for letting things upset my life, He laughed at me, pointed the way, and here I am."

"Well, for someone who couldn't do *anything*, my guess is, there's not much you won't try." Steve smiled at her. He was impressed with this woman who would allow anyone to laugh at her—even God.

"You're probably right. I've always been an optimist with a things-will-get-better attitude. And I have a stubborn streak that sometimes works for me, but just as often gets me in trouble. I had been independent before I was married, but somehow I let Harold take that independence from me. Now I allow God to lead me." Laura paused, feeling the seriousness of the moment. Then she smiled. "Sorry, about the sermonette. What about you two? You don't have the distinction of being the most eligible bachelors in the area for nothing."

Both men coughed to hide embarrassment. Neither one wanted to share deep emotions with anyone, much less this pretty woman preacher, who might condemn and scold. They sat silent for a minute—Todd staring into his cup, turning it around in his hands; Steve staring out the window into the darkness. Laura waited.

Finally, still staring at the window, Steve said, "It's not much of a story for me. I was married very young. The marriage ended in a nasty divorce less than a year later. I decided to never let that happen again. I've been pretty much married to my work since. I understand criminals. I don't understand relationships."

"I think divorce is harder than death to deal with," Laura said. "With death the other is really gone. With divorce the other is always lurking somewhere in the back of your mind, poking and prodding, stirring up old memories, good or bad."

Steve turned sharply to face her. Was she making fun of him? Her eyes were full of compassion and honesty. Maybe she was different. But she was a preacher. It was her job to be compassionate. To get the focus off himself, Steve turned to Todd. "All right, pal. What's your story? You're younger than we are, so you probably have a dozen girls on the line." Steve winked at Todd.

"Me? I had a girl—once. We were supposed to be married when I finished school. She ran off with someone else. I'm not interested in anyone else."

"How awful!" said Laura. "Does she live close enough that you see her sometimes? Is she happy?"

Todd, like Steve, was surprised that Laura would care about something that happened almost a dozen years ago. "Yes, I see her sometimes—not as in dating, but in passing. She's alone again— with a kid to support."

"Have you ever talked to her about what happened?"

"No, and I don't intend to. If she wants to talk, she knows where I am." Pain and anguish filled his voice.

"But, Todd, you're the one who's hurting."

"I'll live." He picked up his cup and started to the sink.

Laura followed and laid a hand on his arm. "I'm sorry, Todd. I get too nosey sometimes. It's really none of my business." She grinned as Todd turned around, "Unless you're one of my church members. Then you're pain is my pain and I'll probably butt in where I'm not wanted. You'll have to tell me to butt out."

Todd laughed in spite of the anger that had flared and died. "Laura, I am one of your flock, and for now you can butt out of my private life."

"All right—for now." She grinned.

"But now," he said, "it's getting late and you're bound to be exhausted. Is there anything else we can help you with tonight?" Boxes were stacked like building blocks all around the kitchen, overflowing into the other two rooms. Upstairs was the same.

"Thanks, but I have enough stuff to get me through the night. I'll just slide something against the doors to keep them closed until I can get someone out here to fix them tomorrow."

Todd and Steve had started toward the front room. "Do you have any tools in your car, Todd?"

"Sure, Steve, what do you need?"

"Something to fix these doors. She shouldn't have to move furniture around to keep the door closed. It won't take long."

"Yeah, with a burglar on the loose, we don't want to make it any easier for him. I'll get the tools."

Todd brought in the toolbox and, between the two of them, they fixed both the doors so they would close and lock. When they finally said good night, Laura realized how tired she was, and with a note of irritation, how much pleasure she felt when Steve Morgan was near.

As she crawled beneath the covers, she whispered, "Lord, that was some welcome I received tonight. What could possibly happen to top that?" Feeling that familiar chuckle in her soul, she knew that whatever came next, God would see her through it.

Another storm system moved into the valley. Laura was oblivious of all the thunder and lightning. Exhausted, sleep came quickly, if not restfully. Not long into slumber, however, Laura picked up her Victorian candlestick and ran in slow motion down the steps, a long braid of red hair and her white gown flowing behind her. A strange, eerie voice called to her from the garage— or was it the belfry? She wasn't sure.

"Lauraaaaaa! Lauraaaaa! Come to me my sweet. Come…"

The candle flickered in the rain, but did not go out. Laura ran like a floating ghost out the front door and across the porch. Bodiless hands hidden in the high grass along the sidewalk grabbed at her ankles. The garage stood open with a laser-like beam flashing on and off in psychedelic colors. Behind her screams from the belfry penetrated the night's already tumultuous disquiet. From inside the garage someone called to her, "Laura! Laura darling come to me."

She hesitated, turned to the eerie sounds from the belfry, then back to the garage. Starting forward, she tripped over the body of her husband, Harold, who lay across the garage entrance and fell silently screaming headlong into strong arms. She looked up into the twinkling blue eyes and smiling face of Detective Steve Morgan. She dropped the candle as he pulled her to him and kissed her. At the high-pitched, witch-like laugh from the center of the garage, they turned to see District Superintendent William Collins kick the candle, igniting the stack of lumber in the center of the garage.

Laura's muffled cry brought her upright in bed. Perspiration dripped from her hair and ran down her face. Outside lightning flashed and thunder rumbled. She looked for her bedside clock and remembered it was still packed. She checked her watch with the flashlight beside her bed. One o'clock. Laura lay with her eyes open, mind whirling, and heart pounding for a couple of hours before weariness settled over her, pulling her once again into the forgetfulness of slumber. New dreams replaced that one—all with screeching voices calling to her and Detective Morgan trying to save her from monsters and fires.

8

"Yowl" Two feline voices from the corner of the bell tower joined forces with the thunder and wind.

"Shut up." Jeb Little threw a shoe at the corner. A growl and hiss answered him. He turned back to watch the house from his makeshift apartment. He was tired of the rain and the wind. His bones ached.

"Colin ought to make Randy live up here. How come he gets a warm bed and hot meals? When this is over, Colin and me are going to have a talk—a real long talk." Jeb growled and muttered sounding a lot like the two felines in the corner.

Finally, he saw what he was watching for—movement again at the house. One cop had gone to the cruiser then returned to the house. Sounds of pounding and scraping drifted to the tower.

"Looks like their leaving this time. Maybe I can get some sleep. No one's going to be prowling around down there in the rain."

Soon, one by one, each room in the house darkened.

"She must have gone to bed. I'll give her a half hour then go rattle a few pipes in the basement."

More yowls and growls from the corner made Jeb laugh. "Hee, hee, hee," he cackled. "Think that's a good idea?" He threw a jar of water on the cats to make their yowls and hisses louder and longer then he laughed some more.

Thunder rumbled closer. More rain followed. Jeb paced in his close quarters to stay awake and stop the pain in his joints. He hated the rain. He would've moved over the house if *she* wasn't there.

"Colin promised me something better when this little game is over. How much longer will that be? He said a couple of months. It's getting close to two years. I'm tired of being cold and wet."

More growls and yowls came from the corner with a hiss or two thrown in for good measure.

"Those blasted cats are constantly complaining. What's their problem? I fed them this morning. At least they help with my assignment—to make sure no one stays in that house."

Jeb was bored. He wanted to sleep in a real bed and get rid of those cats. Most folks in this town seemed to be scared of his *ghosts*, but this woman was different. She didn't scare easily. That made him uneasy.

Lightning flashed across the night sky. Thunder drummed its ebb and flow. Jeb was tired of that, too. The sound made his ears ring. The lightning made his eyes ache. The rafters rattled and the wind sent a sad moaning wail whipping through the crevices transferring its eerie cry to the streets of Cottonville—sounds mingled with screeches and howls like a yard full of Tom cats pursuing a female in heat.

Jeb paced and muttered to himself as he kept watch over the precious cargo stored in the rickety old garage behind the Methodist Church.

"She should've been scared off. Randy must've messed up somehow. Can't depend on kids these days to do anything right."

Suddenly he saw a small circle of light dancing around inside the garage. "What was that?" He waited, peering into the blackness for more signs of unauthorized activity. "Maybe it was just the lightning reflecting on a window. No. There it is again—a tiny flutter of light—a cigarette, or small flashlight? Someone's in the garage."

Jeb cupped his hands like a pair of binoculars and held them against his eyes to get a better focus. "Maybe Randy's back and waiting in the garage for another chance at her. Shouldn't be in there though, not with a light bouncing around for anyone to see. What if those cops come back?"

Jeb knew he would be the one who would feel the brunt of Colin's anger, not Randy, if something happened to the stuff. He'd endured his brother's anger too often not to be concerned now. He swore under his breath. Nothing to do but go down and find out. He checked the collars of Rascal and Mischief, his two performing cats. They were secure. Then he lifted the wooden hatch cover aside and started backing down the ladder, pulling the cover back in place.

Muttering curses at the storm, his arthritic hands, and the person in the garage, Jeb carefully descended the wooden slats from the tower. So many times had he been up and down those rungs, he could easily do it in the dark, although he kept a powerful flashlight fastened to his belt. Once down the ladder, he worked his way through the cavernous bowels of the church structure to a hidden entrance facing the garage. With stealth, he measured each step, not worrying about anyone hearing him. No one would be in the church this time of night and the thunder would hide his steps.

Once outside, great pellets of rain battered him as Jeb ran from the church to the garage. Hearing the grating of a shovel in the dirt, he slipped through the space where the two sliding doors refused to meet. A lantern rested on the ground near the center of the garage pointing an accusing finger of light to the rising mound of dark earth and the young man, digging there. Like an animal ready to pounce, Jeb removed his flashlight from his belt and aimed its beam at the young man's face.

"Randy, what are you doing?" Jeb's voice blended with the rumble of thunder. The light on the younger man bounced around like an angry leprechaun as Jeb's body shook with rage.

Randy, blinded by the light, threw his arms up to shield his eyes, and whirled around. Stupid old man. I thought he was asleep.

"Why are *you* here, Pop?" Randy replied, wanting to avoid a fight, but not really believing he would, nor caring one way or the other. He held the shovel poised for action. No stupid old man who lived in a belfry was going to stop him from getting what he wanted—father or not.

"You know why I'm here," replied Jeb. "I was put here to guard this stuff, and I won't let even you take it out of here." The older man, pulled his gun, and took a step forward. The younger one was quicker—more agile. He swung the shovel like a baseball bat, striking the older man's hand. The gun skittered across the dirt floor landing near the boy's excavation. Before Jeb could move, Randy had the gun in his hand. Jeb lunged at him. The two men— father and son—became entwined in an embrace of death. Thunder boomed, masking the sound as Randy pulled the trigger. Jeb Little crumpled to the floor.

With no concern for the body of his father, Randy dropped the gun beside him, stepped over the body, and returned to his digging. He took what he wanted from the box, which he then replaced it in the grave-like hole. He re-covered the box with the pile of earth. With the skill of practice, he packed the earth tightly, then pulled the stack of old wooden boards and crates to cover the fact he had been digging. To a casual observer it was only a pile of junk. He put away the shovel, stepped over his dead father and without a backward glance, walked away. Lightning and thunder protested the act of violence. Wind howled through the belfry blowing the terrorized screams of the two felines with it.

9

Sunshine poured through the bare window, spilling over onto the bedside table. Feeling the brightness on her closed eyelids, Laura slowly opened them and squinted until she adjusted. Tired as she was from lack of sleep, she slipped from the bed, stretched, and lifted the window. The scent of a freshly laundered world drifted around the room. Below her window, a variety of birds competed for bugs, seeds, and puddles—chirping and singing like children at a backyard pool party.

A prayer of thanks filled her heart as she turned from the window and surveyed the room in the light of day. Her first glance went to the corner for the mouse, not that she was afraid of mice, but she didn't want to be startled by it. It wasn't there.

"The first night in my new home was certainly one to remember. I hope You don't have anymore surprises like that awaiting me." Laura was surprised at the soft feeling of mirth in the pit of her soul.

Snatches of her dreams and the remembered strange sounds from somewhere outside sent a tremble of uneasiness up her spine. Shrugging it off she turned her thoughts to the day ahead of her— boxes to be unpacked, a big meeting with the leaders of the church, and whatever else impinged itself on her unscheduled day.

This room was large enough to hold her mismatched pieces of

furniture with room to spare—queen-sized bed, dresser, bedside table and chest of drawers. They matched in color—dark wood— but not in style. She'd sold most of their furniture when she went to seminary because space was limited. She kept only a few old pieces from her grandmother and bought what she needed at bargain stores. A feeling of gratitude swept over her for the men who had taken time to set up the bed for her. She'd have to do something special for them when she got settled—maybe make some cookies or something.

Sighing with contentment, she started toward the door, stopping beside one of the numerous boxes. She searched until she found one labeled BATH. From its contents, she pulled a jumbo towel then turned to her suitcase for clean clothes and toiletries. Humming to herself, she headed down the hall.

Like the rest of the house, the bathroom had seen better days, although the smell of fresh paint gave an appearance of cleanliness. Inside the bathroom door to the left was a large, shelf-lined closet. Unfortunately, the cabinet door and the main door fought constantly, making it a struggle to use the closet unless she first closed the main door. Across from the closet, a cabinet of white-painted wood of undetermined origin surrounded the sink. The shiny top was a marble look-a-like, in shades of pinks and purples. The toilet, the usual white ceramic, was under the only window in the room—a window encased in the white wood. The bathtub sported a new sliding shower door, which remained open from the night before. Laura knew fancier places existed, but this was serviceable, and it was her new home.

Leaving her jeans and fresh shirt on one of the shelves, Laura hurried down the hall to the stairs. Things certainly looked different in the light of day. The moss green carpet, worn to the bare backing in many places, ran down the hall like an algae-filled stream, spilling over the stairs and spreading into an even greater pool of green at the bottom of the stairs. On it flowed into the living room and even into the dining room where it was finally held back by the slick, white surface of the kitchen linoleum.

Blinded by the brilliance of the white enamel paint and the

uncurtained windows, Laura squinted at the kitchen where even the counter tops glistened white. The room was longer than it was wide, but with plenty of space at the opposite end of the cooking area for a table and chairs. Memories of her grandmother's farm house brought a smile to her lips. She loved eating in the kitchen.

The only light switch for the room was on the outside wall, next to the back door. To turn the light on in the kitchen she would have to cross the entire length of the room, or else enter the back door. Another item for the trustee meeting.

The coffee pot, like a tiny robot servant, waited on the counter top for Laura to push the on button which would send life through its wires and coils. Sparkling clean, it was ready to begin the day. Laura smiled and flipped the switch to send precious water gurgling and bubbling over the fresh ground coffee beans. The aroma reached out to tickle her nose with a promise of the hot, black liquid to follow. She anticipated its flavor, almost as much as she anticipated a hot shower, which she would take while the coffee brewed.

Fresh from the shower, Laura followed the aroma back to the kitchen, filled her cup, then found her favorite chair by the bay window in the living room. Setting her cup on the windowsill, she removed a stack of pillows and miscellaneous articles from the chair, sighed contentedly, and eased onto that chair. Her Bible open to Psalm 46, she read and re-read it until she began to relax into the presence of God.

"Whatever happens in the next few days, months, or years, God, You will be my refuge and strength."

Although it was still very early, Laura couldn't wait to go out into the sunshine and breathe in the fresh morning air. She crossed the porch and waded through the tall grass to her car. Remembering her dreams, she shivered and ran across the hayfield of a yard. She intended to finish unpacking her car, but glanced at the garage and changed her mind.

"Shebop, I'm going to open that garage door, if I have to tear it off its remaining hinge. You deserve a place out of the sun, or rain, or whatever."

Another shiver grabbed her with the memory of her dream accompanied by the eerie noises from the belfry. Shaking away the silliness of letting a dream bother her, she tugged on the garage door. It opened—too quickly. The one remaining sliding hinge, which should have let the door slide to the side, crumbled. Instead of sliding open, the door crashed to the ground, barely missing Laura's foot. She yelled and jumped to the side.

"Lord, I don't think that's a bit funny," she said when her heart stopped pounding. Not at all sure she wanted to face what she thought she saw, she took a tentative step forward. Normal debris found in most garages cluttered the center and sides, but in the corner near the door, she saw a man's feet and legs. Was someone sleeping there? She was more than willing to ignore him and hope whoever he was would go away, but she knew she had to wake him and ask him to leave. At least she would find out if he needed help to get on his way.

Once again the memory of her dream forced itself to her present. She felt again the lurch of her heart as she had when she tripped over the body of her husband, Harold, in that dream. But this wasn't Harold and this man wasn't dead. Or was he?

Shivering as if she had just walked through a winter storm, Laura forced herself to be reasonable. She had to tackle this problem now, before it got worse. Stepping closer to the sleeping man, she nudged his foot with her toe. "Excuse me," she said.

The man didn't answer. She stepped a little closer and tried again. "Excuse me," she said again. "You're in my garage. You'll have to move on."

The man answered with nerve-shattering silence. Laura started to nudge him a little harder but realized no sound would ever again come from the lips of the man lying on her garage floor in a dark circle where blood had soaked into the dirt. Was that a gun beside him? The man was definitely not asleep. He was dead.

Laura's stomach did a flip-flop as her jaws locked firmly together. She would not scream. First a burglar, now murder! What next? She backed out of the garage while keeping her eyes focused on the man's back. "Lord, this isn't what I expected on my first day at my first church. I don't remember any course in my seminary training that covered murder. I need Your help."

She heard footsteps crunching on the gravel behind her and whirled around. Was the murderer back? Frank Jennings stood with his hands in his pockets. "Morning," he said. "You're up early." She hoped he wasn't the killer. She had to trust him.

"Good morning, Frank. I'm glad you're here. I need your help. There's a..."

Before she could finish, Martha, carrying a platter covered with foil followed him up the drive. "We never had a preacher get up as early as we do," she said. "Are you all right, dear? You look like you've seen a ghost. Those noises in the belfry didn't get to you did they?"

"Not ghosts, Martha, but yes, I am a little shaken." She nodded back toward the garage. "I seem to have stumbled on to a dead man in the garage. I was just going in to call Todd."

"Dead man? Are you sure?" Frank looked past her to the feet sticking out from the corner of the garage. "Looks like old Jeb taking a snooze. I'll just wake him and..."

"Believe me, Frank, the man is dead. He's been shot. Excuse me, I'll go call Todd. You might want to make sure no one touches anything." Even though Frank was the only person there, Laura didn't want him messing up any evidence. He nodded as if he expected the whole town to show up and she turned to go back to the house.

Frank stared at the dead man. Then he blinked and remarked, "It's old Jeb all right."

In a flash Martha, who Laura would learn was a take control person, began giving orders. "Frank, you stay here until Todd comes? I'll go with the Reverend." She took Laura's arm with her free hand and walked with her back to the house. Laura bit her tongue to keep back words of irritation and anger.

When they reached the house, she said, "Martha, I'm glad you're here. Would you be kind enough to put on a fresh pot of coffee while I make the call?" Laura smiled at Martha, who returned her smile with a wide, toothy grin. Laura thought Todd would appreciate a fresh cup of coffee, but she was more interested in giving Martha something to do.

"Sure thing, Reverend. I'll just set these rolls on the table."

The phone waited on the floor in the corner of the living room. Laura stooped, picked it up, and dialed, wondering if Todd would be at his office so early. It wasn't quite seven. Three rings. Laura felt frustrated until she heard a click and another ring. The call was being rerouted probably to his apartment. The second ring was broken.

"Good morning, Chief Williams here."

"Todd, this is Laura Kenzel."

"Good morning, Laura. Something wrong? That mouse keep you up last night?" He chuckled at his feeble attempt of joking.

"Mice I can handle. Dead men are out of my league."

"Dead men? Laura what are you trying to say?"

"There's a dead man in my garage."

"You sure he's dead and not just sleeping. Drifters sometimes…"

"Todd," she broke in," the man is dead. He's lying on my garage floor in what looks like a circle of blood that's soaked into the dirt. He has a hole in his chest and there is a gun beside him."

Laura heard a deep sigh before Todd answered. "We'll be there in five minutes or less."

Laura hated to hear the dismay in his voice, but she hated even more to think of that poor man on her garage floor.

10

The last gurgling of the fresh coffee and wailing siren coincided with the scattering gravel in the driveway as Todd slid to a stop. "You can go see what's going on, Reverend," said Martha. "I'll stay here and answer the phone. People will hear the siren and want to know what's happening."

Laura returned to the garage knowing that Martha was probably right. She grew up in a small town and knew what the grapevine was like, better than any phone system. Frank stood motionless as if he had turned to stone. He couldn't take his eyes from the dead form of Jeb Little.

Todd emerged from the cruiser's driver's side, Steve Morgan from the passenger's side. Turning to Frank and Laura Todd said, "All right, where's the body?"

Frank looked like he was about to try to protect the helpless woman preacher, so before he could answer, Laura stepped forward. "Sorry to get you out so early, Todd. It looks like we had more than just burglars last night. I came over to check the garage to see if I could put my car in it and found it occupied by a man who had been shot."

"I'm assuming you didn't move anything," said Steve as he followed them into the garage.

"I only stepped inside to ask him to leave. I thought he was a drifter sleeping in the garage out of last night's storms. When I realized he was dead, I retreated immediately."

Todd started into the garage, and turned back to Laura's neighbor. "Frank, I'm deputizing you to keep any curious folks away from here. Go out to the street and keep them from coming back here."

Frank grinned from ear to ear. "Got ya, Chief."

Todd pulled out his cell phone and called Doctor Cornelius, who doubled as coroner. Then he called Mark Goodwin, and another deputy to help with the crime scene investigation.

"Looks like news travels fast, as it does in most small towns." Laura nodded toward the crowd of curious onlookers gathering on the street and spilling over onto the front yard of the parsonage.

"Maybe I better get some help for Frank," said Todd. He reached for his phone again.

Laura sighed and said, "You really don't need me here, so maybe I can talk the ladies into coming into the house with me. You can handle the men." She grinned at Steve's raised eyebrows. "A little chauvinistic maybe, but it'll work."

"You're probably right," he said.

Laura started toward the women, turned, and said over her shoulder, "There's fresh coffee when you want it."

Martha was just hanging up the phone when Laura entered with several women following her. "I tried to call a couple of ladies on my hospitality committee, but it looks like they're already here. With all the commotion out there, I thought you might need some help in here. We'll help you get unpacked so you can get settled."

Laura wasn't sure she needed, or wanted, help, especially with a murder investigation going on at the same time. She decided not to fight it. If they could unpack, she could put things away later. She sorted boxes and gave directions to her volunteers. Several women began with the stack in the living room, others moved to the dining room, and Martha and Laura went to the kitchen.

Martha talked while she unpacked boxes, setting items on the counter top. "We've had such a hard time getting a pastor. I feel real bad about all this—someone breaking into your house and a man murdered in the garage. I hope you won't be scared off like the rest."

"Tell me a little about what's been happening, Martha. Do you know who the drifter was? Reverend Collins didn't give me many details about this appointment." He hadn't given her any information at all. All she knew was hearsay.

"That man's name is Jeb Little. He's been around for about a year and a half—maybe two years. I don't know much about him, except he put on shows about once a week with two big, beautiful cats." Martha paused with a bowl in her hand.

"Strange things started happening around here about the same time. People had things stolen, eerie noises in the church scared folks away. Todd found our pastor at the time—John Lakeland— hanging in the belfry. The next one left in the middle of the night and sent a van for his furniture the next week. Dorothy, our secretary, refused to work alone in the church. The bishop sent pastors down here—one after another. None stayed long enough to even move their furniture." She set the bowl on the counter top.

"Some folks think our church is haunted. Others say the Devil has a hold on us. And now they send us a woman! No offence Reverend, but if about seventy-five men couldn't take it, what chance does a woman have?" Martha brushed at a couple of tears that slipped down her cheek.

Laura set the picture she had just pulled from a box against the wall, and gave Martha a hug. "Maybe a woman can combine logic and compassion and beat the odds," she said. She heard the front door open and close and men's voices. Assuming some of the husbands had come in for coffee, she wiped Martha's tears and picked up a small box marked cups.

"Oh, Reverend, I sure hope you're right. It's been so long since we had a real worship service. Some of us meet every Sunday and pray. We've tried to keep a Sunday School going for the children and study as best we can. We've been praying for God to send us someone special who can end our misery."

"I don't know how special I am, Martha, but I'm stubborn as a mule. No one's going to run me off. They'll have to carry me out first." Sensing, rather than hearing, someone at the door, she turned to see Todd and Steve. They both smiled.

"I think your prayers were answered when they sent this one, Martha," said Todd. "She's certainly special and I doubt she'll walk away from trouble." He nodded toward the coffee pot. "We'll take some of that coffee, now, if you don't mind."

"Sure thing, Todd. You folks want a roll with it?" Martha nodded toward the platter of hot cinnamon rolls near the coffee pot.

"Maybe later," said Steve. "Just coffee for now, thanks."

Laura let Martha handle the amenities and turned back to her unpacking, pausing to lift her thoughts in soundless prayer. "Lord, what did You get me into? Burglars? Murder? People who expected me to be a man? Wait until I get my hands on Bill Collins. We may have another body to contend with!" She felt the familiar mirthful feeling in the depth of her soul and sighed. "All right, maybe it won't be that drastic, but I sure will let him know how much trouble he's causing me. It's almost as if it were deliberate. I'm sorry, God. Please forgive my paranoia, but I need strength to get through this."

Laura was amazed at how quickly the women put together an impromptu smorgasbord of rolls, coffee cake, and donuts from the local grocery. They were somewhat subdued by the awareness of a murder investigation being conducted, but an undertone of excitement existed. A dead man on church property? Hard to believe. They talked quietly, sometimes even laughed softly then looked embarrassed for doing so.

Laura heard Todd and Steve cross the porch and turned as they came into the living room where the women were eating their brunch. "Investigation done already?" Laura asked.

Steve smiled at her. "We're almost done. We just need to get your statement for the record. If you could just step out to the porch, it might be a little quieter and more private."

"Sure," she said and he held the door for her to precede him. She was suddenly aware of how quiet it had become in the room behind her. A pin dropping on carpet would have sounded like a sonic boom. All eyes were on Steve Morgan. Laura smiled to herself as she realized that every last woman in that room—married or single—regardless of their age, had a giant-sized crush on him. He had that kind of effect on most women. She hoped she was more sensible than most. Steve didn't seem to notice, or if he did, he didn't care.

Steve, however, noticed more than she thought he did. His heart skipped a beat as Laura brushed against him moving through the door he held for her. Catching his breath, he knew he would have to watch himself. He was adamant—no women ever again.

Laura was more interested in getting this investigation over with than she was Steve Morgan's personal feelings.

"Thank you, Laura," Steve said after they took her statement. "You have a good eye for details and a concise manner of reporting them. We appreciate your help. Now, Todd and I need to check out a few more things in the garage. You can go back to your party." He grinned and nodded toward the living room.

"Oh, but we weren't..." She stopped and smiled. He was teasing her. "Well, maybe it is an impromptu welcome pastor party—a little unorthodox, but God-ordained. What can I say?"

She started to go in, changed her mind, and followed him across the porch. "Do you mind if I tag along. I'm curious, or nosy, depending on your point of view." Her dazzling smile extended to her whole face. "It's been hard staying in the house when I wanted to be where the action is."

Casting aside his upside down emotions, Steve said, "We appreciate your effort to keep the curious out of our way, but it is your garage. You have a right to know what's happening. Come on along, just be careful."

"Oh, I won't touch anything."

"I know you won't. I meant be careful you don't stumble over something in the weeds. If you fall, it might take us a week to find you."

"I'll be careful." She grinned then said, "You need to concentrate on dead souls, not lost ones. That's my territory."

Martha followed them out and took Frank and a couple other men back in the house with her saying something about moving heavy furniture.

"This is Doctor Eric Cornelius," said Todd as Laura stopped beside them. "He also serves as coroner."

"Glad to meet you, Doctor Cornelius," said Laura extending her hand to the tall, white-haired man.

"Sorry you've had such a greeting to our community," he said. "There are lots of good folks here. They'll make it up to you if you give them time."

"Thank you, Doctor. I intend to do just that."

Doctor Cornelius gathered his belongings and followed the emergency car with the body out. He would do the autopsy later in the morgue in the basement of Community General Hospital.

"He's had very little experience with murder," said Todd after he left, "but then neither have I. He's a good and conscientious man."

By the time Todd and Steve sent everyone home and came in for another cup of coffee and Martha's cinnamon rolls, Martha and her crew had unpacked most of the boxes on the first floor before they left. They had stacked the contents neatly around the room for Laura to put away. She would do that later. Right now, she poured herself another cup of coffee and sat at the table with Todd and Steve.

"What time did he say the murder occurred? Was the man there when I arrived last night?"

"No, he wasn't there then. Doc said the time of death was probably between midnight and one a.m. He'll know more after he has a chance to do the autopsy."

"Must have been after midnight since it was almost that when you guys left last night." Laura frowned. "I must have been dead to the world. Pardon the pun. I should have heard something, or maybe I did. Something woke me about one o'clock. I thought it was the nightmare I was having, but maybe something outside caused the nightmare."

"Did you dream about burglars and murders?" asked Todd with a short laugh.

"Close," she said, but didn't return the laughter. Instead, she frowned more and shivered slightly as she remembered the dream.

Laura saw Steve looking at her with concern and shrugged. "It was just a typical nightmare. I heard noises outside and went out to see. Someone was crying in the church and someone calling my name in the garage. I tripped over the body of my deceased husband and my district superintendent set fire to the garage." She left out the part about Steve Morgan.

"Sounds like it might be wrapped up in what's going on, either a premonition, or culmination of stories you've heard combined with the trauma of the evening." Steve smiled. He looked at her as if he suspected there was more to the dream than she was telling.

"Anyway, we had quite a storm last night and you were exhausted," Todd said.

"Yes, I guess I was," she said. "I hardly ever have nightmares. But what's all this about noises and haunted church, and a pastor hanging in the belfry and other pastors being scared off? Martha told me some of it, but surely she exaggerated."

Todd heaved a sigh of relief. "Probably not. I'm glad you're level headed and know a little about what you're getting into. Reverend John Lakeland's wife called me. She said her husband went out to answer an emergency call about midnight. Never came home. She was worried. We came out and searched the place and found him in the belfry—apparent suicide."

Laura shook her head. Todd continued, "Since then no one has stayed more than a day—most not even that long. I've been out here many times to answer calls of noises. Never could find anything."

"Laura, do you know something—or suspect it? I saw you shaking your head." Steve waited for her answer.

Laura stared for a few seconds into her cup. Then she said, "Harold and I knew the Lakelands. He would never take his life in the first place. In the second place, it would have been impossible for him—especially by hanging in the belfry."

"People change, especially under stress."

"Not that much. John had severe arthritis in his hands, knees, and ankles. Besides that he was afraid of heights. His hands could never have tied a rope. If that man last night really killed my husband, and lives in Cottonville, then don't you think there is a good chance he killed John Lakeland?"

Todd looked surprised, then chagrined. "Could that be possible, Steve?"

"Sounds possible. But how does that connect with Jeb Little's murder?"

"Is it possible Jeb was living in the garage—or the house? The garage doors didn't even close, and the house doors didn't lock."

"Maybe he was our burglar last night," said Steve, "the one who got away, that is." He smiled at Laura.

"I don't think so," she said.

"Oh?" Steve raised eyebrows registered his surprise.

"The man in the garage was too short—much older. Our burglar was taller and younger."

"Could you give us a detailed description?"

"No, but he was taller than I am, had long unkempt hair, wore jeans, T-shirt, tennis shoes and smelled like he'd been smoking pot—or something." Laura grinned at their surprised looks and added, "Sorry I can't give you colors. It was too dark."

"Todd, if this lady doesn't last as a pastor here, you really ought to hire her. She could be quite an asset."

"Oh, I think she'll last here, Steve. But that's even better. I can get her expertise without hiring her."

"Thanks for the compliments—I think, but I'm not interested in being a detective. I've got my hands full learning to be a pastor."

"You might have a point, though," said Todd. "The man's name was Jeb Little. He was a sort of a drifter—came into town about a year and a half, maybe even two years ago. Didn't seem to bother anyone. Did nothing unlawful to cause me to arrest him. Made a living—if you could call it that—by panhandling or..." He paused.

"Or what?" Steve asked.

"Well, I don't know what this has to do with anything—maybe nothing. We never knew where he lived, so there's no way we can check it out. But he had a couple of trained cats that would do tricks and people gave him money—you know like the old-time organ grinder with the monkey. They were big cats—looked sort of like raccoons."

"That is interesting," said Steve.

"Where are the cats now?" asked Laura.

"Don't know. They probably took off for the woods when their master died. I'm sure they'll find mice and stuff there. Maybe he even had a tent, or shack, or something out there. We could never locate it. It makes sense he would stay in this house, though. It was empty."

"The cats change the picture. If he was living here, there would be evidence of the cats—you know, litter box, food, hair. I haven't seen anything, unless he kept them in the basement. And I don't think they are there, or I would have heard them." Laura glanced from one to the other of the men as they sipped coffee. "And there's the matter of the mouse. With two cats in the house, I doubt a mouse would survive very long."

"It'll only take a minute to check out the basement," said Todd. He went to the basement door, opened it, and turned on the light. No sound followed, but Todd went down and looked around. "Nothing," he said as he returned.

"I hate to think of the poor things cooped up someplace with no food or water," said Laura.

"We'll be back and look around," said Todd. "In the meantime if you hear anything don't hesitate to call."

Todd and Steve left. Strips of yellow tape across the garage entrance were the only reminders of the morning's activities. But where were the cats?

11

Before stopping for lunch, Laura was determined to remove the last of her possessions from the car. She stroked the smooth blue finish as she took the last box from the hatchback. "Sorry Shebop," she said as if speaking to a friend. "Looks like it's going to be a while before you have a place out of the weather. Maybe by winter. That's only about six months away."

Shebop, patient little car that it was, said nothing, but from somewhere nearby came a sound that made her cringe. Low moans, accompanied by what sounded like small chains rattling, drifted across the yard from the belfry. As if a cold wind had suddenly whipped around her, goose bumps rose on her arms. Hair on her neck stood on end.

Must be the wind blowing through the louvers in the belfry. The sound of a hundred fingernails on a chalkboard continued for several minutes. The air was calm—not even a small breeze.

Laura shaded her eyes with her hands and looked up at the bell tower. The sounds stopped, but she was sure something, or someone, was in the church belfry. She knew she would have to check it out, but she was afraid of heights. Not wanting to feel foolish, she never admitted her fear. Certainly, she couldn't ask Steve or Todd, or even Frank, to check it out. Somehow, she would have to make herself do it.

She shivered. The phone rang so she had no time to ponder the situation. She grabbed the last load from the car and ran to answer it. Like a persistent, whining child screaming for attention, the obnoxious electronic device continued to peal. She lifted the receiver from its cradle thinking she would have to set the answering machine after this call.

"Hello," she tried to sound bright and cheery.

"Laura?" Bill Collins' voice was neither bright, nor cheery.

"Good morning, Bill." She tried to keep the irritation from her own voice as she glanced at the clock and looked around for a chair. This would not be a short conversation. Seeing no chair near enough to reach, she slid to the floor, resting her back against the wall, feet stretched in front of her, eyes closed.

Although he was her supervisor, he had insisted she call him Bill rather than Reverend Collins. When Harold died Bill had tried to date her—a thought that still sent a repulsive shiver through her. Laura was a logical, sensible, intelligent woman, but conversations with Bill Collins always left her feeling confused and uneasy. He didn't seem to listen and jumped from one topic to another with no bridge or reference point. Staying focused was difficult to stay the least.

Laura brought her concentration back to the voice at the other end of the line. "I just had a disturbing call from your Pastor/Parish Relations Chairman—a Margaret Jones?"

"That's Martha Jennings," Laura corrected him. Why would Martha call him?

"Whatever. You haven't even been there a day and already you have the PPR Committee upset. Really, Laura, I expected better things from you."

She waited knowing if she spoke she would say things she would regret later. She had enough regrets to deal with already. She didn't need more.

"Laura? Are you still there?"

Laura wiggled her toes and played with the phone line. "Oh, I'm still here, Bill. I have no intention of leaving. If Martha was upset, it's probably because someone gave her the impression that

I was a male pastor. Would you know anything about that, Bill?"

"Don't be ridiculous, Laura. Of course, I know you're a woman. Why would I say you're a man?"

"Bill, you didn't have to say so. You simply gave them my first name and middle initial and didn't explain that it was a man's name spelled differently."

"Oh, Laura, don't be picky. Just get the mess straightened out or we might have to…"

"Have to what, Bill? I've been appointed for a year. I've already stayed longer than anyone else in the last two years."

"Don't get too confident, Laura, and don't let me hear any more bad news about you down there."

"Bill, as far as I'm concerned, you won't hear *any* news at all from me. Nice talking to you, but I have a murder to solve and a belfry to exorcise." She was tired of his innuendoes and condescending attitude.

"Laura, are you sure you're all right? I tried to tell the bishop we shouldn't send a single woman down there. My term ends next June. Maybe we can…"

"Don't even think it Bill. I'm happy being single. Now if you don't mind, I have work to do."

She replaced the phone, turned on the answering machine and got to her feet. The thought of Bill Collins holding a buzzing phone in his hand brought a smile to her lips.

Laura moved to the bay window and stared at the church with its tall steeple. It reminded her of a bulletin cover Harold had once. A coat of paint would work wonders on it. Although the sun reflected on the side of the building and the blue sky behind the tower looked warm and inviting, Laura shivered and hugged herself. She would not let Bill Collins, burglaries, murder, or noises in the belfry put a damper on the excitement of her first church. With God's help she would overcome whatever problems arose. After lunch, she would explore the church—especially the belfry.

She carried a glass of fresh lemonade and a plate of cheese and crackers to the front porch. After brushing the steps with a cleaning rag, she sat with her back against the house, facing the church. She enjoyed the unseasonably warm day. Birds chirped in the trees and a pair of robins gathered material for a nest at the far end of the porch.

Nibbling her crackers, she reviewed the events since arriving last night. She had expected opposition. She knew some women clergy had endured some downright hostility. But murder and violence were different. Even the impromptu welcome party and the noises in the belfry were strange. But the most difficult to understand were the unwanted emotions she felt in the presence of Detective Steve Morgan. Twenty-five years of marriage and four years of singleness had left her unprepared for dealing with those kinds of personal feelings.

As if her thoughts had sent a message to whoever, or whatever, was in the belfry, the yowls and growls once again swept across the space from the church to the steps. She had to check it out. She didn't think the sound was a human, but…

"Hi."

Startled, Laura jerked her head up and gazed into the hazel, almost green, mischievous eyes of a young boy who looked about ten years old. He stood beside his bike glancing from her face to her plate of cheese and crackers on the floor beside her.

"Hi, yourself." Laura smiled at the boy, noting the copper-red, wispy hair and freckled face. "Is your name Tom Sawyer?"

The boy squinted and giggled. "No, are you Becky Thatcher?"

"No," she answered and they laughed together.

"Is school out already?"

"Nope. Didn't go to school today." He looked at her directly almost daring her to rebuke him.

"Oh? I hope you're not sick." The boy was a picture of good health.

"Nope. Just didn't wanna go. Thought the fish'd be bitin'. 'Sides, I wanted to see the dead man in that garage."

Laura set her glass down beside her. The freckled face boy spoke with a definite southern drawl and careless English, but she had the feeling he was far from ignorant, or dumb. He knew better; he preferred not to do better most of the time.

"Really? Well, he's not there anymore. The coroner took him away."

"Oh." The boy looked disappointed. "Who was he? My grandma said it was old Jeb."

"Well, he was a drifter named Jeb something or other. I guess he didn't have a home. Chief Williams thought maybe he lived in the woods." She watched him as he dug his toes into the dirt by the sidewalk, still holding on to his bike.

"Do you live close to the church?" she asked.

"A couple of blocks that way." He pointed to the north end of town.

"Do your parents know you went fishing?"

"Don't have a dad. He got killed in Viet Nam. There's just me and Mom and Grandma. She takes care of me while Mom works at the bank. 'Cept when I'm in school—or supposed to be." He gave Laura a look that clearly said, "You aren't going to tell, are you?"

Laura said nothing and the boy was quiet for a minute. Laura could tell he was considering something. "Where are his cats?"

"I don't know. No one's seen, or heard from them. I hope they find a home."

"Me too. I seen them once. They were big cats—real big. Jeb said one weighed almost twenty pounds and the other close to fifteen. They were gold, brown, and black striped—sort of like a raccoon. They even had a sort of mask like a raccoon. Old Jeb used to make them do tricks, like roll over and wave at the folks—even jump through a hoop. Sometimes they'd dance on their back paws. Once he had them sit up and beg like dogs. He called them Mischief and Rascal."

"Like raccoons? I don't know a lot about cats. A friend once had one something like that. I think she said it was a Maine Coon Cat. Did they have unusual paws?"

"Yeah, Jeb showed us once. They have five toes instead of four on their front paws. Oh, and they had sparkly, green eyes. Sometimes they looked at people cross-eyed."

"Sure sounds like Maine Coons. It might be dangerous for them to be free. Someone might think they really are raccoons and shoot at them."

"Really?" The boy's eyes widened.

"Possibly." Laura grinned and winked at him.

The boy grinned back and then eyed her plate again. "What you eatin?"

"Cheese and crackers and lemonade. Would you like some? I have plenty. Or I have peanut butter if you like it better."

"I like peanut butter and jelly."

"Then, I'll fix some for you."

"Okay. Can I just wait here while you fix it, or do I have to go in and wash up and everything?" The boy held his grimy hands out for her to see.

"You can stay here if you want. I'll bring a wet cloth and you can clean up a little. Okay?"

"Okay." A broad grin spread across the boy's face.

Laura left him parking his bike. When she and returned a few minutes later with a couple of sandwiches, a plate of chocolate chip cookies, another glass of lemonade, and a wet towel, he was waiting for her by the steps. He wiped his hands and said, "Thank you. I didn't have time to fix lunch before I left this morning."

"Why don't you just sit down on the other end of this step? We'll put the food between us and have a picnic."

"I never had a picnic on porch steps before. This is a lot more fun than school." His already familiar giggle reached Laura's heart, melting it to slush.

"So, tell me, were the fish biting?" Laura couldn't help smiling at the boy who looked about the age of her grandson, Josh. His wholesome, straight forward attitude was a welcome relief after the stressful events of the night before, and the confusing double talk of Bill Collins. She glanced over at his bike where he had a stringer of fish hanging from the handlebars.

"Sure were." He smiled back at her. He took a bite from his sandwich, set it down, then jumped up, and ran to his bike. He held the stringer for her to see the six trout and three bluegills hanging on it.

"Looks like a good day's work. Will your mom fix them for supper?"

"Naw, she don't like fish—at least she don't like to clean them. My grandma will though. Would you like one for your supper?"

"I'd like that very much. Thank you…eh, do you have a name, or shall I continue to call you, Tom?"

"That's not my name, but I like it." He laughed at her puzzled look.

"Would you like to tell me your real name?" she asked. "I'll still call you Tom, if you like."

"You tell me yours first," he said. "My mom said I shouldn't talk to people I don't know."

Laura laughed. She liked this truant little boy a lot. "My name is Laura Kenzel. I'm the new pastor of that church." She nodded toward the church behind him.

"But you're a woman!" His eyes got bigger. The stringer of fish dangled as he stared at her.

"Well, yes, I am that, but I guess God didn't mind, so hopefully others won't either."

The boy giggled. "If God says it's okay, then I guess it is." He examined his fish looking for the biggest one then laid it on the towel on the porch. He frowned as he sat back on the step. "Course I really don't believe in God anyway." Laura watched as doubt far too mature for a child spread across his face, clouding his eyes.

"You don't? Would you like to tell me why you don't believe in God—after you tell me your name?"

"My name is Jerome Nicholas McMichaels." He pronounced it as if he expected her to contradict him.

"Well, Jerome Nicholas McMichaels, that's a fine name for a fisherman. Do your folks call you Jerry?"

A sad smile slightly turned the corners of his mouth up. "Sometimes, but I don't like to be called Jerry."

"What would you rather be called?"

"Jerome. That was my uncle's name, too. He died a couple of months ago. That's why I don't believe in God no more." Jerome's lower lip quivered.

Laura glanced away and waited, giving him time to compose himself. Then she asked, "What happened to your uncle, Jerome? Was he sick?"

"No." He spit the word out like it was something distasteful in his mouth. "He was trying to help a kid, who fell in the lake, but the kid pulled him in and they both drowned."

"Oh, Jerome, how awful. Did you know the kid?"

"Yeah. He used to be my best friend." Jerome's voice sounded old and harsh. "But he killed my uncle and God just let it all happen." He looked at her as if to say, dispute that if you can.

"Oh, Jerome." Tears stung her own eyes. "What an awful thing to happen—your best friend and your uncle all at the same time. Do you want to talk about it?"

"What's to talk about? Joey went ice skating when the lake wasn't safe and fell in. He was stupid. I tried to tell him it wasn't safe, but he wouldn't listen to me. He went anyway. Then he fell in and Uncle Jerome would have pulled Joey out, 'cept Joey wrapped his arms around Uncle Jerome's neck and pulled him in. They both drowned before I could get back with the fire department."

Jerome was on the verge of tears and Laura wanted so much to comfort him. But how? She didn't want to embarrass him by hugging him. Instead she just laid her arm across his shoulder.

"I understand what you're feeling, Jerome."

"You're an adult." He spit out the words as if adult was some kind of fatal disease. He jerked away from her. "How would you know how I feel?"

Laura sighed, brushing away the tears which trickled from her own eyes. How would she know? Good question. How much could she share with a child about death and the devastating results? But Jerome had already experienced it twofold.

She sighed again and said, "I lost someone close to me to what they tried to call a stupid accident, Jerome. It wasn't the same, but the hurt is similar."

"You did?" Then flashing a tear-streaked grin at her, Jerome laid his hand on her arm and asked, "Do you want to talk about it?"

Laura laughed at his perception and placed her other hand over his. "No, I really don't, but sometimes we need to talk, even if we don't want to." She paused and looked off into the distance for a few seconds, gathering her thoughts. Jerome waited, eyes wide, watching her every move.

"My husband was a pastor. Part of his work was to help people. One night…" Laura paused and took another deep breath. After all this time she still had a hard time talking about it. "…this kid in the church, who was always in trouble, called for Harold to come and get him at a bar. Before he got there, a car ran him off the road. Someone murdered Harold while he was unconscious. They found the kid behind the wheel of the other car. He couldn't have done it, but it wouldn't have happened if Butch hadn't been drunk and called Harold."

"Did the kid die, too?" asked Jerome quietly.

"No." The bitterness in her voice surprised Laura. "No, Butch had a concussion and was unconscious for three days. When he awoke he remembered nothing."

Jerome pulled his hand back. They sat quietly for a minute listening to the singing of the robins. The breeze felt so much like a caress against her face that Laura put her hand to her cheek as if someone had touched her.

Jerome stared straight ahead. Finally he asked, "Were you mad at God for letting it happen?" He almost whispered the words as if he were afraid of offending her—or God.

"Jerome, I wish I could say no, but to be honest, I was mad at God; I was mad at the young boy; I was mad at my husband for going after him in the first place. But God understands that anger is part of grief. He waited for me to get over it."

"I don't want to get over it." Jerome spoke with such force that Laura had to bite her tongue and turn away to keep from laughing. She could remember her own stubbornness as a child. She could still hear her grandmother scolding, "Laura Ellen don't be such a stubborn mule. Act your age!" She always thought she was acting her age, just as Jerome was now acting out of his ten-year-old understanding.

She gave him a minute or two to get his anger under control then said, "You'll want to put it behind you some day, Jerome. You have to forgive to stop the hurt. When you're ready, God will be waiting for you."

Jerome said nothing, but she knew he had heard and

understood. They sipped their lemonade quietly for a few minutes until a very long, low-pitched groan from the belfry shattered the silence. It sounded more like "Meoower." That was followed by a higher pitched "yeeeeeooool" Even the birds took off in a flutter of fright.

12

"Good Heavens! Is that our ghost—or ghosts—in the belfry again?" Laura shaded her eyes with her hand and tried to see the belfry better. She could see nothing.

"Don't usually hear them in the daytime. Ghosts are supposed to come out at night." Jerome spoke as if he were an expert on the behavior of ghosts.

"You're probably right, Jerome. I've never heard of ghosts who haunt in the daytime. So either the ghosts are very unhappy, or they aren't ghosts at all. What do you think?"

"I don't believe in ghosts anyway. I bet it's the wind."

"But the wind doesn't seem to be blowing right now and…there it is again."

"Groooowelllllllerl"

"Sure sounds weird. Even owls don't come out during the day." Jerome shaded his eyes and glanced toward the belfry.

Laura started cleaning up the remains of their picnic. An idea was taking form. "Jerome, do you like to climb things? You know, like trees, fences—or ladders?"

"Sure. I'm the best climber around here. We have this big old apple tree in our backyard. I like to climb up to the top with my book and just get away when the other kids laugh and tease me." Jerome sat straighter and pushed out his chest. Then sadness flickered in his eyes, as he added, "Joey and I used to sit up there and study together."

"Would you like to climb something for me?" Laura heard his sadness, but decided to side step it for now.

"Sure, you got an apple tree? I'll pick apples and you can make a pie." He looked at her with wide, hope-filled eyes.

Laura laughed at his enthusiasm. "No, nothing like that—at least not today. I want you to climb to the belfry for me."

"You mean where the ghosts are?" His eyes widened.

"I thought you didn't believe in ghosts," she said. "If you would rather not, that's all right. I can do it. I just thought you might like to climb up there for me."

"You want to find out what's making that noise." His tone was accusing, not sure whether to believe her or not.

"Well, yes, I would like to find out. I don't think it's a ghost. And I don't think it's anything that will harm you."

"You don't think—but you don't know." His tone was flat and non-committal.

Laura said nothing. She stood smiling at Jerome, giving him time to think it over. Once again, they heard the high-pitched "meeeeooool" and faint rattle of small chains.

"I think I ought to go home." Jerome started backing away from her.

"That's all right Jerome. Thank you for the fish and for having a picnic with me. We'll do it again some day. Now, I need to go check out the belfry."

Laura took the remains of their lunch in the house and returned to the porch. Jerome was still standing by his bike waiting to see what she would do. She smiled at him, turned, and strode toward the church with determination. She forced herself not to turn around when she heard footsteps behind her. Smiling, she opened the church door. Before she could close it, Jerome was beside her.

"You're a woman," he stated as if that explained everything. "If you aren't afraid, then I'm not afraid neither. I put my fish in your sink."

"Thank you, Jerome." Laura breathed a prayer of relief. She did not look forward to climbing the ladder to the bell tower. Even as a child, she had never liked heights.

They wound their way around the catacombs of the basement of the church and up the stairs, which Laura hoped would lead to the belfry. She opened the last door and saw a ladder fastened to the wall. The hole at the top was big enough for a man to climb into the belfry. The yowelllls and growls were definitely coming from the belfry, but they stopped when Jerome and Laura entered the room beneath the belfry. Jerome looked at Laura.

"Sure you don't want to change your mind?"

She gave him a smile of encouragement and a little nudge toward the ladder. Slowly he climbed to the top and eased himself up to look over the edge. A long hissing sound startled him as he popped his head over the edge. He ducked back, grabbing at the edge to catch his balance.

"Jerome! Be careful. That wasn't a rattler, was it? Maybe this wasn't a good idea after all. You better come down. It might not be safe."

"It's okay, Pastor. It's them—the cats. They're scared. We startled each other." In his excitement Jerome almost let go of the ladder again.

"Jerome, please, come on down. We'll get Frank Jennings to come and see about it." Laura stepped back to look up at Jerome.

"Naw, he's too old to climb this little ladder. I can do it. I'm just not sure how." Jerome called back down to her.

"What aren't you sure about, Jerome?"

"Their chains are nailed to the wall and they looked scared. I don't think I can carry them down the ladder even if I can get them unfastened."

"Stay where you are Jerome and talk to them. They need to know you're their friend. Don't try to touch them. Don't try to go all the way up into the tower. Just stand there and talk to them. I have an idea how to get them down, but I'll need to run home and get something to put them in. Okay?"

"Okay, but hurry. They look so sad and hungry. There's no food or water up here and it's as hot as…"

"Never mind how hot it is. Just talk to them. I'll be back in five minutes, or less."

Laura left Jerome talking to the cats and wound her way down and around the church, retracing their steps to the parsonage. In a spare bedroom, she dumped the contents of two large canvas bags of craft items in a heap on the bed, chose a small ball of yarn, and took the bags back to the church.

Laura leaned her hand against the door to catch her breath at the top of the stairs. She heard Jerome talking to the cats.

"You are such pretty kitties. Someone wasn't very nice to you and when I find out who it was, I'll take care of them. We're going to get you out of here real soon. My preacher lady will take care of it. You'll like her. She's okay, for a woman. She..."

The compassion she heard in Jerome's voice touched her heart. Sure he would be embarrassed if he knew she heard him, she called out to warn him of her return. "Jerome, I'm back."

She stepped close to the bottom of the ladder, gulping back her fear, which rose like a sourball candy in her throat. She called up to the brave little boy, who was half in and half out of the belfry. "Now, Jerome, I'm going to come up the ladder. Can you ease yourself over the edge? Don't get close enough for them to scratch you."

"I think I can," he called back as he hooked a knee over the ledge and pulled himself up. He disappeared through the hole and Laura heard him scooting across the wooden floor. Taking a deep breath, she forced herself to move. Panic gripped her as she put a foot on the bottom rung of the ladder. She took another deep breath and forced a second foot to follow. One more step. Then another. Beads of sweat gathered across her upper lip and forehead.

Don't look down. Don't look down. One step at a time and don't look down. Laura kept up the steady flow of inward, self-encouragement until she reached the top. One more step and she could see over the edge. Already she could smell the litter box—or lack thereof. Jerome inched his way to the two beautiful, raccoon-like felines. Small, short chains hooked their collars to a bent nail on the wall.

90

Her own fears momentarily forgotten, Laura's heart skipped a beat when she saw the cats. They looked as though they had been there for a while and were probably hungry and even more thirsty. They seemed too weak to even hiss or spit at Jerome again. The only sound was a feeble "meow" ending in a question mark, as if asking, "Are you going to help us?"

Jerome reached out to let them sniff his fingers. He touched one and then the other with the tips of his fingers. With gentle strokes, he petted first one and then the other, speaking to them in a whisper. Hastily, he swiped the back of his hand across his face to brush away the sweat and tears sliding down his face, leaving streaks of wet dust and dirt. It was indeed very hot with the sun beating down on them.

"How could anyone do this to them? Where is God? Why would he let this happen to poor helpless animals?"

Laura struggled with her own emotions as she pulled herself up so she could rest her arms on the edge of the hole. This certainly wasn't the ideal place for a theological discussion with a small boy.

"You know, Jerome, God loves His people more than we can ever imagine, but He wants us to choose to love Him. That means we can also choose not to love Him. Some people choose not to love, and do evil things. God allows bad things because He won't make us love him. But do you know something else, Jerome?"

"What?" His face had a defiant look, but he still kept his touch gentle on the cats. Laura knew his anger wasn't with her, or the cats. She also knew God could handle the anger of a small boy.

"God allows things to happen, but He always gives us a way to undo at least some of the evil, if we look for it."

"How? How can anyone undo the evil here?"

"Well, to begin with, God sent you to me. I prayed for someone to come because I thought the cats might be up here, but I'm afraid of heights like this. I couldn't have come up here without your help." She nodded to the cats. "And who knows, when we find out who did it, maybe we can even help them turn their lives around. But, right now, we need to get the kitties out of this heat and get some food and water into them."

"Do you think they'll be all right?"

"They're still alive enough to yell and get our attention. We'll do our best to make sure they survive. Now, here are two bags. Don't even try to unfasten their chains. They look too sturdy and the nails look bent into the wall. Just see if you can unfasten the collars. They must be pretty tight or the cats would have pulled their head through them."

"They are," said Jerome. "I have to tighten it a little more to get it loose. Sorry kitty. Don't want to hurt you."

Jerome leaned back as the big cat jumped against him, sniffing his hand. The cat then tried to get his partner loose.

"Hold on there Rascal," said Jerome. "Let me do it."

Rascal sat back and watched while Jerome stroked the soft, striped fur of the smaller cat. "This one is Mischief." The cat lay on her belly, not moving a muscle as he unfastened the collar and let it fall to the floor. He slid his hands under her. She was limp and almost lifeless in his arms.

"Put each cat in a bag and hand it to me," said Laura. "I will tie the top of it so the cat doesn't jump out. I'm not sure either of them has the strength to do that, but we don't want to take a chance of them falling."

"She's just barely breathing," he whispered as he placed her in the soft canvas bag. "She don't even try to move. The cat did look limp, but Laura noticed her open one eye. She wouldn't swear to it, but it sure looked like the mischievous little thing winked at her.

Laura quickly tied a piece of yarn around the top of the bag slid the loops of each bag up to her shoulder. Laura felt the weight of first one cat then the other as the loops cut into her shoulders. They were certainly not scrawny, underfed cats. She hoped their weight wouldn't cause her to slip. She suddenly felt paralyzed—frozen to the ladder. Her fear had returned.

"It's all right, Pastor," said Jerome, laying his hand on her arm. "Don't be afraid. God got you up here; He'll get you down."

"Thanks, Jerome, but I thought you didn't believe in God." She tried to smile at him.

He giggled. "I don't, but you do."

Laura felt a wave of gratitude and affection for this little boy who had sneaked into her life. She descended one slow step at a time, set the bags down, wiped the sweat from her brow, and sighed in relief.

"All right, Jerome, I'm right under you."

Jerome turned around and backed out of the hole. Soon he was on the last rung and Laura reached out to help him off the ladder. She couldn't help wrapping her arms around him in a tight hug.

"Thank you Jerome. You are the best little rescuer that God could have sent for these poor kitties. Now, let's take them over to the house and see what we can do for them."

"Pastor?"

"Yes, Jerome."

He looked at her with a mixture of awe and respect. "You really are afraid of heights, aren't you?"

"Yes, Jerome. I know it's silly of me, but I'm very much afraid. I could never have gone up there if you hadn't been here to help me."

"But you did it—even when you were scared."

"Sometimes we have to close our eyes and ears to our fears and let God guide us in the scary paths. It helps to have someone to give encouragement." She tousled his hair. "Now, let's get these kitties home and give them some food and water."

13

"You take them out of the bags while I get some water and tuna," said Laura as they carried the cats into the kitchen. She rummaged through the cabinets and found a couple small bowls. She filled one with water, then opened a can of tuna packed in water and put half of it in the other bowl.

"They're shivering. They couldn't be cold as hot as it is today." Fear shadowed Jerome's eyes into a deeper green.

"They're probably scared. Here, see if you can get them to eat, or drink something. I'll go upstairs and get a warm blanket for them." Laura ran up the steps, grabbed an old blanket which she had used to cover some of her furniture during the move and returned to find Jerome trying without much success to coax them to eat.

"Here we go. Are they eating?"

"They can't." Tears gathered on his eyelids ready to cascade down his cheeks. "They're going to die."

"Let me try." Laura sat on the floor beside Jerome and took Mischief on her lap. Holding the cat like a small baby, she forced the cat's mouth open. "Now, Jerome, put a taste of the tuna on her tongue." He picked up a tiny piece of tuna and placed it in the cat's mouth. With one hand, Laura held the mouth closed and with the other hand, she stroked the cat's throat until she felt it swallow. When she let go, Mischief started licking her chops. Jerome took her and held her. She allowed him to feed her a few more bites, while Laura went through the same process with Rascal.

Soon they were both eating the tuna which had enough water in it to help with hydration. With the pangs of hunger satisfied, they were content then to drink some water from the bowl. Both cats took a few catch as catch can kinds of swipes at cleaning their faces then curled up entwined together on the blanket. Laura gently drew the corner over them and they promptly went to sleep.

The smile on Jerome's face was enough to make Laura forget how fearful she had been. "We did it," he whispered. "We did it. Are you going to keep them?"

"I don't know Jerome," I need to call Chief Williams. He'll want to check it out. If Jeb had any relatives, they might want the cats. Until they're strong and healthy again, I'll keep them here...unless you want to take them home with you."

"Oh, no, I can't do that. I don't think my mom would let me." He paused then asked, "Can I come to see them sometime?"

"Of course you can," she said. "After all they wouldn't be here if it weren't for you. And I'll need help with them. You can come after school each day."

Jerome beamed. "Well, you helped too."

"Now, I guess I'd better call Chief Williams and file a report." She picked up the phone and began to dial. After the call from Bill Collins, Laura had placed a small table and chair for the phone in the corner. This time she didn't have to sit on the floor.

"Chief Williams." The voice was warm and friendly while at the same time professional.

"Todd, this is Laura Kenzel."

"Yes ma'am. I hope you didn't find any more bodies." She could hear the amusement with a touch of apprehension in his voice. He reminded her of a schoolboy.

"Well, not exactly."

"Not, exactly? What does that mean?" Suspicion replaced the amusement.

"Well, Jerome McMichaels stopped by and together we solved the mystery of the strange noise from the belfry."

"Oh, really. Had a few bats in the belfry?" A hearty laugh followed his words.

"Close. We had cats in the belfry." She winked at Jerome who covered his mouth and giggled.

"Cats in the belfry? That's a new one."

"Jeb Little's cats. Someone chained them in the belfry."

"Are you sure about that? Why would anyone want to do that?"

"Well, Todd, we found the cats. You can find out who and why."

"Probably kids pulling pranks."

"Maybe, but prank, or not, it would be my guess that somehow their imprisonment in the belfry relates to the death of their owner. You find out who put them in the belfry and why, and I think you'll be closer to finding your murderer."

"I'm sure glad Steve chose this week to help me. We'll both be right over to get your statement. Cats in the belfry?"

Laura turned to Jerome. "Chief Williams and Detective Morgan will be here shortly to get our statements. While we wait, would you mind running a little errand for me?"

"What do you want me do to?" He cocked his head to one side and narrowed his eyes. "More ladders to climb?"

Laura laughed in spite of her own uneasiness. "No. No more ladders. I think I saw a grocery store not far from here when I drove in last evening. Do you suppose you can ride your bike over there?"

Jerome relaxed and a spark of hope replaced the suspicion. "Sure, it's only around the corner—well maybe a couple of corners. What do you want? Ice cream, maybe?"

Laura laughed again at his not so subtle hint. "That's not what I had in mind, but if you can carry it with the other things I want, you can get some. If I'm going to keep Rascal and Mischief for a while, I'll need some cat food—three or four cans should do it for now. I also, need some kitty litter—the clumping kind. My friend says it's easier to clean up. I think that should do until I can get to a pet store." Laura moved to the closet as she spoke. She opened it and retrieved her purse from the shelf.

CATS IN THE BELFRY

"You need a box to put the litter stuff in?" Jerome sounded as if he knew all about taking care of cats.

"Not now. I'll wait and see what happens. I have a plastic storage box I can use—the kind that slides under a bed. Should be low enough for them to get in and out of easily." She opened her purse, extracted a twenty dollar bill from her billfold, and handed it to Jerome. "This should do it. Get whatever kind of ice cream you like. Hurry now, Chief Williams will be here any minute. He'll probably want your statement, too."

"Really? He'll want to talk to me about something besides skipping school? I like the chief, but he's always bugging me about school."

She nodded and smiled at his eagerness and candid remarks, and refrained from adding her own comments about school. Later would be time enough.

"I'm off. Back in a few minutes." He bounded out the door and Laura watched as he sped away on his bike, passing the police cruiser, as Todd pulled into the driveway. At least he didn't have his lights flashing and siren screaming this time.

Laura waited at the door, while Todd and Steve got out of the cruiser and approached the house. "Come in," she said holding the door open. "Sorry to bother you again so soon. Can I make you some coffee? Sandwich? Lemonade?"

"No thanks. We just finished lunch when you called," said Todd.

"After the breakfast we had here earlier, we didn't need much, but lemonade sounds good." Steve glanced around the room. "Looks like you've had a busy morning aside from exploring belfries." He smiled at her and Laura struggled to keep from blushing.

She started for the kitchen and half-turned to them returning a smile. "I guess I did get a few things accomplished. At least there are places to sit this afternoon. Take your pick. Todd, sure you don't want anything?"

"Lemonade does sound good, now that you mention it. Thanks."

97

While Todd opened his clipboard and found his pen, Laura slipped into the kitchen. She returned with a tray of three glasses of lemonade.

"Now, Pastor," Todd began, pen poised over that nosey form of questions, "tell us what happened. Cats in the belfry? I've heard of bats, but not cats." He laughed slightly at his attempt at joking. No one joined him so he cleared his throat and waited for Laura to begin. Steve had his small notebook and pen ready, but as before, he listened more than he wrote.

With as much accuracy as possible, Laura told them about Jerome stopping by, them talking and then hearing the noises from the church belfry. "We decided ghosts don't usually haunt in the daylight hours, so it had to be something else." She then described how she and Jerome had rescued the cats.

"They seemed a little weak and dehydrated, but I have a feeling they were playing possum. They'll be fine. They're resting in the kitchen on a blanket, if you want to question them."

Laura tried to look serious, but had to break into a laugh at the expression on Todd's face. He laughed with her and commented, "Do you think they can be trusted to tell the truth?"

"If they could talk—or rather if we could understand feline language—I expect they could solve a lot of your mysteries, including the murder of their owner." Laura still smiled, but her tone was more serious.

"I don't doubt that one bit," said Steve.

"Well, I guess at least the mystery of the noise from the belfry is solved," stated Todd snapping his clipboard shut. "The kids around here get pretty wound up this time of year. It's warm enough to be out, but school's still in session. So they expend pent-up energy after school. Where is Jerome anyway? Didn't I see him take off on his bike as we drove up? I wouldn't be surprised if he didn't put them up there himself and then lead you to find them. For a little kid, he sure can get himself in a lot of trouble—never anything serious, just little stuff."

Steve saw the anger rise on Laura's face. He sat back to watch the fireworks. The red flush slowly rose up to her cheeks and her brown eyes snapped with anger as her fists clenched and her jaws clamped down.

Laura was unaware that Steve watched her. Her voice was tight and cracked with emotion. "Chief Williams, how dare you judge a small boy who has had so much trouble in his young life already? Of course, he didn't know where the cats were. And I think you had better stick around long enough to get his statement. If it wasn't for him, we would still have a mystery about the noises in the belfry. He'll be back any minute. I sent him to the store for some things I needed for the cats."

"I don't see what a kid can add. You gave a complete report. We thank you for your help, but we have more important things to do. Come on Steve let's take a look at that garage again."

"I think you're making a mistake, Chief Williams." Laura glared at him.

Steve noted she intentionally used his title and not his first name. Amusement and some other emotions he wouldn't even think about rose up within him. He had never seen a woman so angry about what happened to a little boy she hardly knew.

"She might have a point, Todd. Even if the kid had a part in putting them there, you should hear his story. Maybe get him alone and compare stories."

Laura turned her glare at him. "You don't need to sound so patronizing, Detective Morgan." Again she emphasized the title. "Jerome seems to be the only one who's willing to be even a little bit helpful to me." Laura paused. Her anger suddenly subsided.

"I'm sorry. That wasn't fair. A lot of folks have tried to help me, including you two. But Jerome will tell you exactly what I've told you, except he may think he has to tell you what we talked about. He doesn't, so don't ask. That was confidential—had nothing to do with the cats in the belfry."

Steve raised his eyebrow and gave her a quizzical look. "What kind of conversation could you have with a ten-year-old that could be considered confidential?"

"It doesn't matter what the age of a person is who shares painful information with me. If they don't want it spread around—for whatever reason—I consider it confidential. It's the same as being in a counselor's office." Her look dared him to contradict her. Her cheeks still glowed with the residue of her anger.

"Okay." He smiled at her, holding his hands out in front of him as if to ward off angry blows. "If you say it's confidential, we won't pursue it now, but, if the future resolution of this murder case depends on that confidential information, we'll have to dig further."

"It has nothing to do with the case—only the feelings of a small boy who's had too much grief in his short life already. I would never encourage him to withhold any information pertinent to the investigation." Laura turned away from them. He knew she brushed at the threatening tears.

"I'm sure you wouldn't and I didn't mean to question your ministry. I guess I've never met a minister who's so concerned about the feelings of her folks—especially one of the children." Steve felt a strong desire to reach out and touch her—hold her—anything to make the pain in her eyes go away. What he couldn't understand was that the pain was not her own. It was for Jerome, but she bore it as if it was her own. He was intrigued. The sound of gravel scattering in the driveway and footsteps running across the porch saved him from making a fool of himself.

"I'm back." Jerome barged through the door as if he lived there and ran to the kitchen. They heard him place the bags on the table. Then they heard the refrigerator open and close, and Jerome returned to the living room.

"Here's your change, Pastor. I got just plain vanilla ice cream. Hope that's all right. Did you tell them what happened already?" Hopefulness bubbled over the freckle-faced kid.

"Yes, I told them the way I remembered it," Laura said.

"Oh." Disappointment replaced the excitement in his eyes.

"But we need to hear your side of the story—then compare notes." Steve smiled at the little boy.

Excitement leapt back into his eyes. "You mean to make sure we're both telling the truth." His matter-of-fact tone made them all laugh.

Steve glanced at Laura. All it took to take away her pain was to give some attention to this excited, winsome little boy. He would always remember that. He reached out to Jerome and lightly slapped him on the back. "You got us pegged, son. Why don't we walk over to the church? You can tell Chief Williams and me about it while we check out the crime scene."

"Okay." Jerome started toward the door but turned to Laura with a question furrowing his brow. Instead of a question he said, "We'll be back for ice cream in a few minutes. Do you have any chocolate sauce?"

"No, I don't have any on hand, but I think I can make some hot fudge sauce while you're gone." Laura smiled at them. As they started out the door, she called to him, "Oh, by the way, Jerome, you don't have to tell them what we talked about if you don't want to. That's confidential information."

Jerome's worried frown relaxed into a smile. "Thanks."

14

Jerome was breathless and near tears when he finished telling Steve and Todd about helping his pastor find the cats. Todd started up the ladder to the bell tower. Jerome looked up at Steve, who knelt closer to the boy. "Why do people want to hurt helpless little animals and homeless old men?"

Steve laid his hands on Jerome's shoulders and looked into the frightened, sad eyes. "Jerome, I wish I could give you an answer. I've spent my life searching for a reason and haven't found one yet. With your help, we'll find the person who did this and punish him for it. That's a promise."

"Detective Morgan, are you ever scared? I mean, do you ever have to do something you're scared of doing?"

Caught off guard, Steve couldn't imagine what prompted that question. He glanced up at Todd, who was on his way down the ladder. He shrugged in a "who knows what the kid might be thinking" manner. Steve decided the best way to deal with this boy was with an honest, straight-forward answer.

"Yes, Jerome, there are times when I'm very much afraid. And I'm sure I've had to do some things that brought fear to my heart. In our line of business, Todd and I are sometimes in dangerous positions and that can be scary. Why do you ask?"

"I guess I always thought I was a coward if I admitted I was scared, but Pastor climbed all the way up there to help me. She said she's scared of heights and wouldn't have gone up there if I hadn't been here to help her. I thought maybe she was just trying to make me feel better 'cause I was scared to come down the ladder. She said sometimes we have to do things we're afraid of and trust God to help us."

Steve's admiration for that beautiful, lady preacher jumped a couple of notches. "Jerome, from what I've seen of your pastor, you can believe her one hundred per cent. If she shared that information with you, it was because she trusted you. She meant every word."

"If she trusted me, maybe I shouldn't have told you." Jerome dropped his head.

"Your secret—and hers—is safe with us, Jerome. That's not part of the record."

"Thanks." Jerome flashed his boyish, happy grin.

"Steve's right, son," said Todd. "The pastor's secret is safe with us and we'll do all we can to catch the people who did this. I must admit, I thought maybe you had something to do with it, but I was wrong."

"Me?" said Jerome. "Why would you think I had anything to do with it? I love animals. I wouldn't hurt those cats like that."

"Hold on, there kid," said Todd. "I'm not accusing you. It was just a thought because—well, you do seem to turn up where there's trouble sometimes. Although, I have to admit this isn't the kind of trouble you usually get into."

"I can't help it if fishing is more fun than sitting in a stuffy old school room."

"What changed your mind?" asked Steve, winking at Jerome, who relaxed.

"Facts. I was just up there looking into the belfry. Didn't go all the way in. Didn't need to. There's no way this kid could have gotten two lively cats with claws up the ladder in the first place, and certainly he couldn't have chained them to the wall without getting himself all scratched up. I don't see a scratch on him that would match that kind of a fight."

"Good point," said Steve. "We're going to make a first-rate detective out of you yet. Now, what do you say we check out the garage?"

"Then we can have a hot fudge sundae," said Jerome.

"I don't think we were invited," said Steve.

"There's enough and I'm sure Pastor don't mind. She made me a peanut butter and jelly sandwich 'cause I forgot to pack a lunch."

"All right then," said Steve, "but if we get in trouble it's all your fault."

Jerome giggled. "I only get in trouble for not going to school. Pastor won't yell at me."

"You're probably right, Jerome, so let's get over there before the hot fudge gets cold."

"Sounds like a plan to me," laughed Todd. "Come on Jerome— eh, I thought your name was Jerry."

"My name is Jerome Nicholas McMichaels." Jerome stubbornly set his jaw, crossed his arms, and dared them the contradict him. "Some folks call me Jerry, but I like Jerome better. That's what my preacher calls me." Then he giggled like the ten-year-old that he was and added, "She called me Tom Sawyer before she knew my name and I called her Becky Thatcher. Now she's my pastor and I'm Jerome."

"Then Jerome it is," said Todd tousling his red hair. "Let's go."

Steve shook his head and wondered about his own sanity. The more time he spent with this likable little boy, the more he wanted to know all he could about Laura Kenzel. Maybe if he had met someone like her thirty years ago his life would be different today.

* * *

Laura watched Jerome, Steve and Todd cross to the church then returned to the kitchen to make the fudge sauce until the front door banged and Jerome ran through the house to the kitchen. "Is the sauce ready yet?" He headed for the sink to wash his hands without waiting to be told to do so.

"It's ready." Laura smiled at him as she moved the pan from the hot burner to a cold one.

"Can we help?" Steve followed Jerome into the kitchen. "We were invited in for ice cream and hot fudge. I hope you don't mind."

"You might see if you can find some bowls up there. I'm not sure where I put them—or even if I put them away yet."

"Sure smells good." Todd followed into the kitchen, pulled a chair away from the table, and sat down. Laura smiled to herself at the look of boyish anticipation on his face. She watched Jerome enjoy his treat.

Feeling Steve watching her, she turned to him. "I hope I don't have to call you folks out again anytime soon."

"Offer us treats like this, and you can call us anytime. Right, Todd?"

"Sure thing. I don't think I ever had anything so good. This your own recipe?"

"Thank you. My grandmother taught me years ago." She changed the subject to hide the feeling of embarrassment. "Do you think there's any connection between the cats in the belfry and the murder?"

"I doubt it. I know you think they're related and if we find who put them there and why, we'll be closer to finding our murderer, but I still think it was kids pulling pranks." Todd spoke in between bites.

"I don't know, Todd. Don't dismiss the idea too quickly," said Steve. "Sometimes insignificant and seemingly unrelated facts have more to do with clearing an investigation than we think."

A small moan from the corner caught their attention. Jerome looked at Laura and fear flashed in his eyes. "Are they all right?"

"They might want a little more tuna and water," Laura replied "Why don't you finish your ice cream, then get the dish of tuna out of the refrigerator and see if you can give them a bite. I fixed their litter box while you were gone. We'll move them upstairs in a few minutes."

Jerome excused himself, took his dish to the sink and got the tuna from the refrigerator. He took it to the corner of the kitchen. Laura watched as he crooned to the cats and coaxed them to eat.

She turned away and started to clear the table. With her back to the men she dabbed at her eyes.

"How could anyone try to harm those beautiful, helpless animals?" Laura couldn't face them, and she really didn't expect an answer.

Steve clenched his fists to keep back the anger, but more to keep him from doing something stupid—like touching her, or worse yet, taking her in his arms. She wasn't the type to manipulate a man into holding her. She probably didn't even think about the possibility.

"Jerome asked us the same question," he said. "We'll find whoever did this. That's a promise."

Todd and Steve both rose and started toward the living room. "We better get back to work before folks start accusing their police chief of enjoying his work too much," Steve teased.

"Yeah? Since it's your vacation we may as well have some enjoyment," Todd said. "Thanks for the ice cream, Laura. I guess we have all the information we need for now. Call us if anything else comes up, or if you think of something else we need to know."

"Thanks. I hope I won't need to do that. When I get home from the meeting tonight, I'll call it a night as early as possible."

"Big meeting?" Steve asked.

"You might say that. The district superintendent gave these folks the impression they were getting a man for their new minister. Now I have to straighten out the miscommunication and tackle the matter of maintenance. So much needs to be done."

"I'm sure you'll have them eating out of your hands within minutes." Steve laughed as they moved toward the door. "The women this morning seemed to be accepting."

"I don't know Steve," interrupted Todd. "The women might accept her, but Frank Jennings is part of that group and he's one stubborn man."

"Thanks, Todd," said Laura, not meaning it at all. "I needed to hear that."

"Don't listen to him. You'll do fine."

"Steve's right. They're basically good folks. Frank can be stubborn, but he's a good man."

Jerome had followed them to the door. "They're sleeping again." He nodded toward the kitchen.

Todd turned to him and asked, "Jerome, what time does your mom get home from work?"

Jerome frowned and looked up at the chief, then at Laura. "A little after five," he mumbled. "I go to Grandma's until she gets home. So she won't know I skipped school today unless you tell her."

"That's not quite accurate, Jerome."

He jerked around to look at Laura as if he were afraid she was going to tell on him. "Why not?"

"How are you going to explain all those nice fish you caught?"

Jerome relaxed and grinned. "I'll take them to my grandma. She likes fish. My mom likes them, too, but I would have to tell her where I got them."

"And your grandmother won't tell?"

"Not if I ask her not to." Jerome looked uneasy.

"What are you going to tell your mom when she reads in the newspaper all about you helping to solve the mystery of the belfry?" asked Todd.

His eyes got wide. "It's going to be in the paper?"

"Well, sure," said Todd with a grin. "Those noises have been a mystery for almost two years. Everyone will want to know what it was, and who solved it. You're a hero, Jerome, but how will you explain to your mom?"

"Oh. Well…I guess…I guess I'll have to tell her the truth." He finally stated with a note of dread. Then he added, his eyes sparkling, "I'm really a hero? A real hero like my dad?"

"You certainly are a hero, Jerome," said Steve, "and I bet your mom will let you go with just a warning—this time, especially if the chief here talks to her first. Maybe you should call your grandmother and stay here until he has a chance to do that."

Steve looked at Laura for her approval. Laura had never seen such blue eyes. They twinkled as they met hers in conspiracy. She felt herself smile. She also felt that rush of warmth spread across her cheeks. She dropped her gaze to Jerome, hoping Steve Morgan didn't noticed. She glanced at Todd and saw something more like pain mixed with anger. Was he angry that Jerome wouldn't be punished? She didn't think so. He seemed to like Jerome. Before she could ask him what was wrong, Jerome was looking at her with wide, anxious eyes.

"Can I?"

"As long as your grandmother approves. You can help me move the cats upstairs to a spare bedroom and then we'll clean those fish and get them ready to cook. Maybe your mom won't mind cooking them if they're already cleaned."

"You know how to clean fish?"

"Of course, I know how to clean fish," she declared. "When I was your age I fished with my uncle. He always made me clean what we caught." Jerome looked properly impressed.

"You sure are smart for a woman." Jerome grinned.

"Thanks, Jerome." Laura smiled at him. "I *really* needed that." And she meant it with all her heart.

Steve and Todd laughed as they left. "Call us if you need us."

Laura and Jerome went to the kitchen where the cats curled on the blanket in the corner. While they cleaned the fish and they talked about various things: school—he was bored, church—they didn't have much because some folks were afraid of ghosts, his grandmother and mother—they were all the family he had since his uncle's death. When the last fish was filleted, Laura got a plastic freezer container for them. The phone rang.

"You put them in this while I get the phone," she said grabbing a paper towel and wiping her hands as she hurried to the phone.

"Reverend Kenzel speaking...yes...Let me get back to you...five minutes, ten at the most." Laura hung up the phone and went back to the kitchen.

"Jerome, that was the reporter for *The Cotton-Glen Chronicle*. They want to do an interview and picture."

"You mean they want to talk to me? And my picture?"

"Yes. We need to get your mother's permission. Is it all right if I call her, or would you rather do it?"

"I'll call her then you can tell her what they want."

"All right." Laura was pleased that Jerome was willing to take some responsibility. She was sure Todd had already talked to Jerome's mother, so she would know why Jerome was at Laura's house.

"I don't know," said Carolyn McMichaels. "I don't want them making my boy look foolish or anything."

"I'll be with him," said Laura. "I won't allow them to badger him."

"All right. Tell him to go right home after the interview. Mother is concerned."

"Would you like for her to be here for the interview?"

"You wouldn't mind?"

"I'd feel better if she were here."

"Thank you, Reverend Kenzel. I'll call her."

Laura called the reporter back. "You can do the interview, but his grandmother and I will be here."

"They're here," said Jerome bouncing to the door about ten minutes later. Laura glanced out the window and saw two cars pull up behind Shebop. An older woman—Jerome's grandmother?—got out of the first car. She was about Laura's height, but thirty pounds heavier. Her red hair streaked with white and gold was a prediction of Jerome's in years to come. The second woman was much younger, blonde, early twenties. The two women seemed to know each other.

"Hi, I'm Karen Markley," said the girl as Laura opened the door for them. "I'm reporter for the paper during the week and organist for your church on Sundays."

"Oh," said Laura. "I'm sorry I didn't make the connection earlier. I'm sure someone told me we had an organist, but it's been rather hectic since I arrived."

"So I hear. I want to do an interview with you, too, eventually— but I'll give you time to get settled."

"And to make sure I stay long enough to get it in print?"

Karen laughed. "That too. I understand you have a big meeting tonight so I won't keep you."

"I'm Sophia Dugal, Jerome's grandmother," said the older

woman extending her hand to Laura. "Karen will do a good job with the article," she said. "She's lived next door to me with her parents since she was much younger than Jerome is. They will both be at the meeting tonight."

A half hour later, Karen had notes for her article and several shots of Jerome with Rascal and Mischief, who, hearing voices came to investigate. Of course, show cats that they were, they were willing to pose for pictures with Jerome—one on either side of him. Karen thanked Jerome for the interview and Laura for allowing them to meet there. She left and Sophia waited for Jerome to gather his belongings and put his bike in her trunk.

"I won't be at the meeting tonight," said Sophia. "Carolyn will be there though. She's on the PPR committee."

"Yeah," said Jerome, "Grandma has to stay with me." He made a sour face then giggled.

"Well, we don't want you running off after dark to go fishing," said Sophia. She tousled her grandson's hair and laughed. "Let's get out of here so the pastor can get her thoughts together for tonight."

15

Procrastinating as long as she dared, Laura finally pushed back the unsettled feeling in the pit of her stomach and went to dress. At the top of the stairs, the doorknob of the spare room rattled. She and Jerome had moved the cats in there before he left. Startled, Laura stepped back and watched. The knob moved. A white paw slipped under the door pulling at it. Laura pushed the door open enough to ease into the room in time to see a bushy, gold and brown striped tail slip under the bed in retreat.

She knelt in the doorway and waited. Both cats slowly eased out from under the bed and sat side by side staring at her, then inched closer. "You are such pretty kitties," she whispered as she touched first one and then the other with the tips of her fingers. "Do you need more food? Would you like to explore the rest of the house?"

Two sets of emerald-green, unblinking eyes watched her with such intensity, Laura was almost sure they could read her thoughts. She laughed and rose to leave. They followed her across the hall to her room. From the safety of her bed, they watched while she changed clothes. "What do you think, kitties? Will this do?" She turned around for them to observe her yellow dress. Simultaneously the cats cocked their heads to one side and blinked their approval. If they didn't understand her, they put on a good act.

"Thank you," Laura said. "Now, if you don't mind, we'll go downstairs and see what I can find for your supper. I saved some trout for you, if you would like to try it."

"Meowll," replied a duet in harmony—more or less.

Laura started down the stairs. The cats ran around her and waited at the bottom. Before she reached the floor, they trotted ahead of her to the kitchen and waited again. She set their bowl of water on the floor in one corner of the kitchen. The other bowl she filled with chopped fish. "We can't have you choking on bones after all you've been through."

Rascal watched while Mischief moved to the bowl and ate about half of the fish. She moved away and began cleaning her paws and face while Rascal cleaned up the fish. Laura laughed. "Well, aren't you the gentleman. I'll give you both something else when I get home later. You finish your baths and take a nap until I get home."

"Meowll?" Were they worried about her leaving? They followed her to the door. Laura interpreted their stare as one of anxiousness.

"It's all right, kitties. I'll be back in a couple of hours. I promise." She stooped to stroke their soft fur.

Both cats rubbed against her legs and purred. She remembered how Susan when she didn't want to be left with a babysitter, would cling to Laura's legs. "Sorry, guys," she said stroking the backs of Rascal and Mischief. "You probably think I'm going to abandon you like Jeb did, but I won't. Honest. I'll be home in a little bit. Be good kitties."

She turned on the lamp and closed the door behind her. Both cats sat in the window watching her—two silhouettes in a frame. How long they watched, she didn't know.

Laura stepped into the church basement and felt as though she was back in her home church. The only difference was the dingy tile floor and the chipped green paint on the block walls here, versus the clean white and pale green colors then. Florescent shop lights hung from various points in the ceiling providing light, but not much in aesthetics. The kitchen was clean enough, but like everything else, needed paint. A large commercial stove, shiny stainless steel dishwasher, two sinks, refrigerator, microwave and cabinets framed the room while a stainless steel table sat in the middle like an island, isolated and alone. A slight musty odor hung in the air, as did a feeling of dampness. She added a dehumidifier to her list for the trustees.

Laura opened the refrigerator, expecting to find various kinds of foreign matter growing in it. She was pleased to see the inside as clean and shiny as it was empty. Either someone spent a lot of time keeping it that way, or the refrigerator was never used.

The back door opened and closed. Frank and Martha Jennings sauntered into the kitchen. Frank looked around the room sniffing the air. Laura wondered if there was a gas leak that she didn't detect. She smelled nothing. Frank went back into the fellowship hall and returned with a scowl on his face. Laura watched with interest. Did he expect something she hadn't done?

"Where's the coffee?" Frank looked around, sniffing the air again.

Laura started to laugh and realized he wasn't joking. "Pardon me?" She would try the ignorant, newcomer approach.

"The coffee," Frank answered. "The preacher's wife always makes the coffee for our meetings."

"Oh?" Laura could think of nothing more to say—at least nothing more that she dared say.

Martha tried to rescue her. "Oh, Frank, don't be such a jerk. Give her time to get to know us. She didn't know she was supposed to make coffee." Martha's words didn't do much to relieve the creeping tension and anger.

Forcing a smile to her lips, Laura said nothing. She returned to the table where she had left her notes and began reviewing them. With a deep intake of air, she sent a message to her action-oriented mind. Careful Laura. Give yourself some time. Don't react. Just be calm.

Martha became the self-appointed hostess for the evening and introduced Laura to the rest of the committee members as each arrived. "This is Attorney Michael Atkins. He's the best lawyer in town."

He shook Laura's hand. "I'm the *only* lawyer in town. Folks depend on me a lot." He barely shook her hand and pulled his hand back to his pocket. "I'm surprised you've stayed around— what is it—almost twenty-four hours, now? If you need a good lawyer, let me know." His smile remained like a pasted-on addition to a picture. His eyes didn't seem to receive the message that a smile was on his lips. Laura decided not to try to decipher what sounded to her like a mixed message at best or a threat at worst.

"James and Karen Lily are the couple coming through the door," Martha said. "They own a farm west of town." Laura shook their hands and told them how much she appreciated them being there.

One by one—two by two—the rest came in and Martha introduced them. Laura's head was spinning by the time they were all seated. Glancing around the banquet-size table, she tried to recall what Martha had said. At the end was Doris Baker, whose husband doesn't come to church. To her right were Lewis and Mona Hostetler. They have a little computer shop downtown. Next to the Hostetlers were Phil and Paula Jameson. He's the president of Cottonville Savings & Loan. Beside Phil Jameson was Carolyn McMichaels, Jerome's mother. Aaron Blakemore sat beside Carolyn. His wife is a pharmacist. He's a drug salesman. Laura was at that one end of the table, so she started at the other end. On Doris Baker's left was Harry Reading, who lost his wife last year. Jack Durham sat beside him. His wife, Nancy, is in Cottonville Manor with Alzheimer's. Fred Martin was next. His wife, Emma, runs the Sunday School Department. Irvine (Irv) Markley and his wife, Susan, were next. Their daughter Karen is the organist and reporter for the local paper. Jim Keenly, whose wife is homebound in a wheelchair; then Gene Stanley, a member for sixty years and widower for ten came next. Martha and Frank finished that side of the table.

Laura wrote the names on her notepad to help her remember. She was ready to begin when Martha glanced around the room and said, "Well," she said, "This is a first. I think all of both committees are here." She sounded both pleased and surprised.

One more person entered the room at the last minute. "Oh, this is Dorothy—Dorothy Barker. She's our part-time secretary, but the noises have kept her away. I asked her to come tonight. Hope you don't mind. I thought she could take notes better than most of us."

"That sounds like an excellent idea, Martha. Thank you for taking care of it. Why don't you sit here on my left, Dorothy? There seems to be a space just for you." Laura smiled at the pleasant-looking woman who would be her secretary, but she was anxious to get the meeting started—and finished. Everyone was present. The chit-chat had gone on long enough. Since two committees were meeting together, Laura presided. Somehow, she knew the PPR Chair and Trustee Chair, since they were husband and wife, would get into a squabble over who was in charge.

"All right folks," she called over the din of the various conversations while tapping on a table with a wooden spoon from the kitchen. "We have a lot to accomplish tonight, so let us get started. Shall we pray?" It wasn't a question for discussion and Laura didn't wait for an answer.

Before anyone could speak, Laura closed her eyes and lifted her face, "Lord, we're here tonight to do the work of this church. We have some hard decisions to make. We have a lot of work to accomplish tonight. Grant us mercy, wisdom, and patience with one another. Amen."

Laura plunged ahead. "I thought it would be easier to meet around these tables than in the Sanctuary. I hope you don't mind. We need to begin working out some details that should have been worked out before I arrived—misunderstandings and false assumptions."

Laura looked over the sea of scowls and frowns that threatened to wash upon her with waves of protest. Trying not to focus on anyone in particular, but keeping her eyes on the entire group, she continued. "First of all, I have been given the impression the pastor's wife is expected to make the coffee for committee meetings. Two comments: one, I don't remember reading anything in *The Discipline*—our church rule book—that assigns that responsibility to the minister's spouse." Someone started to protest, but Laura held up her hand to silence them and plunged ahead without a break. "And second, I don't have a wife."

An eruption of laughter followed a variety of surprised, shocked expressions. Most were from the women. The men, with the exception of Fred Martin, glared at her. Fred joined the laughter.

"And furthermore," continued Laura before anyone could recover and interrupt her train of thought, "I don't have a spouse at all. My husband died four years ago. However, I agree that the idea of having coffee, tea, and/or punch at meetings is an excellent idea. We'll simply have to delegate that job to someone else — possibly the Hospitality Committee?"

She smiled at Martha, who took the challenge. "I think that's a great idea, Reverend. Most of my committee is here tonight, so we'll meet after this meeting and divide up the responsibilities."

Laura took a deep breath. So far so good. A few dark glares, but no real opposition — yet. "The next mistaken information we need to address concerns my appointment. I understand that Martha received word from the district superintendent giving the impression you were receiving a man as your minister."

Each one had an opinion and a comment and made sure everyone else knew about it. They all started talking at once and the decibel level rose higher and higher. Laura tapped the spoon on the table with no results. She let a book fall on the table. Everyone turned to her — some glared, some smiled, some had a skeptical wait and see expression.

"Now," she said making an effort to speak calmly over her churning stomach and rapid heart-beat, "only one person at a time can be heard. Therefore, please, let's proceed in an orderly manner. Martha Jennings is the Pastor/Parish Relations Committee Chairperson, so she can explain how the misunderstanding came about."

"Well," Martha began. No one ever had trouble hearing Martha. "He — Reverend Collins, the district superintendent — called me last Friday and said Laurance E. Kenzel would be our new pastor and because of all the trouble we've had in the last year and a half in getting, or keeping a pastor, the bishop decided to just appoint someone and we could like it, or lump it."

Laura tried to keep her expression non-committal, but groaned inwardly. She was sure Bill Collins didn't say it quite that way—at least she hoped not.

Again the din threatened to overrule order, and once more Laura used the book to get their attention. There were more glares and fewer smiles.

"Sounds to me like we got grounds for a lawsuit," one of the men said with a sneer. Laura couldn't remember who he was, but thought it was Phil Jameson. "What do you think Mike?" He turned to Michael Atkins, the lawyer, one of the few men with a smile on his face—however plastic it might be.

"Well, Phil, until we hear all the facts, I don't think we can start proceedings. Let's hear what Martha and *Reverend* Kenzel have to say first." The smile still had not reached his eyes.

"Thank you, Mr. Atkins." Laura tried to ignore the patronizing of the men and the sympathetic, poor little girl attitude of the women.

"Please, Mike is what all my friends call me."

"All right. Thank you…Mike. Now Martha, did Reverend Collins say *Mister* Kenzel? My name is Laurance, spelled with an *a*, Ellen Kenzel. If he didn't say *Mister* Kenzel, then he's only guilty of letting you make an assumption—one most people would have made under the circumstances."

"So, like it or not, we're stuck with a woman preacher?" Jameson seemed determined to cause problems.

Laura intended to say, "I don't like to think of you being stuck with a woman preacher," but the words rearranged themselves and stumbled out of her mouth differently. "It seems that's a two-way street, Mr. Jameson. Since I've been appointed for a year, I'm just as stuck as you are."

"Well, we'll just see about that. Come on Paula, we don't have to listen to this garbage." Phil Jameson got up and grabbed his wife's arm.

"Mr. Jameson," Laura spoke slow and even. "Are you resigning from the Pastor/Parish Committee and/or the Trustees?" Laura leveled her gaze and stared at him.

"I'm not resigning from anything, but I won't sit here and listen to any more of this garbage."

"Mr. Jameson, like it or not, as you put it, we are stuck with each other, until Bishop Giles says differently. Therefore, if you are going to remain on the committee and help work through this mess, then I suggest you sit down and help us. If you find that too difficult to do, we'll accept your resignation and you may leave."

"You can't do that." He roared rather than shouted. The other members sat with eyes wide and mouths open.

"A lot of unorthodox things have been done—both in this church and in the conference. What are a few more added to the list? As long as I'm the pastor of this church—and I am the pastor until the bishop says I am not—then this is the way it will be. I didn't travel fifteen hours in the pouring rain, arrive to a run-down church, parsonage and garage, be attacked by a burglar, and find a dead man in my garage and cats in the belfry, just to come to a meeting and be told I can't be the pastor on the technicality of a name and the fact that I am female. I am fully qualified. I am here. This is the way it will be. God made me female. God called me to ministry. Now, please sit down and help us, or turn in your resignation and leave."

Laura hadn't raised her voice or let her anger show except in her snapping eyes and slight color of her cheeks. She stared at Phil Jameson with no hint of a smile or of backing down. She meant what she said and intended to use the authority the bishop had given her when he sent her to Cottonville. A few gasps, giggles, and muffled laughs trickled around the room.

"Boy, does she have you pegged, Phil," said Fred Martin.

"Shut up, Fred." Phil Jameson glared daggers at Laura and then at Fred. He mumbled something unintelligible that sounded a lot like profanity.

"Would you like to repeat that?" Laura still did not blink, as she waited for Jameson to either sit down, or leave.

"No." He huffed and sat down with a thump, almost turning the chair over.

She breathed a prayer of thanksgiving as he took his seat. As evenly as she could manage she said, "Thank you." Laura was glad she was not standing. She didn't think her legs would have held her. One more hurdle crossed.

"Now, that we understand one another, shall we move on to some of the more pressing issues? You know we've had a murder on our premises. Folks are used to pastors coming and going— going more than staying, but why has that been so? Part of the mystery has been solved by finding the cats in the belfry. They provided the weird noises which caused fear and alarm. But why were they there? How come no one knew they were there?"

"Are you accusing me of not doing my job?" asked Frank.

"I'm not accusing anyone of anything. I don't know who's responsible. It seems no one is responsible for anything. For instance, when was the last time the church or parsonage was painted—or the lawns mowed?"

"It's the pastor's responsibility to mow the lawn." Frank said.

"You've not had a pastor for almost two years." Laura stated the obvious.

"So?" He glared at her.

"Has the yard looked like a hay field that long?" Laura couldn't believe what she was hearing.

"Course not." Fred tried to hide his mirth. "Snow covered it part of the time." He couldn't hold back the laughter for his feeble joke.

Laura smiled too. She would learn that Fred Martin was a jokester—not a cruel prankster. He just liked jokes and puns. The others were used to his humor. They smiled, or laughed with him.

"I won't ask who shovels the snow," said Laura still smiling. "I'll wait until fall for that."

More giggles and chuckles, then Laura continued. "All right, the pastor may have accepted that responsibility in the past. This one does not. So, trustees, you'll need to work it out among yourselves who will take care if it—before Sunday if you don't mind." Laura smiled at Frank who glared back at her.

119

"Next, the paint."

"We just painted the church and parsonage not too long ago." Gene Stanley was a quiet spoken man.

"What did you use? Watercolor?" Laura was tired and the words slipped out unbidden.

Fred laughed loudly. "Watercolor. I like that one."

Laura realized her unintended humor would go a lot further than bludgeoning them with words. She smiled at Fred.

Ignoring Fred's fit of giggles, Jack Durham asked, "When was the last time we painted? It seems like it was just a few years ago."

"It was back in 1962," said Martha. "I remember because the men were in the middle of painting and Frank had to quit and take me to the hospital when Marie was born. It ain't been touched since."

"That's almost thirty years," said Karen Lily. "Why, we've painted our barn at least three, maybe four, times since then."

"Well," said Frank grudgingly, "it probably is due for another coat."

"Two or three will be more like it," said Laura under her breath.

"What was that, *Pastor*?" Frank asked.

"Never mind," she said. "I suggest you set a date very soon, appoint your crew, and make your plans now—tonight."

"Well, I have six gallons of paint in my barn," said Jim Lily. "We can start with that."

"Come on Jim," exclaimed Doris. "How long have they been there? Since the last time the church was painted?"

That broke them up again. Everyone had to laugh—even Jim. "Well, maybe it has been there that long."

"Think it might be a bit thick?" said Harry.

"We can always add water and make it a watercolor." Jim winked at Laura. She had to laugh. She knew she had won most of them.

Doris had an idea. "Memorial Day is coming up in a couple of weeks. With all the parades and special stuff going on, wouldn't it be wonderful if we could have a shining new coat of paint on our church. We could have a luncheon here like the Presbyterians do.

While the men are painting outside, the women can clean and spruce up the inside."

"I think that's a great idea." Martha loved anything to do with cooking and feeding a lot of people. "We haven't had a luncheon here for years—'cept for funerals. How about it Frank?" Martha turned to her husband.

"Well, I don't know. That's not much time to do three buildings and do them right."

"You could start with the church," said Laura. "Start at the front so it gives a good first impression, then do as much as you can with the rest of it. I expect the townspeople will be glad to see you doing something and won't mind one bit if it isn't all done."

"I think she's right," said Fred. "Hey, come to think about it, I think Hardy's is having a special on paint this week."

"What kind of paint?" Laura was almost afraid to ask.

"Oh, the best grade of watercolor." That sent them all into fits of laughter again then Fred continued, "No, it really is good paint—*Sherwin Williams*, I think. I'll give Hardy a call as soon as I get home. We can start first thing Monday morning. Matter of fact—some of us can get started immediately with preparations—you know scraping, caulking, fixing broken pieces, that sort of stuff. What do you say fellows. Anyone have time tomorrow?"

The noise level was rising again—this time with the excitement. A few folks looked sour enough to curdle any blood that hadn't been already curdled by the ghosts in the belfry. That look sparked more uneasiness in Laura as she watched and listened. Some, especially Frank Jennings, Mike Atkins and Phil Jameson sent tingles of warning through her. They were unhappy and she didn't know why. Surely it was more than her being a woman.

"One more note of information before we get too carried away." Laura raised her voice to be heard.

Everyone stopped talking and looked toward her with expectation.

"Is this good news, or bad news?" asked Fred with a twinkle in his eyes.

"Both." She smiled. "The good news is, as has been said before, the mystery of the noise in the belfry has been solved. Jeb Little's two Maine Coon Cats were chained up there. The bad news is we don't know who put them there, or why. We need to be cautious, as well as observant. Now, do what you need to do to make your plans."

The noise level rose again until a new voice from the door called them to attention once more. "Anyone want pizza?"

"Pizza? Where did that come from?" Laura glanced toward the door to see Todd and Steve carrying several boxes of pizza into the room.

"We stopped by earlier and heard a lot of yelling. Thought maybe you needed something to calm folks down, but it looks like they're more excited than angry." Todd spoke as he and Steve set the pizzas on a table. Martha Jennings took over and organized her committee to cut and serve. Laura smiled. Martha already had the clean up organized in her mind.

16

"Excuse me for saying so, Laura, but you look like death warmed over. Can't you go home and let them close up?" Steve kept his voice low as he glanced around the room where people ate pizza. The spicy aroma of sauce, pepperoni, and sausage filled the room. Voices rose in excitement.

"The meeting's over and I am tired."

"Come on, I'll walk you over to the house. I need to ask you a couple of questions just to clear my mind. If you don't feel like answering a couple more questions, they can wait until tomorrow." He hesitated then grinned. "I promise I won't question your authority as pastor."

"A couple, but no more. I might drop off to sleep in the middle of a sentence," said Laura. She smiled then shivered and glanced to see if a window were open.

"Are you all right?" asked Steve.

"Just tired, I guess. So much has happened. I keep waiting for another unpleasant surprise. Let me tell Martha I'm leaving. She and Frank can lock up."

Steve and Laura stepped out the door and a strong odor of fresh paint drifted across the driveway. "Has someone been painting?" Steve asked. He glanced around the area between the church and garage.

"Not that I'm aware of, but it sure smells like fresh paint. And it smells close by."

"Maybe something in the air. Sometimes smells are carried by the breezes."

"Probably. I need to check my car before we go to the house. I haven't driven it today, but I want to make sure it's locked." Steve waited while she went around to the driver's side to check the door. Laura reached for the handle and froze. Her face blanched and screwed into a look that meant more trouble. He was at her side in three long strides. The strong, stringent paint odor was so close it stung their eyes and nose. A message in red paint rambled across the side of her car: WE AIN'T DONE YET.

"Laura?" Steve stared at the red paint then looked around the area. He saw no one, but didn't want to leave her to search farther. She didn't answer for a few seconds. Shaking her head, she let her fists drop to her side and she spoke between clenched teeth. "Oh, Shebop, how could they?"

"Shebop?" Steve gave her a curious look.

"My car." She tried to smile. "I call her that." She reached out to touch the car and pulled her hand back with red paint on the tips of her fingers. "It's still wet. Maybe if I hurry I can clean it off."

Steve placed a hand on her arm, not wanting to cause her more pain, but knowing he would. "We'll need to get some pictures and check the scene. I'll wait here. You get Todd and we'll take care of this as quickly as we can, then get it cleaned up for you."

Laura said nothing, but pulled a tissue from her pocket and removed the paint from her finger as she returned to the church. She found Todd just inside the door with a group of the men. Women seemed to gather in another corner. She didn't want to cause a panic and have everyone rushing out to mess up any evidence that might be there, so she tapped Todd on the shoulder.

"Back already?" Todd's smile didn't last long.

"You got a minute? We need to discuss something with you."

"Sure, excuse me fellas," said Todd to the group of men. He followed Laura who had already started out, catching up with her at the door. "What's up?"

"We got more trouble. Didn't want to cause a stampede."

"What kind of trouble?"

"Someone painted a warning on my car. Steve said you'll need to get pictures, prints, check the area, and keep folks from generally messing up evidence. Better call for some back up and ask the folks to leave without trying to see what's going on."

"I'll get Frank to help."

"To help with what, Todd? Thought there might be more trouble."

"Someone sprayed the pastor's car. Don't let anyone near it. I'll call Mark Goodwin to come take pictures and prints."

"Got you, Chief."

"The cats!" Laura turned toward the house with a feeling that something was wrong.

"Surely no one would…" Todd glanced at Steve and nodded at Laura who was already running for the dark house.

"I'll go with her to check," said Steve.

"I'll be there as soon as Mark gets here."

Without thinking of danger, she ran for the house, glad Steve had followed when she stumbled in the tall grass.

"Are you all right?" Steve took her hand and helped her to the porch.

"I'm not sure. Something is wrong. It's too dark. I left a light on."

She ran across the porch to the door, half expecting it to be standing open. It wasn't, but the cats growled, howled, and banged against the door as if they were in distress of some kind.

The door opened and both cats wrapped around her ankles talking to her in their own special Maine Coon language which, of course, she couldn't understand. She would have fallen if Steve hadn't been there. He held her with one arm and reached for the light switch with the other. Laura would have laughed at the effort the cats were making to communicate under different circumstances, but the sight of the spray paint had shaken her more than she realized. The dark house and talking felines only added to her fears.

Oh God, she thought, *help me through this new onslaught of terror. I can't make sense of anything.* To Steve she said, "I'm positive I left a lamp burning." She did a quick survey of the room, mentally checking a list of everything that had been there before she went out. Everything looked normal as far as she could tell.

"Maybe the bulb burned out," suggested Steve. He pushed the switch and more light flooded the room. "It works. Maybe you were worried about the meeting and just thought you turned it on."

"It's possible, I suppose. Anything's possible it seems, but I always turn a lamp on when I leave. It's as automatic as breathing. It's a habit I got into after Harold died. I don't like coming into a dark house." She glanced at Steve hoping she didn't sound like a coward. "It's one of my phobias, I guess." She tried to smile, but didn't succeed.

"It's not a phobia. It's good sense."

Rascal and Mischief still chattered as if trying to get her attention. "All right, I'm listening, fellas, but you'll have to be patient with me. I don't understand feline language very well. I know you're trying to tell me something. Maybe if you lead me instead of trying to tell me. No, I don't suppose that would work either."

Steve chuckled. She smiled at him and shrugged her shoulders, then stooped to pet them. They unwrapped themselves from her ankles and plopped down on their haunches in front of her, staring with their green eyes crossed and unblinking behind their coon-like masks.

"Maybe they're trying mental telepathy," he said.

"Maybe." Laura tried to smile at the cats. She took a deep breath and stood. "Oh well, come on guys. I promised you some more supper when I got home and I could use a cup of coffee. Steve?"

"Sure. Always take a good cup of coffee."

But when she started for the kitchen the cats wrapped themselves around her ankles again making it difficult, if not impossible, to move. Before she reached the door to the dining room Rascal jumped toward her shoulders, not touching her, but making it clear if she moved, he would land on her. Mischief weaved in and out around her ankles. At the same time they were meowing in a duet of Maine Coon felinese.

"Come on guys," said Laura, "you're going to make me fall and then I won't be able to get you anything to eat. You can't be that hungry." She heard Todd run across the porch.

"Everything all right here?"

"I think so," she said over her shoulder, "but these crazy cats won't let me move."

"Speaking of cats, what's with them? They sound like a dozen instead of two." Todd tried to touch Mischief, but she evaded him.

"I don't know," said Laura. "They won't let me move. I just want to feed them and make some coffee."

Mischief had left her post at Laura's ankles and sat side by side with Rascal in front of the dining room door. Laura started once more toward the kitchen and both cats jumped, hitting her chest, not hard enough to hurt her, but executing enough force to throw her off balance. She would have fallen if Steve hadn't been close enough to catch her.

"This is getting to be a habit," he said and held her until she gained her balance.

"Maybe they were up in that belfry too long and it has made them a little crazy—or rabid." Todd wrapped his hand around his gun, as the cats plopped down on their haunches in front of the dining room door looking from one human to another.

"Don't," said Laura, laying a hand on Todd's arm. "They're trying to tell us something. I just don't understand feline language."

"Maybe there's something in the kitchen that's dangerous for anyone walking through that door." Steve frowned.

"Come on, Steve," said Todd. "Cats aren't that smart. Dogs, maybe. Cats, no." He pulled his gun and started for the door. Both cats hit him smack in the stomach, knocking him to the floor.

Steve covered his mouth with his hand to hold back the laugh. "Where's the light switch for the kitchen, Laura?"

"Over by the back door," she said. "Todd, are you all right?"

"The back door? There's none on this side?"

"This is a parsonage," she said as if that explained everything.

"Yeah, I'm okay. Nothing hurt but my ego," said Todd as Steve pulled him to this feet.

"Where's the light switch for the dining room?" Steve was almost afraid to ask.

"On the wall to the right, just inside the room on this side," said Laura. "What was that? I thought I heard something in the kitchen."

Steve reached around the corner and flipped on the light. At the same instant a gun was fired from the kitchen. Steve yelled as he fell, "Laura, hit the floor!"

He needn't have said anything. With the sound of the shot, both cats hit her full force knocking her to the floor, stretching across her.

Todd ran out the front door. Laura heard him cross the porch and start around the house. She knew he was too late. The back door slammed immediately following the shot. Whoever had been in the kitchen was gone.

Steve heard the door close, too, and ran through to the kitchen to meet Todd outside the back door. In the darkness, they saw the form of a man running toward the woods. "Over there," he called. Mark Goodwin ran toward the woods with his powerful flashlight, but they saw nothing. The man got away.

Steve let them chase the shadow and returned to make sure Laura was all right. He started back through the dining room and saw her still pinned to the floor by about fifty pounds of feline. Before he could reach her, she convinced them to let her sit up, but they wouldn't let her all the way up. She sat with her back to him.

He started to say something, but she began talking and there was no doubt to Whom she spoke. He didn't want to interfere, nor did he want to eavesdrop. But she would hear him if he tried to leave, so he waited.

Her face turned heavenward, she declared, "I don't think this is a bit funny. At least You could have warned me what I was getting into. Even Daniel knew he was going into a lion's den. I'm beginning to understand why no one has stayed here." She paused and then continued with a deep sigh, "But I'm here, and You're here. Together we'll work it out, Lord. One way, or another, we'll work it out."

Steve felt as if he had eavesdropped on an intimate conversation, but he was even more fascinated with this woman who refused to let all the trouble drive her away from the place to which she thoroughly believed God had called her. He gave her a few seconds in case she had more to say then, cleared his throat and said, "Are you declaring your authority to your Boss?"

Laura jerked around. Embarrassment then defiance followed her surprise. "Well, sometimes I *have* to let Him know where I stand."

Steve laughed and crossed the room to give her a hand up. Laura glared then smiled as she reached for his offered hand.

"That's the only thing that keeps me sane sometimes—talking to my *Boss*, as you put it. He brought me here, so I expect Him to help me when I'm in trouble. And I feel like I'm in deep trouble and don't even know why."

She paused. "Steve! You're hurt!" Blood trickled down his arm and dripped on her dress as she took his hand.

"It's only a scratch," he said, "but looks like I've ruined your dress. I'm sorry."

"It'll wash and I have a first aid kit in the kitchen. Let me clean it."

"Laura, it's only a scratch." Steve felt irritated as he followed her into the kitchen. She turned to get the first aid kit and he suddenly understood his anger. This beautiful woman whom he thought was so different wasn't any different after all. She had to pull the mothering trick on him. Make him feel like a little boy who can't help himself. Well he never allowed it before and he wouldn't allow it now.

"Laura, it's just a scratch. I can handle it myself."

"Fine, it's your arm." As if she could read his mind she added, "You aren't a little boy and I'm not your mother. I was just trying to save myself some work." She set the kit down on the table beside him and turned back to the counter to make the coffee.

Steve felt confused and asked, "How can tending to my scratch save you work?"

Laura turned back with a grin on her face. "If you bleed to death, I might have to do a funeral and I really have enough to do right now."

Steve's mouth opened, but he was speechless. Suddenly he broke into laughter. He was still laughing when Todd came in the back door. Getting his laughter under control, Steve said, "Laura, I'm sorry. I know you were trying to help, but it brought back painful memories I didn't expect, and that wasn't your fault. If you don't mind, I guess I could use a little help getting a patch on it."

She threw him a clean, wet cloth from the sink. "Clean up your arm and around the cut with this until I get the coffee on. Then I'll patch you up, as long as Todd doesn't try to arrest me for practicing medicine without a license." She turned her grin to Todd.

Todd laughed and said, "I wouldn't think of it, but why don't I do this while you do that?" He took the cloth, then some alcohol and cleaned the cut and put a bandage on it. "If it starts hurting or looks red, better see a doctor."

"Yoo hoo, are you all right Reverend?" Martha Jennings called from the front door.

"We're in the kitchen, Martha. Come on in," Laura called to her.

"We heard a gunshot. The men cleaned up your car and went with Mark to try to track down the man who ran out of the house. Are you all right?"

"Yes, I'm fine. The cats knocked me down, then sat on me so I couldn't move. Detective Morgan got a small scratch from the shot, but I think he'll live." She turned and flashed a smile at Steve who sat at the table, where Todd was just closing up the first aid kit.

"Well, I think you better come over and stay with us tonight. I don't think you ought to be here alone with that crazy man on the loose."

"Thanks, Martha, but I'll be fine. The cats seem to be good protectors. I don't think he'll be back after all the commotion he's caused. He just wanted to scare me."

"Well, if you won't come to our house, I'll come over here and stay the night."

"Martha, please don't misunderstand me, but I really would rather be alone. It's been a very traumatic day and I just need to think and pray it through. I'll be fine, really I will. I have some fresh coffee. Would you like some?"

Frank fixed the back door lock which was broken again. Steve and Todd stayed until Martha and Frank left then checked the rest of the house for other booby-traps. They found none and were ready to leave.

"Laura, are you really sure you won't stay somewhere else tonight?" Todd said.

"Todd's right, Laura. Whoever did this might come back."

"I understand your concern, but where would I go?"

"You could go to Frank and Martha's." Steve looked concerned.

"This house is about as safe as anyplace else. And if it's me they're after I don't want to put anyone else in danger. Besides, I have two good guard cats." Laura stooped to pet Rascal and Mischief, who sat watching the humans with a very wise look on their faces. They purred as she stroked them—one on either side of her.

"One of us can stay here tonight," suggested Todd.

Laura stopped stroking the cats and glanced up in time to see Steve glance at her. She felt a strange sense of panic. He looked as though he shared her panic. Standing, she changed her glance to a glare and addressed Todd. "I don't think that's necessary, Todd. I think I can handle whatever comes along. I have the phone you installed upstairs, and I'll be sure to call if I hear any strange noises." Then she smiled and added, "Other than Rascal's and Mischief's snoring that is."

Todd frowned. "Well, all right, but I don't like it. I feel responsible."

"Why on earth should you feel responsible for me? I'm a capable adult. I'm sorry I've contributed to your education into higher crime, but you certainly aren't responsible for me."

Steve laughed. "I don't like it either, Laura, but you're right.

131

We're acting like a couple of protective old men with a poor, helpless little girl. We overreacted. Sorry. Truce?"

She laughed and relaxed. "Truce. It's been a long, harrowing day for all of us."

"Goodnight, Laura. Lock the doors and we'll check on you tomorrow. Call if you hear anything unusual." Todd and Steve waited on the porch until she locked the door after them.

"Come on Rascal and Mischief. Bedtime. It's been a long day for all of us. Tonight you can sleep on a soft bed if you want to instead of that cold drafty belfry."

Rascal and Mischief followed her up the stairs, tails held high, as if they knew they were home. Laura opened the door to the spare bedroom for them then went across the hall to her own bed. She no sooner laid her head on her pillow when she felt two fur balls at her feet. She smiled to herself.

"All right, guys. I guess I am thankful for real, live, warm bodies near me—even if they are covered with fur." Rascal and Mischief curled up at her feet on either side and purred with contentment.

Sleep began to play at the edges of her consciousness. Steve never did ask his questions. A low rumble like a truck in a distance startled her from the first sinking of sleep. A light flashed through her still curtain-less window. Laura was immediately on her feet, the cats at her side. Was someone in her drive by the garage? She had her hand on the phone next to her bed, when she heard the rumble again, this time a little closer. Light once again illuminated her room. With a sigh of relief, Laura pulled her hand back. It was only another spring storm approaching.

She closed her windows and crawled back into bed. Rascal and Mischief returned to their chosen spots.

"Sorry, God," she said as sleep once again began to overtake her. "I can't stay awake for Your fireworks tonight. I don't know what tomorrow will bring, but I'm sure we're on a roll—and I don't mean a thunder roll."

17

The shrill, nerve-jangling sound of the telephone pulled Laura from the depths of sleep while rain tapped softly at her window urging her to more slumber. The persistent machine won the battle and she forced her eyes to open. Where was the clock? What time was it? Six a.m.?

Suddenly she sat up sending the cats to the floor, tails swishing. Was there an emergency?

"Hello." Her heart thumped against her chest. She wasn't ready for emergencies yet. She didn't even know the people.

"Laura?"

Anxiety turned to anger as she recognized the voice of Bill Collins. What could he want so early in the morning?

Laura swung her legs over the side of the bed and reached for her robe. She glanced at the rain bouncing on her window pane and the cats thumping their tails on the floor.

"Laura? Are you there?"

"Of course I'm here, Bill. Where else would I be at six o'clock in the morning?" She slid her feet into her slippers waiting beside the bed.

"Well, you don't have to sound so snappish. I can't help it if you can't stay out of trouble down there. I don't know what we're going to do with you."

"What are you talking about, Bill?" She really didn't care, nor want to know, but he would tell her anyway.

"Laura, your attitude isn't helping one bit. I just got a call from someone on your PPR and I don't appreciate getting calls at home—especially at this time of morning as you so aptly put it."

"Don't raise your voice to me, Bill Collins. I didn't tell anyone to call you. Who called? Martha Jennings? She's the only one who has the authority to call you on behalf of the rest of the committee."

"No, it wasn't Margaret—or whatever her name is."

"Then who? No one else had any business calling you about anything." Laura frowned. This was going to be another confusing call.

"He didn't give his name, but he was pretty hot under the collar."

"Bill, I can't believe you would take an anonymous phone call seriously. I have no idea what you are talking about." Nothing made sense, but then with Bill it hardly ever did. Was it his intention to pull her from sleep hoping she would be too groggy to pay attention? If he really knew her, he would know she was instantly awake when she opened her eyes.

"Of course you don't. You didn't want them to even talk to me. You're making your own rules down there and that's got to stop. And while I'm at it, what do you mean the conference is doing things in an unorthodox way? Bishop Giles said...the cabinet thought you would...church having a hard time...making them..."

Come on Bill. Get it out of your system and leave me alone, Laura thought as she reached over to pet the kitties, which had jumped back to the bed. Stroking their soft fur helped to calm her.

"Laura, are you listening to me? Laura? Answer me."

"I'm still here Bill. And like I told you before, I'm here to stay."

"Well, we'll see about that. You don't make the rules for this conference. The bishop will jerk you out of there in no time flat."

Laura felt the familiar churning in her stomach and anger building, but she managed to keep her voice at an even level. "Bill, the bishop didn't send me here. God did. And He's the one I answer to. I'll leave when God says leave and not one minute before." The familiar stubbornness stiffened her back and narrowed her eyes.

"Laura, what's gotten into you? I thought when you went to seminary you were going to make a good minister. You certainly had a good role model. Harold was the best we had."

Anger flared. If Harold was the best, then why didn't they tell him that once in awhile? Why...? Laura didn't trust herself to even think about it anymore. "What's your point, Bill? You didn't waken me just to tell me what a good pastor Harold was."

"I want to know what's going on down there. Why did you tell one of your members to shut-up and sit down?"

"I didn't."

"Yes, you did. He said so."

"Oh, so the word of an anonymous man, whom you have never met, is to be believed over the word of one of your pastors, whom you do know?" Did he know Phil Jameson? How? Laura frowned and tried to clear her thinking.

"Well, Laura, you are a little head strong sometimes."

Rascal and Mischief seemed to want her attention. The phone cord dangled and moved just enough to look like a nice toy. Rascal batted and grabbed at it while Mischief nibbled at Laura's elbow. Laura gently shoved them away, but they returned as if playing a game with her.

"Bill, how many pastors did you send here in the last year and a half?" She pulled the cord away from Rascal as she thought about what Bill Collins was saying—or not saying.

"What does that have to do with anything?"

"How many?" Rascal grabbed again as she pulled the cord away. Mischief jumped for it but missed, falling off the bed. She shook herself and jumped back beside Laura.

"I don't know. I would have to look it up."

"Approximately." Laura smiled as she thought about the discomfort in Bill's voice. Mischief nibbled again at her elbow.

Bill mumbled something which Laura could not understand. She knew that was the intent. She shoved the cats away again.

"Would you repeat that?" she asked sweetly. She lifted her arm out of the reach of Mischief.

"About seventy-five," he said.

"And how many of those seventy-five were women?" Laura knew the answer, but was determined to make him squirm a little.

"None—they wouldn't even talk to our women." Mischief stretched across her lap and began purring so loudly Laura could hardly hear her superintendent.

"So seventy-five men and zero women could not even get a foot in the door. And anyone who did, lasted less than twenty-four hours." Absently she stroked Mischief which helped her keep her voice calm. "Bill Collins, I am going to say this one more time, and you can pass the word to Bishop Giles if you want to. God put me here, not you or the bishop. I have been here forty-eight hours, been burglarized twice, shot at once, found one dead man in my garage, found two cats in my belfry, had a warning spray-painted across the side of my car, and only God knows what else I have yet to discover. But, I'm here, and here I will stay until God says go."

"Laura…"

She didn't wait for his response but plunged ahead. "Now, if you and/or Bishop Giles want to come down here and meet face to face with my Pastor/Parish Relations Committee, I will be glad to set up a meeting. If you don't want to meet face to face with them, then please do me the courtesy of not chewing me out for their problems, or listening to the complaints of an anonymous caller."

"Laura, you're asking for trouble." That sounded more like a threat than a statement to Laura, but she let it go without a challenge.

"Bill, I already have trouble and I didn't ask for it. What I need is support from my district superintendent and bishop and I don't feel much of that coming from up there."

"Laura, you know we pray for you every day."

"Sure you do," she replied with heavy sarcasm, not at all sure she believed him. "Then you better get on your knees and double, or triple, your prayers and stay off my back. It's been good talking to you Bill. Call again when you have something to say."

With great self-control Laura replaced the phone very carefully and once again took pleasure in the thought of Bill Collins standing with a buzzing phone in his hand. Rascal made one more swipe at the cord and Mischief purred with contentment on Laura's lap.

"Well, guys," she said, "we're awake. Let's go get some coffee."

Both cats suddenly sat on their haunches and stared at her with crossed eyes. Had she been able to read their thoughts she would probably have heard them loud and clear in stereo, "You've got to be kidding."

She laughed and started for the door, the cats trailing after her like a couple of shadows. "Well, all right. I'll find some kitty food for you, but I want my coffee."

Morning routine behind her, Laura was ready to face the day. She was determined that neither rain, nor Bill Collins, would ruin it.

"This is a day the Lord has made, kitties. What do you suppose it will hold for us? Maybe the rain will wash away some of the mean spirit. The men won't be able to begin the paint job this morning—maybe by afternoon. Anyway, I still have things to put away, a sermon to begin and who knows what else."

Smiling from sheer happiness, Laura began singing familiar hymns as she tackled the tasks at hand. The day would be wonderful—with or without the rain. She had finished setting up her computer in an alcove off the kitchen when she heard familiar footsteps on the front porch.

Opening the door as Todd raised his fist to knock, she leaned back."Whoa! Hold on there. I've had enough trouble without the Cottonville chief of police giving me a black eye for opening the door."

Todd laughed. "Sorry about that, Laura. I just wanted to check and make sure everything's all right. I should have come around earlier, but Steve and I went to the high school this morning and it took longer than we thought it would."

"That's all right, Todd. I would have called if there was any more trouble. Come on in." She smiled at him and stepped aside. Surely he had good news to bring this time and the rain had stopped.

"Thanks, Laura, but I won't stay." Todd entered the room, but stood with his hat in his hand. "Steve and I were talking to some of the kids at the high school and we think we know who sprayed your car. By the way, we were able to clean most of it off. We wondered if you want to talk to the kids when we arrest them."

"You won't arrest them for one incident, will you?" Laura closed the door and turned to face Todd.

"One incident? Laura, have you forgotten a little case of murder, cruelty to animals, mischievous vandalism, breaking and entering, attempted kidnapping—to name only a few incidents."

"Surely the high school kids didn't do all of that."

"Laura, I don't know where you come from, but most places today are having trouble with kids and crime—even mass murders."

"I know, but..." She shook her head and walked away from Todd and straightened a throw that didn't need straightened.

"We don't like to think the kids we know would do anything like that, but facts are facts."

"I know you're right, Todd." She turned back to face him. "I guess I don't really want to believe it, but I know I should." All of a sudden the day didn't seem so bright. The miserable feeling was pushing aside her happiness.

"I know how you feel." Todd turned his hat over and over in his hands like a steering wheel. "We'll hold off as long as we can. We want to make sure we know who did what, and we want to have all of their parents present. We'll let you know."

"Todd, do you suppose there's more to it than just kids playing jokes?" Laura frowned as she thought about the whole scene.

"I don't think so. Why do you ask?"

"I don't know. It just seems too much of coincidence with all that's happened. It's all connected to the church not keeping a pastor somehow. The whole point seems to be to drive me away. Someone doesn't want the church to have a pastor. Why?"

"I don't know, Laura. You could be right. I hope not. I'll run it by Steve. See what he thinks."

Laura smiled trying to regain her happy feeling. "I was just going to have some lunch. Would you care to join me?" She changed the subject.

"Thanks, but I'm meeting Steve at Charlie's in a half-hour. He's talking to some of the parents. Maybe you'd like to join us."

"I've got a lot to do here yet. Appreciate the offer though." Laura felt an odd mixture of emotions. She would have liked to go to Charlie's because Steve would be there, but for the same reason she was afraid to go.

"You're sure everything's all right here?"

"Positive. Besides I have Rascal and Mischief to watch over me. Remember?" She smiled as she pushed aside her thoughts, which she would deal with later.

"Yeah, I remember," Todd laughed as he rubbed his back side.

Rascal and Mischief stopped playing in the empty boxes when they heard their names. They listened, turning their heads from one to the other, as if they fully understood all that the humans were saying.

Laura laughed with him. "They were just trying to be helpful. They'll look after me and Jerome will stop after school."

"Well, don't hesitate to call if anything seems wrong. Don't worry about calling too many times. If I'm not at the office, someone will be. They can reach me anytime."

"Thanks, I'll remember. Believe me, I'll call if I need you. Have a good lunch."

"You too. Don't work too hard. Take some time to rest."

"Sure, I will." Her sarcastic tone told him she would never quit while there was work to be done. The afternoon disappeared before Laura hardly had time to think about it. The rooms downstairs put in order, she tackled the upstairs, hanging some white lace curtains from her former life as a pastor's wife. With some slight alterations, she was able to make them fit her bedroom windows.

"What do you think, kitties?" She stepped back to admire her work. "They're not the fanciest curtains in the world, but they'll do until I can get something better. Hopefully things will settle down and I can get to a mall next week."

Rascal and Mischief blinked at her.

"I know. You don't know what a mall is. You wouldn't particularly care to go if you did. For us humans, it's where we go to replenish our life with *stuff.*"

Laura glanced at the clock and then her watch. They both read three o'clock. "Jerome should be here by now," she said to her two feline friends. "What do you say we go down and see if he's coming?"

Rascal and Mischief sat on the front window sill viewing their part of the world. Rain no longer fell, but clouds still made the day gray and gloomy. Where was Jerome? Laura felt on edge. Maybe she should call his grandmother. Surely, he didn't forget.

She reached for the phone and was startled by its ring. The cats who had been romping and chasing each other up and down the stairs and in and out of the boxes most of the day, now stared out the window.

"Hello," she said, hoping it might be Jerome.

"Is this Reverend Kenzel?" The crackling voice held both authority and age.

"Yes, it is. Who's calling, please?"

"This is SaraBelle Cotton. Do you know who I am?"

Laura hesitated trying to pull the name out of the myriad of names she had been given the last two days. SaraBelle Cotton? SaraBelle..."Oh, yes, Mrs. Cotton," Laura replied, glad she had remembered. SaraBelle Cotton was one of the founders of the town. Her late son, Charlie, was the namesake of many of its businesses and places of interest. She was "very old, very rich and very demanding," according to Martha. "What can I do for you today?"

"Well," SaraBelle huffed. "I thought you would have done it already."

"I don't understand." Laura was as confused by the woman's tone of voice as by her words.

"How long have you been in town, Reverend Kenzel?" It was a demand not really a question.

"I got in Tuesday night. Today is Thursday," Laura answered, feeling tightness in her stomach and realized her hands were gripping the phone as if it would run away from her.

"I know what day it is." SaraBelle's voice, sharp as a razor's edge, broke in. "I would think you could have found time to visit me yesterday—or at least call me since you are still here. I must say I'm impressed you haven't high-tailed it out of here like all the rest."

"Mrs. Cotton," Laura wanted to explain, but got no further.

"No need to apologize, but I need to talk to you as soon as possible. Ten o'clock tomorrow morning will be sufficient. I have an appointment with my lawyer in a few minutes, or you could come tonight. I will see you tomorrow promptly at ten."

Laura stood holding the buzzing phone. "Doesn't anyone say goodbye? And who does she think she is ordering me to a command performance like…like Rascal and Mischief."

Hearing their names, the cats turned to peer at her. "I'm not talking to you. Take a nap until Jerome gets here." They blinked and turned back to watch out the window.

Laura replaced the phone adding this new twist to her life in Cottonville to the worries about Jerome. The phone rang one more time before she had a chance to move away from it. Maybe this was Jerome.

"Hello?"

"Pastor, this is Cora Duncan. You don't know me, yet. I'm a member of your flock. The Lord told me to call you and tell you to hang in there. I don't know what's going on, but I know you need prayers, so let me pray for you."

And she did while Laura listened, overwhelmed. Still dazed she found voice enough to say, "Thank you." Before she could say another word, Cora said, "Bye," and the familiar buzz from the phone in her hand brought her back to reality.

Suddenly both cats stiffened with their fur bushy as if a big dog had just entered the room. Laura watched them wondering what frightened them. They both began yowling much like they had the night before.

"Something is wrong, but what?" Before Laura could decide

what to do, Rascal was at the door pulling at the door knob, trying to open the door.

"Rascal, I can't let you out. Someone might..." Laura didn't finish. She didn't own these animals. They chose to stay with her. If they chose to leave she would have to let them go. She helped him open the door and he took off across the yard. Mischief watched, then took off toward her car.

"Rascal..." Laura called after him, but he was gone. "Mischief?" Mischief was trying to get in her car. Maybe she needed to go with Rascal if she could find him and keep up with him. There was no time to wonder if this was normal behavior for cats.

18

The dismissal bell echoed down the halls of Grayson Elementary. Usually skipping and laughing as he ran from the building, today Jerome poked along. He was troubled. He'd stayed to help his teacher wash the boards and put up a bulletin board, but there was still plenty of time to go help Pastor with the cats before his mom got home from work. First, he would check in with his grandmother.

In his jacket pocket, Jerome wrapped his fist tightly around a threatening note. Someone had left it in his locker. He didn't understand it. His pastor would know what it was all about and what to do with it.

Jerome usually rode his bike, but it had a flat tire that morning. He heard the town clock—quarter to four. It was later than he thought. He ran rounded the corner of North Main and Third Street. Three high school-aged boys blocked the sidewalk. Jerome knew two of the boys from church. Skip Jameson and Johnny Atkins had always been friendly. The third boy was a stranger.

"Hi, Skip, Johnny." Jerome smiled and started to go around them.

"Where you goin' kid?" The ugly tone of that unknown person made Jerome uneasy, but he was with kids he knew, so he wasn't afraid.

"I'm going to my grandmother's then over to the preacher's house to help her with the cats we found yesterday." He glanced at Skip and Johnny who found something beyond Jerome on which to focus their attention.

"Really, now. Where'd you find them?" The tone didn't change. The long, greasy looking hair hung to his shoulders, falling over his face. Jerome didn't like him and wondered why Johnny and Skip were with him. He tried once again to go around.

The boy stretched out a long, tattooed arm and pushed him back. Jerome glanced at Skip and Johnny for reassurance and found none. "Where'd you find them, kid?" the boy asked again as if he had lost something that Jerome had found and he wanted it back.

"In the belfry at the church," Jerome said. "It was in this morning's newspaper. Everyone knows about it."

"Now, ain't that special, boys? He found the cats in the belfry." The sneering boy stood with hands on his hips towering over Jerome, peering down at him like he was some kind of bug to be squashed.

"Excuse me," said Jerome. "I need to get home." He stepped off the sidewalk to go around them, but the stranger extended a foot and tripped him, then laughed a strange, cackling sound as he fell.

"What's the matter, twerp? Can't you stand up?" And he laughed again.

A hole in the knee of his pants exposed raw, scraped skin, but Jerome didn't say anything. Skip and Johnny weren't going to help him. He picked up his books and ran, looking over his shoulder once to see if anyone followed.

Skip and Johnny started after him, but the other boy stopped them. "Let him go. He'll be back this way. The Third Street bridge is out. Once he checks in with his grandmother, no one will suspect anything until it's too late."

"What do you mean too late? We're only supposed to scare the kid." Johnny threw an anxious glance at Skip. He didn't know Randy very well and wasn't sure he could be trusted.

"Yeah, Randy, we aren't going to hurt the kid, are we?"

Randy laughed a strange, maniacal laugh. He shook his head like he thought he was working with stupid amateurs.

"Come on. We'll wait for the kid at the corner by the woods—maybe get him to go over the park to play some ball."

Randy took off at a trot toward the corner. Skip and Johnny had to almost run to catch up with him. "We'll wait behind these trees. He won't see us until we surround him."

Jerome skipped along excited about helping Laura. He hadn't forgotten about his encounter with the bigger boys, but he assumed they were gone by now. He didn't even mention it to his grandmother. He only opened the door, threw his books on the kitchen table, called to her telling her where he would be, then took off. The scraped knee was his only reminder and he would tend to it later.

The copse of trees hid the three tormenters, so Jerome had no reason to expect an extended foot again. This time he was moving faster and his fall was harder. Sprawling on the sidewalk, he sensed they intended to really hurt him this time. He tried to get up, but Randy kicked him in the ribs. Jerome tried not to scream, but couldn't keep the tears from rolling down his face.

"Randy," shouted Johnny. "You're going to hurt him." He lurched forward to stop the older boy. Randy gave him such a venomous look that Johnny fell back as if he were the one who had been kicked. Skip took Johnny's arm to hold him back.

"Yeah, Randy," said Skip. "He's just a kid."

"You guys are such wimps. I don't know why we even keep you around. Pick him up. Let's move over to the park where we won't draw any attention." He nodded to the far end of the ball field near the woods. With Jerome between them, Johnny and Skip half carried, half dragged the struggling boy, unable to face Jerome.

With tears flowing, Jerome looked to first one and then the other of the two boys, who had been his friends. "Why are you doing this? We go to the same church. We heard the same lessons on love and mercy and being a good neighbor."

"Shut up, kid. I don't want none of that religious stuff." The third boy—Randy, whoever he was—was in charge.

"Johnny? Skip?" Jerome kept glancing from one to the other, but neither boy would face him. "Why won't you help me?" They looked away from him and Randy laughed his weird, wicked laugh.

"What's a matter, kid? Your friends let you down? Maybe your God did too 'cause you ain't got a prayer." Randy giggled a childish, manic sound that reminded Jerome of the ghoulish movies his mother wouldn't let him watch, but at which he had secretly taken peeks.

"I don't understand." Jerome turned to face Randy, who had no trouble facing him. The evil look in the older boy's eyes sent a chill through Jerome. "What do you want with me?" His side hurt where the boy kicked him and his knee hurt from the fall. He was scared. He knew they would hurt him more. Maybe if he could tell the boy what he wanted to know, he would leave him alone.

Randy stepped closer and took Jerome's chin in his left hand. He squeezed it so tightly that Jerome was afraid he would break his jaw. Randy jerked his head up so Jerome had to look directly into that evil face.

"We want to know how much you know. What did you see? What did you tell the cops and that preacher woman?"

"What do you mean? I don't know what you want. How can I tell you what you want to know when I don't know what you're talking about?" It was hard for Jerome to talk with his head held up and pushed back at such an angle. It was hard enough just to breathe.

Randy slapped him across the side of his face with his other hand. "You know what I mean, kid."

He let his chin drop and hit him again while Johnny and Skip on either side of him held his arms. Jerome struggled to free himself. He could feel his eyes beginning to swell from the blows. One of the boys lost his grip and Jerome jerked away from the other. Before he could run, Randy grabbed his arm and twisted it behind his back. Jerome felt a snap, followed by an excruciating pain that shot up his arm into his shoulder.

He had tried to be brave, but after all he was only ten. He

screamed. Randy dropped his arm, hit him again and Jerome felt no more pain.

"Shut up, kid. You want to bring the whole town out?" Randy laughed like he had told some hilarious joke. A look of horror spread across the faces of Skip and Johnny. They didn't join the laughter. They looked frozen to the spot almost as if their feet had taken root.

Johnny yelled, "Come on Randy, you're going to kill him."

Randy's fist swung around and landed in the middle of Johnny's stomach. "Stay out of it, wimp."

Johnny and Skip watched Jerome's limp body slide to the ground. They exchanged frightened glances, as Randy kicked the limp body again swearing with words even they had never heard.

"Come on kid. What did you tell her?"

"Randy, he's out. You're going to kill him. Come on." Johnny shouted again holding his stomach from the previous punch.

Skip joined him. "We were only supposed to scare him and find out how much he saw in the bell tower, find out if he saw Jeb's stuff, and if he knew Jeb was using the tower as a home. We weren't supposed to kill the kid."

"Of course, I'm going to kill him. Where's your brains? We can't let him live. He knows who we are. He knows what's there."

Randy's eyes had a strange, wild look in them. He enjoyed hurting people.

"No," shouted Johnny and Skip together.

"Come on Skip. Let's get out of here. He's mad. I want no part of murder."

"Me neither. Let's go."

"You guys are up to your necks in this whether you like it or not." Randy cackled. He really did enjoy seeing people squirm.

* * *

Mike Hostetler parked his bike at the bicycle rack and looked around for other kids. They usually met to play ball after school. Oh nuts. He had forgotten the class tournaments at the school today. The other kids were probably there. He threw his ball into the air and caught it, then started for his bike. May as well go home.

As he turned, movement near the woods caught his attention. Three bigger boys leaned over a crumpled figure. Maybe it was a deer or even a stray dog? Maybe they would play ball with him. "Hey, what you guys doin'?"

Johnny and Skip turned and ran into the woods like rats abandoning a sinking ship. Randy kicked Jerome one more time, then followed them, cursing because he couldn't finish the job. "You ain't heard the last of me, kid," he called over his shoulder as he ran.

Mike ran to see what they had been looking at. If they had mistreated an animal, he would try to take it home. He stopped beside his friend's crumpled body. Waves of fear, anger, and nausea shot through him. He dropped to his knees beside Jerome and swallowed back the bitter tasting stuff that threatened to spew across the field. He would not be sick. His friend needed help and he was the only one there.

Furtively he looked across the field for someone to help. He saw no one. He called out anyway, on the off chance someone would be nearby.

"Help! Help! Somebody help!"

"Oh God what should I do? I have to go for help, but will those kids come back? I can't carry Jerome, or even drag him very far — shouldn't anyway in case he's hurt inside." Remembering his first aid lessons from Scouts, Mike peeled off his jacket and threw it over Jerome and jumped to his feet.

"I'll get your grandmother, Jerome," Mike yelled as he ran for his bike. He called back over his shoulder. "We'll be back in a flash. Hold on, Jerome."

"Oh God," he prayed as he ran, "please let me get help for Jerome in time. Don't let those boys come back."

Mike pedaled his bike faster than he had ever pedaled in his life. Jerome's grandmother was in the yard checking her flowers. "Mrs. Dugal! Mrs. Dugal!" Mike shouted, threw his bike down, and ran toward her

"Take it easy, Mike," Sophia said. "What's wrong?"

"Come quick. Jerome's hurt bad. They tried to kill him." Mike was pale and his words were almost lost in a sob.

"Where is he?" Sophia threw down her tools and ran for her car.

"Ball park, he..."

Sophia had her car door open. "I'll go to the park. You go to Charlie's across from the park and call for help."

Mike didn't answer. He grabbed his bike and ran with it, jumping on after it was moving down the street. He pedaled to Charlie's, arriving about the same time Sophia got to the park. "Quick," he said as he ran into the little diner, "Call 911. Jerome's hurt bad at the park."

Charlie grabbed the phone and made the call, then made Mike sit down and drink a cola.

* * *

Laura followed Mischief to the car. The cat leaped into the back seat as soon as she opened the door and stood looking out the rear window. Laura backed out of the drive and Mischief leaped to the front seat and stood with front paws on the dash. They raced after Rascal. Laura could barely see him streaking down the street and around the corner. He seemed to be heading toward Glenville Road.

When she stopped at the four-way stop, Mischief chattered and meowed. "Which way did Rascal go?" Laura couldn't see him. Mischief jumped across her lap and put her nose against the window. Then Laura saw him heading toward Glenville. Surely he wasn't going across the mountain. They turned left and followed. Mischief moved back to the passenger seat.

Ahead of her Rascal crossed the street and headed for the ballpark without slowing. Laura turned into the park and saw the red object near the woods. Rascal jumped up and down near it. Mischief chattered more. Laura ignored the parking area and drove across the field. Before the car came to a full stop, she opened the door. Mischief sailed over her head and joined Rascal beside the death-like body on the ground.

"Jerome!" Laura fell to her knees beside him. He needed paramedics. If only she had a cell phone. She would have to leave him with the cats and...Another car drove across the ground and stopped beside hers. Rascal and Mischief stretched themselves out beside Jerome on either side to keep his body warm.

Sophia stopped beside Laura's car and jumped out. "Jerome," she cried as she knelt beside him. She looked at Laura through her tears. "Mike Hostetler came for me and I sent him to Charlie's to call for help."

Sirens already wailed in the distance, drawing closer with each second. "I hear them coming," said Laura. "Do you know what happened?"

"No. Mike came after me, said some big kids beat Jerome."

Jerome groaned and Sophia reached to pick him up.

"Don't," said Laura. "I know how you feel. I wanted to hold him, too, but he might have internal injuries."

Sophia sobbed and laid a hand on the boy's swollen face. "It's all right, Jerome. Help is coming."

The wail of sirens screamed closer as the ambulance and two police cruisers raced across the field to join them.

* * *

Joe Parkerson had been driving an ambulance since he graduated from high school—more than twenty-five years now. Trained as a paramedic, he knew how to handle emergencies. His friend and side-kick for the day, Burt Miller, was new on the job and Joe was helping to train him, a job he loved. It was rewarding to help someone else learn how to handle emergencies.

When the call came in that a small boy was down on the ball field, he assumed some kid got hit by a line drive. He had the lights flashing and siren screaming before he even pulled away from the ambulance bay. The park was only a couple blocks away from the fire department, but seconds often made the difference between life and death.

"Over there," Burt pointed to the far edge of the field. They saw two cars and two women beside the downed boy. The police chief's cruiser flew past them and another right behind him.

Pulling up beside the women, they saw the small boy on the ground. Neither spoke. Each knew what he had to do. Before the vehicle hardly came to rest, Burt was out and had the back door open pulling the gurney toward him. Joe set the brake and jumped from his side moving with speed to Jerome. He checked his pulse and blood pressure and his injuries as much as possible.

Todd and Steve leaped from one of the two cruisers that came to a halt beside the ambulance. They ran to the women as the ambulance opened the back for a gurney.

"Laura? Sophia?" Todd looked from one to the other.

Steve checked Jerome's pulse and clenched his teeth to hold back a flow of unsuitable words. He looked at Laura. Tears streamed down her pale face. She was receiving comfort as her lips moved in silent prayer.

"Mike Hostetler came after me," said Sophia.

"Laura?"

She glanced up at Todd. "Rascal brought me."

Steve gave her a curious look then glanced again at Jerome. Both cats were keeping him warm. He had never liked cats and women were off his list, but somehow both were crowding into his heart. He was glad the paramedics were ready to work. He didn't like the directions his thoughts were going.

"Easy does it, Burt. Let's slide the board under him. Know what happened?" Joe spoke to Todd, while he continued to help Burt to get Jerome stabilized for transport.

"Don't know, yet," said Todd.

"Looks like he took a pretty good beating. Ready, Burt?"

"Ready."

Together they lifted the gurney and slid it into the open jaws of the waiting vehicle.

"You go with him, Sophia. I'll get Carolyn." Todd helped the older woman into the ambulance.

"My car..."

"Give me your keys. We'll take care of it," said Todd. He

handed the keys to Mark Goodwin. "You guys search the woods then take her car home. I'll check with you later."

Mike returned from the diner on his bike. He stood back watching when a policeman told him he couldn't go any closer. "I'll take Mike home," said Laura looking toward the pale little boy. "He's had quite a shock."

She approached Mike. "Let's put your bike in my hatchback and I'll take you home," she said. Mike nodded.

"I'll get it," said Steve. "Mind if I ride with you? I might be in the way when Todd picks Jerome's mother up."

Steve put Mike's bike in the car. "Where are the cats?"

They were gone. Laura called to them with no response. "Maybe they went home. They seem to know their way around. Come on Mike." She turned to the boy in time to see him crumple to the ground. She reached him mere seconds before Steve.

"Mike? Come on Mike. You're all right. Wake up." She held him in one arm and patted his face with the other.

Mike opened his eyes and started sobbing. "Is Jerome dead?"

"No, Mike. He's not dead. He's hurt bad, but you did a super job of getting help to him. Where did you learn to cover him with your jacket like that?" Laura wasn't so much interested in the fact as she was in getting his mind off what he had seen.

"From scouts."

"And you rode that bike really fast. The ambulance got here almost before his grandmother. You did a good job, Mike. You probably saved his life."

"Really?" The color was coming back to his face.

"Really. Now let's get you home. The way news travels around here your mother might be worried."

"Okay."

"Steve?" She held her keys up for him. "Please."

"Sure, come on buddy. We'll have you home in no time and your mother can give you some hot chocolate and maybe even a cookie."

"I'm not allowed sweets before dinner. It'll spoil my appetite."

"I'll tell her to make an exception this time," said Steve as he carried the boy to the car. When they got to Mike's house, Steve carried Mike in and settled him on the couch while Laura explained what had happened to Mona Hostetler, his mother. "We'll call you as soon as we learn anything," she said. Then she and Steve left for the hospital.

* * *

Jerome groaned. Sophia placed her hand on his arm. "It's all right, baby, Grandma's here."

"Grandma? Don't let them hurt me anymore."

"You're going to be all right, Jerry. They're gone. You're safe. We're going to see Doctor Cornelius."

Siren off, lights still flashing Joe rolled to a stop. Sliding doors opened. Burt helped Sophia from the ambulance then pulled the gurney out. Sophia trotted alongside of it until they stopped and transferred Jerome to a hospital gurney. Sophia waited in the examination room with Jerome. Burt and Joe left.

Doctor Jonathan Cornelius, white coat open, stethoscope around his neck, silently slipped in beside the gurney. "What happened to him?"

Sophia told him all she knew. "Will he be all right? He's..." The words stuck in her throat.

"Heart and pulse sound good for such a beating. Don't hear anything that would indicate a punctured lung. We'll get him to X-ray and see what kind of internal damage we have, if any. He looks good, but I'll know more in a little bit. Where's his mother?"

"She was at work. Chief Williams went after her. They should be here any minute."

"Can you give us permission to treat him?"

"Yes."

"Then we won't wait. I'll take him to X-ray myself."

"Thank you Doctor." Sophia signed the permission form and watched them wheel Jerome down the corridor and around the corner out of sight. Then she hurried back to watch for Carolyn, who arrived with Todd as Sophia got to the waiting room. Once again she told what she knew about the beating.

"Mrs. McMichaels?" The emergency nurse came toward them with a clipboard. "We need to get some information, if you don't mind."

"I want to see my baby," said Carolyn swiping at her tears.

"He's in X-ray, Mrs. McMichaels. Doctor J is with him. We'll let you know the minute he returns. If you will just have a seat here we can take care of the paperwork."

"Doctor J?" Sophia looked confused. "I thought Doctor Cornelius went with him."

The nurse smiled. "Sorry," she said. "We call Doctor Jonathan Cornelius Doctor J to distinguish him from his father, Doctor Eric Cornelius."

"Oh, I see," said Sophia. "That's all right then."

Carolyn finished the information on the clipboard and went with her mother to the waiting area which bustled with activity—parents waiting with children with fractures, cuts, and bee stings; a man who fell from a ladder had swollen foot; somewhere a baby cried and coughed with chest congestion. Carolyn and Sophia found two seats together while they waited. Sophia told her daughter all that she knew—again.

After what seemed like hours of waiting, but was in reality only twenty minutes, Doctor Jonathan Cornelius came to talk to them. "We'll need to take him to surgery for a broken arm. X-rays don't show any internal injuries, but he's still unconscious."

More papers to sign and once again an orderly rolled Jerome away—this time to the surgery unit. Carolyn took a paper bag with Jerome's meager belongings and she and her mother went to the surgery waiting room on the second floor. Todd had disappeared—gone to check out details with the hospital staff, to give directions to his men for interviewing Mike Hostetler, and to keep check on Jerome.

Full of soft, overstuffed chairs and couches, some straight-backed chairs, and a few small tables with years-old magazines scattered across them, it was not a bad place to wait. Many lamps gave light to the room. Floor to ceiling windows on the outside wall overlooked the parking lot, providing more light during daylight hours.

154

Sophia picked up a magazine. Carolyn paced until she became too restless to even do that. She picked up the bag of clothes, dumped them on a couch and began folding them carefully and methodically. Out of habit of washing a small boy's clothes, she reached into Jerome's pockets, pulling out odds and ends — a bite of sandwich he hadn't finished, a piece of gum waiting to be chewed, a couple small stones, a marble — all the usual stuff. The jacket pocket was different. She found the note which she read. Suddenly, she sat as if her legs had buckled under her. More color drained from her already pale face.

Sophia rushed to her side. "What is it, Carolyn? What..."

"It's nothing, Mom. Just one of Jerry's drawings." Carolyn didn't offer to show her. Sophia knew it wasn't a drawing, but she would wait. They would talk later when Jerome was out of surgery — when they were home.

19

As Steve drove Laura's car into the hospital, they were both lost in their thoughts. Laura spoke first, "Do you think there's a connection between Jerome's beating and everything else that's happened here?" She paused then added, "Of course there is. I should have called someone sooner when Jerome didn't show up after school. Maybe I could have prevented this."

"Laura, there's no way you can second-guess a madman. You can't blame yourself. Don't even try." He glanced at her from the corner of his eye, while maneuvering the car into a parking space.

"When Todd called, he said Jerome is in surgery," Steve said as they hurried toward the main entrance. "Carolyn and her mother are in the surgical waiting room on the second floor."

Laura could feel anxiety building. She tried to avert her mind and think about other things—Jerome, the cats, anything but being in a hospital. Maybe Steve's presence would make a difference. She couldn't have a panic attack—not now, not here in front of Steve Morgan. Silently she prayed. "O God help me!" She tried not to breathe in the smells, notice the white walls, or the nasal-voiced paging of doctors.

Nothing worked. As soon as she stepped inside the doors of the main entrance—even though it was not the emergency room—she stopped, paralyzed. Her eyes felt fixed, unmovable as she stared ahead like an animal caught in the headlights of an oncoming car. She was worse than paralyzed. She was cold as if she had suddenly been plunged into the Arctic Ocean.

"Laura, are you all right?" Steve laid his hand on her arm.

She didn't answer. The scene of Harold on that gurney was more real than the present surroundings. Like an ice sculpture, unable to move or speak, Laura wasn't even sure she was breathing. Miles away, someone spoke her name. Disembodied voices floated overhead paging busy doctors. Antiseptic smells filled her nose, made her eyes water. All messages of death, not healing.

A hand pressed on her arm. The ice that clogged her veins began to thaw. Would she melt like Frosty? She began to tremble. Steve took off his sweater and draped it around her shoulders. "Over here," he said and guided her to a group of chairs and couches arranged for visitors who waited their turn to see a loved one. "Sit here."

Laura obeyed his order because she could do nothing else. Had he not helped her to the couch, she could not have moved. She pulled his sweater tightly around her, but felt as if she had been swept into an icy vacuum—no air, no heat.

Steve left her for a minute. She felt the ice returning to her veins and wanted to cry after him, but had no voice. He returned with a Styrofoam cup of hot coffee. "Careful, it's hot," he said placing it in her hands. He cupped his hands around hers to help her hold it.

Laura still couldn't speak. She managed to sip the coffee. The hot liquid began to warm and thaw her from the inside. The nearness of a warm, live person gave her courage to fight the panic. Her limbs began to feel prickly as feeling returned.

"Do you want a doctor?" The concern in Steve's voice began to penetrate the thawing sculpture. She shook her head. Steve kept his hands cupped around her hands, afraid she would drop the cup of hot liquid on her. She still trembled.

"Laura, what happened?

"I think I'm all right now. I...must have had a panic attack. Thanks, for being here."

"You froze as if you had seen a ghost."

"I suppose I did, sort of." She bit her lip trying to decide how much to share. She had to talk about it sometime—to really put it all behind her. And she did owe him some kind of explanation.

"I…I haven't been inside a hospital since…the night my husband died. I worked in clinics and nursing homes for my seminary training. I thought with time I would get over my fear." She paused, took a sip of coffee. Steve took his hands away from the cup.

"I suppose most hospitals are alike—the sounds, the smells, the buzzing of activity." Laura tried to laugh, but her shudder made it sound like a sob.

"Do you want to go home? You don't have to stay."

"I do have to stay. It's my job. Somehow I've got to get over this hurdle."

"Would it help to talk about it? I'm a good listener. I can even keep it confidential." He grinned at his reference to her comment about keeping Jerome's conversation confidential.

Laura smiled then turned serious. "I've never talked about that night, not even to my daughter, Susan. I thought the picture had been erased, but it hasn't." She shuddered again. Steve took her hand and waited.

Laura took a deep breath and began. "I told you Harold was killed in a car crash that is now an unsolved murder. Haltingly she told him of receiving a call from the hospital, her friend taking her, and discovering that her husband was dead.

Laura took several deep breaths and finished her story. "Until the moment that officer uncovered the body, I was under the impression I was there to help Harold with a parishioner. I have no idea how I got out of there and back home. Since that night, I haven't been able to make myself enter a hospital. I know I have to get over it. I can't minister to people who are hurting if I can't get past my own fear." Tears threatened to overflow and Laura angrily brushed at them with her free hand.

"Laura! What an awful way to discover the death of a loved one. How could they have been so insensitive?" Laura was surprised at the intensity and anger in his voice.

"Thank you for not laughing at me, Steve. I feel so foolish reacting the way I did."

"You reacted the way anyone would under the circumstances. Ministering to people in crises has to be difficult anytime. That kind of memory just makes it more difficult."

"Like I said before, I tend to stubbornly hold on to my feelings. I don't share them easily. I can take care of myself...until something like this hits me. Then I remember I'm only human, not God." She took another deep breath and gave Steve a slight smile. "Thank you for helping me over the hurdle. I think I can manage it now."

"Are you sure?"

"No, I'm not sure, but I have to." She stood and handed Steve's sweater back to him.

"If you need to leave, or go down for coffee, just say so," Steve said as he reluctantly let go of her hand.

Laura was surprised to feel the soft mirth in her soul. She frowned and would have commented if Steve hadn't been so near. Did God think this was funny? Maybe there would come a day when she thought so too, but not tonight.

Steve led her down a long hall which angled sharply to the left. One of the elevators around the corner stood open as someone stepped out of it. They slid silently shut behind them. Steve pushed the button, glancing down at Laura. "Are you feeling better?"

"I'll make it now," she said. "I'm embarrassed that you had to witness that little scene, but I'm not sure I could have gotten through it alone."

There was no time for a response, for which Steve was glad. He might have embarrassed her more. Laura was still pale, but seemed more in control. He was surprised and impressed that she trusted him enough to confide in him. He was even more impressed that, with all she had been through, she could still smile most of the time. The door slid open once more and they stepped out of the elevator to face the surgery waiting room.

20

Todd followed Laura and Steve into the room. He said he'd been taking care of the police work—talking to folks, gathering data, checking on Jerome.

Sophia stood by a window watching the parking lot for signs of life in a place where she feared death. Carolyn, sat on a couch folding and unfolding Jerome's clothes, as if making them neat would smooth out the pain and anger. She was a younger version of her mother except her hair was a dark brown, not red.

Both women looked toward the door when they heard the footsteps. They crossed the room immediately to greet Steve and Laura. Laura, wanting to be a friend to Jerome's family, as well as their pastor, started toward them. Carolyn's hostile words stopped her.

"You didn't need to call *him*. You should have called me first." She glared at Laura and nodded toward Todd. "He will only make matters worse."

Laura was taken aback by Carolyn's anger. Sophia, embarrassed by her daughter's behavior, approached Laura with open arms and tears in her eyes. Laura put her arms around the woman to comfort her all the while trying to understand Carolyn and wondering how she should respond.

Todd stepped forward as if to protect Laura from Carolyn's

bitter words. "She didn't call me, Carolyn. You know that. The nine-one-one call came to my office."

"Jerry was playing with the bigger kids and they just got a little too rough." Carolyn attempted to glare—to stare him down. She dropped her gaze. She was lying and Todd knew that.

"Carolyn!" Sophia pulled away from Laura and stood before her daughter with hands on her hips. "You can't let bullies run your life. Even if those bigger kids were playing—which they most certainly were not—why would they run off without helping him, or getting help for him? He could have died out there if the Hostetler kid hadn't seen him and run for help."

"Stay out of it, Mom," Carolyn shot back. "I care about my son's life. I don't want them to come back and finish the job."

"Then let someone who knows how, help you. Oh, why did you have to inherit your father's stubbornness?" Sophia threw up her hands in despair, turned to walk toward the window. She stared down into the parking lot, not really seeing the activity of cars and people coming and going. Turning back she pleaded once more with her daughter.

"Carolyn, I've tried to help you with Jerry. We all have—even Reverend Kenzel, who has only known him a couple of days. He's a good kid. We want to help more, but you have to be honest with us. We can't deal with lies and half-truths. Carolyn, please, we all love Jerry as much as you do. Please, let us help."

Sophia covered her face with her hands to hide her tears. Carolyn moved to embrace her. "Oh, Mom." The tears, which she had held back by the force of her anger, started flowing down her cheeks. "I'm so scared I don't know what to say, or do. They said they would hurt him more and kill me."

"Carolyn, who said they would kill you?" Todd asked.

Carolyn released the embrace on her mother and walked to the window where her mother had stood. With her back to them, she stared out the window not really seeing anything.

Memories like a circling waterway returned the years to her. She had known Todd since they were kids—even talked about getting married. Then there was the quarrel—something stupid she couldn't even remember. Doran McMichaels offered to show her the world. Todd went on to The Wheeling Police Academy. Like the prodigal son she finally called her mother to beg her to let her come home. Her mother had cried, "Come home, baby, come home." With a year old baby, Carolyn had returned to Cottonville. She had lied—said her husband was killed in Vietnam.

"Carolyn..." her mother's voice pulled her out of that circling stream. Carolyn waited but didn't turn away from the safety of the window. She knew the footsteps approaching her were not her mother's. When she felt Todd's firm grasp on her arms, she wanted to turn to him and let him erase all her fear. She couldn't. Not yet. He spoke in a quiet voice, so close to her ear she felt his breath on her neck, and tried to push aside the memories and the emotions that it triggered.

"Carolyn, you know you can't handle this alone. We're involved, whether you like it, or not. Pastor Kenzel has been threatened, shot at, and her car spray painted. Her life has been pure hell since she drove in here two days ago. Jerome has been one of the few bright spots in her life. He's a loving kid who needs to know he's loved."

Carolyn wouldn't look at him. She couldn't. The old flame wouldn't die, but she was afraid of rejection. "Todd, stay out of it. Just because we were once..." He didn't let her finish. He turned her around to face him.

"Carolyn, this has nothing to do with us. Some day when this is all behind us, we'll talk about that, but, for now, finding who did this to Jerome and stopping the threats, and yes, even murder, is my first priority. You can help us by cooperating, or we'll work around you and take more time than is necessary to bring it to a halt. The quicker we get information and begin moving in on those jerks, the safer everyone will be. Now, are you going to help us, or not?"

Carolyn looked up into his dark, flashing eyes and tried to pull away. He held her with a tight grip of his hands, but even tighter with the compassion in his eyes. She couldn't hold on to her anger any longer. She wanted him to hold her, comfort her, but she had no right to expect it. The tears began to run down her cheeks, her head fell against him. His arms went around her.

"Oh, Todd, what can I do? How can I help? I don't want them to hurt him anymore. He's all I have."

"I don't want him hurt anymore either. None of us do. Do you know who did it? We need to hear everything from the beginning."

While Todd talked to Carolyn, Steve, Laura and Sophia watched and listened. Sophia looked at Steve. "Detective Morgan, do you really think there's a connection between the murder of that drifter and those kids beating up my grandson? It seems so...impossible for kids to be mixed up in such stuff."

"You're right, ma'am. It seems very impossible, but then, so do all the school bombings and shootings. We're living in tough days—even in small towns like Cottonville. I don't know what the connection is, but, yes, I do believe there is one. All I have to go on is an educated hunch. Was Jerome able to talk before they took him to surgery?"

With some reluctance Carolyn moved away from the comfort of Todd's arms. She accepted the tissue Laura handed her from a box on one of the tables and wiped her nose and eyes, then sat on a couch with Todd beside her, Steve across from her. Laura and Sophia stood listening not only to them, but also for any sound of someone approaching them with news of Jerome.

"One of his friends came after Mom," Carolyn began.

"Mike was crying," said Sophia. "He said some big kids beat Jerome."

Sophia continued, "I didn't want to waste time running in the house to make a call, so I told Mike to go to Charlie's and call nine-one-one and I drove to the ball field. Reverend Kenzel was already there. Her cats were helping to keep him warm."

Steve glanced at Laura who looked like she was suffering as much as Carolyn and Sophia. He drew his attention back to Sophia.

"Mike said there were three of them. They were standing over Jerry 'like vultures over their prey,'" Sophia said.

"Did he get a good look at them?" Steve asked.

"Mike said they ran into the woods when he called to them."

Steve glanced back to Todd and Carolyn, remembering Todd's words about having loved someone who now had a son to raise. He hadn't asked at the time who he had meant, but now it made sense. Jerome needed a dad like Todd. He hoped they could work it out.

Carolyn's sobs abated once again and she took the tissue Todd offered. "I'm sorry," she said, blowing her nose and wiping her face.

"Don't be sorry, Carolyn. He's a special little boy. He didn't deserve a beating like that." Laura seemed unaware of her own tears cascading down her face. Steve watched her, envying Todd. He would like to comfort this lady preacher in the same way. He could see the pain and guilt in her eyes.

He couldn't believe that for Laura ministry was just a job. Laura Kenzel had struggled to overcome her own pain to be with these hurting folks.

Sophia continued, "In the ambulance he woke briefly, but all he said was, 'Don't let them hurt me anymore.' Doctor Cornelius met us at the door and rushed him to X-ray." Minutes later Carolyn and Todd arrived.

"The X-rays showed a broken arm and two fractured ribs," said Carolyn. "His skull wasn't fractured, but his head took some pretty hard blows. He probably has a concussion. They took him directly to surgery for the arm. They gave me his clothes stuffed in a bag. When we came in here I took them out and began to fold them. That's when I found the note in his jacket pocket."

Todd clenched and unclenched his fists. Steve realized Todd was much more emotionally involved than if this was just any kid who was hurt. The way things looked it might be his future stepson they were talking about. He continued the questions. "Can I see the note?"

Carolyn reached in her pocket and found the crinkled paper. She handed it to Steve. "I heard the crackle of paper and reached in his pocket—he's always putting something there, homework, pictures he drew, that kind of thing."

Steve looked at the note: FORGET WHAT YOU SAW. REMEMBER JEB. YOUR MOTHER COULD BE NEXT.

"What did Jerome see?" asked Steve.

"I don't know."

"Maybe they thought he saw something which would incriminate them, or lead Todd and Steve to the murderer." Laura spoke softly.

"When? He doesn't go a lot of places. Just school, fishing when he skips..." Carolyn couldn't help smiling at Todd. "...I've warned him about talking to strangers."

Laura laughed. "Yes, I know. He wouldn't even tell me his name until I told him who I was. He said he wasn't allowed to talk to strangers. I guess he thought if he knew my name, I was no longer a stranger."

"He must have been someplace where he either saw something, without even realizing it, or they think he saw something. Can you give us an idea of where he's been in the last couple of days?" Steve felt confused and angry with himself. He should be able to figure this out.

"School, fishing, visiting with the pastor, home, his grandmother's. That's all I know about. They're all usual places, except visiting with the pastor. Since they warned him to stay away from her, it would seem that's where the problem is. I don't mean Reverend Kenzel is the problem, but well, you know what I mean." Carolyn looked flustered.

Laura moved to lay a hand on her shoulder. "I know what you mean, Carolyn. It seems I've caused a lot of problems and I have no idea why. I wish I knew what was going on."

"Well, it looks like we can narrow it down to one or two places where there's a possibility of him seeing something which would be dangerous for them—the criminals, that is." Steve was writing in his notebook.

"What's that, Steve?" Todd looked confused. "No, wait!" His eyes lit up with comprehension. "I think I see what you are getting at. Jerome"—he paused and looked at Carolyn. "He asked us to call him Jerome, not Jerry." She looked surprised, but he didn't explain further. He continued, "Jerome had to have been in a position to see something either in the woods between the parsonage back yard and the stream where he was fishing, or during the time he was with the pastor. Whatever he's supposed to have seen is, or was, in the area around the church, parsonage, or the woods."

"I'm going to make a detective out of you yet." Steve grinned at his friend. "Now, all we have to do is narrow it down to what he could have seen, and where."

"Mrs. McMichaels?" Doctor Cornelius stood in the doorway, his white coat limp, his face fatigued, the traditional stethoscope hung around his neck like a rosary waiting for use.

21

Anxious eyes met the doctor as he glanced around the room. Carolyn jumped up and ran to him. "Is my boy all right? Can I see him now?"

"He's going to be fine. We'll need to keep him here a day or two. We don't want that concussion to cause any problems. He's still drowsy, but he asked for you and his pastor. Follow me. I'll take you to him. Don't stay too long."

Carolyn turned to her mother, who nodded for her to go on. Then she turned to Laura and said, "You're the only pastor he knows." Laura followed Carolyn and the doctor down the hall.

"He's in there." Doctor Cornelius nodded at the closed door. "Please don't panic at all the treatments we're doing for him. The IV is to get medicine in him without waking him up, plus keeping him well hydrated. He's doing quite well considering the severity of the beating he received. I'm glad to see Chief Williams here. I'm required by law to file a report on any child who's treated here for these kinds of injuries. I'm sure you had nothing to do with it, but you would be surprised by the number of parents who bring a child in here under some very suspicious circumstances and vague reports of how the injury really occurred. Sorry, I didn't mean to get so carried away, but I don't like to see kids hurt like this. Don't stay too long."

Carolyn hurried into the room and the doctor turned to go. Laura stayed back to give Carolyn a few minutes alone with Jerome. She called after Doctor Cornelius.

"Yes?" He turned back to face her.

"Thank you for being a caring doctor. I'm Laura Kenzel, the new pastor of the United Methodist church."

He took her outstretched hand in his and smiled. "I'm glad to meet you, Reverend Kenzel. I'm Jonathan Cornelius. I think you met my father yesterday morning, Eric Cornelius, physician and coroner."

"Oh, yes. I didn't realize we had two doctors in town." Laura realized how snobbish that sounded. "I'm sorry. I didn't mean that the way it sounded. I..." Jonathan was tall and thin like his father.

Doctor Cornelius laughed. "Don't worry about it. If you've experienced only half of what I've heard through the small town grapevine, you have enough on your mind without worrying about correct protocol in a self-contained little town like Cottonville."

"Thank you and I do appreciate your position on children. One question before I see Jerome."

"Yes?"

"Would it be possible for Mrs. McMichaels to stay with Jerome tonight?" She told him about the note. "I think they would both rest easier knowing the other was all right."

"We don't have a bed, but she could sleep in the reclining chair if she wants to. Thank you for thinking of it. My mind must have been out to lunch."

"I'm sure you have your hands full and she was too concerned to think. Thank you. I'll tell her."

Laura walked quietly into the room where Carolyn, tears flowing, sat beside the bed holding Jerome's left hand—the one not covered with a cast. Laura's own emotions were on a roller coaster tonight, so she understood Carolyn's need for release. She went to the other side of the bed.

Around the room, machines beeped and clicked. Bags hung from their metal poles with hooks, dripping liquid into a plastic line leading to Jerome's arm. What was outside the window was anyone's guess. It was too dark to tell. Laura took a couple of deep breaths to get her own anger under control. As much as Doctor Cornelius tried to prepare them, she didn't want to see the sight of that small boy with swollen face and cast on his arm. For his sake, and that of his mother's, she forced herself to be professional.

"Jerome, it's Pastor Kenzel. You wanted to see me?" She spoke softly.

Jerome half opened the slits where his eyes should have been. The swelling and the bandage around his head didn't leave much room. "Yeah. Bet I look more like Frankenstein than Tom Sawyer." He tried to laugh. "Oh, that hurts to laugh."

"Well, then don't," said his mother, sounding more cross than she intended.

"Your mother's right, Jerome," Laura agreed. "Save the laughs for later when we can all laugh together. Right now we all hurt together."

"I know. I'm sorry."

"Not your fault, Jerome. And if it is mine, I'm the one who's sorry."

"Not your fault either," he managed. "Why don't they like you? They don't even know you."

"Who are they, Jerome?"

"There were three. Johnny Atkins, Skip Jameson, and another kid I didn't know—Randy someone. Will you tell Chief Todd so he can take care of them before they hurt my mom?"

"Chief Williams and Detective Morgan are in the waiting room with your grandmother. I'll tell them as soon as I return there."

"Can I see Grandma? I didn't know she was here."

"Why don't I get her, then you can get some sleep. I'll be back tomorrow to see you. Okay?"

"Okay."

"Oh by the way, Mrs. McMichaels, I spoke to Doctor Cornelius. He said you can spend the night in the chair if you want to."

"Thank you, but..."

"Please stay, Mom. Then they can't hurt you."

Laura left the room and took a moment to clear the tears from her own eyes and face, then she walked quickly back to the waiting room where three sets of anxious eyes watched for someone to return with information. "He wants to see you, Sophia. He didn't know you were here. Straight down the hall the last room on the left."

Sophia's eyes lit up as she hurried out of the room and down the hall. Laura turned to Todd and Steve. "He said there were three boys—Atkins, Jameson, and another one he didn't know."

Todd emitted a low whistle. "Atkins and Jameson? You realize who they are, don't you?"

"I'm afraid so," said Laura.

Steve gave them a puzzled look. "Kids who are usually in trouble?"

"No, but only because of who they are," said Todd. "Johnny Atkins is the son of the town's only lawyer, and Skip Jameson is the son of Phil Jameson the local banker, Carolyn's boss. I heard Atkins say something about his nephew, or cousin or someone being in town the other night."

"Sounds like we got our trio, or at least two of them," said Steve, "so what's the problem?"

"The problem is we're dealing with the two most powerful men in town and, with the exception of SaraBelle Cotton, the richest. If we even tried to talk to those kids without the parents and/or a lawyer present, we would be digging buckshot out for weeks—if not literally, then metaphorically." Todd paused, shook his head.

"I've had a run in with the two before and can't get much beyond a warning. Not only is Atkins the only lawyer in town, he's pretty smart—smarter than I am when it comes to getting around the law. I know the law and I know how to arrest, but I don't know how to make it stick against that kind of power."

"Are you saying you aren't going to do anything about this?" asked Laura color rising to her cheeks.

Todd sighed again and ran his fingers through his already ruffled hair. "Let's go to Charlie's for a cup of coffee and see what we can figure out. We can't talk here."

"Todd's right," answered Steve. "This is a pretty public place, even though there's no one in here right now."

"So is Charlie's," said Laura. "Why don't you come to my house? Besides, my coffee is cheaper," she smiled.

"Can't beat an invitation like that," Steve said.

"Why don't you two go ahead? I'll check on Carolyn then pick up some folders on these kids from the office. I'll be there by the time the coffee's ready."

Steve pushed the call button for the elevator, which opened as if waiting for them. Seconds later, they stepped out. Laura stopped and looked both ways. Steve saw the confusion on her face, raised an eyebrow, and waited for her to explain.

"I get a little confused on directions inside a building," Laura said. "I always turn the wrong way and end up turning back." She felt the familiar warmth on her cheeks.

"Just inside?" Steve smiled and without a second thought reached for her hand and started down the hall.

"I'm really good with directions on the road, but...oh well, we all have our weaknesses." She grinned at him as they reached her car and he let go of her hand.

He returned her smile. "Do you want me to drive, or would you like your keys back?" He reached into his pocket and dangled them before her.

"I think I can find my way home," she said. He opened the door for her then got in the passenger's side. Steve stared straight ahead—except for a few sneaked glances. As much as he tried to distance himself from the beautiful woman beside him, he found himself drawn to her. He was still amazed that she would share her deepest fears with him. Why would she trust him?

She pulled into her driveway. "I see you left a light on this time." He nodded toward the house where a light in the living room was burning brightly behind the silhouettes of two back-to-back cats which filled most of the window.

"I wasn't sure when I would get back, so I turned the lamp on as I followed the cats out the door. The question is, how did Rascal and Mischief get in the house? I hoped they would come home, but I didn't expect them to be inside."

"Maybe one of the Jennings saw them and let them in."

"Maybe. I'll ask Martha tomorrow. I'm just relieved to see them. I'm getting too attached to them."

"That's not bad, is it?"

"Only if some family member pops up to claim them."

They moved up the steps and across the porch. When Laura opened the door, the yowling duet of the Maine Coons set up such a ruckus she was reluctant to walk into the room. Steve understood her reluctance and stepped around her. The cats greeted him like a friend, but wrapped around Laura's ankles, purring as loud as a swarm of bees.

Steve laughed. "It looks like they're as glad to see you as you are to see them. I'd say you have a couple of pets whether you asked for them or not. Or maybe they have a good human. If that's the kind of greeting you get when you come in after a long day, maybe I need to look into the possibility."

"It is better than getting knocked to the floor." Laura stooped to embrace both Rascal and Mischief and tell them what good kitties they were. Then she moved ahead to the kitchen half expecting them to stop her. They were involved with a game of chase with a ball of yarn Steve found on the floor. The sound of tires crunched on the gravel as the coffeepot gurgled its last. The cats paused in their ball game with Steve, glanced at the door and resumed playing ball.

22

Laura filled three mugs and started to the living room with a tray when she heard Todd's voice. "That coffee sure smells good," he said. "I could smell it all the way out in the driveway.

"Thanks, Laura," he said taking the tray from her, "I think you're right. This is a much better place to try to get all our facts together. I just hope we aren't intruding and keeping you from something important."

Laura took her cup of coffee and sat in her favorite chair. "Right now, except for thinking about a message for Sunday, I have nothing more important to do than help you find the evil behind all this violence. A cup of coffee is a small price to pay for peace of mind. I just wish I could make some sense of it all. It would appear that much of what happened the last couple of days was preceded by more that I don't even know about."

"Probably so," said Todd.

"Could you fill us in from the beginning of this mess?" Steve said.

Todd's face twisted into a frown. "If I can even remember when it started. A lot of little things along the way—nothing dangerous, or even worth tracking down."

"Like what?" Laura and Steve both asked together then smiled at each other.

"Almost two years ago Jeb Little showed up. Actually, he came sometime in mid-June. I told him we didn't like drifters. He said he was settling down for a while, but I could never get an address from him. About once a week or so, he showed up downtown with the cats and a tin cup—kind of like the old-time organ grinder with his monkey. He played music on his boom box and the cats danced and did other tricks. People enjoyed the show and felt they got their money's worth. Jeb said he wasn't begging. He earned a living with his trained animals. I couldn't refute that. I just didn't see how he could live on what it looked like he collected."

"Did he ever have any trouble with the law?" asked Steve.

"No. I tried to run a fingerprint check on him, but every time I tried, they ended up smeared or something. I talked with Atkins about him once. He warned me to be careful with his civil rights— whatever that meant. He didn't harm anyone, so I just kept an eye on him as best I could and let it go at that."

"Did you get his fingerprints after he died?" Laura asked as she sipped her coffee.

Todd and Steve exchanged glances. "Good question, Laura. Did you, Todd? I can't believe I didn't think of it first." He grinned at her.

"Not unless it's routine in the autopsy. I didn't even think about it." Todd looked a little sheepish.

"Has he been buried yet?"

"I don't think so, Steve. I'll get over to Winters Funeral Home first thing in the morning and do it."

"Did he always play the same kind of music?"

Todd and Steve again exchanged surprised looks. "I don't know, Laura," answered Todd. "Would it make a difference?"

"I don't know if it would, or not. It could, if it was a signal of some kind. Did he always come on the same day of the week?"

Todd looked bewildered. "I guess I never paid that much attention, but…wait a minute. I think it must have been Fridays, or holidays, usually when a lot of people were milling around at the town square."

Steve grinned at Todd. "Maybe we need to deputize her. She's becoming a pretty good detective."

"Don't be smart," Laura said. "I've got my hands full just trying to be a pastor." She frowned and changed her tone. "But, the quicker we get this other stuff out of the way, the quicker I can do that. What are some of the other things that have happened? Martha told me there were strange noises in the belfry and things disappeared in broad daylight. We solved the mystery of the noises, but what kind of items came up missing?"

"Nothing significant, I guess. Hostetlers had some tools taken—shovels, rakes, that kind of stuff. Mary Hunter does a lot of needle crafts and someone took one of her big plastic storage boxes—you know the kind with a lid that holds clothes, or whatever. She'd been working on her back porch with the box beside her rocking chair. She went in to get a bite of supper and when she returned about forty-five minuets to an hour later all her yarn and stuff had been dumped on the porch floor and her box was gone."

"That's weird." Laura thought about all her craft supplies upstairs. Remembering the ball of yarn Steve teased the cats with earlier, she looked at Rascal who stared back unblinking as if reading her mind. Mischief ducked under the chair.

"Laura? Something the matter?" Steve asked as he watched her expression change.

"What? Oh, nothing really. Talking of Mary Hunter's crafts just reminded me of something—nothing important."

"Anything might be important at this stage of the game," said Todd.

Laura laughed. "It really is nothing. I just wondered where the ball of yarn came from the cats were playing with earlier. I found out Rascal can open doors—which is probably how they got in the house—so I secured all my yarn."

"Upstairs?" asked Steve, glancing toward the stairs.

She nodded.

The two men glanced at each other and rose together. "Better check it out," said Todd. Upstairs Laura showed them the room where she had her craft supplies. "Everything is where I put it," she declared. "Like I said, it's probably nothing."

Seated back downstairs, coffee cups refilled, Steve picked up the ball of yarn and tossed it in the air. Rascal jumped for it, but Steve grabbed it before the cat could. "Where did this come from if you didn't give it to them, and they didn't take it from your supplies?"

"Let me see it." He tossed it to her and she turned it over and over in her hands. "This isn't mine. I've never used this color in any of my projects. And look," she unrolled it some more, "there are bits of grass in it. Rascal must have found it outside somewhere when they got back from the park."

"But where?" Todd sipped his coffee, looking more confused than ever.

"Suppose there was some yarn left in that box that was stolen. What would the thief do with it?" Steve asked. He opened his hands and Laura tossed it back to him. Rascal leaped from his sitting position beside Laura and caught the ball in his paws before it even came close to Steve. Surprised by the cat's quick action they all laughed. Mischief grabbed it from Rascal and ran up the steps. The chase was on.

Todd shook his head and said, "Back to your question, Steve, I suppose they would throw it away." Then light began to dawn again for him.

"That box must be close by. But why? And where?"

"One more mystery, but it seems to link the peculiar happenings with the murder in some way." Steve was writing furiously as he talked.

"Why would anyone steal something like that anyway? Surely they could get one at the hardware, or over in Glenville. I did see a hardware store last year when I came through the town, didn't I?" Laura couldn't help the sarcasm.

Steve and Todd laughed at her attempt at joking. "It's only been two days, Laura, not a year." Steve grinned at her.

"Could have fooled me," she said with as much seriousness as she could which caused both men to break into laughter again. She smiled. She wasn't really serious, but it sure felt like more than two days.

"Back to your question, Laura," said Todd, "we thought the same thing. We just assumed kids were playing pranks. But neither the tools, nor the box ever showed up."

"Maybe they didn't want anyone to know they needed it." Steve guessed.

"Which means whoever it was is well known," said Laura

"Laura, I really think you ought to consider a career change."

"I just did and look where it got me." She grinned at him.

Steve laughed and looked back at his notes. "Has anything else disappeared?" he asked.

"I can't think of anything else right now, but it's been a long day and my brain is getting numb." Todd rubbed at his temples.

"You're right, buddy. Sorry, Laura, we've taken advantage of your hospitality. Neighbors are going to accuse you of taking in boarders." Steve smiled as he closed his notebook and slipped it in his pocket.

"I don't have any neighbors close enough to even care what goes on here except the Jennings. I've seen more of you two than I have them, or any of my parishioners," Laura said. "As a matter of fact, I had a call from SaraBelle Cotton earlier this afternoon. She's pretty upset with me because I haven't been to see her yet."

"My gosh," exclaimed Todd, "you've only been here two days and I'm sure she knows all about what's been going on down here."

"Well, maybe, but she's issued a command performance for ten o'clock tomorrow morning. But, back to the question at hand, all that seems to be missing are tools to dig with and a plastic box — possibly to be buried with something in it?"

"Laura, are you sure you don't want to be a detective? I hadn't seen the possibility of a connection between the thefts, but it makes sense. But where? And why? And what's in it?" Steve pulled his notebook back out and jotted down some notes.

"I don't see how any of this connects with anything." Todd rubbed his temples, again. "All this thinking is giving me one terrific headache. Do we have any more questions?" He looked at Laura knowing if there were more questions, she would have them.

"Just one, Todd. How do all of the other events fit with this church's loss of pastor and the inability to get a new one?"

"Do you think they're connected?" He glanced at Laura then Steve, who just smiled like a teacher watching his prize pupil perform.

"I don't know," replied Laura. "It just seems more than coincidental that the town's trouble started about the same time the church's troubles did."

"Now that you mention it," said Todd, "Jeb Little arrived in town about a week after Lakeland died. Things began disappearing and noises came from the belfry soon after that."

"You might have a point there, Laura." Steve lifted his pen from the little spiral notebook.

"Maybe…"

The phone interrupted his thought. Laura looked from one to the other frowning. "It's almost ten o'clock. Who would be calling at this hour?" Then a worried frown crossed her face. She jumped for the phone. "Has something's happened to Jerome?"

Laura reached for the phone, expecting Carolyn or Sophia to be on the other end with bad news from the hospital.

"Reverend Kenzel, this is Ed Winters. We haven't met yet, but my brother, Gary and I own The Winters Funeral Home. I apologize for calling so late, but we have a slight problem and wondered if you could help us."

"I'll do what I can, Mr. Winters," she said. She glanced at Todd and Steve hunching her shoulders as if to say, "What's this all about?" They both turned to listen. Why would Ed Winters be calling her at this time of night?

"Excuse me, Mr. Winters. I hope you don't mind if I use the speakerphone. How can I help you?" She didn't wait for his answer, but pushed the button for the speakerphone, opened the drawer, and pulled out paper and pencil.

"Sure, use the speaker if you want to. I hate to ask you, but it seems every pastor in town is tied up tomorrow and we already have the graveside service set for Jeb Little."

Todd and Steve exchanged glances. Laura's eyebrows went up and she cocked her head to one side as if to hear him better.

Ed Winters continued, "I know he was a drifter and it might be difficult for you, finding him the way you did and everything, but could you possibly do a short graveside service tomorrow morning at ten o'clock?"

"Mr. Winters, the fact that I found the body doesn't bother me as much as the fact that I didn't know the man at all. And I'm sorry, but I have another appointment at ten o'clock tomorrow. Perhaps if you changed the time one of the other pastors could handle it."

"No." He answered too quickly. "They're tied up all day."

"And the service has to be done tomorrow?" Something didn't quite fit. She glanced at Todd and Steve who shrugged their shoulders.

"Well, we want to get it over with and we already have the grave dug and everything." Ed Winters spoke in a nasal, whining tone.

"Mr. Winters, I cannot do it at ten o'clock. If you will change the service to earlier, or later, I'll be glad to do what I can." Laura felt uneasy.

"We wanted to do it at ten because…" The whining voice was beginning to grate on her nerves.

"Mr. Winters, I don't need to hear why you have to have it at ten o'clock. I simply cannot do it then."

"Oh, I'm sure Mrs. Cotton won't mind if you're a little late."

Laura heard a smugness in his voice which she didn't like. She frowned and glanced again at Todd and Steve. "I'm glad you are well enough acquainted with Mrs. Cotton to be certain of that, Mr. Winters. However, it's not my style to be late for appointments. My engagement with Mrs. Cotton takes first priority. I'm sorry, but I can't help you."

"Wait, Reverend Kenzel," Ed Winters lost his nasal whine and turned to an almost desperate pleading. "We're really desperate. We've already made all the arrangements. We have to do the service tomorrow. How about if we move it to nine o'clock? Would that work for you?"

"Where is the service? I know you said graveside, but where is the cemetery?"

"Cottonville Memorial Gardens—just south of town about a mile. I'll pick you up so you don't have to worry about getting lost or anything." Ed Winters gave her a nervous laugh and added, "I promise to have you back in plenty of time for your appointment."

"Thank you for your kind offer, Mr. Winters, but I'll drive myself. I prefer it that way. I'll be there early in case you have some last minute instructions, or requests."

"Thank you, Reverend Kenzel. We'll make sure you are well paid for this."

"Mr. Winters, I do not do funerals to be *well paid*. I do them because everyone—even the Jeb Littles of the world—deserves to have a decent burial. Goodbye, Mr. Winters. I'll see you in the morning." Laura pushed the off button.

"What was that all about?" asked Steve. "It sounds like he wants you and no one else. Could he be curious about the new woman pastor?" He grinned at her.

Laura didn't return the grin. "It sounds more like he is trying to prevent me from seeing SaraBelle Cotton tomorrow morning. I don't know the woman, but when someone orders a command performance, I don't think she would take kindly to me being late. And how did he know I had an appointment at ten o'clock with Mrs. Cotton anyway? Something isn't right here. I can't believe every other pastor on his list of pastors is going to be tied up all day tomorrow." Laura shook her head and tried to smile. "Maybe I'm getting paranoid."

"I've known Ed and Gary Winters as long as I've lived in this town. I never knew them to be other than honest, but..." Todd didn't finish.

"You might be more on target than you know, Laura," said

180

Steve. "This is one of those times when it would be a good idea to trust your instincts. Todd, I think it would be a good idea if you take Laura to that funeral tomorrow. Since she refused their offer to pick her up, they can't detain her with false car trouble, or whatever, but they might try to sabotage her car. I have a feeling she would have a couple of flat tires when it was time to leave, or a missing carburetor, or something which would keep her from seeing Mrs. Cotton. Is there any connection between that lady and all the strange happenings around town?"

"I don't see how," answered Todd. "SaraBelle is ninety if she's a day. Sometimes she's cranky, eccentric, but harmless—unless you count the tongue-lashings she can give. But you might be right. It sounds like someone is going to a lot of trouble to make sure you go to that cemetery, Laura. By setting the time of the service before ten instead of afternoon, it would be easy to sabotage your car and make you miss your appointment with SaraBelle. I'll pick you up at eight-thirty in the morning. And speaking of morning, if we don't get out of here it will be morning before we leave."

"You're right. It's ten-thirty already. Why don't we talk more over lunch tomorrow? I'll buy. How about if I bring something from Charlie's?" Steve volunteered

"You know," Laura said as Todd had his hand on the doorknob to leave, "there's one other thing I wondered about earlier. I just remembered it. Suppose kids didn't put the cats in the belfry at all. Suppose Jeb Little did."

"Why would you say that?" asked Steve.

"I don't know, really. Just a hunch. I didn't take a good look around the belfry. I had other things on my mind, but I seem to remember seeing a couple of bowls as if he fed the cats there. And I seem to recall the smell of an unclean litter box. Maybe he put them there so they wouldn't run away from him. Or maybe he camped there, himself."

"Even in the winter? I doubt it. I still go with the Atkins kid and possibly the Jameson boy, especially since we know they were involved with beating Jerome." Todd was insistent.

Steve, deep in thought, pulled at his chin and frowned. "You just might be on to something, Laura. It might be possible Jerome saw something up there and didn't even know it. Like you, he had other things on his mind. I'll check it out. You get some sleep. Looks like you have a full day ahead of you."

"Yes it does. Are you sure I've only been here two days?"

"Today is Thursday. You came Tuesday night. That adds up to two for me." Todd laughed. "A lot can happen in two or three days. I'm going by the hospital to check on Carolyn and Jerome. I'll ask her when things started happening at the church. Isn't she on one of the committees?"

"Yes, the PPR—that stands for Pastor/Parish Relations Committee," she explained for Steve's benefit. "She should know. Tell her my prayers are with her and Jerome."

"I'll do that. Ready to go, buddy." He turned to Steve. The crunching of gravel faded as they left the drive and drove down the street.

"Well, guys," she turned to the cats. "Let's clean up a little and head up the steps. I don't know about you, but I'm exhausted."

Two sets of shiny, green eyes stared at her while she took cups to the kitchen. When she started toward the steps, they raced up them and waited until she reached the top step. When she stepped into her bedroom, they sat on the foot of her bed grooming themselves, which was quickly becoming a nightly ritual with them. Easing between the cool, clean sheets, Laura reached for her bedside Bible and turned to the Psalms which were a part of her nightly routine. God was her refuge and strength, her help in times of trouble. She would not be afraid because God was still God.

"God, this has been the longest two days of my life. I didn't think it was possible to feel so physically, mentally, and emotionally exhausted. Who is trying to get rid of me? And why? I couldn't have done anything to upset the church already. Could I? You brought me here for a reason and I will stay until You reveal that reason, or tell me to go, but it sure would be easier if I knew what was going on. Someone doesn't want me to see SaraBelle Cotton. If You want me to see her, well, I have the feeling we'll have a few obstacles to cross. Todd is taking me to the graveside service, but I still have an uneasy feeling. Clear the way, O Lord, or give me a way around the problems. And one more thing, I'm not ready for the emotions Steve Morgan is stirring up within me!"

Laura turned the light off and through the window watched the stars twinkling in the night sky. Like Jacob of old, she tried to count them. The soft mirthful feeling within her faded and was soon lost in slumber where stars, and cats, and detectives all intertwined in her dreams.

23

By the time Laura finished her shower, the aroma of the coffee drifted up the stairs. Dressed in her favorite mint-green two-piece linen suit, she would be warm enough for the early May morning and cool enough for the warmer afternoon.

She was clearing the table when she heard the sound of gravel crunching in the driveway. The cats' ears twitched and heads turned toward the sound. As if their minds were connected and they thought as one, Rascal and Mischief trotted to the living room door. Todd opened the door, then knocked as he stepped inside, waiting for Laura to answer.

"Come on in, Todd," Laura called from the kitchen. "I'll be ready in just a minute." She hung up the towel and dish cloth and started for the living room.

"I'm in," he called back. "Rascal let me in."

"I'm sure he did," she laughed. "I have some coffee left if you want some." She reached for her Bible, Book of Services, and purse.

"Thanks, Laura, but I have a cup in the car."

"I really hate to put you out like this, Todd. I'm sure I could handle whatever comes up. I could just keep an eye on my car, or better yet take Rascal and Mischief with me to watch the car."

"I'm sure they could and would, but I'm curious to know what kind of game Ed Winters is playing. By the way, I took Mark over there last night to get the fingerprints. Gary Winters was very helpful, but Ed just about had a cow when he came in and found us. He ranted and raved about desecrating a body and leaving ink stains on the fingers. It should be an interesting morning. I'm glad Steve suggested I be there."

Laura laughed. "All right, since you put it that way. Maybe we can find out something from Mr. Winters. I doubt it, but maybe." She turned to the cats as she started out the door. "Be good kitties and look after the house for me."

Rascal and Mischief blinked at her then went to the window to watch. Laura hoped they would curl up on the couch to await her return.

Todd held the door for her then went around to the driver's side. "No more problems last night?"

Todd always looked neat and handsome in his uniform. She thought about Carolyn and the night before. She had been surprised to learn Jerome's mother was the run-away love Todd didn't want to talk about earlier. She really hoped they could work things out. Jerome adored Todd and she was pretty sure Carolyn did too. And Todd would be an excellent dad for Jerome.

"No, none," she answered. "Did you talk to Carolyn? Could she shed any light? And how is Jerome?"

Todd smiled at her many questions, "Yes, I talked to Carolyn. She said the pastor who was here when Jeb arrived—the first after Lakeland—was the first in a long string of pastors to leave. Some came, looked, and left. Some never showed up. Some came, said they weren't afraid, but were gone by the next morning. And Jerome is doing very well. The doctor said he could go home, but I asked Carolyn to see if the hospital will keep him for a couple more days for his safety. She said she would."

"Good idea. At least with him in the hospital, we don't have to worry about him getting into more trouble, or those boys going after him again. Have you come up with any relatives of Jeb Little yet? Someone who'll want the cats?" Despite her resolve to stay calm, Laura felt her voice catch. In the short time they'd been in her home, she'd learned to love them.

"We've checked all the normal avenues — missing persons, FBI, CIA. We keep coming up with blanks. The fingerprints might help. Maybe we can have Mike Atkins draw up some kind of legal paper that will make them yours."

"I would rather keep Mr. Atkins out of it, if you don't mind."

Todd looked sideways at Laura. "Any reason for that? Something I need to know?"

"Nothing but a feeling. Call it intuition. I just feel uneasy around him. I only met him once, but he gave me the impression he could make things nasty if he doesn't get his way."

"I see." He really didn't, but let it drop. "There's the cemetery. It looks like Winters is already here. Maybe we can get started early and get you back in plenty of time for your appointment with SaraBelle."

"Maybe, but somehow I doubt it." Laura tried to laugh, but sounded more like a choke. "I'm sorry. I'm really sounding paranoid and negative this morning. That isn't like me at all. I'm sure everything will be all right."

The lush green grass was dotted by white monuments standing like soldiers in a row. A freshly dug hole was the only variance in the green covering. Not even a dandelion dared raise its golden head to give a spot of color. Two men stood next to the empty grave. A very plain black box rested on the straps stretched across the grave. Laura assumed the body of Jeb Little was inside that box, waiting his final resting place.

"I'll be right here where I can see everyone and everyone can see me," said Todd as he leaned against his cruiser, which he parked near the hearse. "If I feel it's necessary, I'll move in closer. If you want me, just nod, or wave, toward me."

"Thanks, Todd. I'm sure everything will be all right, but I do feel better knowing you're here." She walked across the carpet of green toward the two men standing at the gravesite with as much confidence as she could muster.

"Good morning. I'm Reverend Kenzel." Laura stepped up to the man she assumed to be Ed Winters. He was dressed in the conservative black suit, white shirt, and gray/blue striped tie. His shoes shone as if they were glass and not a dark brown hair was out of place on his head. Cold, steel-gray eyes gave her a good going over, from head to toe and back. He smiled as he took her extended hand.

"Reverend Kenzel, it is so good to meet you at last." The voice was soft and syrupy, leaving Laura feeling the need for another shower to rid herself of the stickiness. Repressing a shudder, she pulled back her hand and placed it firmly around a tissue in her pocket.

Ed Winters turned to the man next to him. "This is Malcolm Atkins, my assistant. Actually, he's just learning the business. I think you know his cousin, Mike Atkins, the lawyer."

"Yes, I do. Good morning, Mr. Atkins." Laura didn't extend her hand. He looked as though he wouldn't have taken it if she had.

"My cousin tells me you're having a hard time adjusting to life in Cottonville. Most folks would've taken the hint and left by now." Malcolm Atkins' eyes were cold and calculating—just like his cousin's—and yet, that was the only resemblance Laura could determine. At least he didn't add the insincere smile. His voice was smooth as butter, but left no doubt in her mind as to the intent of his words. There was something familiar about his face. Had she met him before? He obviously didn't know her, or if he did, he didn't want to acknowledge it. She dismissed the idea. Probably looked like someone else she'd met.

"I guess I'm not most folks, Mr. Atkins," Laura said without a hint of a smile. She wouldn't let them frighten, or unnerve her.

Ed Winters' syrupy voice flowed into the conversation. "I'm so sorry about all the problems you seem to be having. I don't remember any other pastor having so much trouble." His smile didn't change, but the implication was clear.

Laura could plaster a smile on her face, too, when it was necessary. "That's probably true, Mr. Winters. My guess is it has something to do with the fact that no one else stayed around long enough to have any problems."

Laura saw a flicker of something in Malcolm Atkins's eyes— malice? hatred? fear? She decided it would be best to change the subject. "Is there anything I need to know for this service, Mr. Winters? Do you have any information about the man? Family? Friends? Religious affiliations?"

Mr. Winters looked relieved for the conversation to be moving in a safer direction. "Actually we know very little about him. You've probably heard he was a drifter, only been around for a few months."

Laura stared, neither acknowledging, nor ignoring his words. He continued unaware Laura caught him in an intentional miscalculation of time.

"We know of no family. I checked with Todd. He hadn't heard anything. Jeb stayed pretty much to himself, so I don't expect any friends to show up. His only friends were those two cats, which I understand you have now. Even they didn't like him very much. He kept them tied and muzzled like they were dogs. If he ever went to church anywhere, I don't know about it. I go to the Trinity Presbyterian Church and he never came there. My neighbor goes to the Mt. Carmel Baptist Church. He said Jeb never went there. The Methodists haven't had many services since he came into town, so I guess he didn't go there."

"Mr. Winters, if no family or friends are coming, then why can't we get started now? It's almost nine o'clock." She checked her watch as she spoke.

"Well...eh...there is...eh...one other person coming."

"Oh? And who might that be?"

"Mike Atkins...Since he's the only lawyer in town...eh...we...that is...I thought he should be here."

"Why on earth would we need a lawyer here for a graveside service for a man who is unknown, except for his name, which may or may not be correct?" Laura tried not to let her exasperation show. He was stalling. Why? To make her late for her appointment with SaraBelle Cotton?

"Well...eh...you know...eh...just in case." Beads of perspiration began to pop out on his upper lip and across his forehead. Ed Winters took his forefinger and pulled at his collar, as if it had suddenly become too tight. It wasn't that warm. There was a nice breeze blowing, typical of early May.

"In case of what?" Laura continued to stare at him.

"Well…eh…in case…in case…a relative shows up later and wants to know…everything…was…eh…you know."

"No, I don't know." Laura didn't bother to hide the anger building within her. She could feel the color rise in her cheeks and it had nothing to do with heat.

"They might want…to make sure…"

"Mr. Winters," Laura interrupted him, "what time do you expect Mr. Atkins to arrive?"

"Oh, he should be here any minute." He couldn't look her in the eyes. Laura knew he was lying.

"I see. In other words, ten o'clock."

"Well, I did ask you…"

Laura took a deep breath and measured her words like they were drops of water in a desert wilderness. "And I did tell you ten o'clock would not fit in my schedule. We will either do this service now, this very minute, or I will turn around and walk right back to Chief William's car and be on my way." As she spoke, Laura turned and waved toward the car where Todd stood watching. He immediately began walking with a long loping stride toward them.

"Is there a problem, Reverend Kenzel?

"Todd. It is good to see you. Haven't seen you for…" Ed Winters tried to side-track the conversation.

"It seems," Laura interrupted as rudely as she knew how, "that I have been lied to—again."

"Now, wait a minute. I didn't…"

"No, you wait a minute, Mr. Winters," Laura didn't raise her voice, but there was no question as to her anger. "I told you I could not do a service at ten o'clock and you said nine would be all right. Now you tell me we have to wait until ten for Mr. Atkins to get here. What I want to know, Mr. Winters, is why are you stalling and why don't you want me to see SaraBelle Cotton?"

"Reverend Kenzel, I don't know what you're talking about. I never said anything about a nine o'clock service and…"

"Hold it right there Ed," said Todd. "I've known you a long

time and always considered you an honest, upright citizen, but you are lying. Detective Morgan and I were at Reverend Kenzel's house when you called last night. I know what was said. Now *I* want to know why you're stalling."

"Todd, you're mistaken. I didn't say…"

"Mr. Winters, it is nine fifteen," said Laura checking her watch again. "Once again I ask, do you want me to do this service, or not? If you do then, please get out of my way and let me do it. The poor man might not have had a decent life, but at least let me give him a little dignity in death."

"You heard the lady," said Todd, standing with feet apart, thumbs hooked over his belt. He stared hard at Ed Winters, who looked miserable and stepped aside. There was nothing else he could do. Had they been watching Malcolm Atkins as closely as they did Ed Winters, they would have seen him move to his car and pick up his car phone.

"We'll talk more about this, Winters," said Todd as he followed Laura to the edge of the grave. She stood for a minute or two with her eyes closed, willing herself to be calm. Then she opened her Book of Services and began: "This Service of Committal is offered in the name of God, Father, Son, and Holy Spirit. Amen. In the midst of life we are in death; from whom can we seek help…" She continued through the service for death and resurrection from her Book of Worship finishing with a prayer, the committal, and the benediction. "And now may the blessing of Almighty God, Father, Son, and Holy Spirit, be among us and remain with us now and always. Amen."

The service thus ended, Laura turned to Todd. "Let's get out of here."

They made their way back to the cruiser without stopping to chat, or say goodbye to Ed Winters, or his assistant Malcolm Atkins, who stood smirking beside the car.

"Reverend Kenzel, you forgot your check." Ed Winters ran after them waving the check like a truce flag. Catching up with them at the car, he handed her the check for one thousand dollars and stood back glaring at her as she glanced at it. Had the check been in an envelope, Laura would have put it in her pocket and opened it later when she was alone. It made no difference to her what the amount was, or even if the envelope contained a check at all. This check was not in an envelope and it was given to her with the intent of her reading it immediately. She could read the intended message as clearly as if it had been written in bold red letters across the face of the check. "Take the money and run."

Laura didn't think it was possible for her anger to be any greater, but she saw red before her eyes—and it was more than just the intended red ink. Todd looked at her anxiously. He had seen her angry before, but she was beyond anger. She was livid. Eyes narrowed and jaws clenched firmly together, she sucked in enough air to calm her so she could speak. Ed Winters stood before her as if hypnotized, unable to either move, or speak. Fear popped out in great drops of perspiration on his temples. Color drained from his face. Whether his fear was directed at Laura, or some unseen person, she didn't know, nor did she care.

"What is it?" Todd asked.

She held the check for him to see, then began systematically tearing it into tiny little pieces. Speaking through clenched teeth, she said in a slow measured tone. "Mr. Winters, I don't know what this is all about, but I am not stupid. No graveside service is worth this much money. I don't know who wants to get rid of me, or why, but if I were not a Christian, I would tell you what you could do with this check. I don't even have the words in my vocabulary to express the anger I am feeling, so I will simply tell you to gather up all these little pieces and take them back to whomever bought you off and don't you *ever* try anything like this with me again."

Laura released him from her stare and turned back to the car. She got in without another glance at Ed Winters or Malcolm Atkins, who had joined them. She closed the door as gently as she could. She would not stoop to slamming it. Todd got in and turned the key. He glanced at her from the corner of his eye trying to hide the smile that threatened to slide across his face. As he drove toward the exit, he asked, "Are you all right?"

Laura stared straight ahead. She struggled to push the anger back into its little box for safe-keeping. The unwanted emotion refused to be tucked away so easily. Finally winning the battle, Laura whispered, "I'm sorry, Todd. I shouldn't have lost my temper that way. It wasn't very Christian of me, much less ladylike."

"Laura!" Todd exploded into laughter. When he could stop laughing Todd said, "The jerk asked for it. I was ready to deck him myself. You did it much more effectively and I didn't get in trouble for police brutality. I definitely will talk to him later. He knows something and I want to know what. Now, let's get you home."

Todd's laughter brought a smile to Laura's lips. "I guess you're right, Todd, but that doesn't excuse my behavior."

"Well, at least you didn't slam my car door. It took a lot of self-control to close it as gently as you did." He flashed his boyish grin at her.

"Well, it wasn't the car's fault."

They drove in silence except for a chuckle now and then from Todd. Laura's thoughts raced ahead to her ten o'clock meeting. What could be so important that SaraBelle practically demanded Laura be there? Why did Ed Winters try to keep Laura away from SaraBelle?

Todd's phone chirped from his belt. "Yeah, Chief Williams here…Steve! What's up?…We're a couple of blocks away. Be there in about two minutes—or less."

He replaced the phone, switched on the siren and lights, and turned to Laura. "Hold on, we're going to move a little fast. We got more trouble at your place."

"What else can happen?" She didn't have time to even give it much consideration before they pulled into her drive and onto the grass. A fire truck sat in the drive way and Shebop was engulfed in black smoke.

"My car!" Laura jumped from the cruiser and ran toward her car. Two pair of hands grabbed her—Steve on one side and Todd on the other. They held her back. She was too shocked to even think of shedding tears. Feeling like a statue carved in marble, she heard Todd and Steve talking, but they sounded so far off.

"What happened?" asked Todd. "Did you see who did this?"

"Yeah, I saw them and I called the fire department immediately. I think everything's all right. It was only old rags and stuff under the car. The fire department got to it in time, but the car will need to be cleaned to get rid of the smoke and soot before she can drive it."

That brought Laura out of her trance. "But I have an appointment in fifteen minutes with SaraBelle Cotton. Someone sure is going to a lot of trouble to keep me from seeing that lady. I wonder who, or why."

Todd and Steve released her arms since she seemed to be thinking and talking rationally. Laura stared at the car for a minute and glanced at her watch. What were her alternatives? Coming to a decision, she looked from Todd to Steve and asked, "Could one of you to drop me off at Mrs. Cotton's house? It's not that far, but I don't want to be late. I'll walk home."

Without a moment's hesitation, Steve replied, before Todd could answer. "Give me the keys to your car and take mine." He reached into his pocket and pulled out his own keys and extended his hand for her to take them. "It's parked up the street from the church. I'll walk you to it then I'll take your car to J B's Body Shop to get it cleaned up before you get back."

"I couldn't do that." Laura looked like he had offered her his life, instead of his car. Instinctively she pulled her hands back behind her.

"You got something against Buicks?" Steve asked as seriously as he could around the grin twitching the corners of his mouth.

"No, but, what if…"

He took her arm and started walking toward the street. "No what ifs. Just take it and go. I have a lot to talk to Todd about and I have a feeling he has something about his morning's experience to share with me. Don't be in a hurry. I can pick the car up at noon, or later tonight, or even tomorrow. There's plenty of gas in it if you want to just drive around to clear your head after you talk to Mrs. Cotton."

He let go of her arm once they were on the sidewalk in front of the church. She was still hesitant, but she was only going up on the hill across town—not more than two miles round trip. Surely, she couldn't hurt his car in that short time. Could she?

Steve took her hand and placed the keys in it, then closed her fingers around them. "You can't hurt it," he said as if he had read her mind. "It's only a car."

Laura grasped the keys and looked into those twinkling blue eyes. Finally, she lowered her gaze, feeling that familiar rush of color to her cheeks. "Thanks," she muttered, wanting to say more, but feeling her voice choking up again. "I really owe you one."

"Don't worry about it. Todd and I will collect your thanks in coffee sometime. If you want to go for a drive, do it. Todd and I'll go to Charlie's for lunch. We can all get together later this afternoon. So, like I said, don't be in a hurry. Take some time to relax and think if you want to."

He opened the door for her. "Have fun," he said as she slid in under the steering wheel. He closed the door and waited for her to acquaint herself with all the necessary features. She turned the key. He stepped aside as she glided into the street. She wouldn't tell Shebop, but it sure felt nice driving a big car. She glanced in the rearview mirror and saw Steve still watching her. Was he concerned about her, or his car? "Lord, don't let me put a scratch on it." The soft mirthful feeling enveloped her soul.

24

Laura drove past the monument to Charlie Cotton noting a number of cars and pedestrians in the downtown area. Then she remembered. Today was Friday—gathering day in small towns. Maybe she would walk downtown and shop a little this afternoon.

She turned left and went around Cotton Lake and started up Cotton Hill to SaraBelle Cotton's mansion. She wasn't concerned about the wealth of Mrs. Cotton as much as she was the attitude. She wouldn't tolerate anyone ordering, or threatening, her, not even this town's richest resident.

One more worry to add to her list. Things weren't bad enough, now she had to cater to an elderly, eccentric woman with an attitude. And as much as she appreciated Todd and Steve, she felt her hard-gained independence slipping into interdependence. She'd determined she would never *need* anyone's help again. If she couldn't do it herself, it wouldn't get done. So why did she allow Todd to help her this morning, and why was she driving Steve's car now?

The soft mirth in her soul didn't do much to relieve her anxieties. "God, what are You getting me into?" Her only answer was what felt like laughter.

Laura was glad she had only a few minutes with her tumbling, rolling questions. Already she was winding her way up the long cement driveway, easing around the curve by the front door.

A mild headache pricked at her temples as she stopped in front of the towering white Southern-style mansion. The grounds were well manicured, sporting shrubs and flowers of many varieties. A stone path meandered around the side of the house.

Laura's disturbing thoughts stopped as she turned the key to the off position. Sighing, she opened the door and stepped onto the cement. Another deep breath cleared her mind. She closed the car door and unlike Shebop, it made a soft swishing sound and an even softer click.

Massive white columns stood guard at the entrance which was overwhelmingly bright in the morning sun. Laura found the doorbell hidden among the intricate designs of burnished brass on either side of the door. She pressed her finger against the soft red glow from the inner most circle of one of the designs and heard the chiming answer deep within the inner workings of the house.

Laura stepped back to wait for the door to open. With a house this size and the money SaraBelle Cotton was purported to have, she assumed there would be at least a maid, and possibly a butler. The tall young man who answered the door was certainly neither. His jeans were tattered. The T-shirt sported a picture which Laura didn't understand—nor did she think she wanted to understand it. Somehow, this man didn't fit in with her picture of the eccentric woman. He looked to be about eighteen, or so—although he could have been older. Laura began to wonder if she had the wrong house. SaraBelle had no children and certainly none this age.

"Yeah?" The young man glared at her.

Laura took an instant disliking to him—something she hardly ever did. The feeling of animosity surprised her so much that she had to concentrate in order to even sound civil, much less friendly. "Good morning. I'm Reverend Kenzel. I was to meet with Mrs. Cotton at ten o'clock. I realize I'm a few minutes early, but…"

"Reverend Kenzel? Oh, yeah. I know who you are. I'm Horace Cotton—great nephew of the great SaraBelle Cotton." He half sneered as he emphasized his aunt's name. The smell of alcohol permeated the air every time he exhaled. Bloodshot eyes peered at her from half-closed lids. She wasn't sure she even wanted to be in the same house with the strange young man. The eerie foreboding became so strong she was tempted to run back to the safety of Steve's Buick. However, she would not leave without seeing the woman she came to see.

"May I come in?" Laura still stood outside the door and half expected him to say no.

"Come in if you want to, but I don't know why you're here. I'm getting ready to take Aunt SaraBelle to Glenville to get her hair done."

"She called me yesterday and asked me to come this morning at ten." Eccentric old lady or not, why would she call and demand a command performance and then make arrangements to go somewhere else?

"Well, you know how old ladies are." His laugh wasn't very pleasant. He seemed to find a special delight in breathing his alcoholic breath near Laura's face. She clenched her fists and clamped her jaws in an effort to ignore his rudeness, and keep her own temper under control.

The voice of an elderly woman—SaraBelle, Laura assumed—called from the adjoining room. "Who is it Horace?"

"No one, Auntie. Just a salesman. I told her you don't want nothing."

"Horace is correct, young lady." The voice now spoke beside her as the old woman walked briskly into the room.

Laura turned to see a little woman who couldn't have been much more that five feet tall and weighed about as much as her age of ninety-one. Her gray hair was arranged in short, waves all around her face. She wore stylish, wire framed glasses which did not hide the snapping dark eyes. She was dressed in a smart-looking tailored pantsuit of bright red. This woman might have a few years of age behind her, but she definitely lived in the present.

"I don't buy from door to door sales persons. So just take

whatever you have and get off my property before I call Chief Williams to come and throw you off. Didn't you see the signs posted? No solicitors."

Laura pulled her gaze from SaraBelle to Horace who stood behind SaraBelle with his hand over his mouth, snickering at his little practical joke. Laura glared at him, her hand itching to slap the silly smirk off his face.

"Mrs. Cotton, I think your nephew is playing a joke on you." Laura surprised herself. She was able to keep her tone even and civil. "I'm Reverend Kenzel. You called and asked me to come by today."

Deep color rose in SaraBelle's cheeks. "Horace! How dare you treat my pastor like that!"

Horace laughed that nasty laugh Laura was beginning to get used to—and hate at the same time.

"She don't need to see you, Auntie. You're good enough. Besides you do have an appointment in Glenville in an hour. It will take us forty-five minutes to get there unless we get held up somewhere. Then it'll take longer."

"Horace is right, young lady. When your secretary called and said you couldn't make it I had him call and make an appointment for me to get my hair done. Serves you right for canceling and then coming anyway, expecting me to welcome you with open arms."

A smile spread across Laura's face and the furrows of worry faded. The whole conversation was so ridiculous, she could hardly believe it. Someone must be awfully stupid or desperate and this eccentric old woman knew nothing about the plot to keep them apart.

"Well, I'm glad you find it so amusing." SaraBelle sniffed with a hint of amusement in her eyes.

Laura reached over and laid her hand on SaraBelle's arm. "I'm sorry, but with all the things that have happened to me in the last two and a half days, I was beginning to feel very old and worn out. It was good to hear someone call me *young lady*."

"Well, young lady," SaraBelle said it again just to see that beautiful smile. She returned Laura's smile, "everyone is young compared to my ninety-one years." Then she laughed a mirthful, sort of cackle.

"But not everyone has the health and stamina you have. God has blessed you abundantly, Mrs. Cotton, I can tell that. But I'm confused. You said my secretary called?"

"That's right. She called about nine o'clock this morning. Didn't give me much notice." SaraBelle narrowed her eyes and tried to act stern.

"Mrs. Cotton, I don't have a secretary. I'm not even sure if I have an office at the church. I haven't had time yet to go over and see what's there."

Laura's confusion caused SaraBelle to lift her eyebrows, creasing her forehead. "What happened to Dorothy? She used to be the secretary, although the woman who called didn't sound like Dorothy."

"I met Dorothy the other night at the church. Martha Jennings invited her to take notes. She said she stopped coming because of the noises. She's coming back next week."

"Then who called me?"

"I wish I knew. It seems someone's been trying very hard all morning to keep us from getting together."

"Why would anyone not want us to meet? And who?"

"I don't have a clue. I hoped you would have some ideas."

Horace had been leaning against the wall cleaning his fingernails with what looked like a hunting knife. He gave the appearance of not paying any attention to the women, but Laura was certain he weighed every word and the look on his face told her he didn't like what he heard. Suddenly he pushed himself away from his support and spoke sharply to SaraBelle as if he needed to remind her of everything. "Auntie, we got to get going if you're going to make that appointment. You know how Shirley gets when you make an appointment and then don't get there on time."

Laura had a brilliant thought—at least she hoped it was a brilliant idea. "Why don't I take you to Glenville, Mrs. Cotton? We can talk on the way. I'll do some shopping while you get your hair done. Then Horace can get back to school, or wherever."

Horace snorted. "I ain't going to school. I got suspended."

"Oh? That's too bad, Horace."

"Don't matter to me. I have enough to keep me busy here. But we're wasting time. Come on, Auntie, let's go." He grabbed SaraBelle by the elbow and started to force her toward the door.

"Young man, you take your hands off me this instant." SaraBelle didn't raise her voice. She didn't have to. Her cold tone would have frozen him like a winter storm if he hadn't dropped her arm. Laura didn't know a small, frail-looking lady could sound so emphatic. Horace apparently hadn't seen that side of her either.

SaraBelle glared at Horace. "You've been drinking again. Go sleep it off. Reverend Kenzel has graciously offered to drive me to Glenville. I'll not insult her generosity by refusing. Tell cook not to expect me for lunch, or dinner. We might just make a day of it."

She turned from her nephew, dismissing him from her sight and mind, and took Laura's arm. "Come along, my dear. I have a feeling you have a lot to tell me. From what I hear a lot of terrible things have happened to you since you arrived in Cottonville."

If Laura expected to walk slowly and coddle this nonagenarian, she was in for a surprise. SaraBelle was out the door and waiting for her beside the car by the time she stepped from the porch.

"This is a mighty fancy looking car for a young lady pastor," SaraBelle remarked as Laura opened the door for her.

Laura ran around to the other side and opened the door and slid in under the steering wheel. "Oh, it's not mine," she said. "Chief Williams took me to a brief graveside service this morning and when I got back from the cemetery, black smoke was rolling out from under my car. Someone stuffed old rags soaked in something under it and set fire to them. A friend offered me this one."

"Well, it's good you have friends. Sounds like you need some good folks on your side if all I hear is true. Doesn't this car belong to Detective Morgan from Glenville?" SaraBelle gave Laura a sly look.

Laura was surprised. "Well, yes. I didn't know you knew him."

SaraBelle laughed a cackling sound of genuine mirth unlike the artificial, nasty sound Laura had heard so much of lately. "I don't know him, but I know of him. All the single women—and some married ones too—who come into Shirley's go on and on about how handsome he is and how he avoids women. Never heard anything bad about him."

"I've really appreciated having him and Chief Williams on my side the last few days." Laura tried to ignore the slight blush she felt rising in her cheeks. She knew SaraBelle saw it and would assume the worst—or best, depending on her point of view.

SaraBelle laughed merrily again and said no more about Detective Morgan. "Now, young lady, we have about forty-five minutes to solve this mystery. So let's get started by calling me SaraBelle, not Mrs. Cotton. That sounds so stuffy. Tell me everything you know, what all has happened, and why you came here. Don't leave anything out."

Laura sighed and smiled at SaraBelle, who sounded genuinely interested. She started with her long drive from Illinois and the conversation with Nancy. She continued to tell her about the burglary, finding the dead man in her garage, the cats in the belfry, and the spray paint on her car. She glanced sideways at SaraBelle, who listened intently. She told her that someone took a shot at Steve after the meeting at the church and about Jerome's beating. Then she explained the preventative measures to keep them from meeting—Ed Winters, the car fire, and finally Horace's seemingly small part.

When SaraBelle finally spoke, she was very serious. "Reverend Kenzel, you are either a very brave woman, or a very foolish one. Most men would have left after the first threat—and did, for that matter. What I want to know is why you stayed with such odds against you?"

Laura glanced at her, then back at the road. She saw in her eyes the honest search for truth and answered very quietly, "SaraBelle, my friends call me Laura. I was not prepared for my husband's death—not that we are ever prepared for the death of a spouse, but I was determined to become independent. I turned my back on people who wanted to help me. I ignored my only source of comfort—my God. But He didn't ignore me. He waited for my acute grief and anger to abate and then He told me loud and clear what I was to do.

"When I heard about this place, I knew I would go even before the bishop appointed me. I've told my district superintendent—he tried to get me to leave after someone called him—I told him neither he, nor the bishop, sent me here. God did. And here I will stay until God tells me to go. The only way I can do what I have done, and what I will do, is through the grace of God. I'm not a brave woman. I'm scared to death. A fool, maybe," she flashed a smile at SaraBelle, "but didn't Paul say we should be fools for Christ?"

"That's what I wanted to hear," said SaraBelle. "I believe you and I believe I know at least one person who's behind some of these things, but I don't know why. Why don't I tell you...what was that?"

A small ping sounded from the hood of the car. Then, suddenly, Laura's side window shattered. What sounded like a giant bug whistled through the opening and SaraBelle's window also shattered into the proverbial million pieces.

"Someone is shooting at us," said SaraBelle.

"Duck down in your seat," yelled Laura. "I think he just hit a back tire. I'll try to keep us on the road. See if you can use that car phone and call for help."

SaraBelle obeyed without question. She grabbed the phone as she slid down into the seat as far as possible. She might be ninety-one years old, but at one hundred pounds, she was small, quick, and agile when she needed to be. Laura heard her dialing, but had to keep all her concentration on keeping the car on the road. They were on Gopher Mountain Road with all its deadly curves, fifteen miles-per-hour speed limit, and no guardrails. It was a long way to the bottom of the mountain from anywhere on the road without much to stop a moving vehicle except a few small trees. She felt another tire go—a front one this time. Steering became more difficult. If he hit the gas tank...but she wouldn't let herself think about that. She would have to do the best she could.

"O God," Laura prayed, "don't let us down now. I'm doing all I can, but I can't keep it on the road much longer. Whatever happens, help Todd and Steve find the people behind this."

"We're going over the edge," Laura said. "I can't guide it anymore. The tires won't turn."

SaraBelle removed her glasses, closed her eyes, and made herself as limp as possible. The car bounced off the road, followed by a crash that shook the car and inflated the air bags.

25

"SaraBelle?" Laura sent out a tentative inquiry, not even sure if she spoke aloud or if the words were simply echoes in her frightened mind. SaraBelle didn't answer. Laura felt the air bag begin to deflate like a huge balloon with a long slow hiss, relaxing the uncomfortable pressure against her chest. If only the fear and pain that gripped her mind and body could evaporate as easily.

She was alive, but what about SaraBelle? "Oh, Lord, don't let me face another dead body." She slowly turned toward SaraBelle, not sure what would meet her eyes. It probably wouldn't be good, but she had to know the truth.

SaraBelle also waited for the giant balloon to release her, hoping and praying that Laura was still alive. She, too, was afraid to speak for fear there would be no answer. "God," she prayed, "it's not fair for this brave lady to have to endure so much. She's a good woman and You brought her here to help us. Now, keep her alive long enough to do it."

SaraBelle had no trouble rebuking anyone, including God. She always said she and God had an understanding—she could say what she pleased and God would do as He pleased. While she had a close relationship with her God, SaraBelle never had fanciful thoughts, visions, or audible suggestions in her religious life. However, at that moment she could have sworn—had she been a

204

swearing lady—she heard a voice say something to the effect that, "Laura Kenzel is in My hands. She has some lessons to learn and some lives to touch before this case is closed."

Both air bags deflated, Laura and SaraBelle looked at each other. SaraBelle tried to smile. Her glasses were gone and a slow trickle of blood oozed from her nose. She raised a hand to touch the lump rising above the corner of her eye. It wasn't as large as she thought. It was probably beginning to turn a nasty shade of red or purple. She winced and tried to put on her best confident manner for Laura's sake. Since she couldn't see much without her glasses, she assumed her preacher looked about the same as she felt, except she could sense Laura's guilt, remorse, and fear.

The poor dear probably feels responsible for wrecking Morgan's car and half-killing me. Just wait until I get my hands on that sniper. But there was no time for pity-parties. SaraBelle cleared her throat and spoke in her best I'm-in-charge, matter-of-fact voice. "Well, young lady, I think we're alive, thanks to your superb job of guiding this tank."

Laura tried to laugh, but the sound caught in her throat and sounded more like a sob. "I'm afraid I didn't do it all by myself. I don't know how we stayed on the road as long as we did. Do you know where we are? We can't be at the bottom of the mountain. I think we hit a boulder."

"I can't see a thing without my glasses," said SaraBelle. "I know you're there because I see a form and some movement and hear your voice. If you can help me find my glasses, I'll take a look." SaraBelle patted the seat between her, searching for her glasses. "I took them off when we started over the edge and laid them on the seat. I didn't want glass in my eyes, you know."

SaraBelle's everything-is-normal attitude made Laura laugh through her pain. She helped SaraBelle look for them. Sure enough, the glasses were safely tucked in the crack between the soft seats. She handed them to SaraBelle who placed them on her face with a grimace.

"Humph!" SaraBelle snorted. "If I don't look any better than you, we certainly won't win any beauty contests. Now, we're alive, but I don't think we're out of danger. Do you think any of your bones are broken? I seem to be intact—a little scrambled maybe, but nothing feels broken." She had been flexing and stretching her arms and legs and moving her head from side to side as she talked.

"I think some ribs are either bruised or fractured, but I can move my legs and arms. My left arm hurts, but it moves." Laura also tentatively moved her limbs and head. "How well do you know this road, SaraBelle?" she asked.

"As well as anyone. I used to walk to Glenville in my younger days. There was a boulder about the size of a small shed we used to climb on and sit to rest awhile on our way to and from Glenville. We called it the Bethel Boulder because it reminded us of Jacob and God's promise to be with him. It's the only place like it on Gopher Mountain. Looks like God led us to the right place to stop." SaraBelle laughed her soft cackling laugh.

"I think you're right. I noticed the boulder the other day. It's not very far off the road. Todd won't have any trouble finding us. If that sniper's still up there, he won't have any trouble finding us either. We don't want to get out of the car and let him know we're still alive. Maybe we should try the phone again. Let Todd and Steve know where we are. I hear sirens."

SaraBelle took the phone and pushed the emergency button, which dialed 911 immediately. Suddenly, her bravado slipped and her hands began shaking. She couldn't hold the phone still, so she handed it to Laura. Todd was trying to get an answer, "Hello...Hello...Who is this?

Laura could hear the panic in his voice, but she was having a hard time finding her own voice. Between the panic, the pain, and the dryness in her throat, she couldn't immediately get a sound past the lump in her throat.

"Todd." She finally made a sound more like a croak.

"Laura? Is that you? Where are you? What's happening?"

Before she could answer Todd, Steve apparently took the phone from him. "Laura? Are you all right? Where are you?" Was he excited? Anxious? Angry? She couldn't tell.

"Steve?" Her mind felt a fuzzy. Thoughts wouldn't focus. How could she tell him she wrecked his car?

"Laura, where are you?"

She gulped back the knot in her throat that threatened to cut off her breath as well as her sound. "Do you know Bethel Boulder?"

"We're almost there."

"We…we…crashed into it."

"You *what*?" She could hear the panic—or was it anger—in his voice. "Are you all right?"

"I think so." The tears would no longer stay back. The strain of the last two days came crashing in on her as surely as Steve's Buick crashed into that boulder. Gulping a swallow of air she tried to continue. "…but, your car…I'm sorry…tried to keep…on the road."

"Laura, don't worry about the car. Hold on, we'll be there in less than three minutes."

"Steve?" No matter how much it hurt, she had to warn him. "Yes?"

"We were shot at…sniper might still…be out there…and when you get here…act as if SaraBelle didn't make it."

"Laura, have you completely lost your mind?"

"No." She was gaining a little more control of her voice as long as she stayed with facts. "But, if he's still there, we don't want him to finish the job…SaraBelle has information…and he knows it…Please, Steve, humor me…I've really had about all I can take of this mess." The pool of tears once again started their relentless trail down her face.

"We can fake it if we need to. Hold on a couple more minutes."

SaraBelle listened with interest to the one-sided conversation. Steve? Now, that's very interesting. He lends her his car. She calls him Steve. Has our unapproachable detective been snagged?

When Laura replaced the phone, SaraBelle reached over and squeezed her hand. "There, there child, everything's going to be all right." She tried to laugh, but only gave a hoarse kind of sound. Still holding Laura's hand she said, "Our God certainly has a great sense of humor."

Laura surprised by her words, glanced up at her questioningly.

"Well, He does," went on SaraBelle. "Think about it. First, He sends us a woman preacher—no offense there. Then, He sends an old lady and that same green preacher on a joy ride in a big fancy car and then brings us crashing into the only boulder on this entire mountain. Do you realize what we would look like if we had been in your little Chevette? Oh, yes, I know your car," she said in response to the surprised look on Laura's face. "Or, if we had gone off at any other point on this road there wouldn't be much left of us, big car or not. And besides that," she cackled again and continued in a conspiratorial tone, "I've never known Steve Morgan to even give a woman the time of day, much less the keys to his car." She winked, or tried to, at Laura. Her swollen eyes made it an interesting gesture.

Laura really looked surprised and dazed. "I understand the sense of humor, but a flat tire somewhere could have been a lot safer." Laura's tone was more than a little sarcastic.

"Sure," cackled SaraBelle, "but there's more adventure this way. For an old lady in Cottonville, there isn't much chance for adventure these days."

Laura had to laugh, and immediately grabbed her ribs and winced.

"By the way," said SaraBelle, "that was a smart idea, making that sniper think he got us. Now, we only have about a minute before help gets here. When we get to the hospital, this is what I want you to do." And she quickly laid out a plan that caused Laura to gasp, but she had no chance to answer because screaming sirens whined to a stop just above them on the road.

Laura reached to open the car door when she heard someone sliding down the hill. The door opened and she was in Steve's arms before she knew what was happening. The tears kept rolling in spite of her resolve not to be a weepy woman. "Steve...I'm sorry...your car...SaraBelle..." She wasn't coherent, but the words just wouldn't come out right. The pain made it difficult to breathe and another strange emotion she felt with his arms around her added to her confusion. It threatened to take her breath away completely and yet it felt so comfortable that she could have stayed there forever.

"Laura, cars can be replaced. I hate to think of the outcome if you had been driving your car. I'm glad it was mine." She started to protest.

"Never mind," he said as he caressed her hair away from the angry red lump above her eye. For a brief second she thought he might kiss it. "We'll sort it all out later. The ambulance is here. Let's get you ladies to the hospital."

While Steve helped Laura, the paramedics went to the passenger side and lifted SaraBelle onto the gurney, but not before she observed the scene between her pastor and Detective Morgan. She smiled to herself and tucked the picture away in a special place in her heart. She hoped she lived long enough to see the outcome of this strange, budding romance. She loved happy endings.

"Come on," said Steve. With his arm around Laura's waist, he helped her up the hill. "You can sit in the back of the ambulance with Mrs. Cotton and Burt."

"No. I'll ride with you and Todd. We need to talk."

"Laura, you're hurt. You need to…" Steve stopped. He saw the clenched fists and the set of her jaw. He'd seen it before and while he had known her only a short time, he knew he would only waste precious time if he tried to argue with her. "At least let them check you over first." He nodded to Joe who put the blood pressure cuff on her and checked her eyes, and asked pertinent questions.

"Blood pressure's a little high. Vision seems clear. Should be all right to go with you. Follow us and don't try to be heroic and fly on these curves." Joe grinned at Steve, then closed the back door of the ambulance and jumped onto the driver's seat. He hit the siren and lights and took off for Cottonville Community Hospital.

Steve opened the passenger side of the front for Laura. "I think I could talk to both of you better if I sat in the back. It hurts to turn around, like I would have to do in the front."

"Laura, if you hurt that bad, you should have gone…"

She didn't let Steve finish. "We're wasting time."

"All right." He opened the back door and helped her in. Then he went around and got in beside her. "You don't mind if I sit beside you do you? Now, let's have the facts, ma'am." He winked at her and she returned his smile, then told Todd and Steve what had happened from the time she arrived at SaraBelle's to the crash. She told them SaraBelle's plan to make everyone think she was nearly dead. Laura would continue to be stubborn about leaving Cottonville. The hope was that the person in charge would show his hand and try to make her leave. They were pretty sure Horace was the only one who knew she was driving SaraBelle to Glenville in Steve's car.

"I don't like it. You both could be killed," Steve said after she explained SaraBelle's plan.

"We almost were," she reminded him. "And it isn't going to stop until we can come up with some hard evidence to convict whoever is behind it all."

"She's right, Steve. I don't like it either, but I don't think we have any alternative at this point. We'll have Doctor Cornelius keep both of them in the hospital for a couple of days with no visitors and…"

"No," Laura was emphatic and a note of panic made her voice sharp. "I will not stay in the hospital. The whole plan depends on me staying at home and being my old stubborn self. Besides," she added, "I have two cats at home that need me." She tried to laugh, but grabbed her ribs and clenched teeth to keep back the tears. Taking as deep a breath as she could, she said, "I feel like Jerome. It hurts to laugh."

"Then don't." Steve and Todd both spoke together.

"I don't think you'll have any trouble convincing anyone you are your stubborn self," Steve said half under his breath.

"Very funny," she said.

He smiled at her.

26

Joe killed the lights and siren as he eased the ambulance to the emergency doors. Nurses and orderlies rushed through the open doors to take the gurney with SaraBelle back to the row of examining rooms. Todd pulled the cruiser around the ambulance and stopped. He and Steve jumped from the car at the same time to help Laura. Steve opened her door while Todd went for a wheelchair. Laura clenched her teeth and stood at the curb as he returned with it.

"I don't need that. I'm not helpless," she snapped at them, pain clouding her thinking. She was determined to take care of herself. Todd glanced at Steve. Steve smiled, picked her up, and put her in the chair.

"What do you think you're doing?" Laura didn't raise her voice, but her eyes snapped and her jaws clenched.

"It's apparent your stubborn self is in control and your rational self is out to lunch," answered Steve. "This is no time for an argument, so just sit back and enjoy the ride." Steve then proceeded to wheel her into the ER and down the hall to the room appointed for her.

Laura still fighting her jumble of emotions kept her teeth clenched so she wouldn't say things she would later regret. She knew he was right, and it made her even angrier that he was. She also knew she couldn't easily get out of the chair without a lot of pain. Besides that, the sounds and smells sent a flutter of panic to her aching mind. Now she had to fight off a panic attack as well as her other fears.

"God, what are You doing to me? How can I help others, when I can't even help myself?" A soothing feeling in her soul let her know that God was there, but she still had to suffer on her own.

In the eight by ten foot cubicle they called an examination room, the nurse asked her to get on what looked to her like a very narrow bed made of stainless steel—or a morgue slab. Of course it was covered with the traditional white. Laura froze. She closed her eyes and fell back into the chair to catch her breath and wait for the pain to abate. She felt Steve's arms around her once more, as he lifted her from the chair to the table/bed.

Steve ignored the nurse, who waited to tend her patient. He stayed beside Laura, his hand on her arm until her muscles began to relax. When she seemed to be breathing more normally, he and Todd retreated to the waiting room and left Laura alone with the large woman in white whose dark skin stood out in stark contrast. With gentle hands she helped Laura into a hospital gown. Her gentleness sent the panic further into the shadows—at least for the time being.

"Do I really need to do this?" asked Laura. She tried not to sound too angry with this stranger who was only doing her job and trying to help her.

"It'll make it easier to get x-rays, and if you are admitted, you'll be all ready," the nurse answered flashing a broad smile at Laura.

"I won't be admitted," Laura stated.

The woman laughed. "Honey, I think the doctor has already decided you will."

"Then he can just undecide. I won't stay." Laura knew she was being obstinate, but spending a night in one of those small, white, antiseptic-smelling rooms was unthinkable.

"Why does everything take so long?" Laura asked when she returned from X-ray. Maggie, the nurse, took her blood pressure and checked her IV. "And why do I have to have this thing in my arm? What's in it? You aren't putting drugs in it are you?"

Maggie laughed a jolly laugh of a person who is content with her life. "You ask a lot of questions for someone who just tried to fight Gopher Mountain's Bethel Boulder and lost. But that's a good sign, Reverend. It means you can still think. It'll help you recover faster. The IV is to help with any dehydration and shock and it's in place if we need to give you any medication. We aren't giving you any yet, but it's available and will make it easier when we do. Doctor J should be here any minute. He's getting your friend admitted.

"Doctor J?"

Maggie laughed and explained why they called Doctor Jonathan Cornelius, Doctor J.

"Oh...Can I see SaraBelle? Is she all right?"

"She seems to be doing very well for a woman her age, but the doctor wants to keep her at least overnight. I'll see what I can do about getting you in to see her."

They heard footsteps and Maggie peeked around the curtain. "Looks like your friends are back. I'll leave you with them for a few minutes while I check for you."

"They're admitting SaraBelle," said Todd. "But she won't go to her room until she sees you. Doctor Cornelius will limit her visitors—especially not to include the nephew."

"That's good. I'll see her before I leave," said Laura.

Todd and Steve exchanged a meaningful glance. "I don't think you'll be going anywhere," said Steve.

"You want to bet?" She glared at him.

He smiled back at her. "No, I would probably lose, but you ought to stay at least overnight."

"I ought to get dressed and go home. I have things to do." She glanced around the room to see where they had put her clothes.

"Detective Morgan is right, Reverend Kenzel." Doctor Cornelius spoke as he came around the curtain that served as a door to the cubicle. He stood at the foot of her bed. "Mrs. Cotton is pretty shaken up, and so are you for that matter, but at her age we have a little more concern. She wants to see her pastor then I want her to sleep. Then we'll give you a shot to help you..."

213

"No! No shots. I just want to get dressed and get out of here." The panic rushed in once more and Laura fought to keep it at bay.

"Reverend Kenzel, you've had a severe trauma. You need to…"

"I need to get out of here. I'll be fine. I'll take a couple of aspirin when I get home. Now, if someone will give me my clothes and leave me alone, I'll get dressed and go see my parishioner."

"Can you guys talk some sense into her?" Doctor Cornelius looked first at Steve then Todd.

Steve recognized the signs and understood why she wanted out immediately. He moved to her side and took her hand. "Laura, you're all right. It's not the same, but you are shook up and close to shock."

Laura closed her eyes but squeezed Steve's hand. "I know," she whispered, "but…please…I can't stay…"

"She's right, Doctor," said Steve. "It's rather important for her. We'll make sure she gets home and right to bed."

Laura unable to speak squeezed his hand again to let him know she was grateful for his help.

Shaking his head Doctor Cornelius turned back to his patient. "Reverend Kenzel, I think you'll need something stronger than aspirin. If you won't let me give you a shot, then take these pain tablets. There's enough for three days. If you need more, let me know."

"Thank you, Doctor." She took the packet of pills from him. "Can I see Jerome for a few minutes? I told him I would see him today. He'll be worried if I don't."

"Reverend Kenzel, you need to go home and rest." Doctor Cornelius sounded like a stern, exasperated parent, but accepted defeat. He shook his head again and smiled. "It wouldn't do any good to say no. Go see him, but only for a few minutes. You really need to rest." He looked past her to Steve and Todd.

"Maggie, will you help Reverend Kenzel get dressed then take them to Mrs. Cotton's room?"

"Yes, Doctor." Maggie winked at Laura as she entered the room. "If you gentlemen will step outside, I'll have her ready to go in a few minutes."

"Thank you, Maggie."

"You're welcome, Reverend." She helped Laura get dressed then said, "Now, I know you don't want any help, but since you're going to visit a couple of folks, it might make for a long walk. I would suggest you let these gentlemen feel useful. You sit in the chair and let them push you."

"Thanks again, Maggie." Laura knew she didn't have the strength to walk to SaraBelle's examining room then up to Jerome's, but she would have refused an order to get in the wheelchair. Maggie seemed to know that, also. She pulled the curtain and asked Todd to bring a wheelchair that was beside the nurse's station.

"Now, be a good girl and let these fine gentlemen help you in the chair and save Maggie's poor back." She laughed and winked at Laura who smiled at her.

"Only for your back, Maggie," she said. Steve picked her up, put her in the wheelchair then they took her to see SaraBelle.

"I'm glad you weren't hurt much," said SaraBelle. "I was afraid for you and it would all be my fault. Please forgive the stubbornness of an old woman."

"SaraBelle, it wasn't your fault. I offered to take you to Glenville. Now don't worry about me. You rest and stay put for a few days until we can get this sorted out."

"Pastor?"

"Yes?"

"Thank you for being more stubborn than I am and for staying beyond all odds." Then she began to drift into sleep.

"See you tomorrow, SaraBelle."

"Hmmmm." And she was sound asleep.

They entered the elevator and rode to the second floor. "Do you mind if we tag along?" asked Steve as they came to Jerome's room.

"Are you afraid I'll do something stupid, like faint on his bed, or have hysterics?" She glared at them.

"No, nothing so dramatic. We just want to see Jerome, too," he said.

"Oh. I'm sorry. I'm not thinking too clearly."

"I wonder why?" Steve said as he wheeled her through the door.

Jerome sat up in his bed, looking a little less swollen. He grinned broadly as the three friends entered his room. Then his grin turned to a horrified, wide-eyed stare. "Pastor, what happened to you?" His voice was just above a whisper.

"Oh, you looked so handsome yesterday I thought I would see if it would help me to try your secret formula." She tried to sound teasing, but the words came out a little choked.

"Did they..." he couldn't finish.

"No, Jerome," said Todd. "She took Detective Morgan's car for a joyride with SaraBelle Cotton down Gopher Mountain and ran into a little boulder."

"You crashed into the Bethel Boulder?"

"I guess I did." Laura felt miserable and not just because of her injuries.

"Does it hurt much?" Jerome asked with genuine concern.

"A little—well, a lot if I laugh."

"I know what you mean." He paused. "Gee, that old Bethel Boulder would make kitty litter of your little car. Thank you, Detective Morgan, for letting her crash your car instead of hers."

Laura bit her lip. Steve said, "I'm glad it was my car, too, Jerome."

"We've all had a long day, sport," said Todd. "I think I hear your supper coming and we need to get your pastor home so she can rest. I'll see you later."

"Okay. Pastor?" Laura sensed that Jerome didn't know how to ask the grown-up question which would give him the assurance he needed. With teeth clenched, she pulled herself out of the chair to stand beside Jerome's bed. Ignoring her pain, she wrapped her arms around this little boy who had stolen her heart. She felt his tears on her shoulder and knew hers were running down their well worn path.

"I'm all right, Jerome," she whispered. "I'm in good hands. And so are you."

"I know," he whispered back, "and God gave us the chief and

Detective Morgan, too. So we're in lots of good hands."

"That's right. Now, I've got to go. See you tomorrow. Okay?"

"Okay, but Pastor…"

"Yes?"

"Try to stay out of trouble until I get out of here to help you." Then he giggled and held his side. She laughed and immediately wished she hadn't, but she wouldn't let him know how much she hurt. While Todd and Steve said their goodbyes, Laura stepped outside the room and leaned against the wall. She couldn't hold back the tears while she gasped for breath.

Laura still leaned against the side of the wall when she heard Todd and Steve behind her. Her breathing was coming a little easier, but she felt Steve's arms around her and let him help her into the chair without struggle. Maybe she should have stayed overnight, but she just couldn't face that possibility. Anyway her choice was made. She would live with it.

"Come on. Let's get you out of here," said Steve. "If Doctor Cornelius saw you now, you would be in a bed whether you wanted one or not." He wheeled her to the elevator and then to the car.

The afternoon had slid into early evening by the time they left the hospital. Laura had been right about her injuries. A couple of ribs were bruised and her left arm sprained. She would have a black eye for awhile, but she was able to walk on her own—more or less.

They arrived at her house and Steve helped her out of the car and walked with her to the house. She'd left early that morning, so hadn't left a light burning. Steve opened the door and flipped on the light. Yowls, howls, and chattering from the cats greeted them. Two felines immediately surrounded Laura, but it felt like a dozen. They rubbed against her ankles. She grabbed the back of the chair as wave of nausea and dizziness swept over her.

"I need to feed them and…"

"Laura, you're as pale as the white paws on Rascal and Mischief. You need to take a couple of those pills Doctor Cornelius gave you and go to bed immediately," Steve said.

Todd went to the kitchen and returned with a glass of water. "You might need this to take the pills," he said as he offered her the glass.

"Thanks, Todd, I'll take them later."

"Where are they?" asked Steve.

"Right here in my pocket." She glared at him as she pulled the little envelope from its resting place.

He took the packet from her, opened it and removed two tablets. He held them out for her to take.

"I'll take them later," she said through clenched teeth.

"You'll take them now and go to bed, or I'll have to resort to physical measures." Steve's eyes were not twinkling with the teasing she was used to seeing.

"I'll feed the cats," said Todd. "Come on guys. We'll let them battle that one out."

Rascal and Mischief looked anxiously from Laura to Steve. "She'll be all right, guys," said Steve. "I won't hurt her. I'm trying to make her feel better." They blinked at him, swished their tails against Laura's legs and trotted off to the kitchen.

"Even your cats are trying to tell you you're being stubborn for the sake of being stubborn. Now, take these pills—please." Then he smiled and glistening tears ran over the brims of her eyes. She took the pills with no comment.

"Thanks." She felt like she was close to passing out. Once again, she felt Steve's arms around her as he carried her up the stairs. He set her down on the bed and waited.

"Are you all right? Do you want me to call Martha to come and help?"

"I think I can take it from here," she murmured. Steve went back downstairs where Todd waited.

"Want to stop at the office or go to the apartment?"

"Neither," said Steve. "I'm staying here tonight—not here in the house," he hastened to add, "but in the belfry of the church. I was up there this morning and I have an idea I want to explore. You go ahead. I want to make sure she's asleep and all right before I turn off the lights and lock up."

218

The cats zipped past them and up the stairs. Todd grinned at his friend. "I understand," he said.

"Am I losing my mind?" Steve asked, not really looking for an answer. "I've managed for almost thirty years to ignore women, but there's something about her that I can't ignore."

"Oh, I wouldn't say you're losing your mind, my friend, but the heart is long gone." Todd chuckled.

"Is it that obvious? But I can't let that happen. I won't be hurt again."

"Sometimes, my friend, the hurt is not in the losing, but in the fear of losing again. Don't fight it. If it's God's direction you can't lose. If it's not, you can't win."

Steve laughed. "I thought the theologian was upstairs. I'll see you tomorrow. I'll go make sure she's all right then head for my camping quarters."

Todd left and Steve checked on Laura, who was asleep with a cat stretched out on either side of her, paws extended across her body as if protecting her. He smiled and left, turning off the lights and locking the door on his way out.

27

Gray overcast skies projected dim prospects for a sunny day. Robins ignored the predictions and did their best to chase away the clouds which let bits of sunlight through tiny openings. The chirping morning song reached Laura's groggy brain, prodding an awareness of the day's planned activities. The men were to start the delayed preparation of the church for painting. Would they be waylaid again? One thing after another had prevented them from working—the rain on Thursday, then the fire truck yesterday. What could go wrong today? Maybe she didn't want to know.

Laura opened her eyes and tried to sit up. Suddenly she remembered yesterday's ride over the side of Gopher Mountain. Doctor Cornelius said her bruised ribs would be as painful as fractured ribs and would take about as long to heal. She agreed as unbidden tears filled her eyes.

Both cats eased back on the bed, tucked their front paws under them, and squeezed their eyes shut. They prepared to wait as Laura ignored the pain as far as possible and gathered her clothes. She would shower before going downstairs in case she couldn't make it back up the steps. She took a deep breath and started for the bathroom. Was that the aroma of Martha's cinnamon buns wafting up the stairs? But how…? Never mind. First thing's first. The hot water cascading over her achy body would give her a good start on the day.

"Okay, kitties," she called a few minutes later as she started toward the steps. "I think I feel human again. Let's get some breakfast." Two blurs of gold, brown, and black sped past her. By the time she trudged into the kitchen, they sat near the cabinet where she kept their food, chattering to one another in their special Maine Coon language.

The strong cinnamon aroma became stronger until she reached the kitchen. A covered plate waited beside the coffee pot. A note peeked from under the plate: "Sorry about your accident. We have a key to your house, so let myself in. Didn't want to disturb you. Made these this morning. Enjoy. Martha Jennings."

Laura swiped her finger across the edge of the plate. "Ummmmmmmmm," she sighed as she licked her finger, and replaced the towel. "These will taste so good this morning when my coffee is done. I must remember to thank her..." Rascal and Mischief tapped at her leg and chattered. "Okay...Okay, I'm coming."

Cats fed and coffee brewed, Laura juggled her steaming hot mug in one hand, a plate with two sweet rolls on top of her Bible in the other. Cautiously she opened the back door and eased down the three steps to the back patio. Neither the backyard, nor the patio was much to look at, but she enjoyed the fresh air, birds, and whatever animals came along. This morning Rascal and Mischief followed her out.

"Stay in the yard," she said as they ran past her. "It looks like the sun is going to chase away the clouds after all. Wonder what time the men will be here?"

Rascal and Mischief would not have answered her, even if they could speak her language. They bounded across the backyard and were lost to sight in the tall grass, except for the tip of a tail here and there, as they jumped and chased one another. Despite her injuries, Laura felt content. Whatever happened, God was with her and she had her two furry friends to share her mishaps and give her comfort. She began to sing softly: "Morning has broken..."

Suddenly both cats stopped racing and stood up on their back legs, reminding her of the groundhogs on her grandfather's farm when she was a child. They looked toward the church. Someone was coming. Laura rotated her body gingerly in time to see Steve come around the corner of the house. He wore the same clothes he wore yesterday. His hair was neat, but not the way he usually had it combed. A stubble of beard clung to his chin.

"You sound chipper this morning after all you've been through," he said. "I would have thought you would be singing, 'Nobody knows the trouble I've seen…'" In his mellow baritone voice he sang the first few measures of the song.

Laura smiled at him—she knew better than to try to laugh. "Very funny." Then she changed the subject. "You're out early yourself. Rascal and Mischief told me someone was coming, but I thought it was the men ready to work on the church."

"I have a lot to do. Besides, I smelled your coffee and I saw Martha Jennings bring a plate of something over here. I thought I would invite myself to breakfast."

How could he have seen Martha? Where was he? Had he stayed in her house somewhere?

"If you want breakfast, you'll have to help yourself. I'm not up to playing hostess this morning. For some reason, my muscles are a little stiff and don't want to move. Just look until you find what you need. Cups are in the cupboard, rolls on the table. Bring a chair with you if you want to sit."

"Thank you," he said. He returned a few minutes later with coffee, rolls, and chair.

"Ummmmm. Delicious. I must remember to tell Martha. Now, we need to talk." He became more serious.

"First, tell me how you could smell the coffee and see Martha Jennings bring the rolls over."

He laughed. "You won't believe me."

"Try me. After these last few days, I can believe almost anything."

"You said something to the effect that it might be possible someone other than the kids tied the cats in the belfry—maybe even Jeb himself. The more I thought about that, the more sense it began to make. I was up there yesterday when the boys set fire to your car. I decided to spend the night in the belfry."

"The belfry? You slept up there in the belfry?"

"I told you you wouldn't believe me." He grinned that special way that made his eyes twinkle.

Laura tried to ignore the effect it had on her. Now she understood his appearance. "Oh, I believe you—I think. But...what did you find out?"

Steve took a sip of his coffee. "I think you were right. Not only are there bowls and a litter box up there, there's also was a sleeping bag and knapsack with Jeb's belongings. Apparently he lived up there most of the time—if not permanently. That's why there were noises from the belfry. What the cats didn't make, Jeb himself came up with. When he knew Todd was coming to check it out, he hid stuff in a trap off the side."

"But why? What would be the point of scaring people away from the church?" Laura asked as she nibbled at the warm cinnamon roll.

"Well, I think I can answer that one, also." He spoke around the bite of roll he had just bitten off. "Last night I saw people in your garage."

"Last night? While I was sleeping?" Laura held her cup half way to her mouth. She thought she was beyond being surprised by anything going on, but people coming and going right under her nose? While she slept yet.

Steve nodded. "'Fraid so."

"Oh, great. Next they'll carry the house off and I won't even know it."

"They didn't go near the house. If they had, I would've been down here a lot faster than it takes to tell you about it. No, I think they were counting on the doctor giving you some heavy duty pain medication, or a shot to make you sleep."

"Who were they and what did they want?"

"Unfortunately, I can't answer either of those questions right now. It looked like a couple of kids and an older man. They went in with something and came out empty handed. By the way, the men won't be working today. Those men last night took all the tools—including the ladders."

"What? Someone really doesn't want the church to improve, do they? Why do they want to get rid of the church? Or is it just me they are trying to scare off?" Laura sat shaking her head trying to understand. "What did I say, or do, to cause all this trouble?"

"Laura, I don't think you said, or did, anything. It started before you came, remember? And I don't think it's you, as a person, they want to scare off. The position of pastor—possibly. They just don't want to take a chance of someone finding Jeb's belfry apartment, and/or whatever they have in the garage. I intend to have a look around that garage as soon as I finish my breakfast."

"Help yourself to more rolls. They won't be near as good when they are cold."

Steve got up and started for the kitchen and reached for her cup. "More coffee?"

"Thanks." She handed it to him, glad she didn't have to move.

"What are the felines up to out there?" he asked when he returned. He nodded toward the cats, as he handed her the coffee cup.

"I don't know." She sipped her coffee. "They've been chasing each other and jumping around ever since we came out here. Maybe they found a mouse."

"Not unless you have purple mice around here." Steve watched.

"Purple mice?" Laura frowned and glanced at him to see if he was teasing her. He was serious.

Steve set his cup and plate on his chair. He was already striding toward the cats when Laura got up to follow at a more leisurely pace. It wasn't easy to wade through the tall grass, when every breath felt like a sharp knife jabbing her lungs.

"What have you got there, Rascal? Can I see it?" Steve approached the cats then squatted and held out his hand. Rascal ignored him. Mischief brought her toy over and dropped it at his feet. Rascal turned his head and watched as Steve praised Mischief and stroked her shiny fur. "Good kitty, Mischief. Thank you."

Rascal then brought his *purple mouse* over for Steve to see, dropping the ball of purple yarn at his feet.

"Good kitties. You can have them back in a minute." Laura stooped to pick up one of the balls, took a deep breath, and gritted her teeth as she stood.

"These aren't mine," she said when the pain subsided and she was able to talk. "I've never used these colors. I wonder if there are any more around."

Steve reached in his pocket and brought out a couple of treats for the kitties. "Good kitties. Can you find some more?" Rascal ate his treat and pawed at the pocket which held the treats.

"Not yet, smarty. Find me some more yarn, first." Steve laughed as Rascal sat on his haunches, blinked, and waited. Steve blinked back at him and waited. Finally, Rascal swished his tail and turned to explore the yard. Mischief followed him. They found a couple more balls of yarn a little closer to the garage. Steve gave them each another treat.

Laura gave him a quizzical look. "Do you always carry kitty treats in your pocket?"

"They were part of the stuff in the belfry. Jeb probably used them to train the cats."

Laura shook her head and smiled. "It looks like they want in the garage. Maybe they figure they'll find something in there worth more treats."

"Now is as good a time as any to check it out. I'll finish my rolls later. Let's try the door to see if it's locked."

"That would be rather redundant, since the front door is off its hinges." Laura couldn't keep the sarcasm from her voice.

Steve grinned at her. "I know, but we'll try anyway—to please the cats." Rascal and Mischief paused at the door. "Need some help over the weeds?"

"No, I'll make it. Don't wait for me, though, or you'll be here all day just getting to the garage."

Steve stomped through the grass, breaking it down and leaving a path for Laura to follow. He reached the door and turned the knob, which fell off in his hand. "Well, so much for locks," he said holding the knob out to Laura as she eased up beside him. "I'll see if it will open from this side, if not, I'll go around." He hooked his finger through the circle, where the knob should have been, and pulled. Slowly it moved with a groan. He tried again, pulling harder. The door opened with a squawk. "No one went out that way last night. I would have heard them."

"At least it didn't fall off its hinge on top of you," said Laura, remembering the door that almost fell on her when she discovered Jeb's body.

"I guess we have to be thankful for small favors," he said.

Rascal and Mischief ran past them into the garage. Steve followed. "There's no light in here so we'll just have to depend on the outside light."

"Looks like a dirt floor. Why am I not surprised? I was only a few feet inside briefly Wednesday morning, so I didn't notice it before. Looks like a few muddy spots; I suppose the roof leaks. Wonder what's under that pile of wood and why it's in the middle of the floor."

"Todd and I checked everything over good Wednesday. I don't remember it being arranged exactly like that. There was a pile of stuff, but it seemed more orderly—like it had been stacked there for some time." Steve examined the pile of lumber as he talked.

Both Rascal and Mischief climbed around the wood, then got down and started to dig at the edges with their backs hunched, tails bushy. A low growl rumbled from their throats.

"What's wrong with them, now?" Steve moved closer to see what the cats were digging.

"It's usually a sign of fear, or some perceived danger. They were bushy like that when they started out to find Jerome." Laura couldn't stop the small shiver that ran up her spine. "I hope there's not another body."

28

Steve laid a hand on Laura's arm. "Are you all right? If you want..."

"Don't even think about suggesting that I leave. I'm here and whatever is under that pile of junk can't be any worse than what I've already experienced." She didn't sound very convincing, but Steve smiled and turned back to the task of moving the junk.

"Do you have a shovel? Never mind there's one." He reached for the shovel leaning against the wall.

"Not mine. One of the missing tools, maybe?" Laura shifted to the side where she would be out of his way.

"Could be." He started digging. "Dirt's soft—been dug recently."

Rascal and Mischief pawed the dirt and threw it behind them like a couple of pups digging a hole in a flowerbed. Suddenly the shovel struck something solid a few inches down. Steve moved the dirt aside and pulled out a piece of plywood about four by six feet.

"I think we found the missing plastic storage box, too. And I would almost stake my life that it's full of cocaine." Bags of white powder were heaped inside the clear, plastic container.

"Cocaine?" Had she heard him correctly? Cocaine in her garage?

"Sure looks like it. Makes sense now that they would steal a useless plastic box. They store the stuff in the box until time to move it. That way nothing, man nor beast, would be able to get into it. Jeb probably saw something going on down here and came to investigate."

"Or else, he was in on it from the beginning, creating a diversion while it was delivered, keeping folks away with the noise. That explains why they—whoever *they* are—don't want a pastor here. Maybe he got scared, or wanted more money, or…"

"Laura, you've been reading too many mystery novels, but you could be right. For now, I'll put things back the way we found them and call Todd. We now know far more than we did, but we still don't know enough. Like, who? And why this particular place? Why not one of the other churches, or someplace else in town?" Steve covered the box with the plywood which he covered with the dirt, packing it down with the shovel.

"Good kitties, Rascal and Mischief," Laura called to the cats. "Come on let's get out of this place. You don't like that stuff, do you?" Both cats snorted and sneezed as if to rid themselves of the smell. "Maybe Jeb used the stuff and was abusive to them." Laura didn't want to think that they were abused, but knew they probably were.

"It would make sense. They're smart animals. They knew it was bad stuff. There, I think it looks pretty much the same as it did," he said, as he placed the last piece of wood on the pile. "Let's go call Todd. Come on kitties. I'll give you some more treats when we get in the house."

Rascal and Mischief loped to the house ahead of them and by the time Steve and Laura reached the back door two furry tails disappeared into the kitchen.

"How did they do that?"

"I told you Rascal can open doors—especially this one. The handle pulls down to open it." Laura laughed and grabbed her side.

Steve winced with her, and picked up their cups and plates, while she opened the door. "I can hold the door." She smiled, after her bout with pain. "After all, your hands are full."

"I'll make a fresh pot of coffee while you call Todd," said Laura reaching for the glass carafe. Steve went to the living room to make the call. The last gurgles coincided with Todd's arrival. They heard him walk across the porch, and before he could knock, Steve went to open the door.

"Good morning, Todd," Laura said over her shoulder as he ambled into the kitchen. "Coffee just finished brewing. There are some fresh cinnamon rolls on the table. Help yourself."

"Cinnamon rolls? Laura, I hope you haven't been up baking already this morning. According to Doctor Cornelius, you should be in the hospital."

"Not me! Martha Jennings brought them over. Coffee is about my limit this morning," she answered, handing him a cup of the brew. "We may as well sit here in the kitchen."

"Would it be more comfortable for you in the front room?" Steve asked.

"Thanks for the concern, but actually these kitchen chairs are easier to get in and out of with less pain."

"Ummmm. These are good. Now, what's going on so early in the morning? You see something last night, Steve?" Todd glanced at Laura, then back at Steve. "You did tell her what you were doing?"

Steve laughed. "Yes, I told her, although I'm sure my appearance must have given her some clue." He smiled as he ran his hand over his scratchy chin. "And yes, I saw something very interesting. Rascal and Mischief helped us find something even more interesting in the garage this morning—a cache of cocaine."

"Cocaine? No kidding?"

"No kidding." Steve then filled him in on where it was, how they found it, and why they missed it on Wednesday morning.

"Maybe I'd better go see for myself and then decide what to do. We'll need to get it out of there before some kids find it."

"Todd?" Laura had listened while Steve explained.

"Yes, Laura?"

"I'm not a detective," she smiled at Steve, "nor do I want to be one, but my guess is that they've been using that garage for almost two years and no one's found the drugs yet. I don't think another day will make any difference."

"You have an idea?" He looked at her as if she were the expert and he the novice.

"As a matter of fact, I do, for what it's worth. I think we need to have a conference—the three of us with Jerome and SaraBelle. SaraBelle had something important to tell me, but we were run off the road before she had a chance to say it. She was too drowsy last night from the medication Doctor Cornelius gave her, and I wasn't all that alert myself."

"We noticed," said Steve.

"I'm sure you did. I hope I didn't give you a hard time, but I'm sure I must have. I vaguely remember you bringing me home. I don't remember much after that."

"You should have stayed at the hospital last night," said Todd glancing at Steve. "Steve and I took care of your cats and locked up when we left.

"I know and I appreciate that. Sometimes I'm too stubborn for my own good—and I don't need any comments from either of you." She glared at them as if she expected them to agree with her.

They both laughed. Laura tried to join them but winced, bit her lip and waited a few seconds until she could talk again. "I spent too many years letting someone else take care of me. I've worked hard to overcome that feeling of helplessness. I'm determined not to let it happen to me again…and…I guess I just panicked. Until night before last, I hadn't been inside a hospital since Harold's death." Laura took a deep breath, or tried to. She got up and walked to the coffee pot, stopped, and stared out the window. "It was too traumatic and…I'm sorry, you didn't ask for my tale of woe, but I couldn't have gone into the hospital to even see Jerome if Steve hadn't helped me. And there was no way I could have stayed last night. I just couldn't." Laura tried to smile, but bit her lip. She gave Todd a shortened version of her experience.

"Laura, we appreciate you trusting us enough to share such horrors. I still can't believe they could be so insensitive." Steve's anger and compassion were as unsettling to her as his teasing.

Laura picked up the coffee pot and returned to the table trying to smile through the tears that threatened to overflow. Blinking them back she said, "Anyway, back to the problem at hand, I think Jerome probably saw more in the belfry than he realized. Possibly he even heard more than he knows he heard. Maybe if we can all get together, start at the beginning, and organize what we know and what we need to know yet…" She shrugged her shoulders and held her hands in a helpless way in front of her.

"She's got a point, Todd. That stuff in the garage isn't going to go anywhere in the middle of the day. You can set a guard in the belfry to alert us if anyone should try. Make sure it's someone you would trust with your life."

"Mark Goodwin, one of the best officers I have. I'll give him a call and get him right over here. Then, why don't we call Doctor Cornelius and see if he can set us up in a room for early this afternoon. We could say we're having a visit with our friends and need some quiet place where we won't be disturbed."

"Good idea, Todd," said Steve. "As soon as you call Mark, I'll call the hospital."

"Why don't I call the hospital?" Laura said. "It would seem more appropriate and usual for a pastor to request a visit with two patients together than for a police officer. We don't want to alert anyone to the fact that we're having a conference. Todd can take me over because…Doctor Cornelius doesn't want me to drive for a couple of days. Steve can use my car if it's running after the fire and come to bring Todd some information, or something. By then we'll all be there and if anyone outside the hospital is alerted, we'll be done before they could do anything about it. Doctor Cornelius needs to know what we're doing, maybe even be there in case it's too much for SaraBelle. If he's present, there would be no need for a nurse, or anyone else, to enter the room."

"Do you always organize your thoughts so completely?" Todd blinked and shook his head in amazement.

"Well, yes, I guess I do." Laura laughed. "My friends used to kid me about having a computer for a brain. I guess I learned that from my grandmother. She would always say, 'Think it through, child, so you don't have to waste time and effort.'"

Steve laughed. "I still think you ought to consider a career change. Your car is still in the shop, but I have a rental car coming. I called Enterprise last night. They should be along soon. I'll go over to Todd's and get cleaned up." He rubbed his chin again to emphasize the point. "I'll meet you at the hospital at one o'clock. And get that guilty look off your face, Laura. It wasn't your fault. I can't say enough how glad I am that you had my Buick instead of your Chevette."

"But, I still feel responsible." No matter what he said, Laura felt miserable and guilty about wrecking his car. SaraBelle's words about Steve Morgan never letting anyone drive his car continued to haunt her.

"Steve's right, Laura," said Todd. "That sniper is responsible, not you. Now, it's nine o'clock. I've got a few details to take care of at the office. I'll pick you up about twelve-thirty. Why don't you get some rest until then?"

"Sure, I will." The sarcasm was not lost on them. They both shook their heads as they left, knowing she probably wouldn't rest. They were wrong. She sat down in her recliner for a minute after they left and didn't wake until three hours later when she heard Todd's car pull into the driveway. She grabbed a glass of milk for lunch and took off.

29

The spacious and elegant conference room added charm and mystique to a topic already overcharged with mystery. Laura and Todd arrived shortly before one o'clock and were in the conference room when Carolyn and Sophia wheeled Jerome and SaraBelle in. Doctor Jonathan Cornelius followed them.

Steve entered behind him in time to hear him ask, "Is all this intrigue necessary? I could have just as easily discharged both patients. Then you could've had your meeting wherever you want for as long as you need."

Laura opened her mouth to answer, but Todd raised hand, palm outward, suggesting she should let him explain. "The patients may be well enough to go home, Doctor, but you have to remember Jerome was beaten to within an inch of his life, and Mrs. Cotton was shot at and run off the road with the intention of her not living through it. Until we wrap up this case, the safest place for both of them is right here—except maybe in a jail cell."

SaraBelle sat up straight and wagged a finger at Todd. "Now you wait just a minute there young man. I may be old, but I'm not heartless and ignorant. This young boy has been through more than anyone should have to endure. You certainly will *not* put him in a jail cell, even for his own safety." SaraBelle looked and sounded like a mother tiger protecting her cub.

Doctor Cornelius threw his hands up in surrender and laughed. "All right. All right, I give up. You've made your point. Now can we get on with this meeting? I do have other patients who need my attention. However, I have to admit that I'm as fascinated and excited with the mystery as the rest of you. Thank you for inviting me. Peace and quiet are the trademarks of most small towns. Any change in routine is welcome, but violence goes too far." The others nodded in agreement.

"Since this was Laura's idea, why don't we let her start us off." Todd winked at Steve who nodded.

"Make fun all you want to," she replied in pretended pique, "but you'll be glad we did this when we're through. I will take credit, or blame, for this meeting, though. I thought we needed to start at the beginning and list what's happened to whom, and by whom. Then, maybe we can see some kind of pattern forming and get some idea of who might be responsible for it all. We have some of the pieces of the puzzle, but the picture is still incomplete. The trouble started before I came. When? Who was involved? And what preceded these attacks on Jerome and SaraBelle? Todd can probably fill us in with the beginning as well as anyone. If what any of us says triggers other thoughts, please speak up."

"I think you forgot a major detail, Laura."

"Oh?" She glanced at Steve. He wasn't teasing. He was serious.

"You left yourself out of the list of those attacked. You may be new here, and it might be simply because you're in the wrong place at the wrong time, but you are a victim along with the other two, nonetheless."

"You're probably right. I don't like to think of myself as a victim." She dropped her gaze. She didn't want Steve to see how troubled she really was. He was right. Someone wanted her out of the picture—one way or another.

Todd cleared his throat and checked his notes. "Steve's right, Laura. We need to keep in mind how the church is involved, which seems to be simply because of its location. As far as I can remember, our troubles began almost two years ago when Jeb Little showed up with his two trained cats. He set up a stage and

234

set out a cup for money. The strange noises from the belfry of the Methodist Church started about the same time. People got scared and wouldn't go near the place."

"That's it!" Jerome got so excited he bounced in his chair. "That's what those boys thought I saw. The belfry. When I got the cats down, I was so interested in them I didn't think about anything else. Now, I remember. There was lots of other stuff up there—you know, like food and bowls and litter box and…and…it looked like a sleeping bag in the corner. Old Jeb must have been living up there, helping the cats make all those noises."

Steve beamed at the boy. "You've got it, son. That's exactly what happened. Laura figured that out, too, and I spent last night up there. Sometime around two-thirty or three a.m., I saw three men go into the garage. This morning Rascal and Mischief led Laura and me into the garage where we found the plastic storage box that was stolen. It was full of what I'm certain is cocaine."

He grinned at Jerome. "You know, Jerome, those cats would make a good feline patrol. When they sniffed out that drug cache, they looked like they'd stuck their paws in a light socket."

Jerome giggled. "They're smart cats all right. I'm sure glad we found them." His expression sobered. "Is that why those boys beat me? Are they involved—Johnny and Skip, I mean?"

"We'll know soon enough, but it doesn't look good for them. They're the ones Steve saw sabotage Laura's car."

SaraBelle sat with her eyes closed for so long the rest thought she had fallen asleep. She wasn't asleep—just thinking. She had missed none of the conversation. When she spoke, the rest turned to her in surprise.

"You know, my nephew Horace—if he is my nephew—arrived about the same time Jeb Little did."

"You have some doubts as to whether he's your nephew?" Steve questioned.

"I know I have a nephew named Horace—grandson of my husband's youngest brother. I never met him. This boy appeared one day, said his father told him before he died if he ever got in trouble to go see me and I would help him out. I heard of his father's death and that was the last I heard from any of the family until Horace showed up on my door step."

"Didn't you try to check it out?" Laura realized that sounded like she was questioning SaraBelle's ability to think sensibly and added, "I'm sorry, I didn't ask that very well. I know you would do that, but…"

SaraBelle laughed her soft cackle. "Don't try to explain. I know what you mean. We're both a little scrambled, so we don't think as clearly as we want. Yes, I checked it out—or tried to. That's part of what I wanted to talk to you about yesterday. I don't know if it has anything to do with what's happening or not. I asked Mike Atkins to check into it for me. About a week later he gave me glowing reports about Horace and how his parents had died, and how he looked after himself for several months until he remembered he had a great-aunt somewhere in Cottonville."

"But you didn't believe him?" Steve asked.

"I had no reason not to, but all the same something didn't feel quite right. Horace isn't exactly the kind of person who would take any initiative to look after himself. He needs to be told to come in out of the rain if he doesn't want to get wet. Then he started getting into trouble at school, little things that grew into big things. He started drinking heavily. Sometimes I'm actually afraid of him, although I would never let him know that."

Sophia sat between Jerome and SaraBelle. She laid a hand on SaraBelle's arm and smiled at her. "You probably gave him the benefit of a doubt, while you waited for proof."

"I tried, Sophia, but lately Horace has been badgering me about my will, wanting to know where it is, who gets all my money and land. I told him most of it will go to charity since I have no close relatives. That made him furious. He shouted at me, 'What do you think I am? Garbage?'

"When he cooled down, he said he thought I should see that lawyer in town and change my will. Since I have a relative now, I needed to leave everything to him. He was especially interested in a piece of land that he wanted. I told him it was already taken. He became even more enraged and said he would break the will and get it. I said, 'Over my dead body you will,' and he answered, 'That can be arranged.'"

"Let me guess," said Todd. "He wants the land behind the church where the parsonage and garage are."

"Yes, as a matter of fact, that's exactly what he wants. He said the church doesn't need it anyway. No preacher is ever going to stay there again. That was just a few days before you came." She smiled at Laura.

"Things are beginning to add up," said Steve. "Go on."

"Mike Atkins came to see me Thursday evening. He said Horace had been to see him and asked him to stop by and talk some sense into me. He agreed that my estate should go to Horace, even the land behind the church. He had drawn up a new will for me and wanted me to sign it that night. I told him I had to talk to Reverend Kenzel first. If she had any idea that she would be staying, the land would still go to the church."

SaraBelle frowned and then went on, "He said I was being very foolish and senile. Said it would be no trouble for Horace to have me declared incompetent and take over my affairs. I told him to let me think about it. I would call him the next day after I talked to Reverend Kenzel."

"So now we know why someone didn't want me to meet SaraBelle," commented Laura. Then she continued to list the facts. "So far we know: one, Jeb Little and Horace arrived about the same time and both were strangers; two, the Atkins boy, the Jameson boy, and one other unidentified boy beat Jerome; three, Mike Atkins seems to side with Horace; four, someone didn't want me to meet with SaraBelle. Now we know why, but not who. Who all knew I was going to see SaraBelle? Todd, Steve, SaraBelle and now it seems Mike Atkins. Who else knew? Did Horace know?"

"Yes, he knew. He told me I was foolish. Then I got that call from your supposed secretary and he really ridiculed me."

"So now we have an unknown woman and Mike Atkins. Apparently, Malcolm Atkins, who is supposedly Mike's cousin, and Ed Winters both knew. It would seem Ed Winters received his instructions from one of the Atkins. Why? Is there something for which he could be blackmailed?"

"Good point, Laura," said Todd. "I'll check it out. I still need to talk to Ed Winters anyway."

"Can any of them shoot a rifle?" asked Laura.

They all laughed and Laura looked confused.

"Everyone—well almost everyone—in Cottonville can shoot a gun from the time they are grade school age—or before." Todd smiled at her. "Present company excluded, of course."

"Young man, I hope you're not referring to me. I can pick the eye out of a crow on a fence the other side of my lot without ever missing. But I didn't get out of the car and shoot at myself yesterday." SaraBelle sat up straight, hands on hips, and glared at Todd.

Jerome thought that was funny and giggled, then winced, holding his ribs. "Will you teach me to shoot when my arm gets better?"

"We'll see, lad, we'll see," said SaraBelle smiling at Jerome.

Laura felt a pang of guilt. She also knew how to shoot a gun, but saw no reason to say so. It wasn't something she took pride in. It was her grandfather's choice. He insisted on her learning as a child. Someday she might tell Todd and Steve, but for now, she saw no reason to share that part of her life.

A sudden thought sent a sobering look across SaraBelle's face. "I just thought of someone else. Phil Jameson, also, knew you were coming to see me. I opened an account for Horace at the bank soon after he came here. I instructed Jameson to put five hundred dollars a month in it out of my account. Yesterday morning, he called and said that Horace had overdrawn the account by three thousand dollars. He wanted to know if he could make it right from my account. I told him no; he got irate and wanted to know how a young boy was supposed to get along without money. I said he could find a job. He was incensed and called me a senile old hag. I told him I had to go, I was expecting my pastor. He wanted to know why she was coming. I told him it was none of his business, but we were going to talk about the future of the church and some improvements I wanted to see done. A few minutes later—not more than three or four—I got the call from your so-called secretary."

"I was talking to Judy, his secretary, yesterday morning, while she made coffee. Mr. Jameson yelled for her to get in his office. He had an important call she had to make right then. She looked anxious—like she was afraid of him. I asked if she was all right. She said she was, but that Jameson was going to be a real bear today—yesterday." Carolyn looked at Todd as she spoke.

"That's interesting," mused Laura. "We have the Jameson boy and the Atkins boy who beat Jerome. We have Mike Atkins and Phil Jameson who knew about my visit and made it clear at the meeting the other night that they didn't want me to stay. We have another Atkins, who just happened to show up when Jeb gets killed. And we have an unknown boy who beat Jerome. Would you recognize that boy, if you saw him again, Jerome?"

"I sure would. He is real tall with stringy hair down to his shoulders. He sneers a lot and laughs like a fiend out of a horror movie."

SaraBelle and Laura exchanged looks. "Do you have..."

Before Laura could finish her sentence, SaraBelle answered, "No, I don't have a picture of Horace, but I would bet my bottom dollar he was the third kid."

"Horace? Your nephew, Horace?" Todd was looking from SaraBelle to Laura and back again.

"And I would almost be willing to bet he was the intruder Tuesday night—the one that got away." Laura grinned at Todd and Steve. Both returned a smile.

"You sure?"

"Not positive, Todd, but the height, the hair, the smell of marijuana and/or alcohol all fit."

"It makes sense, Todd," said Steve. "Horace seems to be in this up to his eyeballs. He wants that land pretty bad for some reason, obviously a storing station for the drugs between runs. The money wouldn't be bad either. But, if Jameson and Atkins are involved, we're going to have to have some pretty hard and fast evidence. Atkins is slick from what you told me."

"You've got that right, buddy." Todd nodded. "Any ideas on how we capture these rats?"

"Maybe you can set a trap for them in the garage," said Jerome.

"A rat trap," said SaraBelle. "I like that."

"What kind of trap?" Carolyn looked at her son like he was a hero.

"You know, make them think you're going to tear it down or something," he said. "Then they'll want to hurry and get their stuff out."

Steve raised his eyebrows and glanced at Todd, who also looked surprised. "I think the kid might have something there, but how can we set it up without being obvious? Anyone have any ideas?"

"I think I can handle that," said Laura. "I'll call a brief meeting after church tomorrow morning and tell them I want the garage removed immediately. It's a dangerous eyesore."

"You think they'll cooperate, Laura? Atkins and Jameson are both on your committees."

"I'm pretty sure I can." Laura didn't feel quite as confident as the words she spoke. She didn't dare look Steve in the eye, feeling he could see into the depth of her emotions. SaraBelle's voice pulled her back from the brink of her emotionally charged thoughts.

"I can make sure it happens." SaraBelle had been furiously writing something on a slip of paper. "Here, show this to Frank Jennings. I'm sure he'll go for it." She handed the paper to Laura.

Laura read the note and a broad grin spread across her bruised face. "I think you're right. We've got them. There's no way they'll pass this up. I won't let them."

Todd and Steve waited expectantly for her to share it. Jerome was too impatient to wait. "What does it say?"

Laura read the note aloud. "It says: I think the state of disrepair of our residence for a pastor is a disgrace. Get rid of that awful-looking garage, where that man was killed. Put up a decent one with a solid cement floor, electricity, and garage-door opener. Do it immediately and I will pay the full amount. Every day you wait, I will deduct ten per cent. Signed: SaraBelle Cotton."

"Yes!" exclaimed Jerome. "Can I come and watch?"

Laura frowned. "I would rather you and SaraBelle stay here until Monday. I have a feeling someone will show up Sunday evening. It should be all over by Sunday night or Monday morning."

"I hope you're right, Laura," said Todd.

"So do I, Todd," she whispered, more to herself than to anyone there, thinking no one heard her. Like a cat drawn to catnip, she turned her head to glance at Steve. Their eyes met. He'd heard. She couldn't read his expression, but the room suddenly got several degrees warmer. Beginning to feel the effects of her terror-filled week, Laura began to feel light-headed and moved to an empty chair. She dropped her head in her hands. Vaguely she heard Steve speak to Doctor Cornelius.

"I think that about wraps it up for now. Thank you, Doctor, for your help. If all goes well, we'll have these patients off your hands by tomorrow night, or Monday morning. Laura, Todd, and I will need to finalize some plans. Then all we can do is wait for tomorrow. In the meantime, don't take any chances here. No visitors except Jerome's mother and grandmother. We'll wheel them back up to their rooms and then we'll be on our way."

"I'll walk with you," said Todd as Carolyn and Sophia took their places behind the wheelchairs. "Steve, why don't you take Laura home? I'll meet you there in a few minutes."

"Does she have a choice?" Steve teased. Had he known her a little longer, he would have realized she was too weary for teasing.

"Sure she does," Todd answered. "You can take her home, or she can wait for me."

Laura's weariness mixed with all the other raw emotions, prompted unexpected anger and annoyance. "I'm not an invisible object, or a rag doll you can toss from one to the other. Maybe I'll just walk—that is if I have the permission of you two gentlemen who seem to think you have to take care of this poor little girl." She stood, picked up her purse, and marched for the door trying to ignore the pain that the sudden movement generated.

"Whoops! I think we goofed. You straighten it out, buddy," Todd said to Steve as he left with Carolyn, leaving Steve standing in the conference room alone.

Thanks a bunch, pal. Women! Who can ever figure them out? Suddenly he remembered why he swore off them and why he had stuck to it until…until he remembered his smashed Buick and the panic he felt when he thought Laura was hurt bad, or worse. He remembered her words about her struggles. He remembered her weariness and hurried after her.

30

The elevator door closed behind Laura as Steve reached for it, but the other one opened, so he was only a few seconds behind her. Laura leaned against the side trying to understand her run-away feelings. Why was she so angry? Why did she snap at Steve that way? The pain in her side added to her frustration. She simply would not let anyone order her around. The movement stopped and the door slid open. She stepped out feeling more confused. Which way was out—left or right? Steve stepped off the second elevator and reached for her hand. Startled Laura pulled away, then looked up into his twinkling eyes and let him take it.

"Unless you want to go to the cafeteria," he said, "we need to go this way." He started toward the exit.

Her anger had died as quickly as it had risen. Still holding her hand, Steve led her outside to the curb. He hesitated for a second then took her across to the parking lot, took the keys to his rental car from his pocket, and placed them in her hand. "You take the car. I'll walk," he said.

Laura dropped the keys and jerked her head up to see if he were making fun of her. He was serious. Her jumbled emotions turned to horror.

"Steve! I wrecked one car for you. How can you trust me with another?"

"Laura, you didn't wreck my car. You were run off the road by a sniper, but that's beside the point. I won't let you walk home." He stooped to pick up the dropped keys.

"Steve..." she took a deep breath, winced and said, "will you take me home...please?" She didn't want to look him in the eye, but couldn't stop herself.

He grinned as he opened the door. "Promise you won't get mad and jump out of the moving car?"

"I'm not that unstable!" Then she added in a softer, more serious tone, "I hope." She waited until he was behind the wheel and said, "Please don't be angry with me. I don't understand myself anymore. I could always keep my emotions under control. I had no right to speak to you and Todd like that." She turned to look unseeing out her window, afraid of what she might see in his eyes.

Steve said nothing—afraid he might say too much—or the wrong thing. The car pulled smoothly into her driveway a few minutes later. She reached for the door, but he took her hand and held her back. "Laura, I'm not angry—not with you. You were right to remind us of our inexcusable and insensitive behavior. I am angry with myself for putting you through more grief and I'm sorry. You're exhausted. You should be in the hospital with Jerome and SaraBelle. We ought to postpone our meeting until later—at least until tomorrow afternoon. Like SaraBelle said, you were both pretty well shaken up in that wreck yesterday."

"We can't wait. Tomorrow might be too late. I'll be all right—honest. Shall we go in and make some coffee?"

As the door opened they were met by a cacophony of meows, purrs, and guttural chattering. Rascal and Mischief entwined themselves around her ankles until she could hardly move. They seemed to be pushing her toward her recliner. Steve laughed and helped them.

"Why don't I make the coffee? You can rest for a few minutes. It looks like your two friends want you to do that."

"Oh, I can't. I'm all right now, really I am."

"Are you trying to convince me, or yourself?" He grinned and the familiar sparkle lit his eyes. "Now, do you want to sit, or shall I pick you up and put you in the chair?" Steve gently helped her ease back in the recliner. About fifty pounds of feline fur pounced to her lap.

"I guess I'm stuck," she said. "All right, I'll rest until Todd comes, or the coffee is done, whichever comes first."

Smiling, Steve went to the kitchen to make the coffee. He stepped back to ask where she kept the coffee filters and Laura was already sound asleep. His smile increased as he rummaged for the filters. The coffee finished brewing and he took two cups to the front porch. As Steve reached the steps, Todd pulled in beside his car. They sat on the steps and talked quietly for a half hour, or so. Reluctantly, Steve rose. "I suppose we ought to wake her and get our planning over with so she can prepare for tomorrow."

"We should wait…"

"That's what I thought, but Laura is afraid tomorrow will be too late. Much as I hate to admit it, she's probably right."

The door closed softly behind them and Rascal and Mischief stirred. Nap time was over. They chased a ball of yarn Todd rolled across the floor, while Steve got Laura a cup of coffee. She sat up with a start and groaned.

"You all right?" asked Todd.

"I think so. What time is it? I didn't mean to go to sleep."

"It's time to stop being lazy and start thinking like a detective." Steve smiled and handed her the coffee.

"I'm not a detective. I'm a preacher—and not a very good one at that. Tomorrow is my first Sunday and I don't even have a sermon. Do you suppose I can preach about murder in the garage, cats in the belfry, or something like that?"

"You could try. You're certainly qualified and can preach from experience." Todd laughed.

"Thanks, Steve—for the nap and the coffee."

"The coffee I'll take credit for," he said. "I had nothing to do with the nap. I think your two feline friends instigated that one."

"You're probably right. Whatever, I feel almost human again, at least for a while. I'm sorry about my theatrics at the hospital."

"Laura, I think if I'd been through all you've had to endure since Tuesday night, I would've given it a lot more punch. We're your friends. We can handle a little temper once in a while. Right, Steve?"

"Right, Todd." Steve was glad Todd had answered her.

"Now, let's figure out what we're doing." Todd was all business.

Their plans were made when the mantel clock struck six. Where had the time gone? Laura offered to fix supper for them, but they declined, so Laura opted for a sandwich. The house had become quiet. Rascal and Mischief tired of their games, slept intertwined on the couch.

Laura, weary and achy, felt a sense of panic begin to jar her nerves. Tomorrow her first Sunday—Mother's Day. She had no message and not much time to prepare. She ate her sandwich, sat in her recliner with her notepad and pen on her lap and closed her eyes in meditation.

"God, this isn't the way the seminary taught me to do ministry. They didn't teach me what to do with murder, drugs, and threats to my life. Somehow, the lives of a small boy and an old woman got in the way of the teaching. I have a feeling that's all right with You. The question is, what do I say tomorrow? Will I even be able to get out of bed? Will anyone be in church to hear me anyway? I guess even if I am the only one there, I still need to hear Your word."

Laura thought the earlier nap had refreshed her, but when she opened her eyes, everything was dark. The clock on the mantel struck one. "Good heavens, I've been asleep again—for hours. I guess I needed it, but now what will I do?"

Before panic took control, she heard deep in that special pocket of her mind, "Don't worry about what you will say; words will be given to you."

Everything was so quiet that Laura suddenly was afraid. Where were the cats? Had they left? Had someone come in, while she was sleeping, and taken them? With her heart pounding, she straightened and reached for the lamp and felt Rascal and Mischief stretch beside her—one on either side. She breathed a sigh of relief as they opened their emerald green eyes and blinked at her.

"Come on guys. Let's go to bed. We'll worry about tomorrow when it gets here—well, it's already here, but we'll wait for morning."

She turned off the lamp and started for the steps, her guard cats on either side of her. She decided against any more pills, not wanting to oversleep. Even with her naps, however, sleep came immediately. She knew the next day would bring disagreement and more confrontations, but it would be a good day. God was in charge. She had friends in her corner. How bad could things be?

31

Laura stopped at the full-length mirror on her bedroom door. She didn't look too bad in her navy blue suit, except for the purplish color around her eye. She had chosen a simple gold chain with a small cross and gold earrings as her only accessories. The black eye and vague headache didn't do a lot to elevate self-esteem. Sore ribs made it difficult to breathe deeply, but that long-awaited first Sunday on her own in her first appointment sent a tingle of joy through her, filling her heart with a prayer of thanksgiving. It had been an impossible week, but God had prevailed. He wouldn't desert her now.

One last look around the room for forgotten items and Laura opened the front door with as deep a sigh as she could manage. Rascal and Mischief, coats groomed to perfection, sat beside the door ready to go.

"Sorry guys, you can't go to church with me today. Maybe tomorrow I'll take you over for a look around." Laura closed the door firmly behind her. However, as she opened the church door, she almost stepped on two streaks of raccoon-color fur that whizzed past her.

"Rascal! Mischief! What are you doing? I thought I..." Laura was left talking to herself. Maybe they would be good. At any rate, she couldn't possibly chase them over the entire church in heels, take them home—assuming she could even catch them in the first place—and get back in time for worship.

Laura soon forgot the cats as she walked quietly and reverently into the sanctuary. Her days had been so full of murder and chaos since her arrival in Cottonville, there'd been no time, or opportunity, to even explore the church. Now she took her time ambling about. Sunlight through the stained glass painted swirling pictures across smooth light oak pews—like a reflection on still water. Would it disappear if she touched it? The satin finish of the wood felt cool beneath her fingers—the colors playing across the back of her hand.

Words of Katharina von Schlegel's *Be Still my Soul* welled up within her soul and tumbled out unbidden in response to her awe. The pungent aroma of grape juice and the smell of fresh bread drew her attention to the communion table. She hadn't planned for communion, but, of course, it made sense to do so.

Laura stood before the altar lost in her song and prayer. Suddenly, she sensed someone behind her and fell silent in embarrassment. A young teenager huddled in the corner of the front pew. "Oh, I'm sorry I didn't know anyone was here," said Laura.

"Please, don't apologize. I heard you come in. I would've said something sooner, but you started singing. It was so beautiful, I couldn't interrupt." The speaker was a pretty girl with braces and dark brown braids. She swiped at her brown eyes, embarrassed to be caught crying. "You're the new pastor, aren't you?"

"Yes, I am. And who are you?" Laura recovered from her surprise, sat beside the girl.

"I'm Jody Atkins. You know my father."

"Yes, I met him." It was difficult to keep her voice even when her suspicions about Mike Atkins were so strong.

"He doesn't like you. Neither does my brother. I don't know why, but please don't judge them too harshly until you get to know them."

"Jody, I try to give people the benefit of the doubt when we meet. I know it's difficult for some folks to accept a woman as a pastor, but they'll get used to it. I hope things will work out for your father and brother." She really hoped so, but thought there was more involved than just not liking a woman pastor.

"Pastor, I'm really worried about them—not because they don't like you. They don't like much of anyone anymore. There's something more. I'm not even sure what, but I'm so afraid they're in trouble of some kind."

Laura unconsciously rubbed a hand across the other arm. The skin on her arms and back of her neck prickled. This was Mike Atkins' daughter talking. She forced herself to be calm. She didn't want to frighten the girl anymore than she already was.

"What kind of trouble, Jody and what makes you think so?" Laura held her breath. Jody seemed like a sensitive young girl seeking help, but not knowing how to ask for it.

"I don't know. Just...sometimes Johnny—he's my twin brother—sometimes he seems so...so...spacey. You know what I mean?"

"I think I do. Do you think he might be on drugs?" She hated to ask, but what else could she say?

Tears trickled down Jody's face again. Her head bowed, her voice was so low Laura had to lean forward to hear. "I think he is. He denies it. He yells at me when I try to talk to him about it." Jody lifted her head and the look in her eyes reminded Laura of a small animal caught in a trap. "He didn't used to be that way."

"How long has this been going on, Jody?"

Laura sensed Jody's need to talk. Her heart went out to the young girl. It was tough enough being a teenager, but to have this kind of worry was beyond the coping skills of most adults. She could feel the tension as Jody struggled with how much she could trust her new pastor. Apparently she decided she would take the chance and a load of care the girl had carried for a long time tumbled out at Laura's feet. Laura moved closer and put her arm around the thin shoulders.

"It started a little over a year ago. Johnny and I used to be so close. Now he hardly talks to me. And Dad won't even think about the possibility of trouble. Chief Williams has tried to tell him several times that Johnny is in trouble and he thinks it's drug related. Dad just tells him to mind his own business and won't listen to anyone except Johnny. When Johnny says he didn't do something, Dad believes him. I used to, but I don't anymore. I've caught him in too many lies. His best friend, Skip Jameson is involved too. It all began when they started hanging out with Horace Cotton. I don't like him. He scares me."

"Oh God," Laura silently prayed, "help me to know what to say to this child. It's going to devastate her if her father and brother are involved in murder."

"Where's your mother, Jody? What does she say about all this?"

More tears slid down her face as Jody tried to talk. Finally, she said, "She left about a year ago. She tried to tell Dad Johnny needed help. He got real angry and told her to get out. She said she would take us with her and get help for Johnny. Dad said he would kill us all if she tried. We haven't heard from her since. I think she tries. I see him tear up letters and once I heard him on the phone say, 'I told you what I would do if you tried,' and he hung up."

Laura was appalled. "Jody! What an awful thing to take place in front of you."

"Oh, they didn't know I heard. I didn't mean to listen. I was in the walk-in closet off the study looking for something when they came into the study. I couldn't move. I was too scared. Dad told us later Mom ran off with another man."

"Oh, Jody," Laura swiped at her own tears, "it sounds like you've given this a lot of thought. What do you think we can do about it?"

"You're right. I've thought a lot about it. I can't say anything to Chief Williams because all I have is feelings. I can't prove anything. And I know I can't do anything about it until Dad and Johnny are ready to face reality. All I can do is pray, but I wonder if God really cares about my prayers. I'm only a teenager. Does God care about kids on drugs and dads who don't listen?"

"Jody, I don't know a lot about drugs and kids who use them. I do know about God, and I can say with all the assurance I have, God cares about you, your brother, your dad, and your mom. He cares about all kids on drugs. God doesn't want anyone to suffer, but God doesn't want to take away the freedom he's given us, either. We can pray that God will send someone to help them see the road they are on, but we have to be prepared to be that someone. We can pray that they, like the prodigal son, will come to themselves and seek help. Whatever happens, Jody, God is in it with us, suffering with us, rejoicing with us."

"Thank you, Pastor." She dabbed at her eyes with a well used tissue. Laura pulled a handful of folded tissues from her pocket and placed them in Jody's small hand.

Jody took them and gave Laura a small, grateful smile. "I know you have things to do to get ready for church, but is it all right if I just sit here? I won't bother you, or get in your way."

"You can stay there as long as you need to. You won't bother me at all. I can pray with you while I go about my preparations." Laura smiled and patted the girl on the shoulder. The song became a hum and she prayed silently then went to her office. Martha Jennings found her there a few minutes later.

"Pastor," she called from the office doorway. "Can I see you for a minute?"

"Sure, Martha, come in. By the way the rolls were delicious. Nothing could have helped more to make me feel better. Detective Morgan and Chief Williams also enjoyed them."

Martha beamed. "I love cooking and especially baking. Doc says I shouldn't eat so much of the stuff I cook, so I give it away. That way I can still enjoy baking it. I set out bread and juice for communion. I hope you don't mind. I would've called to ask, but figured you had enough on your mind. We haven't had communion for over two years and some of us ladies thought maybe you wouldn't mind. If it's not all right, I'll go take them off the altar."

Laura smiled at her. "Martha, I think it's a marvelous idea. I'm just jealous that I didn't think of it myself. I appreciate your thoughtfulness. How is it usually served?"

"We like to come to the altar and kneel. Some folks have trouble kneeling anymore, but we still like to do it that way. Whatever you want will be fine with us."

Laura did not hesitate. "We'll come to the altar. However," she added, remembering her sprained arm and sore ribs, "I will need some help with the communion cup tray. Do you think you could help me serve this morning?"

Martha grinned from ear to ear. "I never done that before, but I'm sure I can hold a tray while folks lift a cup from it. I'd be pleased to help you."

After Martha left, Laura sat in her office thinking and praying until she heard the organ begin to play. Where did the time go? She gathered her notes and moved toward the pulpit.

"Well, God, this is it. Should I say wish me luck?" The familiar mirth touched the depth of her soul.

32

The first half of the service unfolded without incident. Worshipers filled the sanctuary, even though Laura had feared people wouldn't come at all. She knew many were there out of curiosity, wondering about the woman preacher who refused to be scared away. Some were there to scoff, some to ridicule, some to pity her, but most, she felt, were there to truly worship God in spite of all the troubles and difficulties they had experienced the last two years.

Laura glanced over the congregation, surprised to see so many familiar faces. In less than a week, many folks had already become her friends. Fred Martin and his wife Emma sat near the front on the pulpit side. The women who helped her unpack, the committee persons, all were eager to hear their friend. Although she knew Todd and Steve would be nearby, she was surprised to see them sitting on the back row where, she assumed, they could watch everyone. She couldn't have explained, if she tried, how pleased and safe she felt with them there.

Jody Atkins with her young soprano voice, sang a solo, *Fill My Cup* which moved Laura to tears. She knew how much the young girl really meant the words she sang and how much she reached out to the deaf ears of her father and brother. Mike and Johnny Atkins sat in a pew at the back of the church glaring at Laura. She knew, also, the song was for her mother, wherever she was. Jody sat down and Laura stood.

"And all God's people said..." Laura looked over the sea of confused faces. No one said anything. "All right, I guess I will have to explain," she said. "Some churches automatically say, 'Amen,' when they are moved by something in the service. Some need a little encouragement. So when I say, 'And all God's people said' you respond with 'Amen' if you really mean it. So, let's try it again. And all God's people said..."

"Amen," the congregation responded, followed by a nervous laugh because it was something they had never done before.

"Don't worry," said Laura smiling. "You'll catch on. This morning, even though it's Mother's Day, and even though it's my first Sunday here, I'm not going to give you a sermon. So, if you came to see how a woman preaches, you'll just have to come back next week."

There was another small ripple of laughter around the room.

"This morning I do need to say a couple of things, however. First, I want to explain about the black eye. I could say I ran into a door, but I think most of you already know about all that has been going on here since my arrival Tuesday night. For those who don't know, I'll give a brief synopsis, not that I want to give it too much importance, but because as members and friends of this church, you need to know the truth first hand. I surprised a burglar twice, found a dead man in my garage, two cats in the church belfry named Rascal and Mischief, and spray paint on my car. Someone stuffed rags soaked in oil under my car and set fire to them. When I borrowed a friend's car, SaraBelle Cotton and I were shot at and run off the road on Gopher Mountain. That's where I got the black eye and a couple of bruised ribs. So please don't hug me when you leave."

At the mention of their names, Rascal and Mischief slid from under Laura's chair where they had hidden. With the grace of flying trapeze artists, they landed simultaneously on the pulpit where they sat like royalty on either side of her notes. This brought more laughter. To try to remove the cats would only cause more commotion so Laura decided to take a chance and leave them in their glory.

"They take seriously the old story about you save my life and I'm yours forever."

More laughter. How could this lady preacher still have a sense of humor in the midst of it all that had happened to her?

"All that I've mentioned was done to scare me away for whatever reason. I was tempted to ask this morning if you want me to stay, but decided I won't because, one, you might say no, and I would really feel unloved and unwanted." The laughter was a little louder and longer.

"And two, you might say, yes. Then I would get a big head, and I don't know what that would do to my black eye."

Most of the congregation was laughing, not because she had been hurt, but because she could make light of it all. Some, of course, glared and would gladly have accepted her resignation. It didn't make sense. Why was she staying?

As if she read the minds of those who wanted her gone, Laura became very serious. "But the real reason I won't ask is, it wouldn't matter how you answered. I believe very firmly that God sent me here, and here I will stay until God decides it is time for me to leave. So, if anyone has a problem with that, take it up with my Boss. You do know Him, don't you?"

Laura's gaze went to Steve and Todd, who returned her smile.

Several members said, "Amen." More laughter followed.

"Now, folks," Laura continued, "that's enough about the bad news. The Good News is God is alive and well in Cottonville. Today is Mother's Day, so honor your mother, wherever she is. Honor that person who substitutes for your mother if she is gone. Most of all, honor God who created mothers, fathers, and families, God who loves us more than any mother ever could—whether we are good or bad, in trouble, or helping those in trouble, kids on drugs, parents afraid to ask for help, even people who find it impossible to live with good and feel they must destroy it. Yes, God loves us all—not that God likes everything we do—but God sent his Son, Jesus Christ, that we might all have eternal life. On that night when he was betrayed..."

Rascal and Mischief sat like ceramic statues until Laura moved to the altar for the service of Holy Communion. Both cats eased down on their stomachs, tucked front paws under them, and half-closed their eyes. Laura, aware of their relaxed stance, ignored them and began the liturgy of the sacrament. With Martha's help, she offered the bread and the cup to each who came to the altar and took it to the pews for those who were unable to walk to the altar.

Following the hymn, Laura announced the brief meeting of the Pastor/Parish Relations Committee and the Trustees. After the benediction, she went to greet the people. Rascal and Mischief stayed at their post until they saw her move toward the fellowship hall in the basement.

"Pastor." A heavy-set lady with very curly gray hair and a bright red dress with large yellow daises on it, approached her as she turned to go downstairs.

"Yes," she answered hoping this wasn't another diversion tactic.

"I know you're in a hurry. I'm Cora Duncan and I just wanted you to know I'm praying for you each day. The Lord told me you need a lot of prayers. Now I know why." And she smiled and turned to go.

"Wait, Cora." Laura stopped her. "Thank you. You don't know how much your call meant to me the other night."

Cora smiled and waved as she turned to leave. Laura went to the meeting with a lighter heart. She knew she had a prayer partner who would never let her down.

33

Committee members gathered around a long table in the fellowship hall waiting for Laura—some bored, some anxious, some with a let's-get-this-over-with attitude. Fred Martin stopped to speak to Todd and Steve who stood by the exit door of the fellowship hall.

"More trouble?"

"No, we're just here to watch."

"Making sure no one runs out before we finish?" Fred laughed.

"Hadn't thought about it Fred, but might not be a bad idea," said Todd. "Reverend Kenzel's had enough trouble. She doesn't need her committees deserting her."

"You got that right. Any closer to putting a stop to it all?"

"We hope so, Fred—at least some of it. We can't change people's attitudes."

Laura walked past them, nodded, and went to start the meeting. Rascal and Mischief followed Laura in, but sat beside Todd and Steve to watch.

"Better get over there before she starts without me," said Fred. "See you."

Todd and Steve leaned against the wall. No one else questioned their presence.

"Friends, I won't keep you long," she began. "We talked the

other night about cleaning and sprucing up around the church and parsonage. I know you've tried, but everything from the weather, to the fire truck, to stolen tools have kept you from it. I have reason to believe it was all a part of a plot to drive me away as the other pastors were driven away—all that is except the weather. I won't even try to interpret that one. As I said before, I don't intend to give up. I hope you're with me."

Around the table nods and affirmation sounded from some—glares and scowls from others.

"I know this is a sudden request, but I want that garage torn down. It's a reminder of all that has happened here, it's an eyesore, and it's dangerous for any of the kids who wander by on their way to the woods to go fishing. I received an offer which I think is too good to refuse."

Mike Atkins spoke through his plastic smile. "What's the matter? City girl like you can't handle country living?"

Laura tried to ignore him, but he continued, "If you don't like the way things are here, maybe you need to take the hints and to go back to the city where you came from. That garage has been good enough for all the other pastors we've had. I'm sure your little bug would fit in it with no trouble."

Laura clamped her teeth together and drew a deep breath. Steve would have given anything to deck him one. He felt Todd's hand on his arm. They hadn't been present at her first meeting, so didn't know how she would handle this man's animosity.

Laura wasn't concerned with handling the meeting. She didn't want to lose her temper and blow it. Still recovering from her injuries, she wasn't as much in control of her emotions as she would liked to have been. But she could hold her own without help. Rascal and Mischief kept their eyes on her, tails swishing, ears back. No one had even noticed them, except Steve. He watched with interest. They would be at Laura's side in a split second should she need them.

"*Mister* Atkins," Laura said. "Not that it matters, but I was raised in a rural village surrounded by coal-mining towns in the mountains of southern West Virginia. I've lived in houses that weren't in much better condition than that garage. I'm well acquainted with wealth and poverty, urban, sub-urban, and rural living. What I'm asking for has nothing to do with who I am, or what my background is. It has to do with who we are as a church in this community. What kind of image of God are we projecting to the people of Cottonville? SaraBelle Cotton has generously offered a gift…" She handed the note to Frank. "…and I think we ought to accept that gift. And Mr. Atkins," she added, "it will take a lot more than the few hints, as you call them, to drive me away."

Todd and Steve exchanged glances, grinned and relaxed. Laura could handle these people quite well.

"What is it Frank?" asked Fred. "SaraBelle give us another *twofer* offer? You know, she gives two dollars for every one we provide? She gave us that offer once before."

"Yeah, we turned her down then, and we'll turn her down now." Phil Jameson's face was getting red as he pounded his fist on the table.

"Let's hear what she has to say, Jameson. I think we were too quick to turn her down before. We could have used the last offer of a ramp for the church." Jim Keenly was a soft spoken man who took care of his wheelchair bound wife, and still had time for his church.

"Come off it, Keenly," roared Jameson. "We don't need a ramp. When people get too old to come to church, let them stay home."

Jim Keenly looked like he had been kicked in the stomach by a stubborn mule.

"Mr. Jameson," said Laura between clenched teeth, "that was a rude and thoughtless remark. If we were offered a ramp before, I would be willing to say SaraBelle will reconsider it. And I hope age is kinder to you than you are to those who are afflicted. Please read the message from SaraBelle, Mr. Jennings." Her eyes flashed and never left Phil Jameson as Frank lifted the note and glanced over it.

"Remind me never to get her angry," whispered Steve.

"You and me both," replied Todd.

"Well, folks," drawled Frank. "It looks like SaraBelle isn't too pleased with the state of things here. Can't say as I blame her." Then he read the note.

"SaraBelle is getting senile," said Mike Atkins. "She doesn't even know how to handle her own money anymore. Why should she tell us how to run the church?"

"Oh, she knows what she wants, Mr. Atkins, but it isn't what Horace wants. There's nothing wrong with her mind. We would both be dead right now if it hadn't been for her quick thinking and acting." Laura's voice was still quiet and controlled, her eyes narrowed.

Frank broke in, "What's all the jabbering about anyway? The building's an eyesore—not fit to put a car in. If SaraBelle wants to replace it and is willing to foot the bill, I say let's do it."

"I agree," said Fred, "and furthermore, I think we ought to consider a Capital Funds Drive for a new parsonage and the renovating of the church.

"I'm with you, Fred," interjected Lewis Hostetler. "We've let fear keep us bound up like Lazarus too long. Where's our faith?"

Mike Atkins stared, fists clenched, eyes cold, smile plastered in place. "Well, it seems our professional suggestions aren't worth a lot, Jameson, but we're team players. I'll volunteer to get some bids and…"

"And it will be taken care of a year from now?" Laura finished for him. "I don't think so, Mr. Atkins. If I don't see you folks tearing it down by nine o'clock tomorrow morning, I will personally call a wrecking company to come and take care of it immediately."

Phil Jameson, his face beet-red and perspiration standing out in beads over his face, looked as if he would have a stroke. "You can't do that," he sputtered.

"I can and I will." Laura's eyes flashed.

Frank Jennings smiled. "I'll be there as soon as the sun's up. Anyone care to join me?"

"Count on me," said Fred. "I was one of those kids who enjoyed taking things apart. Hated putting them back together. Always had pieces and parts left over. It'll be a pleasure to take something apart and not worry about putting it back." He laughed at his own ineptitude. The others, knowing Fred, laughed with him.

"I'm in," said Irvine Markly.

"Can't be there that early, but I'll be there." Jim Lily had farm chores to take care of first.

"The Hospitality Committee will provide coffee at six a.m. and rolls for coffee break at nine o'clock here in the fellowship hall. We'll also have lunch at noon," said Martha.

Laura left the fellowship hall smiling. She heard bits and pieces of conversation as she met Todd and Steve at the door.

"...can't do that!"

"...think she is?"

"...coffee cake..."

"...sausages..."

"...coffee—lots of coffee..."

"...and ice tea..."

"...bring some chickens—sandwiches..."

"Are we all ready?" she asked.

"As ready as we're going to be. Do you really think they'll be there tonight?" Steve took her arm as they left the church. Rascal and Mischief followed.

Laura glanced up at the gathering clouds. "I think they'll try this afternoon, or early evening—especially if we get a storm to hide their activity."

"Then we better get in position. We might not have much time," Todd said as he drew out his cell phone and started calling his back-ups.

"Laura..." There was so much Steve wanted to say to her, but this wasn't the time.

"Yes?"

"Be careful. We'll be watching, but if something goes wrong, don't take any chances."

"I won't. I have two kitties that need me." She glanced down at the two cats who sat on either side of her staring at her with their adoring, eyes.

"And a police chief and detective?" Steve asked.

"I don't know. Do they need me—or do I need them?"

Steve smiled. "A little of both, maybe."

Todd and Steve went to their appointed posts and Laura with the cats on either side of her went to her house to wait for what was sure to be a horrendous afternoon. Already the dark clouds moved in from the west. The early morning breeze had picked up fury and little cyclones blew debris across the yard. No thunder or lightning, yet, but it wouldn't be long before a spring thunderstorm would also add to the mystique of the afternoon.

34

Dark gray thunderheads rolled in to replace the earlier bright skies and white clouds. Too restless to sit and wait for something to happen, Laura paced; Rascal and Mischeif kept in step beside her. Would they wait for nightfall to move the drugs? Would they be bold enough to try before dark if they were covered by the storm? They would need some light to see what they were doing in the garage. If they waited for nightfall, someone might see their lights.

Lightning flashed across the sky followed by a thunder roll that sounded like it bounced from mountain to mountain. Laura glanced toward the bell tower. What if…She wouldn't let her thoughts stray into what if territory. She forced herself to move away from the window. Fear and anxiety surged like bitter bile, not only fear of danger, but also, fear of giving in to her desire to run to Todd and Steve to escape the loneliness of waiting.

"God, I need courage to get through this. And if it's not asking too much, keep Steve and Todd safe." The sky darkened to an almost twilight blackness as she prayed.

A loud clap of thunder coincided with the pounding at the front door. Rascal and Mischeif stiffened, fur bristled, backs arched. Nervous about their plan, but anxious to get it over with, Laura reached for the door.

Deep in the recesses of her heart and soul she felt that spiritual mirth and what amounted to "When you go through the fires, I will be with you. There is much work to do here."

Another bang against the door startled her. She stepped back as the door flew open. Horace stood, gun in hand, facing her.

Before she could move he grabbed her wrist with his freehand. "We're cleaning out the garage before they tear it down tomorrow. Thought you ought to be there."

"Suppose I don't want to go."

Horace laughed—a cold, hard sound. "Let's go." He jerked her out the door. He was stronger than he looked and her injured ribs and arm made it impossible to fight him. He was definitely older than seventeen.

"We want you where we can keep an eye on you. Don't want those stupid cops hanging around." He jabbed the gun into her bruised ribs. Laura bit her lip and held her breath to keep from crying out in pain. She had no choice but to go with him.

Horace, dragging his captive with him, ran to the garage as the dark clouds opened their locks, letting huge drops of rain plummet to earth. From the corner of her eye Laura saw two raccoon-colored animals streak across the backyard. She hoped they would stay hidden.

Horace pulled her closer to the garage where a car waited, its motor running, front end inches inside the garage, headlights lighting the area where Steve found the drugs. Malcolm Atkins, with hands in his pockets, watched several others as they dug.

"Well, Reverend Kenzel, we meet again." He emphasized the Reverend as Horace pushed her into the garage. "You know, you are one stubborn lady. You should have taken the gentle hints and left when you had the chance. Now we have no choice but to make it a permanent departure." He laughed with that same chilling laughter that Horace had earlier.

"Mr. Atkins—if indeed that is your name—I'm surprised to see you here. What interest would you have in an old garage that's going to be torn down tomorrow?"

"You're sharp, lady, too sharp for your own good. So you

figured out that I'm not who I said I was. How'd you know? Not that it makes any difference, but I'm always curious about where I slipped up. It'll help me the next time."

"Oh, nothing you said, or did," said Laura surprised that she could keep her voice even knowing the man intended to kill her. She had to keep him talking in order to get as much information from him as she could. She hoped Todd and Steve had wired the place like they'd planned to do. Would the storm cause any problems in carrying the sound?

"You don't look anything like Mike Atkins. Actually you look more like Jeb Little. And it was a little too strange the way you just happened to show up when things got more weird around here. What I don't understand is how Ed Winters is connected to anything."

"Shut up, Kenzel." Phil Jameson stood in a darkened corner of the garage. Laura, surprised to hear his voice turned to get a better look at those by the wood pile. Skip Jameson and Johnny Atkins shoveled dirt.

"Mr. Jameson. I thought you would be here. Where's Mike Atkins? Surely he should be here helping you."

"Leave my dad out of this." Johnny stopped digging and shot daggers at her.

"Shut up and dig," Phil Jameson said. Turning back to Laura, he said, "Mike Atkins is a sissy-fied, panty-waist."

Johnny looked like he would go after Jameson with the shovel. Skip pulled him back.

"But he is involved," said Laura.

"How do you know that?" asked the man who called himself Malcolm Atkins.

"Well, that's obvious," said Laura turning back to Atkins. "When Jeb Little arrived with—I'll call him Horace for the lack of his real name—Mike Atkins had to give some kind of credence for him being here. What I don't understand is why SaraBelle and what happened to Mr. Little—if that is his name."

"You're as curious as my brother's ignorant cats," laughed Malcolm.

"I wouldn't give her the time of day if I were you Boss," warned Phil Jameson.

"Well, you aren't running this operation, Jameson. I am—at least while Colin's not here. What's it going to hurt to let her die with all the knowledge she wants." He ogled Laura from top to bottom. She was glad she had worn jeans with her T-shirt and sandals—not shorts. Malcolm stepped closer and ran his hands over Laura's torso. She clamped her teeth together to keep from cringing and shuddering. "She's not wired," he said.

"So, you want some answers. It should be obvious, even to you, that SaraBelle's money is the only reason we needed her. She's an old lady with millions and no one to leave it to except her nephew Horace, who does exist, by the way. He doesn't have the foggiest idea that his aunt is still alive. He's a typical teenager who can't think beyond today."

"So this man, whoever he is, came to town and pretended to be Horace. Jeb Little was what? His father? Uncle? Cousin?"

"You really *are* good, lady." Horace sounded surprised and impressed. "He was my father. How did you figure that one out?"

"I saw the resemblance the first time I saw you. Jeb might have been dead when I saw him, but I don't forget a face. So, Mike Atkins falsified papers to prove that you were SaraBelle's nephew?"

"He's not that smart, lady," said Phil Jameson. "He thinks he's a hot-shot lawyer, but he wouldn't last any time in a *real* law practice." Laura glanced at Johnny and saw Skip once again hold him back. "No, Atkins' only part in this operation is his ignorance and a little blackmail. I made up the papers and gave them to Atkins. He said they weren't legal. That's when I had to resort to blackmail. Told him his precious son was into drugs big time and if he didn't go along he would find him some day with an overdose. I got the cooperation I needed. It helps to have a lawyer on your side." He snickered.

"So that's the reason he sent his wife away. He didn't want her involved."

"What do you mean?" asked Johnny. "My mother ran away with another man."

"No, Johnny. She left because your father threatened to kill all of you if she didn't leave."

"Did he tell you that?"

"No."

"Then how…?" He didn't finish the question, but turned back to his digging. Laura saw the troubled look in his eyes.

"Maybe the man has some guts after all." Malcolm sounded impressed. "But you asked about Ed Winters and how he got involved. That was a stroke of pure luck. Jameson stumbled upon the fact that Ed was having an affair with Jameson's secretary. It was easy to get his cooperation when we threatened to tell his wife and the community. We convinced him he wasn't doing anything wrong, or illegal, by delaying you. No harm in holding up a funeral for a nobody. It would give Randy—that's Horace's real name, by the way—a chance to get the old woman away before you could get there. It was another stroke of luck that Jameson called her and found out she expected you to visit that morning. The secretary wasn't too anxious for her husband to know about her affair, so she called and said she was your secretary and canceled the meeting. Randy only pretended to call for a hair appointment. Would have worked fine if you hadn't been so bull-headed and taken that stupid cop with you."

"And the fire under my car?" Laura asked, but she already knew. "It was just more diversion to keep me away from SaraBelle?"

"That's right. We planned to let the air out of your tires or something so you couldn't get back in time. When you showed up with the cop, I had to do some quick last minute changes. So I got on the car phone and called Skip. Told him to get Johnny and get over to your place and create a diversion of some kind. I thought they were pretty ingenious. I would've put the rags inside the car myself, but I guess there was enough smoke rolling around the car it looked like it was on fire. Whatever, it would have worked if that other cop hadn't given you the keys to his car. I told the boys to hang around and let me know what happened."

Thunder rolled closer and louder. Without the headlights of the car, it would have been impossible to see anything in the garage.

"So you called Horace—Randy—and warned him I was coming anyway. He was to get SaraBelle out of the house before I got there."

"That's right. But you showed up before he could get her away and insisted on taking her to Glenville, yourself. The old lady refused to change her will, but Randy had been practicing her signature. Atkins left the new will there for her to read and think about. All Randy had to do was sign her name to it and get it notarized—by Phil Jameson, of course—and he was home free."

"But only if SaraBelle was dead." Laura couldn't believe people could be so cold-hearted.

"Well, that was only a matter of time anyway," said Randy. "She's an old lady. If she had a heart attack and fell over the wall at Lookout Point, who would question?"

"When that didn't work out, you followed and shot at the car."

Randy giggled like a child who had just played a trick on someone. "Yeah, I thought sure I hit her. She fell forward. Then I started shooting tires, figured I may as well get rid of both of you at the same time. If the car went up in flames, or rolled to the bottom of the mountain, no one would ever know."

"But it didn't," Laura said softly.

"I don't know how you did it. I never saw anyone control a car like that before. It was pure luck you ran off the road at the only place on the mountain where you would be stopped before rolling to the bottom."

"No, Randy, it wasn't luck, but you wouldn't understand about miracles, would you? What happened to your father? Did you kill him, too? Because he caught you stealing some of the cocaine?"

"You're nuts." Randy started to sweat.

"Is she right, Randy?" Malcolm suddenly seemed more interested in the conversation.

"So what? The old man had set up living quarters in the belfry. He kept those stupid cats tied up there." He giggled that manic, child-like giggle again. "It was a great stroke of real genius. When the cats didn't make enough noise, he added to it to keep people away from the garage."

"That's why you, Johnny, and Skip beat Jerome. You were afraid he might have seen something up there that would tell us someone had been living up there."

"Yeah, we warned the little rat. He kept saying he didn't know what we were talking about."

"He didn't. He only saw the cats because that was his concern. You almost killed him. It *was* you who did the beating, wasn't it?"

"Yeah, those two sissies were afraid of hurting the kid."

"And your father—Jeb Little—created diversions by having the cats do tricks. People watched the cats and no one would see the shipments come and go." Laura wanted to be sure they got everything on tape—if it was being taped.

"Yeah, he lived in the belfry so he could watch the garage. He could see and hear everything within a block of here. I thought he was out, or asleep, so I came over to check on the stuff—make sure it wasn't getting wet, or anything. We were having a bad storm. It looked so inviting I had to have a little of it. It was only a small bag. I was going to tell you about it." He glanced at Malcolm.

"But he wasn't out and he saw you go in the garage," said Laura.

"I turned around and saw him. He looked like a crazy old man. Accused me of stealing the stuff. Said he would tell my uncle. Didn't matter I was his son, he pulled a gun on me. I knocked it out of his hand with the shovel, and picked it up. We scuffled. The gun went off. I didn't mean to kill him. He was my father." Randy didn't look, or sound, very sorry for his deed.

A look of knowing crossed between Malcolm and Jameson. "You shouldn't have done that kid," said Malcolm. "Steal our stuff, that is. What you did to your old man is your business, but you don't steal from us. We'll take care of you later."

"You attacked me earlier that night and took a shot at Detective Morgan the next night, didn't you?" Laura was determined to get every bit of information from them.

Randy sneered. "Yeah, I had my orders to make sure I either scared you away or killed you. I would have succeeded if those cops hadn't showed up."

"How did you know a woman was coming?"

Randy laughed that maniacal cackle again. "My uncle told me."

"Malcolm?"

"That's enough questions," said Malcolm. "Let's get this stuff out of here. We've wasted enough time talking. The storm won't last and we don't want the Jennings to come nosing around. We gave you enough to satisfy your curiosity." He smiled a crooked, cold smile. "I'm sorry you'll have to come with us. We can't afford to leave you behind since you know everything. Randy will enjoy your company before he disposes of your remains."

Malcolm looked out the front of the garage. The rain was falling literally in buckets—visibility next to zero. "Damn rain," he said. "Never saw it rain so heavy. You can't see anything out there."

He turned to the two teenagers. "Johnny, turn the car around. Back it up so the trunk is inside the garage. We don't want this stuff to get wet."

Johnny glanced at Laura, ducked his head, and ran out into the rain. Thunder boomed and rolled overhead. Rafters of the old garage vibrated. Malcolm leaned toward the door, watching Johnny back the car and turn it around. The car stopped in the driveway. "What's that kid doing?"

Phil Jameson moved to the door. The rain was still falling like a waterfall. Thunder boomed and rumbled. The headlights pointing toward the street, but the car didn't move.

"Maybe it got wet and stalled out on him," said Skip. He glanced at Laura with a look that said, "I'm sorry."

She felt sorry for both of the boys. They were good kids who got in over their heads with the wrong crowd. Of course, it didn't help to have their fathers involved.

He said, "I didn't know all the stuff that was going. Johnny didn't either. We only wanted a good time—not murder."

Phil Jameson clapped his son hard on the back. "Too bad kid, that's life. Learn that lesson now. It won't get any better."

Anger flared in Laura. How could a father treat his son that way? "That's not true," she said. "Life doesn't have to be this evil. God didn't intend..." she didn't finish her sentence as a hand landed hard across her face.

"Shut up," said Randy. "I heard enough of that kind of stuff from the old lady."

"Skip, get out there and see what's keeping that boy," Jameson ordered. "We got to move this stuff before Jennings sees activity up here and calls the cops."

The rain continued to drum on the roof while they waited. Malcolm paced back and forth before the open door trying to see and hear the car. Randy nervously juggled the gun in his left hand while keeping his right hand on Laura's shoulder. He pulled her closer to him. It took all her willpower and concentration to keep back the shudder.

"Where are those boys?" asked Malcolm.

"That car never stalled out in rain before. If they ran off and left us, I'll thrash them both." Jameson pounded a fist into the waiting palm of his other hand.

A deep frown covered Malcolm's face. "Something isn't right here." He glared at Laura, his irritation turning to suspicion. "Wait a minute. They didn't run out on us. The cops grabbed them. This is a set up. You set us up, you…"

Malcolm didn't get a chance to finish his accusation. Steve's fist landed on his jaw. At the same time, Todd took care of Jameson. "Just like rats in a trap," said Todd and Steve together. They turned to take care of Randy, but they hadn't planned on Randy having a gun. He pulled Laura closer to him and hooked his arm around her neck.

"Don't move cops, or she's a goner," he warned as Todd and Steve both lurched forward. They stopped, waiting for a chance to move. Randy backed toward the door dragging Laura with him. He didn't get far. Two raccoon-like blurs dropped from the rafters. Rascal landed on the outstretched left arm with tiny swords drawn for battle, while his teeth clamped down on the hand that held the gun. Mischief, claws also protracted landed on top of Randy's bare head. He screamed, as the gun fell from his injured hand. Pushing Laura away in an effort to shake his assailants loose, Randy continued to scream and claw at the furious fur balls. Laura fell to her hands and knees. Todd grabbed the gun. Randy screamed while blood flowed from his head and his left hand. The other hand looked like he had been through a briar patch from trying to get the animals off him.

Steve ran to help Laura up, but she shook her head, turned, and sat on the floor. "I don't think my legs will hold me yet," she said, trying to catch her breath around the pain in her ribs.

He knelt beside her, turned her face toward him, and saw the hand print. Blood trickled from the previous cut over her eye and now from the corner of her mouth. More anger flashed across his face.

"I'm all right," she said. "Just shaky"

"Laura, I'm sorry…" He was interrupted by Todd.

"Excuse me, Laura, but would you call them off?" asked Todd. It was difficult to speak around the wide grin that covered his face.

Laura answered without a hint of anything other than dead sincerity. "I don't know. They're ignorant and stupid cats, who don't listen to human commands, but I suppose I could try." She turned to her two furry protectors. "Rascal, Mischief, let the men take over from here. Good job, kitties. Come on, we'll go home and get a treat."

They let go of their captive, dropped to the floor, and bounded over to Laura, who embraced them. They stood on their back legs on either side of her with front paws on her shoulders, licked her face, and purred in her ears.

"Stop it, you silly cats. You're going to knock me over."

Laura laughed at them until pain and reality took over. Tears of relief came unbidden as she buried her face in their fur. They patted her face with soft pads of their paws and licked at her tears. She sat unable to move until strong arms carefully lifted her to her feet. The cats moved out of the way for Steve, as if they knew he wouldn't hurt their human.

"Come on, Laura. Let's take these feline heroes home and give them a treat. They deserve it and you've earned a break. Todd and his men have things under control. They can clean up this mess. I don't know about you, but I could use a cup of your coffee. We'll need to have a conference to fill in the rest, if you're up to it, that is."

The storm passed as suddenly as it had arrived leaving a gentle spring rain. Thunder rolled into the eastern mountains sending a few echoes back as if to say, "Our job is done for now."

The sun poked its fingers of light through the few remaining clouds, arching a perfect rainbow across the belfry of the church as they left the garage.

"Oh, Steve! Look!" In that sacred hollow of her mind, Laura heard, "My bow is in the cloud...a sign of the covenant between me and you."

35

Laura shuddered, remembering Malcolm's hands on her and Randy's gun in her side. Steve drew her closer to him. "Are you sure you're all right?"

"Yes, just trying to erase the memories, but not being very successful." She tried to smile but even that brought some discomfort at the side of her mouth where Randy slapped her. "But you're soaked. You'll get pneumonia."

Steve laughed. "I doubt that. Besides, Todd and I put some dry clothes in my car in case we got caught in the rain. I'll go get them, unless you want to call it a day. We can tie up loose ends tomorrow."

That brought a real smile. She winced. "Steve, you know as well as I do that SaraBelle and Jerome won't wait until tomorrow. I am weary, but I can't rest until all the loose ends are tied neatly in a knot and everyone who's been involved knows what happened. I'll be all right."

"I'm sure you will, but..."

"But what?"

"Never mind. We'll talk later. I'll get our clothes." How could he say all that he really felt? He wished she didn't have to suffer at all and he wanted to always be there to make sure she would be all right.

"Are you parked close by?"

"Just up the street. I'll pull into your driveway."

Laura followed the cats into the house and had the coffee on when Steve came in carrying an overnight bag. "You can use the guest room at the top of the stairs if you want to," Laura said as she returned to the living room.

"Looks like you have some messages," he said as he started up the stairs.

"I'll get them as soon as I take care of the kitties. They deserve a special treat. Come on, Rascal and Mischief."

Steve came back down the stairs in dry clothes as Laura pushed the play button on the answering machine. "That's strange, two hang-ups. Well, I guess they'll call back."

"Probably someone who dialed a wrong number," he said and sat down on the floor with the cats. While the coffee brewed, he held a ball of yarn while he listened to Laura. The cats, tired of waiting for him to throw the ball, both jumped for it. They missed the ball, but hit each other, sat back in surprise, then started boxing at each other, spitting, and chattering. Steve and Laura laughed until they felt tears in their eyes and Laura held her sides.

Steve saw her agony and asked, "Are you all right? Maybe I'd better put the yarn away."

She shook her head, then when the pain had subsided said, "I'm all right. I just have to remember not to laugh so hard. It makes it hard to breathe. Let them play; they deserve some fun."

He threw the ball of yarn, but continued to watch her. The cats stopped their boxing match and ran for the ball. Rascal got it and brought it back to Steve who threw it again. This time Rascal let Mischief get it. They continued to play while Laura listened to her messages.

"The next one has to be Susan. She won't bother to identify herself. She'll jump right in and tell me about her latest adventure—or her next one." She was right.

"Mom, where are you? Surely you don't have any social life down there. I really needed to talk to you, not your machine. Norman and I have a fabulous chance of a lifetime. We've been invited to spend a year in Europe. Norman will be an exchange professor at a university in Germany. I didn't think it would be good for Joshua to go so far away from home, so I thought, since you don't have anything to do, and must be bored to death down there, Joshua could come and stay with you for a year. We'll make sure he has all the money he needs and you have permission to do whatever needs to be done in case of an accident, or discipline, etc. Call me later and let me know when you can come and get him. We need to leave by the middle of June. Bye. Oh, by the way, happy Mother's Day. Norman bought me a beautiful new diamond necklace. Wasn't that sweet of him? Joshua made a cute little card. Got to go. Bye. Call me."

Laura shook her head and frowned at Susan's call. She pushed the button for the next message.

"Reverend Kenzel, this is Doctor Cornelius. Our patients are threatening mutiny. They're going to sign themselves out. I can bully Jerome, but SaraBelle is a little out of my league. Call me as soon as you can at the hospital."

"Great," said Laura, "now we have mutiny on our hands." The thought about SaraBelle threatening Doctor Cornelius brought a smile.

Steve laughed. "Better call him as soon as you hear your last message. He sounds desperate."

"I will." She pushed the button for the next message.

"Pastor? This is Martha Jennings. We saw cars and men running over by your garage. Is everything all right? Frank's getting ready to go check it out."

The last call was more confusing. "Laura, what are you doing down there? I don't like the reports I'm getting and the Bishop is concerned. I'll talk to you later, but if you expect to stay there you better straighten up."

"What was that all about?" asked Steve. He got up and went to stand beside her, placing his hands on her shoulders. He felt a small shudder. "Laura? Who was that?"

"District Superintendent Bill Collins and I have no idea what he's talking about. He's always confusing, but this makes no sense whatsoever. It's almost like he knows someone here who keeps him informed about me, but he told me he'd never been down here."

"It sounds like he and/or the bishop don't want you here."

"I don't know why, but...oh, well, sounds like someone on the porch. That's probably Frank Jennings," she said. "Do you want to get the door while I call Doctor Cornelius?" Laura pushed the button for the tape to rewind.

"Sure," he answered giving her a curious look. He threw the ball toward the dining room. "That's all kitties. No more playtime for now."

Both cats plopped down on their haunches and stared at the door. They didn't bother to chase the ball if the game was over. Steve opened the door for Frank. "Come in, Mr. Jennings. Laura is on the phone."

"I talked to Todd out there. Did you folks know about all this drug business?" His tone bordered on an accusation.

"I'll let your pastor fill you in," said Steve winking at Laura as she finished dialing the hospital. She tried to glare at him, but it hurt too much, so she just held up one finger to Frank, indicating she would be with him in a minute.

"Could I speak to Doctor Cornelius, please," she said to the person at the other end. He must've been very close, because he answered almost immediately. "Doctor Cornelius, everything's all right," Laura said. "You can dismiss SaraBelle and Jerome, but would you mind asking them to come to my house? You're welcome to come, too, if you want. We thought they would want to hear all the details as we tie up loose ends. Thanks. Bye."

"Mr. Jennings," she turned to her latest guest. "I just listened to the tape on the answering machine and was going to call you next. Everything's all right now. I appreciate your concern. A couple more minutes over there and I probably would have needed your help."

"Todd told me we had a drug ring operating in that old garage."

"That's right, but he has everything under control. If you and Martha want to come over in about a half an hour, the others will be here and you can hear the whole story. I think you need to know and I would like very much for you to be here."

"Sure, we'll be here. Thanks for asking us. Martha's got some dough rising over there. She was going to make rolls for tomorrow. Why don't I have her make some pizza and bring it over. She says, conversation is always better with food." He smiled at her and she felt the last of his hostility fall away.

"By the way," he said, "I just want to say I admired the way you handled that meeting this morning. Atkins and Jameson have hood-winked us for a long time, keeping us from doing what we knew we should be doing. That's no excuse, I know. We let them do it to us. Thanks for helping us cut the rope that was choking the life out of our church." Frank Jennings looked embarrassed at having given such a long speech — especially one with such feeling. He nodded and left.

The phone rang and Laura pushed the speaker phone on.

"Hello, Reverend Kenzel speaking."

"Mother? Where were you? Didn't you get my message? What do you think? When can you come and get Joshua?'

"Susan, it's good to hear from you, dear. Yes, I got your message. I was out rounding up a drug ring. And I think it's a marvelous chance for Josh and me to get better acquainted. But you'll have to bring him here. I can't come and get him."

"Mother, we have so much to do. You have more time than we do," Susan whined.

"I'm sorry Susan, but I have a full time job now. I can't up and leave whenever you think I should. I'm sure you and Norman can take a few days to bring Josh down here. Why not Memorial Day weekend? I understand we have a lot of things going on in Cottonville that weekend and he should be nearly through with school by then. When can I expect you? Friday? Saturday? Sunday is my busiest day, remember, so if you come then my time will be limited."

"Mother!"

"Sorry Susan, that's the way it will have to be. If you can't bring him, then put him on a bus. I could pick him up in Glenville, or have a friend pick him up, if I'm busy. The bus doesn't come through Cottonville. There's no airport close by and trains stopped running years ago."

She looked inquiringly at Steve, who smiled and nodded

"Mother, you're being impossible."

"Oh really? I didn't know I could be impossible." She grinned at Steve who watched with a mixture of curiosity, awe, and affection. He placed his hand over his mouth to mute his chuckle.

"*Mother*. Oh, all right. We'll bring him down on Friday of Memorial Day weekend. Joshua doesn't go to public schools. He has a tutor. We'll work out details for getting him one down there. We probably won't be able to stay the whole weekend. We have too much to do to get ready to leave by June 15. If you change your mind, let me know."

"I won't change my mind, dear, and Susan, don't even think about sending a tutor down here. Josh will go to school in town. Look forward to seeing you."

"We'll talk about it. Good-bye, Mother."

Laura frowned as she pushed the off button. "Looks like I'm going to be the parent of a ten-year-old for a year. I hope he'll get along with Jerome."

"You don't look too happy about it. You like kids, don't you?"

"Sure, I like kids. And I love my grandson. I just wish Susan and Norman would spend more time with the boy. They give him everything money can buy, but hardly give him the time of day. Surely they could take him with them. A whole year! That's a long time for a little boy."

"Sounds like the best thing that could happen to him would be to spend time in Cottonville with you."

"Maybe you're right." She smiled. "Well, since I have a house full of people coming in a little bit, I better get organized."

"Aren't you always? Organized that is." He laughed.

"Well, maybe." She grinned back at him.

The sound of a car arriving prevented any more conversation.

36

Rascal and Mischief entertained the guests with their dancing and acrobatics. Jerome, his mother and grandmother, SaraBelle, Doctor Jonathan Cornelius, Martha and Frank Jennings, Steve, Todd, and Laura all were eager to hear the last word and put to rest the fear and chaos of the last two years. Spicy aroma of pizza wafted from the kitchen, some ready to eat, some in the oven cooking. Martha made sure everyone had a plate and a cup of cola.

Jerome sat on the edge of the chair beside his mother. He was eager to hear the complete story. Steve grinned at the boy who seemed so unaffected by all that had happened to him, but he knew better. Jerome was only ten. He would carry the scars of more than just a broken arm for many years.

Taking an audio tape from his pocket, Todd tossed it to Steve, who caught it as Rascal jumped for it. Rascal sat, swishing his tail. "Sorry, Rascal, this isn't a toy. It's a valuable tape."

"A copy," Todd said, as Steve placed it in the tape player Laura had set out for him.

"Did it work?" she asked.

"Got every word, Laura," said Todd. "You were marvelous. You got them to tell you everything. This tape with the confessions will convince any jury."

"Can we hear it?" Jerome asked.

Steve pulled some notes from his pocket. "Before we hear the tape, you need to hear a story. I had no idea of a tie-in until Laura asked if we had fingerprinted Jeb Little's body. Her question prompted Todd to get out to the funeral home before they buried Jeb and get his fingerprints. I still say, she would make a great detective." Steve's eyes twinkled as he teased her.

Laura felt the familiar blush. "I'm *not* a detective. You can do the detecting. Just let me be the pastor I came here to be." She paused. "All right, I know you are waiting for me to ask, so did you get anything on the prints?"

Steve and Todd both laughed.

"Yes, we got some fingerprint information back from the FBI, but you need to know the whole story first." Steve started the narrative.

"In the mid to late fifties there was a Jacobson family who caused quite a stir in Glenville. The three Jacobson brothers, Colin, Dalton, and Hugh, were nothing but trouble from the time they were small. Colin, about eight years older than his brothers, seemed to delight in thinking up ways to cause someone grief. The younger brothers looked up to him and followed his every wish and command.

"They were into the general stuff of teens in trouble—shoplifting, smoking, drinking, and using drugs. When Colin discovered the money that could be made with drug trafficking, he was hooked, not on the drugs, but the money. He was intelligent enough to know he couldn't use the drugs and still remain smart enough to sell them and make a fortune. The younger brothers had considerably less intelligence and common sense. They were soon in trouble with the law for more than just shoplifting.

"They turned to big time theft. At first, they robbed convenience stores and gas stations, adding payrolls and banks as they got bolder. The inevitable happened. Someone was shot in a robbery attempt. The two younger brothers were sent to prison for a long time.

"In the meantime Colin had managed to escape the arrest, either because he wasn't there, or because he was able to buy off the authorities and his brothers. No one really knew. After he shot and killed his parents, whom neighbors found in their home several days later, Colin disappeared. For whatever reason, the law enforcement folks never got his fingerprints. He couldn't be traced."

"I remember that case. Martha and I were newlyweds and looking for a place to settle down. We considered Glenville, but decided on Cottonville, because we didn't want to raise kids in a town where bullies, like the Jacobsons, were a part of it."

Martha laughed. "But we had plenty of bad apples in our own little barrel. And it looks like the drugs followed us."

"I bet those Jacobsons were behind our drug ring." Jerome stated with his ten-year-old authoritative voice.

"Right on, Jerome, maybe I'll make you into a detective like Steve Morgan someday." Todd grinned at the boy.

"Now," continued Steve, "a little explanation of our preparations before the tape."

"What about the fingerprints?"

"Laura, didn't they teach you patience in seminary?" Steve gave her a look of mock sincerity.

"No. Do we need a drum roll to get this story moving?"

They all laughed. "Are you adding comedian to your list of talents, Reverend Kenzel?"

"No, but since you're being so melodramatic and these folks need...never mind. Continue."

He continued his story.

"First of all, you need to know what we did and why. After yesterday's meeting at the hospital, Todd, Laura, and I came back here and laid the plans to trap the rats as Jerome said. You already know Jeb Little had been living in the belfry. You know, also, I spent some time up there, but the criminals didn't know that. They thought their secret was still safe. Todd had his experts out here late yesterday afternoon and into the night wiring the garage so we could tape from the belfry. It took some pretty powerful batteries since there's no electricity in the garage, but we did it. Then Laura baited the trap this morning by making sure they knew the building would be coming down first thing in the morning."

"That was some bait." Frank Jennings actually laughed, a much more pleasant sound than the growls and complaints Laura had heard from him when she first arrived. "I thought Jameson was going to have a stroke right there on the spot."

"And Mike Atkins wanted to stonewall us again, but she set him straight too," Martha added.

Laura felt uncomfortable and tried to shift the attention away from her. "We still need to tear it down," she said.

"We will," said Frank. "Now, let's hear the rest of this story. Sorry, Detective Morgan."

"No problem," he said. "Laura was sure they would come this afternoon, or tonight, to get the stuff out. The storm was a God-send."

"Yes, it was, wasn't it?" Laura murmured.

Steve smiled at her and continued. "The storm helped to hide their actions, somewhat, but didn't seem to affect the tape at all. Horace took Laura at gun point to the garage, while the boys dug up the box of cocaine. It was clear they intended to kill her—either there and leave her, or take her with them and kill her later. We started the tape recording as soon as we saw the men and boys go into the garage. Listen to the tape and then we will tie up any loose ends."

The tape played to a deeply entranced audience. When it finished the silence was almost deafening. Then questions began to roll like the former thunder.

"Wait," said Todd. "One question at a time. Steve and I were in the belfry and when we heard them tell Johnny to turn the car around, we signaled the men hiding down there to grab him. Then we headed down ourselves in time to see them grab Skip as well. We thought it would be a matter of seconds before someone figured they had been set up. We were right. That's when we came in at the end. The two fur balls were the real heroes who saved Laura's life, though."

"How did they do that, anyway? I never knew cats were so intelligent, or capable." Sophia stroked Mischief who apparently decided she had a nice lap that needed to be kept warm.

"When Pastor said they were Maine Coon Cats, I looked them up in our school library. They're known for their size and their long, sharp claws and teeth. Some folks believe they're a cross between a raccoon and a cat. They're intelligent just because they are. Maine Coons don't usually have very loud voices. Pastor said they probably have some Siamese in them. She saved their lives and loved them, so they saved hers and loved her back." Jerome beamed.

"I'm sure Randy will always remember the claws and teeth part," said Laura. "I'll always remember they saved my life. I guess we're more or less even."

"What will happen to them—not the cats, the people?" Jerome became more serious. "Johnny and Skip were good guys before Horace, or Randy, or whatever his name was, came along. Will they go to jail?"

"It seems Johnny's only involvement was buying, using and helping to transport the stuff. Mike's involvement was forced. His only real sin was stupidity. Skip's problem was he loved his father and the drugs were given to him by Phil. Neither of the boys had any idea Jeb—whose real name, by the way, was Dalton Jacobson was killed because of those drugs."

He nodded at Laura. "That's right. The fingerprints came back from the FBI as those of Dalton Jacobson."

"Then Randy is a Jacobson, too?"

"That's right, Jerome," said Todd.

Steve picked up the narrative again. "Horace—or Randy Jacobson—was Jeb's son, but that didn't prevent him from killing his father. He will be tried for murder. Jameson will go to prison for a good long time, as will Malcolm Atkins—who is really Hugh Jacobson, the other younger Jacobson brother. Johnny and Skip will go to a hospital to help them kick the cocaine habit. They'll probably get probation. Mike will face some disciplinary action from the Law Board. Ed Winters did nothing illegal—immoral maybe, but not illegal. My guess is he'll give some second thoughts to playing around again.

"How did you know Jameson was involved?" asked Frank.

"We didn't exactly," admitted Laura. "I really thought Mike Atkins was behind it all until SaraBelle said yesterday she had a call from Jameson and then immediately after he hung up she had a call from someone who said she was my secretary. Then I could see his involvement in other smaller ways. So I knew one, or both, of the men were involved in some way and would make sure word got to the right person."

"I hate to say this," said Steve, "but I have to throw this out for consideration. Two of the Jacobsons were involved. There's a third brother, and unless I miss my guess, Colin Jacobson is the real mastermind behind all that's happened here."

"You mean we might hear more from him?" Laura could hardly speak above a whisper.

"I don't want to be an alarmist, and you've certainly had more than your share of trouble at the hands of this band of thugs, but I have to at least warn you of the possibility. Hopefully, this will end it. With all his serfs either dead, or in jail, and the drug traffic interrupted, there would be no point in trying again, at least in this place." Steve hesitated then glanced at Laura.

"Laura, don't worry…"

She forced a smile, but couldn't control the shudder that slid down her spine. "It's all right. With two guard cats and the best homicide detective in the area and a police chief who goes over and above the call of duty, what can happen? I guess I just hoped we could put it all behind us. But evil is ever with us and, with God's help, we'll deal with it."

She wished she felt as confident as she sounded. Her mind raced in reverse to a previous conversation. Who knew a woman was coming to Cottonville besides Bishop Giles and District Superintendent Collins? She felt Steve's eyes burning deep within her and was certain he could see the uneasiness.

"What about…?" She took a deep breath and forced herself to look into Steve's eyes. "How did my husband's death fit in?"

Steve shook his head. "I should have known you would tie it together."

"You're right, Laura," said Todd. "Randy confessed to that

murder as well. Said his Uncle Colin paid him big bucks to get Butch drunk with alcohol and drugs. Randy ran your husband off the road, got out of the car, and broke his neck while he was unconscious. Then he pulled Butch under the steering wheel and Colin picked Randy up. They called the police and left."

"But why? Harold wasn't..."

"No, he wasn't involved with anything. Somehow he found out Colin Jacobson's identity. They had to kill him before he told anyone."

"Then that's what Harold wanted to tell Bishop Jarvis and that's why they're after me."

"If they are really after you, why did they wait four years?" Steve wanted to direct the aggressive action away from her and onto the drugs.

"Because as long as I was in seminary, I wasn't a threat. But when I heard about this church from some of my seminary buddies, I asked Bishop Giles to send me here."

"Why?" several asked at the same time.

"Because, I believed that is what God was telling me to do."

"Laura, if you're right, then..."

"Colin Jacobson thinks Harold told me about him and he won't give up until I'm dead."

"But who is he?" Jerome stared wide-eyed at his pastor.

"We don't know," said Todd, "but we'll find out."

Laura shivered. She was sure she knew, but had no way of proving it. She would talk to Todd and Steve later.

"So the reason we've been without a pastor for so long was because Jameson blackmailed Atkins into siding with him to stop anyone who would even consider coming here?" Frank Jennings had a hard time believing it.

"That's right, Frank," said Steve. "Randy confessed to killing Reverend Lakeland, also. The ones they couldn't intimidate, Randy and his father scared away. Laura wouldn't be scared off." He chuckled and Todd joined him. Laura smiled, knowing they were remembering her first night in Cottonville.

"Then it didn't have anything to do with our church? I mean

those preachers didn't leave, or stay away, because we were such a bad congregation?" Martha dabbed at the corner of her eyes with a tissue she pulled from the box on the table next to her.

"Right again," said Todd.

"You're a good congregation," said Laura. "All congregations are made up of good and bad. This one just happened to have one that sought evil ways of living. You couldn't have known. You trusted your people the way we are taught to trust."

"Even I was taken in," said SaraBelle. "And I have been around longer than any of you. I didn't suspect Jameson of such horrid stuff and Atkins sure put on a good act. It must've been tough to send his wife away. I remember when those two got married. You couldn't ask for a more loving couple. Maybe she'll come back when she hears what's happened."

"SaraBelle, you're a hopeless romantic," laughed Carolyn. "But this time I hope you're right. Poor Jody, she'll need all our love and support."

Carolyn took a deep breath and held Jerome's good hand in hers. Hesitantly she continued. "Now, it's my turn. You've all loved and supported me and Jerome. I don't know where we would be without you. I guess, this has brought home to me what lies and anger can do to people. I have to confess to you, my friends and family, the truth. I've been living a lie for over ten years and I'm tired of it."

Tears began to trickle down her cheeks. Jerome reached to brush them away. "Mom, you don't have to tell anything…"

"Yes, Jerome. I can't live a lie any longer. It's not fair to you, or me, or…" She didn't finish the sentence, but glanced at Todd, who moved to her side and placed his arm around her.

"I was never married to Doren McMichaels. We ran off together. Because I was young and stupid, I believed he was going to give me the world. Todd and I had quarreled—I don't even remember what we quarreled about. When I got pregnant Doren wanted me to have an abortion and I refused. He left. I managed as long as I could, then played the prodigal daughter and called Mom. I learned Doren was killed in a robbery attempt."

"But your name…" Sophia couldn't finish her sentence. If her daughter wasn't married to McMichaels, then what about Jerome?

"I had my name legally changed when I found out Doren was dead. I invented the story about him dying in Vietnam. I didn't want Jerome to grow up without some kind of a father, even if it was only a make-believe one."

Carolyn placed her arms around her son, "I'm so sorry, Jerome. I wanted you to have the kind of life you deserved. I shouldn't have lied to you. I loved you too much to cause you pain and grief, but I know I've hurt you anyway. Can you ever forgive me?"

Jerome scowled and then his tears started flowing. "I want to be angry. First my best friend dies and causes my uncle to die along with him. Now you tell me the father I thought was a hero was only a crook. I want to be real angry, but Pastor says I have to forgive to stop the hurt. I don't want to hurt anymore, so I will."

"Jerome," Todd knelt in front of the boy and wrapped his arms around him. He spoke very quietly, but they all could hear him. "You don't need a hero in your family. You are the hero. Without your help we could never have cracked this case and those two animals would be dead cats in the belfry. Not many boys your age could take the beating you did and still be concerned about what would happen to the perpetrators. Your mother made a couple of mistakes. One was running away from me and the other was a big mistake in judgment. But I made a big mistake too. I should have gone after her, so I take some of the blame. However, since you're the man of the house, with your permission, I would like to begin where we left off years ago."

Jerome brushed aside his tears and smiled at Todd. "You mean, you might be my dad someday?"

"Jerome!" Carolyn tried to hide her embarrassment, but her pleasure was too great.

"If it's all right with your mother. We'll see what happens."

"Well, I don't know about his mother," said Sophia, brushing at her tears, "but his grandmother is sure in favor of it."

"Me too." Jerome giggled and put his good arm around Todd's neck.

The phone rang calling Laura away from the sounds of

happiness. "Hello, Reverend Kenzel speaking…Just a minute, please…Todd, it's for you."

"Yeah?" The smiled faded and was replaced by a frown. "When?…How?…Okay. I'll be right there."

"Trouble?" asked Steve.

"Yeah, Randy Jacobson escaped. He'll probably try to get out of town as fast as he can, but we'll find him. And…" he paused trying to find the words to say what he had to say, "Skip Jameson was found dead in his cell. Drug overdose."

37

Time stood still. There must be some mistake. How could Skip get any drugs, much less enough to overdose?

"Oh, no," they finally all moaned together.

"Steve, will you see that these folks get home?" Todd stepped toward Carolyn. He kissed her and said, "I'll call you later."

She nodded

"Sure, buddy," said Steve trying to keep his disappointment from showing. He had hoped to have some time alone with Laura. "I'll stop by the station later."

Todd left and the others began gathering their things to leave.

"Paula is going to need a friend, Frank," said Martha. "With her husband in jail and her son dead, she doesn't need to be alone right now. I'm going over there."

"You go ahead," he answered. "Take the car. I'll take your pans and things and walk home. Call me if you need anything."

"I'll stop and see if Jody will come home with me for a few days," said Carolyn. "With her mother gone, her father and brother in jail, she doesn't need to be alone either."

"Thank you, Carolyn and Martha," said Laura. She should be the one going to Paula and Jody, but she suddenly felt very weary and drained. "Tell them I'll see them in the morning unless they need me tonight. Call me if they do."

"Detective Morgan, if you don't mind, I think I would rather have Doctor Cornelius take me home," said SaraBelle. "I think I need to have my blood pressure checked. Besides," she chuckled softly, "I'm sure you have other things you would rather be doing." She grinned, winked at him, and nodded toward Laura, who blushed.

Doctor Cornelius laughed and took SaraBelle's arm. "Come on, we don't want you having a stroke here. I think Reverend Kenzel's had enough trauma for one day."

"Thanks," Steve said smiling as Doctor Cornelius escorted SaraBelle out the door. "I do have a few loose ends of my own to tie up."

When everyone was gone, Steve helped Laura carry dishes to the kitchen. "Laura, we do need to talk. I know you need to rest and I would wait until tomorrow, but my vacation is over and I need to go back to Glenville tonight."

"It's so frustrating thinking everything is all wrapped up and then…"

"The Jacobsons are like that—slippery as eels, deadly as vipers."

"Steve, what about Colin? Is it possible…?" She wasn't sure how to say she thought her bishop or district superintendent could be involved.

"We have nothing on him—no fingerprints, no pictures, no known address."

"How did Harold find out who he was?"

"I wish I knew," said Steve. "He didn't leave any message, note, cryptic words?"

"Nothing—I didn't know he had called the bishop until Bishop Jarvis returned his call after the accident. What really bothers me is, I keep wondering who besides the bishop and district superintendent knew a woman was coming to Cottonville?"

"I can't believe a bishop and district superintendent could be involved, but I'll check into it. However, I don't want to talk about murder; I want to talk about us—or at least about me. I can't speak for you."

"Steve, don't…" He could see the panic building.

"Please, let me finish," he took her hands in his. "If I don't say this now, it may never get said. You know about my divorce and my vow to never even think about another woman, much less fall in love. I kept that promise—until last Tuesday night. I don't know what happened. You caught me off guard. I even thought you felt it too. I keep fighting with myself, but the feeling won't go away. I'm falling head over heels in love and I'm scared to death. I don't want to be hurt again."

Unconsciously he fingered her wedding ring as he talked. "I know you aren't ready for involvements. I'm not either. We've known each other less than a week. It seems longer because of all we've been through. When you were in that wreck and I realized that I could have lost you without ever really knowing you…"

Laura started to speak, but he shook his head, took a deep breath, and continued. "I had to say something before leaving for Glenville, or I might lose my nerve and never call. I still might lose my nerve, once I'm away from you. I'm not asking for a commitment of any kind. I just need to let you know where I stand and ask if I can call you sometime? Will you give me a chance? Or would you rather I just get out of your life, and stay out?"

"Steve, I…don't know what to say. Like you said, so much has happened in such a short time." She paused then looked into his blue eyes. He continued to hold her hands, their eyes held by unacknowledged desire.

"When Harold died, a whole new life opened for me. I never intended to even think about another man. You're right, however. I was attracted to you that night. I don't understand it, but I feel like a school girl with a giant crush on the star quarterback every time you're near me. I know I'm not ready—you're right, neither of us are—to think about a commitment of any kind, except friendship. I would feel a deep void if we were no longer friends. If that friendship progresses to love, I won't be disappointed, but we need time."

Steve had been holding his breath. He exhaled slowly and returned her grin. "That's all I need to hear for the present. I won't push or hurry you. The ball is in your court. When you feel we can talk some more, give me a call. Okay?"

Laura nodded. She couldn't speak around the lump that suddenly closed her throat.

"Now, I hope I don't blow it," said Steve, "but I'm going to kiss you good night and be on my way."

Before she could refuse him—which she wouldn't have done anyway—he slipped his arms around her, pulled her close. She felt his lips on hers and slipped her arms around his neck.

"We'll talk more, later," he said and started for the door.

Laura nodded and followed to see him out.

"One more for the road?" He kissed her again. "Goodnight, Laura."

"Goodnight, Steve." She closed the door and leaned against it, afraid her knees would buckle.

"Rascal, Mischief," she said to her furry friends as they climbed the stairs for bed, "what do you think? Am I making a mistake by leaving the door open—metaphorically speaking, of course—for romance at my age? After all, I'm hardly a teenager."

Two sets of green eyes peered at her. They blinked then raced her to the bed where they settled down to their nightly ritual of grooming themselves and each other. Laura went through her nightly routine as well. As she brushed her hair, she remembered Steve holding her hand and fingering her ring. Holding her hand before her she pondered what to do. As long as she wore Harold's ring, she could keep suitors away—which was fine while she was in seminary. If she put it away, would that mean she wanted men—especially Steve Morgan—to notice her?

She slipped the ring off her finger and pressed it into a velvet slot for rings. She would never again wear that ring, or possibly any other, but she would be open to whatever happened. She couldn't be open as long as she was tied to the past.

The soft chuckle in her soul caught her attention. She could almost hear, "Didn't I say I would provide? Now there is still another little matter of the past—forgiveness. You need to listen to what you told Jerome."

"Later," she whispered. She would have to call Butch Martin with a word of forgiveness as well as the truth about that night.

She began to drift into sleep. Visions of Randy Jacobson and a faceless Jacobson mingled with visions of Bishop Giles and Bill Collins and floated over her like mists over the creek in the woods. What sounded like an eerie laugh reached her internal hearing and brought her upright in bed, sweat pouring down her face. Rascal and Mischief were asleep at the foot of her bed. It had only been a dream, but it was nearly dawn before she could sleep again. Then pleasant dreams of Steve Morgan replaced the nightmares.

Printed in the United States
111694LV00003B/85-93/A